Mosaic

Cindy Koepp

Des Moines, Iowa, USA

Mosaic

© Copyright 2024 by Cindy Koepp

For permissions and queries, contact the publisher at:
C_Koepp@yahoo.com

PRINTING HISTORY
First Edition
April 2024

ISBN-13: 979-8-9903197-0-7

CREDITS
Cover Art by: Rowell Cruz

PUBLISHER'S NOTE

Contents

Forward

This collection of stories came from sources as varied as the subjects. Some were contest entries. A few were slated to be in anthologies that never came to be. One started off life as a serial on my (now defunct) blog. Many are spin-offs of novels I've written. One even started off life as a fanfic of a somewhat obscure TV show from, oh, before I was born, anyway.

Altogether, they represent some of my favorite short stories. Would be a shame if no one else ever got to read them.

So here they are.

Origin:
I was headed to a writer conference, the cost of which was a bit $$$. When I heard about a contest with a prize of a scholarship to the conference, I went for it. The requirements were a flash fiction (under 1000 words) piece about a weird way to get to there.

Old School Moves

The bellhop ushered me through a steel door marked "Employees Only" then closed it behind me. I found myself in an alley, as expected, but with no vehicle in sight. Just a guy in faded jeans, a denim jacket, and a green polo shirt over a blue one. All collars were turned up. He sported a mullet of light brown hair and enough product to poof up the front and make lighting a match a fire hazard.

How ... retro.

The throwback sat on a padded hotel chair, eyes glued to a TV on a milk crate that also held a well-maintained Atari 2600 running *Frogger*. I'd preferred *Asteroids* myself.

"You headed for the Old School Gaming conference?" His frog got squashed by a car and restarted.

"Yeah." I checked my jacket pocket one last time for my notecards. I knew enough about old console game trivia that I could probably wing it on running the activity I was in charge of, but the cards had source references in case someone challenged my official answer. "I'm supposed to find my ride to the new location out here." I took a step closer as the newest frog became the hood ornament for a sedan with the first move the guy made. *Not your game, huh?* I restrained the developing smirk. As a teen, I'd rolled the score over on *Frogger* regularly.

"Chill." He aimed an elbow at the folding chair next to him. "The GarGuile will be with you in a sec."

GarGuile? Is that an old BBS alias? I smiled. I couldn't fault him, though. I used to go by Squawkatiel on the old dial-in bulletin boards.

When his next frog went the way of the first two, GarGuile frowned.

"GAME OVER!" splashed across the screen.

He shrugged and powered down the Atari before he pulled the *Frogger* cartridge out and inserted an unmarked one.

I leaned forward. "I'd like to get to the conference, please."

"Yep. Gimme a minute." He powered up the 2600.

Was that going to be the same "minute" my ex had meant before he spent hours playing some other hokey game?

His TV went from static to vertical stripes and a hum that said communication with the cartridge had failed.

GarGuile grumbled and turned off the system before yanking the cartridge loose. "It was working just a few minutes ago." He blew on the copper contacts and plugged the game back in. "Stay still."

Acrid smoke burst from the cartridge. That explained why we were outside. The hotel probably didn't want the smoke alarms going off every few minutes. When it cleared, GarGuile and the hotel alley were gone. I stood in a pixelated gray brick box, and the only way out was an opening directly in front of me.

I looked down at a version of me that was composed of tiny squares in a sixteen-color palette I remembered so well from the years I'd spent playing vintage games. Things never went easily for the player in those games, and three lives could flash by in a second. I hoped GarGuile was better at this game than he was at *Frogger*.

"I have a bad feeling about this," I muttered.

"Don't have a cow," GarGuile's sourceless voice said. "The portal to the conference is in the game."

"Why would you code it into a vintage game?"

GarGuile snorted. "Keep out the sort of bogus airheads who invaded last year."

I hadn't been there last year, but I'd heard the tale. Some group of brat kids had shown up and trashed an exhibit on the original *Pong*.

"Terrific. So, am I battling Yorgle, Grundle, and Rhindle for a chalice or what?" I asked.

"This isn't *Adventure*, so, no."

I rolled my eyes. "That's a relief."

"Just down the hall. No sweat."

I slid forward as if on one of the moving walkways at the Dallas airport. At least, that's what I assumed was going on. The floor didn't change at all, but the pixelated walls slid past on either side of me. As I moved, patterns in the pixels emerged, showing GarGuile's artistic side in a few of the more common sideways emoticons. I picked out a chef, a wry smile, and a left-handed smilie.

"See? Easy." GarGuile's smirk was evident in his tone. "Hey! Don't touch—"

Forward momentum stopped.

"I didn't touch anything!" After a couple seconds of listening to myself breathe, I looked up at the solid gray ceiling. "Hello? What's going on?"

Nothing. My voice didn't even echo.

After what felt like an eternity, I scowled. "Decided to play *Centipede* instead?"

Well, he had said the portal to the conference was down the corridor. Hopefully, not an exaggeration.

As I walked forward, the brick wall patterns alternated and the floor pattern flipped left to right with each step. Repetitive, but at least I knew I was moving. A dozen steps further, I came to a perpendicular passage, giving me the option to turn left or right. In these games, I tended to stick to the right wall, so I turned that way but didn't get too far. The new corridor went a few steps to a dead end, which had been decorated with an almost comical skull and crossbones.

The game beeped high, then low, then lower.

The hairs on the nape of my neck prickled. Okay, that was ominous.

When I turned to go back, nothing blocked the way, but the game only let me see a couple steps forward before the scenery grayed out. I tip-toed along, watching the art flip-flop in the characteristic way. Queasiness unsteadied my hands.

I reached the intersection. Ahead, a blue box with square dots for eyes and a downward curved line for a mouth advanced a step then stopped.

Thank God for turn-based movement. If I could avoid any dead-ends—but this maze was nothing but dead ends so far.

"Nice play, Shakespeare. You should've stayed put," GarGuile said.

"Where have you been?" I frowned at the ceiling.

"Fire department dweebs came to investigate the smoke and unplugged my extension cord. Again. I'll take control. Now that you woke the beast up, I'll have to get rid of it. It's blocking the portal."

I slid up the main corridor then turned left, which gave me an extreme close-up of bricks. GarGuile moved me through the secret door to a room just big enough for me and an arrow made from a dash and a greater-than sign.

"Grab the spear," GarGuile ordered.

I picked it up, expecting it to have some mass, and almost tossed it. Should've expected that. Seriously. It was made of light. How much could it weigh?

After another extreme zoom of the bricks, I was back in the main corridor staring eyeball-to-pixel with a blue box. The same "beast," I assumed. I gasped and nearly dropped the ASCII graphics arrow, but I tightened my grip on the dash making up the spear's staff.

"Stab it fast!" GarGuile hollered.

Why? If we really were using turn-based movement, it wouldn't move until after I did.

I shoved the pointy end of the greater-than sign at the box. A downward sliding note ended with the box's disappearance.

"Good. Now drop the spear."

"You sure that thing has no friends?" I asked the ceiling.

"Yeah. My game."

"Then why put a monster in it?"

GarGuile sighed. "I told you earlier. I don't want party crashers."

I looked at the "spear" and let go. It went noiselessly from in my hand to on the ground in an instant. The moving walkway effect returned as I went to the crossing corridor then turned left. Directly ahead, a brown door with a few jagged stripes meant to look like wood grain.

"When you're ready to come back, gimme a call. 867—"

"5309?"

"Totally."

I snorted. That figured.

After another real close look at GarGuile's artistic abilities, I stepped out into a larger, real-world room decorated in the latest hotel chic and populated by people I recognized from social media.

To get back, I think I'll take a cab.

Origin:
After the amazing success of *Condemned Courier* on JukePop Serials, I decided to try my hand at another serial to keep my blog more active. One problem. I was in the middle of the school year, so I didn't have time to start from scratch.

Like many writers, I have more ideas living in a folder than time to write them. While I was sorting through wild story ideas, I came across City of Refuge. It was supposed to be set in ancient Israel, only my research had stalled out, so I'd shelved it for later.

No reason I couldn't change the venue, so I moved the story to a science fiction setting and away it went.

After completing its run on my blog, I canned it for future repurposing. Here it is.

City of Refuge

Chapter 1: Fatal Accident?

Jeremiah Baruch guided his engine-drawn, flatbed hovercart into Bethlehem City, a rather generous name for a frontier town with one dirt-packed street bordered by shops. A few other hovervehicles of different sizes and configurations parked along each side of the street. Folks walked on the sidewalks in front of the stores, which were elevated a couple feet to stay above the water and muck after a storm.

He parked the hovercart in front of the general store and powered down. The cables connecting the two cylindrical engines to the wagon whined and settled onto their support struts. The flatbed wagon, little more than a bench on a low-walled open box, floated down onto its landing gear. The dull hum faded out, leaving the more distant noise of other hovercarts and the sounds of people doing business in the local shops. Music from the saloon's synthesizer carried down the street in spite of the early morning hour. How people could drink and carry on like that before lunch was beyond him, but the sheriff allowed it so long as those partaking kept the "partying" in the saloon.

In the seat next to Jeremiah, Dave looked down the street at the Rusty Robot Saloon and grinned like a kid with a new lollipop.

Knew I should've left you home. Jer grabbed his cane. "Stay with the wagon."

Dave sneered. "Stop treating me like Ethan."

"Maybe if you acted like you were six years his senior, that'd be easier to do. Stay put. We don't need trouble today."

Jer swung his left leg over the side of the hovercart and grimaced as he helped his right one with his hand. Weather would change soon, and as stiff and sore as his leg was today, the approaching storm would be a bad one.

Need to secure the animals, close the cover on the crops ... He stopped the list of storm preparations. The town errands needed doing while there was still time to get them done. He'd left Haddy and Tamar at home with Lemuel and Ethan. They'd organize the ranch hands to finish the chores.

Bracing himself with the cane and the side of the wagon, Jer stood. In spite of his effort to keep as much of his weight on the cane as he could, a sharp pain shot from his knee to his hip.

Yeah, there's a storm coming all right. That's the only time the ache gets this bad. Better hustle and get the errands done. Maybe Dave can take care of the bank.

Jer paused and glanced at his middle brother. Yeah, he *could* stop at the bank, but how much of Pa's money would make it into the account, and how much would end up in Dave's pocket?

Jer sighed and continued on to the general store. Anything he wanted done right he'd better do himself.

The general store, like nearly all the structures on Gibeah, had been built from panels of the generation ship that had brought the first colonists. The periodic storms on the planet had weathered the shine off the metal.

The three steps up from the street to the storefront would have been murder, but Jer took his time, stepping up with his left foot and lifting himself up onto the step then balancing on his right leg and cane to step up with his left foot again. At the top of the short run of steps, he paused for a moment to collect himself then entered the door. A bell over his head rang.

The inside of the store had been reorganized, probably by Mr. Rubin's wife while he'd been away at the New Jebus hospital week before last. All the premade clothes and cloth had been moved to the shelves filling the middle of the store along with lanterns and other gear. Anything small enough to disappear into a pocket or pouch had been sequestered to shelves behind the counter. Prudent, really, more than one family in the area had their own version of Dave.

Old Man Rubin came out of the back. His white hair was confined to a ring that connected his ears, but he looked good, not nearly as pale as he had a few weeks ago. "Morning, Jer. Got your email with your order. I saw you pull up, so I got the boys loading your wagon."

"Thank you, sir. How's the new shoulder?" Jer limped forward to the counter.

Mr. Rubin moved the new cybernetic replacement through its range of motion. "Not bad at all. The surgery didn't hurt near as much as I expected. All that new-fangled medical technology on New Jebus was something else. I was in and out in two days. Good as new. Better maybe. Your Pa is getting his heart replaced?"

"Yes, sir. That last heart attack scared Ma. They're on New Jebus now."

"He'll be fine, I'm sure, but I'll say a few prayers for him tonight." Mr. Rubin dug out his ledger from under the counter. "Not to be telling you your business, Jer, but you might consider a replacement for that, um, weather detector of yours."

Jer smiled. "Yes, sir. Saving for Pa's heart surgery was first. We're scraping mites together for Haddy's eyes next. Then we'll decide if my bum leg is worth the fee."

"I'd say it is, but you and your folks will have to decide that." Mr. Rubin scanned through all his clients and stopped on Pa's name. "That's two hundred sixty-three fifty this week."

Jer pulled out his credit chip, set it on the ledger, and tapped his payment code. The display showed the money transferring to Mr. Rubin's account.

With a loud scuffle of feet, Aaron, the older boy in Mr. Rubin's family, rushed in from the back and skidded to a stop before he swept his blonde hair out of his eyes with a swipe of his hand. "Mr. Baruch! Mr. Baruch! Your brother's in an awful fight with Mr. Lindemann! Micah already went for the sheriff, but come quick!"

There was no such thing as "come quick" on days when his hip was acting up, but he limped along as best he could. Mr. Rubin's strong left arm, the recently repaired one, caught Jer under the right elbow and helped bear his weight down the stairs.

Halfway down the street, Kane Lindemann and Dave were throwing fists at each other while Kane's two pals, Nahum and Vashti, stood off to the side cheering their friend on. The gathering crowd stayed well back. Nearby, Jessie Zimmel, the Rusty Robot's head barmaid, leaned on a light pole and watched the fight with a grin on her face. Sheriff Weisser, a short man with an athletic build and a dark beard that reached to his shoulders, ran down the street.

Dave's fist connected with Kane's jaw and sent him sprawling in the dirt. Kane came back up with a knife in hand. He thumbed the switch and energy crackled down the length of the blade. Jer reached for his pistol, but from his angle, he'd have to aim past too many people.

Sheriff Weisser pushed his way through the crowd and shot the dirt at Kane's feet. "Put it away, Kane, before I stun your hide and stick you in a cell."

After turning off the plasma edge of his knife, Kane slammed it into its sheath. He jabbed his finger in Dave's direction. "You stay away from Jessie."

"Or what?" Dave spat at the ground.

"You won't always have the sheriff and your kin around." Kane made a fist. "Then we'll see."

"Oh yeah, we'll see."

Sheriff Weisser stood between them. "That's enough." He pointed at Kane and his pals. "You three, get outta here before I decide to put you in a cell for disturbing the peace."

Jer wove his way through the dispersing crowd. "Dave, I told you to stay with the wagon."

Dave gritted his teeth and clenched his fists. "I'm not your boy!"

"No, but he talks sense," Sheriff Weisser said. "You know Kane is sweet on Jessie, so–"

"And you aren't," Jer chimed in, looking pointedly at Dave.

Sheriff Weisser raised an eyebrow at Jer then frowned at Dave. "Why are you coming onto her so strong that even I can see it on other end of the street?"

Dave shrugged.

"Words, boy. I'm not your pa, but I'm the law. Unless you want a night in a cell for disturbing the peace, you'll answer with words, not head jiggles. Why you coming on to a girl you don't even like?"

"Joking with Kane."

Jer rolled his eyes. "Only Kane's not joking." He turned to Sheriff Weisser "I'd be obliged if you could sit on Dave until I'm done with errands. Shopkeepers don't want him around after last month, and looks like I can't leave him with the wagon."

Sheriff Weisser nodded and got a good grip on Dave's upper arm. "Yep, me and Dave here are going to have a nice little chat about a man's responsibilities, just like I promised the last time you came in here and started trouble. Let's go, Dave."

Jer watched them leave and blew out a sigh.

The crowd went about their business, except for Jessie who still leaned on the lamppost. Her dress, transparent except for a few strategically placed decorations, shimmered in the orange-tinted light of the sun overhead. Her artificially ginger hair was piled in neat little curls on top of her head. Her eyes sparkled with equally artificial glitter in her makeup.

She smirked, pushed off from the pole, and practically slithered over. "Poor Jer. That brother of yours is like a stampede waiting to start."

"This is all one big game to you, isn't it?" Jer adjusted the grip on his cane. "Do you care at all for either of them?"

"Those two?" She snorted. "Boys have been fighting over me for years. I have never belonged to any man, and certainly never will belong to some penniless asteroid herder like Kane." She reached for him. "Now a ranch owner like yourself ...."

He stepped back. "Good day, Ma'am."

Jessie's laugh followed him back to the wagon. Mr. Rubin's boys had done a fine job packing the supplies. Jer tightened one of the bands securing the load and increased the power on another. Both adjustments probably weren't necessary, but he felt better to have done something. The remaining errands to the church, the bank, the butcher, and the dairy went smoothly, and the supplies were added to the wagon.

That left one more stop, and Jer was of a mind to leave his brother in a cell until Pa got home next week. Dave would stay out of trouble, and everyone else would have some peace. Everyone except the sheriff. Maybe Dave would go out on one of his asteroid-herding runs and give everyone a break that way.

Jer hobbled across to the sheriff's office and took the steps one at a time. Inside, Sheriff Weisser sat on one side of his desk. Dave sat on the other, sulking while the sheriff worked at his computer. His plaid shirt sported a torn seam at one shoulder. Ma would be thrilled. It wasn't like she didn't have work to do aside from perpetually repairing Dave's shirts after he got into a dust-up with someone, usually Kane. Pa, though, had been as good as his word. He would not be buying Dave any new clothes to replace what was damaged by stupid choices. Dave, himself, couldn't be bothered to buy his own. Maybe Ma should make him do his own repairs, too.

Now, almost two hours after the fight, the side of Dave's face had swelled some, and a shiner was developing under his left eye.

"Sheriff, can I take Dave home?" Jer asked.

"Yep. Lack of common sense isn't a crime." He looked up from his computer and drove a hard glare into Dave. "But the next time you come into town and instigate a problem, David Obadiah Baruch, I will find something to charge you with. You got me, boy?"

Dave pushed off from the chair. "Yes. Sir."

"Let's go, Dave. Storm's coming, and we need to get ready for it." Jer indicated the door with a twitch of his head. "Thanks, Sheriff."

"Don't mention it."

They walked to the wagon in silence. Dave grabbed the side and vaulted up and over with an ease Jer hadn't known in ten years. Jer set his cane behind the seat and grabbed the side.

Dave offered his hand. "Come on, Gimpy, or we'll be here all year."

You're joking with me, aren't you? Gonna throw me in the dirt soon as I trust you? Jer clasped his brother's wrist with one hand and rocked back for momentum. Dave pulled as Jer pushed off with his stronger leg. He turned as he got up onto the wagon and planted himself in the seat.

"Thanks."

"Oh, no. Thank you, big brother. Don't know when I've ever had so much fun in town."

"No one told you to start a fight with Kane." Jer flipped the switches for the engines.

As they wound up and lifted off from the dirt, the wagon floated upward, too. Jer took the control sticks in hand. The cables connecting the two motors to the wagon scooted forward until they were taut then picked up speed as Jer increased the throttle.

"Why'd you make me come in the first place?" Dave asked.

"You were one more innuendo short of Tamar's fist up your nose, that's why." Jer glanced at his brother. "I was trying to keep you from a fat lip and a black eye. Lot of good that did."

Dave planted his elbow on his knee and his chin on his palm. "No one around here knows how to take a joke."

"No one around here thinks your jokes are funny. Flirting with a girl you have no interest in just to get Kane's goat, or making fun of Tamar one moment and grabbing her butt the next while suggesting a roll in the hay? Don't know many who'd find that funny, Dave, and certainly no girl worth having."

"Maybe you and I like different kinds of girls."

"That may be, but you need to look further afield than Tamar. She's had it up to the gills with you."

Dave sat back, kicked his feet up on the front of the wagon, and crossed his arms over his chest. "Sounds like everyone's had it up to the gills with me. Fine by me. I'm tired of everyone treating me like a kid. I'm going to herd some asteroids to the refinery."

"Just get your supplies honestly this time. Take them from our storeroom, not a merchant."

Dave sat up straight again and jabbed his finger at Jer. "Stop needling me, you self-righteous jerk. What I wanted on that trip wasn't in the storeroom, and those merchants got paid back for everything I borrowed and gained another twenty percent. They made money off the deal. That left me with almost nothing to show."

"Yeah, because the judge gave you a choice of that, ten years in prison, or thirty-nine lashes. How much would those merchants have gotten back if you hadn't been caught? Anything?"

After glaring for a moment longer, Dave crossed his arms over his chest and stared straight ahead.

A cool wind picked up from the north bringing a scent of ozone. A blue-black storm cloud loomed. That storm would hit by tonight.

Jer sped up.

📖

Kane hustled around the ship he called home. *Imperious* had been a gift from his grandmother to get him to do an honest man's work. Herding asteroids to refineries paid decently for him, Vashti, and Nahum, even if it wasn't always the safest job.

Vashti's footsteps, softer than Nahum's, ran up the loading ramp. "Kane! You were right!"

"About Dave Baruch?" Kane closed up the engine maintenance hatch and dogged it.

"Yeah, he's just filed flight plans," Vashti hollered. "Where are you?"

He left the engine room and met her at the ramp. "Where's Dave headed?"

"Nain, according to my contact," she said.

"That's perfect. Let's get there." Kane jogged toward the bridge. "Get Nahum and button it up. I'll file plans."

📖

The storm raging outside rattled the house with bursts of thunder. The winds shrieked. Jer had gathered not only his own hired hands but also the surrounding neighbors under his roof, the only shelter for miles around rated to handle the worst weather. This one, a category eight, ranked high enough for the record books. He prayed earnestly for the safety of those who hadn't yet made it to his house—the Michalsons, the Greenburgs, and at least four others. Maybe they had found somewhere else safe.

Jer sat in his room, reviewing the ranch's financial statements on a battery-powered handheld computer. The power supply for the building could conk out any moment now with a category eight raging outside.

A strong knock banged on the door. Jer looked up from his handheld. "Come i–"

The door flew open and Ethan, the youngest of his brothers, charged in. Dark hair, blue eyes, same build, he could be a doppleganger of Dave six years ago. "Jer, we're getting a message over the FTL."

"In this weather?" He set his computer aside.

"It isn't clear at all but sounds like it might be Dave." Ethan waved for Jer to follow. "Come on!"

Jer grabbed his cane and hobbled after Ethan to the radio room at the end of the hall. Haddy sat there listening intently to a static-riddled transmission that sure sounded like Dave's voice.

"...in troub...ran into...maj...amage..."

Jer snatched the microphone and squeezed the transmitter button. "Dave, we got a bad storm here. Your message is all static. Soon as the storm lets up, I'll come get you, all right? Get somewhere safe if you can and sit tight."

"Wha...Jer, I c...ear you...ran into K...out...I–"

The light on the FTL transmitter went dark. A second later, thunder shook the house. The lights guttered then went out, leaving everyone in darkness for a few moments while the house system turned on the red emergency lights and ignited the backup generator. All the talking in the house went quiet before resuming at a lower level.

Haddy turned toward him and pushed her thick glasses further up her nose. "Sounds like he's in trouble."

"Seems like it, but we're guessing. There wasn't much to that transmission. What'd he say before I got here?"

Haddy frowned, which made her glasses slip. "Not much I could make out. I recorded it, but we'll have to wait for main power to listen to it."

Who would've thought we'd need the FTL radio on the emergency power grid. "Fair enough."

"But what do we do?" Ethan asked.

Jer gripped his brother's shoulder. "The only thing we can do. Take care of our guests until the storm passes, and pray everyone stays safe. Once the weather clears enough for me to launch, I'll fly out to Nain and find out what's happened."

The wind shrieked outside the house, and the thunder roared.

The quantum drive dropped Jer's ship at the edge of the asteroid belt orbiting Nain, a red dwarf further out from the galactic core than his own home system of Gibeah. The asteroid belt took up the space of four planetary orbits, the largest collection of asteroids anywhere in the theocracy's holdings. With the densest asteroid field, Nain was both the most lucrative and the most dangerous. A man could make good living here if tumbling rocks didn't kill him first.

Jer unhooked his flight harness and pushed off from the chair. The sense of flying in zero G was the only chance he had to move without pain. If he didn't have obligations at home, he'd happily brave the risks of asteroid herding. When he arrived at the scanner station, Jer called up a reading of the Nain belt. Five ships aside from his own were in the system, all congregated on the near side of the ring, which was odd by itself.

Asteroid herders tended to maintain a greater distance from each other to prevent getting caught up in stampedes, runaway chain reactions that happened when one misstep with a tractor or repulsor beam sent asteroids smashing into each other or anything else in the way. Jer switched the readout on his screen to show vectors, which made the odd choice clear. The far side of the belt tumbled at a greater speed in random directions, the telltale of a stampede dying out.

The dull ache of tension spread across Jer's shoulders. Had Dave been caught up in that? Jer called up a transponder readout and searched for a familiar code. The tension became a tremor. Maybe Dave had left the system. He was a good pilot and an experienced herder.

The communication system pinged.

Jer pushed off from the sensor station and flew across the bridge to the communication console. It pinged again before he had himself settled properly. The code on the screen identified one of the other ships in the system.

Jer punched the Accept Call button and identified himself. "Who is this?"

"Name's Zack. Just a friendly bit of advice for you. Stay this side of the belt. Couple o' fellas got into it just yesterday on the other side, started a stampede, and ended up getting one of the ships blowed up. The other one lit out on a course for Shechem."

"Sir, you didn't happen to catch the name on those ships, did you?"

"Yep. One of them. *Imperious* was the one what lit out of here. Just about ran over old Adon on the way out."

Kane. Ma will be devastated if the other ship was Dave. "I hate to be a bother, mister, but last night I got a message from my brother. He was supposed to be here at Nain, and he sounded like he was in trouble, but a storm kept me pinned down. If–"

"I hope that other ship wasn't your kin, but let me get the transponder number outta my sensor log."

"I'd be obliged, sir." Seconds passed like decades. Tension in his shoulders became a persistent ache. He whispered prayers that the most obvious answer wasn't the real one.

"All right. I'm sending you the transponder number of the ship what got caught in the stampede." Zack's voice startled Jer out of his thoughts.

Jer swallowed hard and checked the readout screen.

"Sorry, but that code's only a couple digits off yours." Zack's voice held equal parts certainty and condolences. "If you both registered near the same time or place, I'm afraid it's not good news."

"Yes, sir. Thank you for your effort." Jer rubbed his forehead and shut off the system.

He was the nearest kinsman. Chasing Dave's killer was his job, but first he needed Sheriff Weisser to deputize him.

📖

Jer parked his wagon in the barn and hobbled inside. His shirt weighed more with a couple ounces of titanium pinned to it. Sheriff Weisser's imprimatur had turned Jer from ranch boss to avenger of blood. Now all that remained was to chase Kane down and see justice done according to theocracy law. First, though, he had to pick two people to crew with him. Short runs by himself were fine, but this hunt for Kane might take a while. Ethan and Haddy, along with the managers of their Pa's hired hands, Tamar and Lemuel, sat in the front room. Ethan tinkered with one of his mechanical widgets. Haddy's brown eyes were red from weeping and her hair was well on the way to escaping from the braid she put it in every morning, but she had composed herself as well as could be expected. Lemuel sat still as a board with his hands folded in his lap, while Tamar stared out the window.

Ethan set his widget aside and bolted to his feet. "Take me with you. I'm really good at fixing stuff, and he was my brother, too." His words came out faster than last night's wind.

"Calm down, Ethan." Jer patted the kid's shoulder. *Eighteen makes you a man by law, but you're still my kid brother.* "I haven't decided who I'm taking."

Tamar turned away from the window. "You know there's no love lost 'tween me and Dave, but if you need a medic on this trip, I'm with you."

"With a snake like Kane, you might need someone who knows weapons." Lemuel rested his hand on the butt of his pistol.

Haddy said nothing and pushed her glasses up again. Words had rarely been necessary between them on important matters like this. She was a real jack of all trades, and that familiarity with a little of everything made her valuable, but she would trust his judgment and go along with his choice no matter what it was.

Chapter 2: The Taxman

Jer considered his options. He was not just choosing his crew. Whoever he didn't take would be left here to run the ranch and all the complexities that brought. With Ma and Pa still away on Theopolis in the New Jebus system, there was only one person who really knew the ins and outs of the ranch well enough. Haddy could keep things running just fine. The hired hands respected her a lot more than Ethan, and she was family, unlike Tamar and Lem. She had the authority to act as needed.

Now, who to leave with her? Tam and Lem were tough as nails, and either could back Haddy just fine. Bandits popped up in the area, off and on, and for all the theocracy's efforts to convert everyone to the true religion, there were still holdouts. The Squatters, the unauthorized colonists who'd tried to claim land without theocracy permission, surfaced now and then to register a violent complaint, contracts notwithstanding. If something or someone riled up those unauthorized colonists, Haddy needed someone who knew the defensive systems as well as he knew how to put on a hat. That meant Lem.

So, Haddy and Lemuel would keep an eye on things here while Jer, Tamar, and Ethan chased down Kane and made him pay for the crime of killing Dave.

"Haddy, I'm leaving Lem here with you to watch over the homestead. Keep your eyes open. We haven't heard or seen much of the Squatters lately, but that don't mean they aren't planning something."

"That means I'm going?" Ethan grinned.

"You and Tamar. We're leaving as soon as you're packed." Jer clapped Ethan's shoulder.

Brow furrowed, Haddy hid her quivering hands by crossing her arms over her chest.

"Meet you back here in fifteen." Tamar stood.

Ethan followed her to the second-floor stairs. After they disappeared around the corner, Jer sat where he could see both Lemuel and Haddy without straining something. "Sorry to leave you two short-handed. Haddy, you just need to keep things running. Put off big decisions until Pa's back. I'm leaving Lemuel with you in case someone riles up the Squatters."

"They have been remarkably quiet lately." Lemuel rubbed his stubbly chin.

Jer nodded. "Don't expect that to continue."

"Patrols will happen as planned. We'll keep eyes and ears open." Lemuel stood and tugged his pants up and jacket down. "Speaking of which, if you'll excuse me, sir, patrol's due back shortly." He settled his hat on his sparse hair and nodded once to Haddy. "Ma'am."

Jer waited for him to leave. "You'll be okay, Haddy. There are good folk here to help you out until Pa comes home."

"I've only run the place for a day or two before. How long will you be gone?"

"I can't say for sure, but Ma and Pa will probably get back before I do. A lot depends on what the judge decides."

"Do you really think you'll catch Kane before he gets to Refuge?" she asked.

"No, but the judge will give me a week to get there before hearing the case without me. I'll stop and break the news to Ma and Pa on the way."

She shook her head. "I already told them. Ma called to give me an update earlier and wanted to know why I'd been crying."

Jer leaned forward with his elbows on his knees. "How'd she take it?"

"Better than I expected, actually." Haddy sniffled and wiped her nose with an embroidered handkerchief. "I guess no one's too surprised. She said for you to watch yourself with Kane and forget planning any kind of memorial until they return by the end of the week."

"Makes sense, but probably shouldn't wait for me and Ethan to get home. If the judge rules it an accident, or if Kane rabbits out of there after the trial, we might be a while. We'll pay our respects when we get back." He stood. "Anything you need me to do before I leave?"

She hesitated and sniffled again then threw her arms around him for a hug tight enough to impress a grizzly. "No, I think I can do this, but come back soon. Be safe out there."

"I'll be home as soon as I can." He kissed her forehead.

📖

When the solar gravity numbers reached the safe zone for the quantum drive, Jer engaged the stabilization systems. Retrorockets fired, and *Yireh* slowed to a stop. At least it felt like they weren't moving. They had a long way to go before the quantum drive would be satisfied. He entered the coordinates for Shechem.

"I'll see you at Shechem," Tamar said before she slipped out of the room.

Jer turned to his brother. "Glad to see you're looking less green."

"Yeah, sorry, Jer." Ethan stared at his shoes. "Zero G just turns my guts."

"Happens to lots of folks, kid. Don't fret over it."

Ethan sighed. "Yeah, but I know your leg doesn't trouble you as much at Zero G."

"True, but if a half G Keeps your dinner in its place, I'll be fine." He turned back to his console and called up the holoreader. "Go lie still somewhere so the quantum drive can cancel out our movement."

"M'kay. See you when we're there."

As Ethan left the bridge, Jer watched the estimated stabilization time climb upward. Even the minimal force of walking across deck plates had to be zeroed out before the quantum drive would engage. Once the drive established the ship's momentum at absolute stop, their location could be anywhere in the universe. This time, it'd be Shechem, the star system where the theocracy's courts were located.

The holoreader scrolled at a comfortable rate so Jer could read without any motion. With a page width of only one to two words, he didn't even have to scan left to right with his eyes. Meanwhile, miniature thrusters all around the ship fired in different directions, at intermittent durations. After he'd read for a while, Jer refocused his eyes on the instrument panel beyond his book. That miniscule motion added a couple hundredths of a second to the countdown. He watched the last few seconds before everything went black.

The darkness cleared, and Jer looked out the viewscreen at a yellow, main sequence star with its collection of planets: Shechem. The quantum drive powered down. Jer keyed the shipwide PA: "We're here. I'm taking us into Refuge."

He powered down his reader and engaged the thrusters. With continuous acceleration, he closed the distance quickly at an increasing rate and adjusted course for Refuge, the one terraformed planet in the Shechem system. As he passed the system's fifth orbit, four small fighters rose from the planet's surface. Jer checked the radar and keyed the identification protocols.

Bailiffs. Probably coming to see what our business is.

Tamar walked onto the bridge and perched at the communication station just moments before it pinged.

She answered the call. "This is the Gibean ship *Yireh*. Please identify."

"City of Refuge patrol group Theta. State your business."

"Jeremiah Baruch is onboard pursuing Kane Lindemann who is responsible for the death of David Baruch at Nain."

"Standby."

As *Yireh* passed orbit four, Jer reduced his acceleration.

"*Yireh*, we have record of Kane Lindemann's arrival. All cases involving the Nain asteroid field are settled in Heptam City. We will send you coordinates and the approved course. Do not deviate."

Jer looked back at Tamar and nodded.

"Understood," she said.

The radar showed Theta patrol keeping pace with *Yireh*. The communication system pinged again.

"Got the course. Sending it your way." Tamar hummed as she tapped the computer keys.

The course appeared in the radar a moment later. The required route, almost as complicated as breathing, took them all the way to a specific landing hangar. Jer adjusted course and speed to match the specifications before the patrol returned to the planet by a different route.

When *Yireh* entered the atmosphere, the attitude jets fired to turn the better-armored underside to the reentry burn. Orange and red haze filled the screen for almost a full minute before it faded, and the jets fired again to turn *Yireh* back into flight mode.

Most of the colonized worlds of the theocracy were terraformed into ranch and farmland, but Shechem was the exception. The rocky surface had been leveled for industrial purposes, and the eight Cities of Refuge had been built as judicial and manufacturing centers. A gray haze filled the air in spite of scrubbers scattered all over the planet working full time to keep the air breathable.

The course led Jer around to the day side of the planet. Heptam City grew larger on the horizon. Factories reached up through the smog blanketing the city, but there was no obvious sign of pollution sources. No smokestacks belched black clouds. Modern vehicles had no exhaust fumes, and yet the pollution was worse over the city.

Jer landed the ship in the designated hangar and set all systems in standby mode. He'd never been to Shechem, but merchants who did business here had renamed it City of Refuse. There had to be a reason why.

"Take me with you," Ethan pleaded.

Jer startled and spun toward his youngest brother. "Y'know, one of these days I'll get used to how quiet you move."

"Sorry." Ethan's goofy grin had nothing like an apology in it. "Really, though. I want to go to court with you."

"Nothin' doin', kid. You and Tamar are staying on the ship. Only avengers of blood, the accused, and members of the court are allowed in the court itself."

Tamar shook her head. "Tales I've heard about these cities? Uh-uh. No way, Ethan. I'm not leaving this ship, and neither are you."

Ethan frowned. "If it's that bad, shouldn't we go along to protect Jer?"

"And come back to *Yireh* totally stripped of all useful parts?" Tamar asked.

"Wait a minute." Ethan propped his left hand on his hip and pointed with his right. "Shechem is the legal center of the theocracy. Shouldn't there be more law here?"

Jer smirked. *Such innocence.* "Maintaining law and order requires something like ninety-eight percent of the population to be law-abiding citizens. When somewhere between one-third to one-half of Shechem's population is criminals, who beat the court waiting for the high priest to die so they get their pardons, what do you think that amounts to for those trying to maintain order?"

"Oh." Ethan flopped in the nearest chair. "Guess that means I'm stuck here. Why'd we come if we're just going to sit on the ship?"

"Get going, boss." Tamar indicated the loading ramp with a twitch of her head. "While you're gone, I'll explain the likely scenarios to Ethan here. We'll make sure you have a ship to come back to."

"Good. Button it up and use the ship's defenses if you need to. I'll be back when I can."

Jer grabbed his cane and headed aft with Tamar on his heels. The half-gravity gave an extra bounce in his step, which complicated using the cane, but the pain wasn't so bad. He could tolerate more weight on his bad leg without the pain getting the better of him.

Tamar lowered the ramp, letting in a gust of Shechem's air. The chemical stench threatened to turn Jer's stomach. He hobbled down the ramp as quick as he could, pausing at the end and making a deliberate downward step as if he were on stairs instead of level ground. The increased gravity pulled at him, and he gritted his teeth against the persistent ache in his leg. After making sure he'd gotten the pained expression out of his face, he turned back to the ship and waved. Tamar closed everything up.

"Jeremiah Baruch."

He turned toward a voice deep enough to come from the center of the planet. A lean man in a dark green uniform stood nearby with a demeanor of careful confidence.

Ready for trouble and capable of handling it? Jer limped forward, switching the cane to his left hand and offering his right to the man. "I'm Jeremiah Baruch."

The man kept his own hands loose at his sides. "Physical contact with court officials is strictly forbidden. Come with me, please. The court was alerted to your arrival. Your case will be heard as soon as you arrive at the judge's bench."

Jer followed the official out of the hangar complex and into the open air. If it were possible, the stench outside was worse than inside. The official stopped at a heavily-armored car and reached into his pocket. The hovercar beeped twice and two doors opened.

"Get in." The official pointed to the nearer open door.

Jer sat on the heavily cushioned seat and swung his left leg in before lifting his right leg with his arm. He set the cane next to him. The official climbed in the other side and tapped a button on the control panel. The hovercar beeped as the doors slowly closed and sealed. Cool air smelling of a sweeter chemistry blasted from the vents for ten seconds, eradicating one disagreeable stench with another that was only somewhat better. After the official entered information into the navigation system, the hovercar lifted off and drove itself.

"I am authorized to accept your tax payment." The official pulled out a ledger.

"Tax payment?" Jer asked.

"Yes. To support your use of the court system, there is a voluntary tax in any amount you wish to contribute."

Jer thought back through his civics classes in secondary school. "The court is supported by the theocracy. Otherwise, justice would only go to the wealthy."

The official snickered. "That's what the textbooks say, don't they? The real world doesn't work like the textbooks. Consider it like a donation to a church. It's not required, but the judge loves a generous giver." He leaned closer. "For an extra ten shekels, I'll tell you what the accused paid for his tax."

Chapter 3: Order in the Court

Jer struggled to think clearly with the official staring at him. The courts were supposed to be free to everyone to prevent justice going to the highest bidder. Tithes to the church were meant to take care of all government. Ten percent of all transactions public and private. That was all anyone was expected to pay. Was this some kind of test? Pay the "tax" and prove just how dishonest he could be? Maybe the system was corrupt now and he would only get justice by playing along?

Whatever it was, this whole situation smelled worse than the compost pile rotting behind the shed.

"I'll pass." Jer crossed his arms over his chest.

The court official tapped a few times on his screen. "You sure you want to do that? The judge will not be impressed."

"It's not in the budget, friend."

"Not even a mite?" The official frowned.

"There's no oxygen in a vacuum."

He put the ledger away. "Well, I guess if you haven't got it, you haven't got it."

The hovercar turned onto a wide street. The dinginess of the surrounding area gave way to a level of shine even Ma would approve of. The crowds here thinned so a man could walk easily without brushing anyone's shoulder. At the end of the street, a low granite building reached four spires toward the gray clouds hovering above.

Once the hovercar parked in a large lot next to the building, the doors opened with a hiss of equalizing pressure and hydraulics. Cane firmly in hand, Jer swung his legs out and rocked back before levering himself up.

Other hovercars in the lot clearly belonged to people with an excess of income. Jer identified several of the vehicles by year and make, and just the import fees to get one of them here from Earth were more than the ranch earned in a whole year, before expenses.

The court official secured his hovercar and came around. "Follow me."

He set a quick pace, and Jer hobbled along as fast as he could. They entered the building through a side door. The air inside had an antiseptic smell to it. Bright lighting reflected off gilt surfaces, including a collection of brass statues of men and women in judicial robes and miters. Each held a gavel and a book, symbols of their office. Personalities shown ranged from stern to somber to jovial.

The court official looked over his shoulder at Jer with a smirk full of mischief. "Quickly, now. Shouldn't keep the judge waiting." He hurried down the hall.

Jer grimaced. "I'd go faster if I could."

The official stopped next to a statue of a short, older woman whose beauty had the artificial look of surgical perfection.

"Right through here." The official opened the door beside it.

"Thank you."

Jer stepped through into a space five meters square. Purple and gold brocade curtains hung from the walls on the left and the right. Directly ahead, a gold-inlaid desk sat in front of a mural of a hand reaching out of a cloud to give a scroll to a judge who resembled the statue outside the door. Halfway across the room, a brass bar split the space.

Kane stood on the left side of the bar, looking more smug than he had a right to, considering the reason for the meeting. "Afternoon, Jer."

"Kane." Jer walked up the right side of the bar, where the accuser stood to present his case.

"Pity about Dave, but it was an accident."

Jer's shoulder and chest muscles tensed. "I think that's what we're here to decide, isn't it?"

The curtain in the far corner of the room fluttered.

The official who had given Jer a ride came out and stood at rigid attention. "The Honorable Sarah Sterman."

The subject of the statue and the mural entered and took a seat at the desk.

She tapped the surface. "Jeremiah Baruch, you chose not to pay the tax."

"I paid my tithe for this quarter before I left home. Now, with final expenses for my brother and this unexpected trip, there's nothing left for another tax."

"I see." Her stern look matched the one on the mural behind her. She pointed at Kane. "What evidence do you have that this unfortunate death was, in fact, an accident?"

Kane produced a data chip. "Statements from my crew. We were mining the same area of Nain as David Baruch. My ship malfunctioned. The repulsor beam I used to move an asteroid jammed. That caused a stampede. Dave was caught up in it."

The official retrieved the chip for the judge. She slid it into her desk's data port. A screen tilted upward, and the judge read the information.

She nodded. "Any other evidence?"

"Just those statements." Kane shook his head. "The malfunction that affected the repulsor wiped out sensor logs."

Convenient. Jer clenched his jaw to avoid speaking out of turn.

"Jeremiah Baruch." The judge turned toward him. "You may offer one piece of evidence to counter what Kane Lindemann provided."

Only one? What happened to hearing all available evidence before making a decision?

Jer pulled two chips from his pocket. He had statements from the miner who'd told him about the accident and from the sheriff. The miner was a first-hand witness, but the evidence was hardly conclusive. The sheriff's testimony proved hostility between Dave and Kane, but that was before the Nain event. He looked at both chips. Which one would give him the best chance of getting justice?

Chapter 4: Verdict

Jer shifted his weight and looked at the two data chips. "Sorry, ma'am, but I don't follow. Why only one?"

The judge huffed. "Mr. Lindemann provided one piece of evidence. You provide one piece of evidence. Equal time. It's only fair."

"Begging Your Honor's pardon, but Mr. Lindemann gave you two eyewitness testimonies on that data chip. If it's to be equal time, shouldn't I also get to provide two witnesses? I just have mine on two different chips is all."

The judge's face scrunched up like someone had handed her a warm glass of sour milk. "I suppose I see your point."

She pointed to the official who collected both chips. Once she had all three, she turned her attention back to Kane's evidence. The images played right there on the judge's desk, but the distance rendered the low volume into murmurs that meant nothing.

Kane's chip showed Vashti and Nahum in turn, talking for minutes at a time, undoubtedly portraying their boss as innocent of all wrong-doing. The judge drummed her fingers on the desk while she listened. Sheriff Weisser's report came next, and Jer mentally replayed the description of the brawl in the street over Jezebel. That testified to the bad blood between the two. Finally, the old miner's report and sensor log revealed Kane setting up mining too close to where Dave had already established himself. That just begged for trouble as any seasoned miner would know.

The moment the second video ended, the judge jabbed her finger at Kane. "I find that you were negligent, and your lack of diligence resulted in the death of another." She swiveled and pointed at Jer. "An argument over a girl is not sufficient to establish premeditation. Tempers may have run high, but people often say what they don't mean." She picked up her gavel. "Kane Lindemann, you are guilty of manslaughter. You will be implanted with a location chip. Any attempt to leave Shechem, alter or damage the chip, or remove it will result in forfeiture of the court's protection. David Baruch's next of kin will be notified and authorized to hunt you down." She banged the gavel on the desk and hustled out the back door hidden by the curtain.

The court official took Kane by the arm and turned to Jer. "If you want a taxi, they're usually waiting at the end of the cul-de-sac. If you'd rather save a few shekels and walk it, there's a map in the hall showing several routes." He herded Kane out the same door as the judge.

Jer stood in the empty room. That was it? A few video clips, a quick lecture, and done?

He pivoted in place, using his cane like the third leg of a tripod, and grimaced against the ache that started below his knee and ended just above his hip. The wide corridor outside the courtroom was empty now, but voices carried from some of the rooms. Apparently, some judges were into stern lectures but others were hosting a comedy. Jer found the map at the end of the corridor. Different-colored lines traced paths from the courthouse to the hangar. Some paths were less direct than others, but he didn't feel up to sightseeing. A slot in the wall offered a portable version of the map in exchange for more money than Jer had spent on supplies last month. Taxis were probably worse, given the local anything-for-a-shekel mentality. Walking would hurt and run the risk of finding some unsavory elements of society. Taxis had their risks, too. Dishonest drivers or criminals looking for an easy mark were just two possibilities. Jer memorized the most direct route and started for the end of the cul-de-sac. He'd decide when he got there.

Kane stepped out of the taxi and paid the driver almost a month's income for the ride. He tried to slam the door but a fit of coughing took over, rendering the act useless. The hydraulics pulled the door down as Kane stumbled into the hangar where the air wasn't entirely toxic. As he approached the ship, the ramp lowered, and Kane jogged up. Vashti stood at the top, waiting to button it up.

"How'd it go?" Vashti asked.

In his absence, she'd dyed her hair again, changing it from electric blue to moss green. As often as she tweaked her hair colors, he was amazed any of it was still attached to her head. At least the green matched the camouflaged fatigues that were effectively her uniform most days.

Kane rubbed the back of his neck where the chip had been inserted. The anesthesia used to numb the area was wearing off already. "Manslaughter."

Nahum leaned out of the cargo bay door. "That's good, ain't it?"

"It means I'm not dead yet, but I am stuck on this planet until the high priest dies. Can't say that prospect thrills me. He's an old guy, but he ain't that old."

"High Priest might need to have an accident." Nahum waggled his eyebrows.

Vashti rolled her eyes. "Bodyguards?"

"Eh, there are ways."

She shook her head. "We could distract Jer long enough for you to hightail it out of here. The universe is a big place to get lost in."

Kane considered both ideas.

Chapter 5: Unexpected Encounter

Jer shook his head and stepped back from the cab. "Thanks anyway."

"Suit yourself, mister." The driver tapped a button on his dashboard and the door swung closed.

A quick look down the block in both directions confirmed what Jer already knew. He'd talked to all the taxi drivers. The cheapest rate had been the cost of two weeks' supplies for a ride in a cab that smelled of old tobacco.

Jer tugged a handkerchief out of his pocket and held it over his mouth and nose. *Looks like I'll be walking this time.*

Normally he wouldn't have minded. The shortest trip was only a few blocks, but with his gimpy leg acting up and air that smelled worse than a caged skunk in a sewer, a ride would have been much nicer.

"Throw hay bales in one pile and wishes in the other and see which one gets the tallest," he muttered.

That was one of Pa's favorite sayings whenever one of them got to bellyachin' about what needed to be done. Jer could even hear it in Pa's voice.

How was Pa doing now, anyway? The heart surgery on Theopolis should be finished by now. He might even be on the way back home if all had gone well. He offered a quick prayer for Pa's recovery. The family wouldn't handle two tragedies back-to-back very well.

Jer sighed and recalled the shortest map path on the map in the courthouse. With his back to the building, he got his bearings then started off to the left.

Many of the locals he passed walked hunched over. Their clothes were serviceable but plain, and the looks on their faces resembled their clothes. They went about their business without making eye contact. Most were silent, and the few who weren't grumbled incoherently as they trudged along. Although the majority of the inhabitants either breathed through a cloth like him or used nothing at all, a scattering had some sort of breathing device that fit in their noses like a plastic moustache. Whether it actually filtered the air, got rid of or masked the stench, or just made a fashion statement, Jer couldn't say. The folks wearing them didn't look like they'd be up for an interview.

He turned his attention from the people to the environment. The area near the courthouse was in relatively decent repair. Buildings were clean and well maintained even if the people looked more like the most destitute of a major city's homeless population. What sort of intelligence lurked behind the tired, lonely expressions? How many doctors, engineers, or scientists were stuck here because of an accusation? How many were parents separated from their children? All of them waited for the death of the High Priest, which signaled an automatic pardon to all Shechem's temporary residents.

Two blocks away from the courthouse, the scenery changed as abruptly as flipping a switch. The people all shared the same drab appearance and joyless demeanor, but the buildings around him morphed from clean and orderly to pockmarked stone, broken windows, and graffiti.

Jer's stomach turned as he began to consider whether forgoing the cab would prove a mite wise and a shekel foolish. What good would it do him to save money on the cab fare only to get mugged or killed while walking?

He dismissed his fears as foolishness. No one was even looking at him, and the hangar was only a couple more blocks away.

When Jer turned the corner, the sight of the hangar buoyed his spirits. He grimaced and adjusted the grip on his cane as he renewed his speed.

A man stepped out of a shadowed doorway and blocked Jer's path. When Jer stepped aside, the man moved with him.

"Excuse me." Jer moved the other way.

The man blocked the path again and another person moved up behind Jer.

Tension radiated down Jer's back from his shoulders. "Now look, fellas, I ain't carryin' much of value, and I don't want trouble."

"Hand over what you got, and there won't be trouble."

Jer gripped the head of his cane more tightly. They didn't know who they were messing with, but they might have friends, more than Jer could deal with.

📖

Nahum stared out the transport's window as the ship entered the New Jebus system. A yellow-white main sequence star herded only a few planets. One of those, Theopolis, was their target. The two outer gas giants in the system might provide an interesting mining opportunity or two, but that would have to wait until they got the boss out of his current jam. He should have left the mess with Dave Baruch alone, but get a pretty girl involved and the boss's wits went lightyears away.

Vashti tapped his arm and leaned closer. "Your plan account for Pa Baruch being in Theopolis somewhere?"

Nahum rolled his eyes. "Four billion people on this planet and you're worried about running into one old man? You this paranoid all the time?"

"Just wondering how far you thought this out is all." Vashti shrugged. "If this were as easy as you make it out to be, why hasn't it been done already?"

"Because people like you jump to the conclusion it can't be done!" He squinted at her. "Go home if you'd rather."

Vashti snorted. "Oh no. I'm dying to see you pull off this caper."

The transport captain came on the PA. "Prepare for landing."

Nahum leaned back in his seat and closed his eyes as the ship rumbled through re-entry burn and settled on its gear scant minutes later. The ship had no sooner touched down than most of the passengers were on their feet, rooting through bins for their carry-on luggage, and shuffling for the exit.

Nahum stayed still. No sense herding like cattle through a gate. Five minutes later, the line cleared and Nahum and Vashti collected their things before disembarking.

The spaceport wasn't as crowded as Nahum had hoped for. Crowds offered a form of anonymity, a way to get lost from security cameras. Maybe Vashti was right. Maybe this would be harder than he thought.

Someone grabbed Nahum's arm and spun him around. He jerked free and stepped back.

Pa Baruch beamed a huge smile. "Well, if it ain't Nahum Rotenberg and Vashti Osgood. Didn't expect to see you here. What brings you to Theopolis?"

Chapter 6: Looking for Trouble

Nahum's shoulders tensed. He ignored the smirk on Vashti's face and scrambled to come up with a reason for them to be in Theopolis that didn't involve an untimely death of a certain priest.

"Um, we're, um, we're on an errand for Kane, seeing as he's stuck on Shechem for a while." Nahum rubbed his upper lip.

Vashti stepped forward. "Terribly sorry about what happened to Dave. Those asteroids got to stampeding, and he just couldn't shake loose of them. Such a tragedy."

Ma Baruch's eyes teared up, and she took an embroidered handkerchief from her purse.

"Thank you." Ol' Man Baruch drew his wife into a one-armed hug. "So, what are your plans now?"

"At loose ends for a while." The tension in Nahum's shoulders faded. "If Kane finds decent quarters on Shechem, we'll probably keep our mining business afloat. We'll know more once this errand's done."

An announcement over the PA called all passengers to Gibeah for boarding.

Old Man Baruch looked up at the ceiling for a moment. "That's us. You two have a good trip now."

"You do the same," Nahum said.

As the pair walked off, Vashti backhanded Nahum's arm. "'We're on an errand?' That's the best you could do?"

He scowled at her. "It worked, didn't it? Now let's go. We need to do some data collection before we finish the errand."

Vashti shrugged. "I guess everyone's vulnerable somewhere. We just have to figure out where."

Jer settled his weight on his stronger leg and raised the head of his cane above his shoulder. "Now, I told you I've got nothing of value in my pockets today. I don't want trouble, and you can't afford trouble, so let's just part ways."

"Mister, if you don't hand over what you got, I'm gonna break that cane over your head and take what I want," the guy in front said.

"This cane?" Jer triggered the LEDs built into cane just below the handle.

Fiercely bright light cut through the smog like a laser. The thugs cried out and so did a few others nearby.

Jer swung the cane like a bat, catching the spokesman above the ear with the metal cap on the cane. Before the spokesman hit the ground, Jer pivoted and jabbed the other thug in the belly. When the guy doubled over, Jer slammed the cane against the back of the mugger's head, dropping him to the pavement. Jer switched off the LEDs. Blinking away after images, he stepped around his would-be attacker and continued on his way.

The remaining couple blocks passed without incident. In fact, many people gave him more space as he passed. Jer entered the hangar complex and hobbled around to the bay where he'd left Ethan and Tamar keeping an eye on *Yireh*.

A man leaned against the door. Unlike the usual denizens of the area, he wore a uniform. The patch on his arm identified him as an employee of Grace Interstellar Works, the biggest commercial passenger carrier in the region.

The man pushed off from the wall and looked Jer up and down, taking particular notice of the cane. "You the kin of Dave Baruch?"

"Who's asking?" Jer stopped and planted the cane directly in front of him, leaning on it with both hands.

"My name don't matter." He came a step or two closer but stayed out of arm's reach. "I got important information for the kin of David Baruch."

"All right. I'm Jer Baruch. What's the problem?"

"It'll cost you twenty-four shekels."

Jer frowned. "What will?"

"The information."

"Mister, I ain't never bought anything sight unseen. My daddy taught me better'n that."

The worker shook his head. "I could get in trouble for just talking to you. Pay up front or I walk."

Chapter 7: Weighing Options

Jer studied the space line worker through narrowed eyes. Paying up front for unknown information sounded like the perfect way to separate a fool and his money. Jer didn't have any delusions about being the sharpest spine on the cactus, but he knew better than to buy from a stranger without inspecting.

He tugged his wallet out of his pocket and withdrew twenty-four shekels. The would-be informant's eyes lit up like a ship's running lights. He came forward with his hand extended.

Jer put his wallet away and closed his fist around the money. "Information then money."

"Now look–" He propped his fist on his hip.

"No, you look." Jer jabbed his cane at the other man's chest. "For all I know, you're running some kind of hustle. If your information is worth it, you'll be paid."

The space line worker glared for a few moments before he turned and walked away. He only managed a few steps before he stopped. He sighed and stared at the ceiling before he turned and came back. "All right. I was working at the security checkpoint. Two men and a woman approached. The woman and one of the men had tickets for Theopolis. Their IDs said Vashti Osgood and Nahum Rotenberg. They addressed the other fella as Kane. Told him to sit tight and he'd be free in no time." He extended his hand. "Pay up."

"What's any of this to me?"

"Your brother's killer is sending two people to Theopolis to secure his release. There's only one thing they could do there that would get Kane and almost everyone else on this planet a free pass off world."

Jer nodded. The current high priest notoriously refused to grant pardons or appeals. By law, only the priest's death would release Shechem's inhabitants. "So why are you talking to me instead of the priest's bodyguard?"

"Who said I didn't? They don't pay for tips, and I got rent due. Just thought you'd like to know what they're planning."

Uh-huh. Somehow, I don't believe your altruism came first. Jer pocketed half the money and tossed the rest to the informant.

He snatched it out of the air and counted the coins. "Where's the rest?"

"That's all it's worth to me. Take it or leave it. You're lucky I'm carrying any real money."

Another hard glare threatened to incinerate Jer. Jer left the man standing there and turned into *Yireh's* landing bay.

The ramp lowered as he approached. Ethan stood at the top. "So, how'd it go?"

Jer stepped into the lighter gravity of the ship. Within a few steps, he went from leaning hard on his cane for support to just needing it as a reminder to be careful. The pain in his leg lightened up gradually, but after so long in normal gravity, the ache would be a while. Maybe tomorrow.

At the top of the ramp, Jer smacked the button to close up the ship. "Let's find Tamar, and I'll tell you all about it."

Ethan darted ahead to the bridge, each step launching him further up and forward in the low gravity. Jer followed with extra springs in his step, too, but not nearly as exuberant as his little brother.

On the bridge, Tamar sat at the communication board and watched the external cameras. She greeted them with a smile and an unspoken question in her eyes. Jer settled into the pilot's chair and swiveled it around to see the others. While Ethan found a spot to lean against the back wall, Jer began his explanation of the court case and the informant. He skipped over the account of the muggers. No sense in worrying folks without cause.

He rested his cane across his lap. "So, that's where we stand. We can stay here and keep an eye on Kane or head home and wait for the court to send us word that he fled the planet."

Ethan pushed off from the wall and came a few steps closer. "What about the high priest? Shouldn't someone warn him?"

"I reckon we could." Tamar shrugged. "But what could we do that his whole collection of bodyguards can't?"

Ethan thought for a moment. "Pick Vashti and Nahum out of a group."

"So, we send a picture along." Tamar smirked and leaned forward. "You don't really think Kane's the first guy to come up with an assassination plot against the high priest, do you?"

Jer shook his head. "No. I 'spect several have tried that particular gambit."

"The priest will be fine." Tamar leaned back in her chair and crossed her legs. "The real issue is whether we sit here counting our hair and burning through resources waiting for Kane to make a run for it or we head home, get back to useful work, and probably lose Kane when he does take off."

Jer nodded once. That just about summed up their options.

Nahum ordered some fancy kind of coffee for Vashti and a good, ol' fashioned iced tea for himself. Once his thumbprint had paid for the order, a slot in the wall opened and a tray slid out. He left the tray and took both cups. That was against protocol, sure, but someone else could deal with the tray. He scanned the cybercafe and found his partner waving from a computer in the back corner, a perfect spot for their afternoon chore. By the time he made it to her chosen location, the coffee-heated ceramic had become unpleasantly warm against his fingers.

He set her cup next to her and slid his in the holder beside his seat.

"Am I flying this thing or you?" Vashti pointed at the computer.

Nahum fished his most recent purchase out of his pocket. "You are, unless you want to be here until next week."

"Right." She sipped the coffee and looked at the tiny chip in his hand. "You sure that thing works?"

He shrugged. "They say you get what you pay for, so this should work flawlessly."

After a quick glance around the café, he inserted the chip into the data port on the front of the computer. Now, if the thing behaved the way it was advertised, they could look up whatever they wanted without triggering any warning systems.

Nahum sat back and watched Vashti navigate to the high priest's official page. Next, she tapped a link to his personal appearances. The list showed location, date, time, and purpose.

"So, dinner with Earth's ambassador is out unless you have diplomatic credentials you haven't mentioned before," Vashti whispered.

Nahum sipped his coffee. "Blessing the sick might work. Think you could fake bein' deathly ill?"

"Sure, but then what? Say we successfully manage what we're here to do." Vashti swirled her coffee cup. "How're we gettin' out of there? I ain't lookin' for the gallows. Are you?"

"Wasn't part of my plan." Nahum chugged a couple big swallows of his tea. "We need something with a time delay, so when he keels over, we're nowhere around at all."

Vashti grabbed his arm. "I got it!"

Chapter 8: Best Laid Plans

Nahum stood outside a general store near the center of Theopolis. Why Vashti wanted to stop here was a total mystery to him. After her major epiphany in the café, she hadn't been forthcoming with details. Annoying, but what could he do but follow her to this store? Here she'd left him on the street wondering what exactly was going through her mind. She'd be getting a piece of his if she didn't let him in on the secret soon.

After what felt like a couple months, Vashti came out with a vial in her hand.

He took it from her and read the label on the clear fluid. "Almond extract, huh? And what's this supposed to do?"

"Don't you remember? On the news a few years ago, there was a story about our favorite high priest and his nut allergy." Vashti tapped the vial. "That there is concentrated almond in alcohol. Clear as it is. We could pass it off as holy water or something else harmless."

He nodded and pocketed the vial. "Then we can find some way to add it to something he's eating."

Vashti shrugged. "Doesn't have to be that complicated. The article said just being around nuts can set off the reaction. Get it on something he touches, and we're all set."

"Well, then let's get to the cathedral and pay the old man a visit." He stepped to the curb and hailed a taxi.

The trip to the cathedral took too long for the distance, but Nahum didn't mind the sightseeing. He'd never been to Theopolis, and they had an hour to kill before tonight's dinner. Playing tourist was as good a way as any. The taxi dropped them off at the cathedral with only a half hour to go. Nahum let Vashti cover the cab fare.

She waved for him to follow. "I saw the catering truck around back as we came around the corner."

Nahum caught up with her and took the lead. They rounded the corner at a speed he hoped split the difference between urgent and suspicious. An unmarked truck halfway down the block had an ant trail of servers in red jackets and black trousers carting sealed containers into the back of the cathedral.

Nahum glanced at Vashti. They weren't dressed for their part, but borrowing a uniform from someone shouldn't prove any more difficult than a whack on the head of a couple workers.

They slowed to a steady walk and approached the catering truck. Some workers offered a squint-eyed look as they carried a container inside. Moments later, a white-clad guard appeared and strode toward Nahum and Vashti.

Nahum smiled and showed both hands were empty. "Hey, I know we're late. We got hung up in traffic."

The guard's hand rested on the butt of his pistol. "That's far enough. Who are you, and what's your business?"

"We're part of the catering crew, and–"

The guard scowled. "The catering crew all came together after being thoroughly checked at another site."

"We were late." Vashti waved in the direction of the spaceport. "Got there just as the van pulled out then took a cab."

The guard's eyes darkened. "Turn around and walk away before you find yourself in a cell with an interrogator."

"Could you just cut us a break?" Nahum took a step closer. "I need the–"

The guard drew his gun and aimed.

"Okay, okay, we're going." Vashti tugged Nahum's arm, and they retreated back around to the front of the building.

"That worked well," Nahum muttered.

Vashti sighed. "Guess we should have expected tight security. So what now? Go spread almond oil extract on every surface he's likely to touch?"

"Doubt that'll work any better, but we can try that then come up with some other idea for the blessing of the sick."

At the front of the cathedral, they joined the line of tourists outside the gate into the courtyard. A gal at the gate accepted payment while a hidden speaker played a continuous loop of instructions.

"Do not leave the tourist areas. No food or drink of any kind allowed past this point. This is a weapon-free zone."

At the gate, Vashti paid their admission. As they stepped through, a small, curly-haired dog on a leash sat down next to a guard and howled pitifully until the guard snapped his fingers.

"Empty your pockets, please." He held a plastic tray as another guard joined them.

Vashti dropped her ID, a few coins, and a data disk in the tray. Nahum left the vial in his pocket but emptied his own assortment of odds and ends.

The guard held the tray under the dog's chin, but after a cursory sniff, the mutt lost all interest.

The newly arrived guard grabbed Nahum by the arm. "Step over here, please, sir."

"Stay very still, please." The first guard released the clasp on the leash and gave a sharp order in a language Nahum didn't recognize.

The dog sniffed Vashti first then trotted over. Nahum's shoulders tensed, and he willed himself to relax. What dog could get a whiff of anything through a sealed glass vial?

The fuzzy mutt sat at his feet and howled. When the dog handler snapped his fingers, the dog retreated to his side.

"Are you carrying anything else, sir?" the new guard asked.

Nahum patted his pockets, ignoring the vial. "Nothing."

"Very well, sir. I will have to ask you to leave. You may return tomorrow and try again." The guard ushered Nahum toward an exit gate.

Nahum shrugged away. "What's this about?"

"You must have handled or eaten nuts today, sir, unless you're carrying something you haven't declared. Come back tomorrow, and perhaps you can enter then."

"This is ridiculous." Nahum frowned.

"I'm sorry, sir, but it's a health concern. I'm sure you can understand. This way, sir." The guard herded him toward the exit.

Vashti followed after collecting their things.

Once they were back in a cab on the way to the hotel, she frowned. "This is going to be harder than we thought."

"We'll contact the boss. There might be another way that doesn't involve getting past security."

📖

Jer weighed his choices. Some part of his conscience told him he had to stop the assassination attempt, but were Nahum and Vashti really that potent a force? The theocracy had been established a few decades ago. As Tamar had said, Kane was hardly the first to come up with the notion of assassinating the high priest to win a pardon. The chances of finding a unique idea the bodyguards hadn't considered was pretty slim. Nahum and Vashti weren't that smart, and Kane wasn't rich enough to hire a pro.

Staying here was a waste, too. Ship's stores wouldn't last forever, and prices on Shechem were insane. Sure, Kane might slip past the patrols, but he wouldn't be the first to try that either. Escapes from Shechem were rare. Kane might still try, though, especially if he thought he could get away before Jer mobilized.

He turned to his console and powered the systems up. "Ethan, contact flight control and get us a departure window."

"We're leaving?" Ethan asked.

Jer looked back over his shoulder and smiled. "I got an idea. Tamar, find us a hiding place."

Tamar smiled, nodding. "Going to draw Kane out?"

"If he'll take the bait."

"Flight control says launch when ready. They don't get much traffic, I guess," Ethan said.

Jer smirked. "Don't suppose they do. Tamar?"

"Not much for hiding spots, boss. Backside of a moon leaves us half blind. Gas giant rings are like mini asteroid fields, and not much safer. We could just hover somewhere and kill all our running lights. Long as we stay out of the sun, we'd be pretty near invisible, but that goes for friendly traffic as well as Kane."

Chapter 9: Not Quite Clear

Once Jer cleared the atmosphere, he swung around onto the course that took them into the planet's shadow. He eased them into position and came to a full stop.

"A'right. Kill running lights, leave the engines on standby, and cut power usage as much as possible." Jer pivoted his chair toward the others.

"How long are we just going to sit out here?" Ethan drew back a slider that turned the cabin lights down to barely enough to see.

Jer shrugged. "Probably longer than we want, and hopefully long enough to get the job done."

"Just play it by ear, Ethan," Tamar growled.

The engine hum dwindled.

"Is it safe to talk?" Ethan asked.

Tamar snickered. "Sound don't travel in space."

"Just askin' is all." He glared at her.

"You two go get some rest. I'll take the first watch and send for one of you later."

Ethan rushed out with Tamar on his heels.

Once they were gone, Jer looked out of the viewscreen at the planet ahead. Only a thin crescent showed. Kane might consider sneaking out the other side of the world. If that happened, the court would alert him to Kane's escape. By the time Jer mobilized and got around the planet, Kane could be well gone, but he couldn't watch *all* sides of the planet by himself. Keeping an eye on this part would have to be enough.

📖

With nothing to do but watch rust form on the ceiling, Kane reclined in his quarters and stared at the green light on the communication board. Either Nahum and Vashti would be calling to give the all-clear, or an informant would be letting him know Jer Baruch had left the planet. Kane hoped the first call would come from Nahum. Paying the informant would drain the pocketbook.

When the green light flared, tension fluttered in his gut. Kane reached over and slapped the communication switch. "Say yer piece."

"You wanted to know if *Yireh* ever left? Well, they just zoomed on out of here." The nasally voice meant Kane was out a few thousand shekels. "Sending you the surveillance video now."

The computer's ping let him know the upload was complete. Seconds later, a new window opened showing *Yireh* on an outbound course.

"So, when do I get paid?" the informant snapped.

"As soon as you stop transmitting." Kane frowned. "Can't send you a payment and keep blabbing."

He smacked the toggle to end the call, and then he set up the fund transfer, less a trade "handling fee." Let the guy complain. In fewer than ten minutes, Kane would be gone.

He jogged up to the bridge and slid into the pilot's seat. He hit switches and turned dials to bring the engines, navigation, and tactical systems online. The communication system demanded attention with an incessant beep.

Kane groaned and flicked the switch to acknowledge the caller. "Yeah?"

"Kane? Nahum. Me an' Vashti have run into a small problem with security here."

"What kind of problem?" Kane asked. *If you've gotten yourself in a legal mess, you're going to sort it out yourself.*

"Can't get past it to gain access to the priest. I 'spect it'll be the same no matter how we try it."

"Skip it." Kane shook his head. "I'll come pick you up, and we'll get out of town."

"Wait, wait, wait." Vashti's voice came through clearer. Perhaps she was getting closer to the mic. "You can't leave Shechem. Isn't that why we're on this little errand?"

"I can now. Jer's left. See you at the spaceports soon." Kane switched off the system and gripped the controls.

He lifted off and headed for space. The communication stations system beeped again. That would be the control tower complaining about his sudden, unauthorized departure. The radar showed a small craft giving pursuit, but if they managed to break through his shields before he left the atmosphere, they deserved to get him.

With continuous acceleration, Kane left Shechem behind like so much manure in a pasture. The planetary police chasing him gave up.

He smirked. "Knew you didn't have it in you."

Kane brought the ship around on the outbound course.

The empty space ahead of him lit up and solidified into *Yireh.*

Chapter 10: Fatal Escape

Jer would have given up his favorite walking stick just to see the look on Kane's face when *Yireh* powered up. *Imperious* yawed almost one hundred eighty degrees and darted away.

Jer threw the throttle forward and chased after his brother's killer. The door behind him whooshed open, but Jer kept his eyes on the viewscreen.

"Want me on tactical, boss?" Tamar asked.

"Yes, ma'am, but no kill shots unless he starts shootin'." Jer gritted his teeth as he followed Kane through a tight turn.

She snorted. "You know he wouldn't be that considerate if the roles were reversed."

"I know it, but if we ain't better than him, we might as well let him go." Jer spared a look back at her, regretting it when he returned his attention to a blank viewscreen.

The radar showed Kane heading across the system. Jer banked into a turn and followed, gradually closing in. The door behind him opened again.

"Ethan, have a seat at cartography and tell me what's ahead of us."

"Uh, sure."

At the far edge of Jer's peripheral vision, Ethan slid into the seat and called up the map.

In front of him, Kane had stopped trying to shake *Yireh* and now raced a straight course.

"Gas giant with rings," Ethan reported.

"What are you up to, Kane?" Jer mumbled.

"Hide in the gas giant?" Ethan asked.

Jer shook his head. "Atmosphere'd crush his ship like a paper cup."

"Computer say how thick that ring is?" Tamar asked.

The stripy gas giant was the size of a kid's marble in the viewscreen and getting bigger by the moment. The rings at that distance were thinner than a sheet of paper.

Ethan tapped the consoles keyboard a few times. "Computer makes it about a hundred meters or thereabout. Way too dense to fly *Yireh* through."

Jer smirked. "Ma didn't raise anyone dumb enough to fly through rings."

"Anything in that ring big enough to trigger a stampede?" Tamar suggested.

Ethan drew a breath through teeth. "Yeah, I think so, but he'd have to get opposite us for it to do any good, wouldn't he?"

The gas giant now filled most of the viewscreen. Had Vashti and Nahum gone for reinforcements rather than on a mission to kill the high priest? Was Kane planning to use the planet's rings as a weapon?

The comm system pinged. In one terrific leap in the half gravity, Ethan pushed off from cartography and landed at communications. "It's Kane."

"Let's hear it," Jer said.

"Back off, Baruch." Kane's voice came through the system with just a touch of distortion. "The only thing waiting for you at that planet up ahead is a one-way ticket to join your brother."

"Shut down your engines or turn back to Shechem," Jer ordered.

"Yer funeral."

The connection broke with a click.

Kane cut communications with *Yireh*. He'd known Jer wouldn't spook easy enough to fall for a bluff, but there was no harm in trying. Leaving the system on autopilot, Kane called up the ship's manifest. *Yireh* was a bigger ship, so a shoot-out wasn't likely to end well. Plenty of natural weapons circled the planet up ahead, and Kane knew how to use them, but first, he had to buy time to get in position.

The ship's holds only had a few tons of new ore, some personal effects, wastewater, and other garbage. That'd be good for a few seconds.

Kane adjusted course to come in parallel to the planet's ring but above it. The radar showed *Yireh* right on his tail. As soon as he was over the gas giant's ring, Kane jettisoned the ore, wastewater, and garbage. He dove down and cranked up the repulsor to push a hole through.

The collision alarm registered a strong protest against the plan. Myriad pings and a couple loud bangs rattled *Imperious* but no hull breach alerts went off. The front viewscreen grayed with static. One section in the top right corner went black.

Lost a camera.

Annoying, but not bad, all things considered. Once through the ring, Kane slowed to a stop and yawed to face *Yireh* as the bigger ship started toward the edge of the ring.

What's the matter, Jer? Too scared to follow me through like that?

Kane picked out several larger chunks of rock and ice in the ring and aimed the repulsor at them. Some he hit straight on, but others he hit from an oblique angle. The big pieces moved, colliding with each other and with smaller debris. He kept agitating the larger parts of the ring until the whole section ahead of *Yireh* was a spinning, crashing mess bulging out in Jer's direction. A smattering of rocks broke away and shot out like projectiles. Kane smiled and continued nudging his missiles like several-ton billiard balls. More chunks broke loose, hurtling in *Yireh's* direction.

Jer dodged the first few, but as the flying rocks grew denser, the pale haze of the repulsor beam reflected off the dust from collisions. Rocks and ice re-entered the chaos from the other side.

Kane watched the screen for stones coming his way and deflected them with his own repulsor. The stampede, now driven from both sides of the ring, became more frantic. He kept one eye on the radar and the other on the targeting system.

His heart raced and his hands shook. "Too close. I'm too close to the ring."

Kane deflected a large rock and grabbed *Imperious's* controls. The collision alarm blared. At the edge of the blackened viewscreen segment, the shiny, white edge of a rock loomed. Some distracted part of his mind tentatively identified the mineral as silver, maybe even platinum, but he dismissed that thought and scrambled to get the repulsor into position.

📖

Jer squinted and turned his head away from the brilliant flare of light.

"Shockwave!" Tamar yelled.

Spinning *Yireh* on its vertical axis, Jer accelerated away from the gas giant's ring before the shockwave from *Imperious's* exploding reactor pelted them with debris and an electromagnetic pulse guaranteed to fry the computers. He eyeballed a course around to the backside of the gas giant, using the massive planet as a shield.

"Ethan." Jer cast a glance at his little brother. "Set us a course for Gibeah. Let's go home."

On the way out of church the next Sabbath, Jer stopped in the graveyard at one of the two newest markers. Neither marked an actual burial place, but they served as memorials to the deceased all the same. He took off his hat and a held it down by his side.

Using his cane for support, Jer knelt in front of Dave's gravestone. "You an' me never did see eye to eye on much, and that's a fact, but a man still grieves the loss of his brother. Hope t' meet up with you on the other side, so's we can get to know each other proper." After a couple moments of silence, Jer grimaced and used his cane to lever himself back up. On the way out, he paused at the other new stone. "You were a murderer and a thief, Kane Lindemann, but for your sake, I hope you made your peace with God before your reactor blew."

As Jer hobbled out of the graveyard, he settled his hat on his head. The Sabbath was not a day for work, but it was a day for planning the work for the week ahead, and there was no shortage of that. He and Pa would spend the day showing Ethan the way of it while Ma and Haddy got Sabbath dinner going. Just wouldn't be the same without Dave there, but with or without him, plenty needed doing. That hole where Dave used to be might never get filled properly, but they'd have to continue on, just like always.

Origin:

After the release of *Mindstorm*, a prequel story about Thomas, "The Negotiator," appeared in the anthology *Aquasynthesis Again* from Splashdown Books. For a while, I tossed around an idea that provided a bit of Calla's history, too. While she didn't have quite the family trainwreck that Thomas did, her medical training did put her in a mess a time or two.

After I finished writing one of those adventures for her, I never quite found the place to put "Crisis" until now.

"Crisis" takes place after Calla completes her medical training but before *Mindstorm*.

Crisis

Calla dashed into the Medward and clutched the corner of the wall to swing down the hall faster. When she reached the emergency room, the staff of Medward 8 scrambled in the organized chaos of packing gear and supplies into bags and crates.

She scanned the room for the gold armband among the different-colored scrubs and white lab coats. The armband on Xava Vandamir marked her as the expedition leader for this team. Calla wove through the crowd. Xava held an electronic clipboard and checked off tasks as people completed them and signaled her.

"Hey, kid. I should have sent someone for you. I keep forgetting you have that Power Deficit thing and don't teleport." She acknowledged Nikk's hand signal and checked two boxes. "Short version: major earthquake on Dapri. Earth is sending help, but they're thirty-six hours away."

"And they don't trust us to get them there quicker, so we're in first."

"Yep, but only until they arrive. Dapri doesn't approve of us, except in a disaster." Xava marked another box.

Calla nodded. "So we're all headed there for a day and a half."

"Not all of us. You and a handful of others are staying behind to hold the fort here." Xava checked off a few more tasks. "I sent you a list of everyone I'm taking. You're in change of Medward 8. Work with Andy to set a master schedule with the rest of the wards. Overnight will be handled by the odd-numbered wards this time, but staff from the even numbered wards will be taking their turns there, too."

Calla recalled the emergency protocols and scanned through the stored images in her mind to bring herself back up to speed on the details. She finished and blinked a few times. "Understood."

Xava smiled. "Y'know, it's creepy how you do that."

"What?"

"You know what. Access that perfect-image memory of yours. It's creepy, but I like it. Wish I could recall that perfectly." She marked one last box. "Okay. That's everything. Andy knows the drill so check with him on what to do next."

"Thanks, Xava. Be safe out there." Calla stepped back.

The departing team gathered around, each holding or touching a bag or crate. They teleported away, leaving Calla with a general practitioner named Will, two nurses, and the random scraps and wrappers from the hastily packed equipment.

"Ok, let's get this mess picked up," she instructed. "Then we'll review the protocol." Calla grabbed the nearest scrap of paper and pitched it in the trash.

📖

After just a few hours of sleep, Calla's alarm went off. She growled and rolled out of bed. The usual business for a ward with five doctors had fallen entirely on her yesterday, and even with most of the routine appointments rescheduled, she had spent most of the day flitting from one patient to the next.

At least she could do her work in the climate-controlled, familiar environment of the med ward. The expedition team would be dealing with much more instability.

Calla yawned her way through breakfast, nothing more exciting than a bowl of cereal and a cup of tea. She had just put the dirty dishes in the washer when someone knocked on her apartment door. She reached out with her mind and recognized the unique mental signature of one of Haidar's emergency services dispatchers. Matt, wasn't it? He worked as a dispatcher to pay his way through school to become a nurse. He took two classes per year because he couldn't afford to go faster. He was a vegetarian by personal choice and—

Okay, brain. That's enough trivia for now.

A warmer than average sense of anxiety warbled in his thoughts. What kind of crisis brought the dispatcher to her door? He'd been around long enough to know psionic medicine specialists used old-style communicators.

Calla hustled to the door and triggered the release. "Good morning."

"Hi. I'm looking for Dr. Geisman." His broad smile and relaxed body language exuded a confidence that didn't match his thoughts.

"'You found her."

He leaned to one side to look past her. "Doctor Calla Geisman, the psionic medicine specialist."

"That's me." She raised her right hand and waved.

He had the decency to blush. "I'm sorry. I didn't expect—I mean—"

You didn't expect someone with Power Deficit Syndrome to be a psionic specialist. Right. You and most of the rest of the station. You'd be amazed at what I can actually do. She sighed and leaned against the door frame. "You're here for a reason?"

Matt nodded. "They need you on Dapri."

"And did they say why?" An uncomfortable tension settled in her shoulders.

"I don't know." He glanced away. "I'm sorry. They just sent me to get you. Dr. Petrov will take over your duties here."

"All right. Let me get my trauma kit and a lab coat." She pushed off the frame and gestured for him to have a seat in the living room. "Back in a bit."

Calla retreated to her bedroom and closed the door. The dress she wore today wouldn't work for crawling around in earthquake debris. She grabbed black jeans and a long-sleeved shirt from her closet and quickly changed. Athletic shoes replaced the flats that went with her dress. Then she grabbed her oldest lab coat and the backpack that held her trauma kit.

When she rejoined Matt in the living room, he stood up as if spring-loaded.

"I'm ready if you are," she said.

He offered his hand and accepted hers without any of the squeamishness that most people showed.

Well, he is studying medicine. He probably knows Power Deficit Syndrome is genetic.

Further thought along that line was cut short by the swirling mass of color that started out as her living room then mutated and resolved into a tent interior. An intense wave of dizziness and nausea doubled Calla over.

"Whoa!" Someone's supporting arm helped her to a stiff, cold chair. "Hey, Calla, it's Xava. Lemme see if I can back that off some."

The familiar and strong mental touch of her colleague drove some of the nausea into the background.

"Better?" Xava asked.

Calla blinked hard. "Yes. Thank you."

Xava gripped Calla's arm. "Take a few minutes to put your head back together, then we'll tell you what the story is, okay?"

"Right." She nodded.

Calla kept her breathing steady while the nausea faded. Before she was totally ready to face the world, she stood slowly enough to keep the planet from twirling backwards.

Xava leaned against a table in a dark gray canvas tent. A map of what had once been the capital of Dapri was tacked to the fabric wall behind her with sections of the city marked out in red. Around them, medical supplies were stacked on tables. Dispatchers coordinated rescue teams and nurses handed out equipment as people asked for it.

"Ready?" Xava cradled her ever-present clipboard in one arm.

"Close enough."

Xava smirked. "I don't believe you, but let's get moving. What do you know about Dapri?"

"Humanoid population. They get part of their mineral requirements by ingesting rocks. Tectonically active planet. Xenophobic to a degree. Psionophobic in many places—"

"Bingo! That's where you come in." Xava pointed at her. "We're running into folks who don't mind us helping out if we promise to limit telepathy. A lot. That's the majority, actually. For the rest, if they're out cold, they don't get a say. There are about a dozen who won't let us glowing-eyed freaks near them, but they won't last until the group shows up from Earth."

"And with my disability, the glow in my eyes isn't visible in a lit room, so I'm it," Calla concluded. She fished her anti-psionic generator from her backpack's front pocket. "This will hide someone else's eye glow."

"Yeah, except we were all together when they freaked out, except—"

Matt shook his head. "Except for us dispatchers. We were here in the tent for a briefing."

"True. You up for helping Calla with the psionophobes?" Xava went over to the supply boxes and returned with a pair of surgical caps. "Her widget will take care of your glow-in-the-bright eyes, and this cap will hide the skull ridge."

Matt grabbed both caps and handed Calla one. "Sure, but what about just bringing a human doctor in?"

"Tried that, but they wouldn't go for teleporting. They're about as psionophobic as the locals, but we told the fearful bunch that we were bringing in a human team. So congratulations! You two just became honorary humans."

Calla fitted the surgical cap over her short hair. "Let's go. They're not getting any healthier while we chat."

📖

Matt walked with Calla to a newly raised tent where their specific patients were gathered. He darted ahead and held the tent flap open for her then ducked inside. Three rows of five camp cots each lined both the longer walls and the middle of the room. Eleven of the beds were occupied. Normally, Matt's telepathy filled him in on the general state of people around him, but the anti-psionic field generator armed in his pocket robbed him of those perceptions.

For the last couple years, he'd wondered at the purpose of the rigid protocols. Now, without his psionic senses, he could only rely on those standard rules. The general protocol for this kind of situation put the most critical patients on the left and the least on the right.

He followed Calla to the nearest occupied bed on the left. The patient was so heavily bandaged, Matt could only guess at gender. The lower right hand was missing two fingers. The pale gray skin had a greenish cast.

Calla sat on the stool next to the bed. "Hello. I'm Dr. Calla Geis—"

"You are one of those-those—" the patient glared at her. The voice identified him as male.

"Haidarians? Do you see my eyes glowing?" Her tone lost all sense of diplomacy.

"No, guess not," he croaked.

"Have you seen Haidarians whose eyes don't glow?" She leaned closer, an offensive gesture in Daprian culture.

He shrank back from her. "No, can't say as I have, but they say the human doctors are still more than a day out."

"Yeah, well, you and your friends here wouldn't let them help you, so they got me. Can't even start to tell you how much I hate teleporting. Just about makes me puke, but I'm here now. So, are you going to let me help, or would you rather bleed to death?"

The man managed a half-smile. "Sorry, Doc. I just don't want those brain freaks touching me, and you look young for a doc is all."

She sat back, opening the space to a more respectful distance. "I graduated last summer, and no one else on the team would agree to teleport, so you're stuck with me. Can you tell me what's going on?" Her voice turned gentler.

"Ground started shaking. I went to get my ancestors and the ceiling fell on me." He lifted his injured hand. "I may have lost them and my fingers for good, may they forgive me. I got all scraped up. Splitting headache. Woke up with one of those glowing-eyed freaks staring at me."

Calla reached toward the end of the bed. Matt grabbed the electronic clipboard hanging there and handed it to her. He read over her shoulder. The report showed a low blood count, high pain level, concussion, and abnormal brain wave activity in addition to minor abrasions and bruises.

Instinctively, he tried to read the brain patterns telepathically but ran into a stiff wall of blackness. The device in his pocket stole his ability.

Calla slipped a small flashlight out of her backpack's side pocket and flashed it at the man's eyes. One pupil, already wide, showed no reaction. The other responded normally.

Matt leaned closer. "Do we need to check for a skull fracture?"

"Not necessary on a Daprian." She glanced up at him. "Anything that hit him hard enough to crack his brain case would have left him dead" She rooted through the main section of her pack and sighed. "Can you see if there's a portable EEG on hand?"

No, of course there wasn't, and she'd know that. Her own specialization rendered such devices useless. What was she playing at? Trying to get rid of him maybe?

His surgical cap slipped to his eyebrow. As he adjusted it, he remembered. A human doctor wouldn't know, not for certain. She was playing her role as a human doctor. He was supposed to be her nurse. Best to play along.

"I'll check." He hustled out of the tent and just stood there, taking in the rubble-strewn skyline and sunlight blazing red with all the dust in the air.

Matt reached into his pocket and tapped the button that turned off the anti-psionic generator. His powers flared back into existence, relieving the silence of his own thoughts. While on this useless errand, he peeked into the minds of those inside the tent. Pain, uneasiness, anger, and even delirium came from each in varying degrees.

"Careful, Matt." Calla's thoughts broke through his perceptions. *"Even a nontelepath will perceive contact above a certain power level. If you're going to try to take a reading, you need to back way down. A tenth of the power you're currently using would be safe enough."*

Rather than scolding him, her soft mental touch carried the warning without any added force. Was that gentleness an artifact of her low power level or a feature of her personality? Either way, one of his instructors could take lessons from her on effective correction.

"I don't know how to do that."

"Then leave the sneaky psionics to me. Remind me later, and I'll show you how to restrict your power level. In the meantime, I'll try to find ways to pass on the sort of information you might be missing without telepathy. I'm sorry. I know this isn't ideal, but I do appreciate your willingness to help."

After a few more minutes to make his errand seem realistic, Matt triggered the generator in his pocket and blocked out the telepathic world, leaving him mentally drowning in darkness. He shuddered and blew out a breath before rejoining Calla.

Back inside the tent, Calla had moved down the line two beds. She perched next to the third patient and slapped a drug capsule into an injector.

Matt jogged over to her. "That's a 'no' on the portable EEG."

Calla rolled her eyes. "That figures. Well, then we'll have to keep an eye on him. Watch for seizures."

And if he has one, then what? If we stop it telepathically, then our little charade is up.

Maybe she'd be able to manage it without his help and without blowing their cover.

"For now, I'll keep working on the two left rows." She pointed across the tent. "You take care of the far right. Let me know what you find."

Matt nodded and headed over to the first occupied cot.

📖

Calla finished the last of her eight patients who were in the worst condition. While Matt put the surgical sterilization field away, Calla rechecked the sutures. Digging bits of rock and metal out of the woman's injuries hardly qualified as major surgery, but the lengthy process in less-than-ideal conditions could lead to complications. She checked her watch and yawned. Aside from a couple visits to a latrine, she'd been at work for ten-and-a-half hours. Muscles she had forgotten about had developed colossal knots. She stretched to work the stiffness out of her shoulders.

"I don't know about you, but dinner is calling." Matt closed the surgical field box and secured the flaps.

Calla stood. "We need to see about dinner for these fine folks first. Then I'll see about my own."

Matt shook his head. "A local humanitarian group is taking care of the patients. The Haidarians' food is not welcome. We just have to stop at the dispatcher's tent and let them know."

"All right, then let's report in and see what's food." She led Matt out of the tent.

The open area in the middle of the camp was chaos as Daprian hover vehicles brought in more casualties and paramedics. Doctors and nurses scurried around assigning triage levels and directing patients to various places.

Calla paused. "They look like they could use an extra pair of hands."

Matt gripped her shoulder and steered her toward the dispatcher tent. "Not our assignment. We've got enough challenge with our own task. If you wipe yourself out taking on extra duties, who takes care of the psionophobes? The team from Earth is still almost twenty-four hours away. A lot can happen in that tent during that time."

"You're right, of course." She continued on to the dispatchers.

A handful of people were milling around. Some were sorting equipment. Others were restocking the sparsely populated supply tables, and one dispatcher stood near the map on the wall, which showed a lot more red.

Matt nodded toward the map. "They've almost got the affected parts of the city cleared."

A tall graying fellow in a paramedic's black and blue uniform turned toward them. "Yeah. Funny. The same telepathy that scares the Daprians is what lets us find and rescue them so fast."

The dispatcher smiled and made a notation on an electronic notepad. "Matt! Dr. Geisman! You two decided to come up for air?"

Calla yawned. "We finally caught up to ourselves."

The paramedic smirked. "What's the matter, Doc? Can't handle a full day's work?"

"Ease off, Pearce." Matt stepped in front of her. "Just because your full day's work doesn't look like ours doesn't mean we didn't have one."

The dispatcher reached across a table and backhanded Pearce's arm. "You and Mick get section thirty-two next."

Pearce snorted and shouldered his way past Matt. "Enjoy your beauty rest, Doc."

"Yeah, and forget you just woke up from a six-hour rest break," the dispatcher said before she muttered, "Jerk." She looked at her electronic clipboard. "You two have missed lunch and both scheduled breaks. Go get dinner and see how much sleep you can get before you're needed again."

Calla pulled off the surgical cap and tucked it into her backpack.

"Mess tent's this way." Matt led her out of the dispatcher's tent to the one next to it. "I hope they've got something I can eat."

"Diet restrictions?" Calla asked. She already knew, but the question was logical enough after his comment.

Matt held back the flap for her then ducked in. "Voluntary. I'm a vegetarian. Options on the expeditions are pretty slim sometimes, but I can always teleport home, grab something to go, and teleport back."

In the back of the tent, plates of bread, lunchmeats, cheese, and sliced vegetables were arrayed down the length of the table. Calla built a decent-sized sandwich with a little of everything then found a place to sit. She waited for Matt to join her with some bread and an impromptu salad. Too tired for much conversation, they ate in a comfortable silence before Matt took her to the next tent over where camp cots were set up for anyone who wanted to catch a quick nap. In spite of the background noise, she fell asleep almost as soon as she stretched out on a cot.

When Calla walked into the mess tent the next morning, the place was full. Pearce and two other paramedics were in the back dishing up eggs and bacon from large, heated trays and plunking a muffin and fist-sized apple on the plates.

Pearce smirked. "Mornin', Doc. You ready for another exhausting day of sitting around on your—"

Someone leaned into the tent. "Pearce, Simmons, Baker. More survivors in section forty-five. Let's hustle."

Pearce shoved the plate into her hands and jogged out. A quick scan of the room turned up Matt in the far corner. He waved her over. Not surprising, his eggs and bacon were untouched, but the apple and muffin were gone, including the crumbs.

She offered him her muffin and fruit. "Trade you?"

He pushed the plate toward her and took her offer. "Joyfully. So, what do you do for fun?"

He led the conversation, staying to light topics like hobbies and favorite music. They continued for a while after they had finished eating until she started feeling guilty about leaving their patients unattended. Matt dropped their trash in the bins by the door. Calla led the way to the dispatcher. The map tacked to the inside of the tent had only a few white areas left.

The dispatcher on duty, a different one from the night before, marked on his electronic clipboard. "Try not to skip your breaks today, okay? I can't send someone to remind you, so you're on your own."

Calla smiled. "I'll keep him honest."

Matt snickered. "That'll work well. I'll remind you. You remind me."

"Right. See you two tonight." The dispatcher winked.

As they left the tent, a disconcerting uneasiness radiated from Matt, growing worse by the second. Calla endured it for a few more steps before she turned to face him. "Are you okay?"

"Yeah, I think breakfast isn't sitting right." He pressed his hand on his abdomen.

She shook her head. "That's a lot stronger than indigestion, and it's hitting too fast for the typical types of food poisoning."

She wrapped her arm around his shoulders and led him back toward the dispatcher's tent. An intense tremor built up in his muscles. Two steps inside the tent, his knees buckled.

Calla caught him and lowered him to the ground only marginally slower than gravity.

She shrugged out of her backpack and snatched a blood test kit from the side pocket. "Dispatcher, do we have any toxicologists here?"

"Harry Mitsumi. I'll get him."

Calla used a lancet to prick Matt's finger and filled a capillary tube with his blood. After slipping the tube into the analyzer, she set it on his chest and reached into his mind. *"Matt, do you hear me?"*

No answer.

She called up a visualization of the mental structures. The glass-paned maze of his memories took shape, but clouds shrouded most of it, and the entire configuration shook.

That's a poison of some kind.

To stabilize her own presence in his mind, she visualized herself as her bird avatar. With her power level, her avatar was the size of a sparrow, but then she didn't need to do more than observe. A sparrow was too small to do further damage to his already fragile state. She flew down to the mid-level of his mental structure. Fears, joys, likes, and dislikes etched into the columns supporting the outer level were blurred, and the columns themselves were no steadier than the maze above.

"Dr. Geisman, I'm Harry Mitsumi. Your analyzer is still working on a solution, so bring me up to speed."

Without withdrawing from Matt's mind, Calla recapped the morning for Harry from breakfast to the current moment. "All the structures are grayed or blurred and terribly unstable. I'm headed to the inner level now."

"Your guess of a toxin is a good one, but that still leaves a lot of territory."

The analyzer pinged.

Harry cursed under his breath. "Yeah, and we didn't bring the antidote for that one with us. I'm going to have to go back to the station for the antidote. Try to redirect the metabolic pathways if you can." A power surge nearby signaled his outbound teleport.

"You might have told me what it was," Calla muttered.

She fluttered into the innermost level where dendrites connected by their axons sputtered and glowed. Without knowing what she was up against, she couldn't pinpoint her efforts, but she knew what normal looked like, and she didn't have to purge the poison. She just had to keep Matt alive until Harry got back. From the look of the sheer bulk of misfiring nerves, that would prove troublesome.

The part of his mind that registered and controlled vital functions was a collection of expected contradictions. His heart raced but his breathing had slowed and become shallow. Muscles quivered. Calla focused on redirecting energy. She slowed the tachycardia to slightly above normal and encouraged deeper breaths. Matt's breathing and pulse leveled out closer to normal, but the rate and intensity of the tremors shot up. A group of neurons started firing at the same speed and gradually recruiting the ones near them.

Oh no you don't. He does not need a seizure to complicate the day.

A quick burst of psionic energy into that group dispersed the synchronized cluster, but the moment she diverted attention from controlling his heart rate, that rocketed back to where it had started. She reapplied the effort to drag his pulse back toward normal and spotted another group of neurons falling into a pattern. Faster this time, Calla shot the disrupting bolt through the neurons then returned her attention to his heart rate before it could get too far out of hand.

The sudden changes in direction threatened the psionic equivalent of whiplash, and a headache hovered in the background.

Harry, where are you? I can't do this indefinitely, and I can't not do this indefinitely. Switching off with another psionic specialist would be dangerous in Matt's current state.

As she continued trying to balance everything out, a timid, jittery mind reached out to her.

Matt?

The acknowledgment came without words.

While disrupting another building seizure, she walled off the growing headache and projected a calming influence.

Stay with me, Matt. You're going to be okay.

Power surged nearby. Harry? It had to be.

A hand touched her shoulder. "Okay, I'm back. I've got it. Injecting it now."

Monitoring him closely, Calla withdrew her efforts while his body entered a stable rest state. Calla flew back up to the outer level, pausing long enough to confirm the structures were steady, then withdrew.

Harry handed her the analyzer. "I'll put him to bed. He just has to sleep it off."

"Thanks, but how did he get poisoned?" Calla asked.

"Breakfast is my guess, but then that begs a question of why aren't the rest of us dropping? Maybe someone had it in for him or you. You said you gave him part of your breakfast?" He and the dispatcher picked up Matt. "I'll fill in Xava and see if we can get an investigator here. In the meantime, I'd teleport home for food." He left.

"Except I can't teleport." Calla put the analyzer away and went to check on her patients.

Calla completed her rounds with the human physicians who would be taking over.

"Okay. It all looks really good. Thanks." The humans shook her hand and dispersed among the wounded.

After a few moments, Calla slipped out of the tent and returned to their temporary sleeping quarters. On the way, she passed the food tent, and the smell of roasted chicken and potatoes made her stomach growl. But after this morning's adventure, she'd eat at home.

Haidarians scrambled to get their equipment out of the humans' way. Many grabbed a closed crate, teleported away, and returned seconds later empty handed. Calla found Matt sitting on the edge of a cot. His hair was all ruffled, and his clothes were a wrinkled mess, but he was alert and a lot steadier in her telepathic senses than he'd been this morning.

She plopped down on the cot across from him. "Hey, how are you?"

"Much better than earlier for sure." He clasped her hand. "You have a remarkably gentle touch. I just barely perceived your presence."

She smiled. "You were a little preoccupied."

"Yeah, but I'm usually hypersensitive when I'm sick."

Calla patted his hand. "Well, when you don't have much power to start—"

Xava leaned into the tent. "All right, you two. Last train's leaving on the teleport express. You coming, or do you like it here that much?"

Matt stood up. "Coming, definitely. I'm done here." He gestured for her to go ahead of him. "Ever figure out my breakfast issues?" he asked Xava.

"No, Daprians wouldn't let us bring in an investigator, we couldn't find that poison anywhere else, and no one got sick but you." Xava scowled and shook her head. "We think a miffed Daprian had intentions of poisoning our breakfast and got interrupted after dosing just one muffin. Unfortunately, you drew the short stick."

"That just seems awfully coincidental to me." Calla frowned.

Xava shrugged. "Yeah, I know, but they're not letting us get any closer to real answers."

Calla rolled her eyes. "So, we're just supposed to be okay that someone tried to kill Matt?"

"Or you. We were sharing breakfast parts, remember?" he said.

"I'm not okay with it, and I don't think anyone else is, but by the time we get the Magistrates to negotiate the right to investigate, whatever evidence there is will be colder than a polar ice cap." Xava clapped Matt on the shoulder. "Sorry. That's not much of an answer."

He blew out a breath. "Not the answer I was hoping for, that's for sure."

Calla slid her hand into his as they joined the rest of the departing group with the last of the equipment.

"*Y'know, you two would make a cute couple.*" Xava smiled and picked up a box of bandages.

Before Calla could respond, colors swirled around her.

Origin:
One of the challenges I perpetually deal with as a writer is figuring out where to start the story. As a result, I often end up with scenes that I intended as a prologue or even as a chapter somewhere in the work, and they later get cut because they don't quite fit with the new place it starts.

Lines of Succession was one of those novels that had multiple starting points, and consequently, I ended up with a couple extra scenes that still fit with the novel but were never used.

"The Choice" and the next story "The Griffin Quill" are two of those.

The Choice

Elaina raced across the grounds side-by-side with her twin while Mother followed along behind them. Her dreaded, long skirts caught on her legs and rustled as she struggled to keep the brutal pace Errol set. Twenty yards to go, and her leg muscles burned. Errol pulled ahead and reached the aerie door first.

She slapped the door to the aerie half a moment after Errol. "Tie!"

Her twin shook his head. "Nope. I win."

Only because Father makes me wear dresses all the time, except when me and Lyssa practice. Elaina's jaw tensed. "I'll win next time. You'll see."

Leaning her back against the aerie wall to catch her breath, she watched Mother waddle closer. She was heavy with child and ready to deliver any time now. Lyssa, Mother's gray-haired maid, hovered nearby.

"What color griffin are you going to get?" Errol asked. "I want a tan one to match my hair. You should get a black one."

Elaina grinned. "I want a good one, no matter what color she is."

Errol cupped his hand around her ear and whispered. "Father will not be happy if you get a girl griffin."

"Yes, I know, because 'girl griffins are for fighting.'" She lowered her voice to mimic her father's deeper tone. "I just want a good one."

By the time Mother and Lyssa arrived, Elaina's labored breathing had eased. Errol opened the door with a flourish and bowed the ladies through. Elaina followed them and waited for Errol to pull the door closed while Mother went on ahead.

The inside of the aerie smelled of griffin dust and a well-stocked butcher shop. A multi-pitched rumble of chattering griffins filled the room.

"Come along, children," Mother called without glancing back.

Elaina clasped her twin's hand and skipped down the main walkway. Rows of stalls lined the right side of the huge room, each with an adult griffin chirping, preening, eating, or napping. Without pausing, she glanced at the griffins they passed. The griffins were tall, even taller than

Father, and the girl griffins were heavier than the boy griffins. She'd learned pretty early on how to tell the boys from the girls just based on their size. Their forequarters, wings, and the tips of their tails were feathered, but the rest of the hindquarters was furry. They looked like they had feathery ears sticking up on their heads, but that wasn't their real ears. Just feathers.

At the end of the walkway, the griffin master waited in a large, square stall with half-height walls. Elaina darted ahead and leaned against it. A dozen griffin kits milled around the nursery stall. Most weren't any taller than her knee. Some played tug with knotted ropes. Some slept, a paw twitching here and there from dreams. A few wrestled.

"Look at all of them!" Errol scrambled over the shortwall like a trained acrobat.

"So, time for you to pick your griffin, is it?" the griffin master asked. He shook his head. "Seems like just last year you were taking your first steps." His big hands wrapped around Elaina's chest and lifted her into the stall.

"Aw, no tan ones?" Errol frowned and looked up at the griffin master.

"No tan as a main color in this lot, but if you want a pale-colored one, there's this little girl over here." He pointed to a mostly white griffin with a few black splotches playing tug with a bigger gray kit.

"Father said no white ones. He said they're sometimes sickly." Errol frowned.

"But she's not just white. She's white and black." Elaina walked past him and crouched next to the pair playing tug.

The white-and-black one's opponent dropped the rope and hissed. Her feathers all stood on end and her eyes pinned. Elaina scrambled to her feet and took a step back, landing her heel on the back hem of her skirt. The gray kit lunged as Elaina fell.

A small black-and-tan blur, a male kit, interposed himself, wings and feathers flared. He swiped his foreclaw, catching the gray across the beak. She reared to return the attack, but the male dodged aside then struck another blow in the same spot. The male kit screeched a warning, a pitiful sound coming from such a small griffin.

Errol swept up the white-and-black kit in his arms and retreated from the battle.

The griffin master stepped between the combatants, using his big boot to push the female toward the wall and the male to the center of the pen. "That's enough of that."

The black-and-tan, speckled male smoothed out his feathers and lowered his wings. He trotted over to Elaina and crawled into her lap.

She preened his little ear tufts, causing him to happily grind his beak. "I think he likes me."

"I should say he does." Lyssa smiled.

"You'll want that one right there, Elaina." Mother pointed to the kit in Elaina's lap. "No question about it."

Lyssa chuckled. "Yes, plenty of spunk, that's for certain."

"Bring yours over here where I can see her, Errol." Mother beckoned him closer.

He carried his little kit and held her up to Mother. "Is she a sickly one?"

"I wouldn't bring any sick ones for you to choose, Your Highness," the griffin master said.

Mother's eyes softened. "I know what your father was wary of. This one shows none of the signs. You may choose her if you'd like."

Elaina hugged her kit and stood, careful to make sure she wasn't standing on her hem again. She handed him to Lyssa then pulled herself up to perch on the half-wall before the griffin master got there to lift her over.

"Don't let your father see you do that." Lyssa gave the kit back as the griffin master helped Errol out of the stall.

Elaina held the griffin out at arm's length as it squirmed and kicked. "He kind of looks like one of the falcons in the mews, in the face I mean."

Mother leaned closer. "He does at that."

"I think I'll call him Tiercel."

"That's a good name for him." Mother rose and turned to the griffin master. "Thank you."

He bowed. "My pleasure, Your Majesty."

Elaina set Tiercel down next to her and preened his head while he purred. "I think we'll be great friends."

The Griffin Quill

Elaina Constance Aquilane swung herself up into her griffin's saddle with a flair that many considered old-fashioned.

Her griffin twisted his head toward her. "Fly, Tiercel?"

She checked her safety tether. "Not yet, you big goof. We have to wait for the horn."

Lyssa, Elaina's nanny-turned-maid, stood outside the roped off area. Her gray, utilitarian tunic-dress matched her braided hair. "Keep your head about you," she warned. "That female griffin is bigger than most, so you'll have to use Tiercel's speed to your advantage."

Elaina nodded. "I'll remember."

"Take good care of her, Tiercel." Lyssa reached across and tapped his flank with her wrinkled hand.

"Good gerfin, yeah." Tiercel whistled.

The assistant marshal standing nearby drew a breath. "Your Highness, are you prepared?"

"Yes, marshal." She sank lower into the saddle.

He raised a flag.

Seconds passed as the surge of excitement energized her. The horn sounded a long, low blast. Tiercel reared back and leapt into the air, spreading his huge black and tan wings as he flapped hard to come up to speed. Their massive opponent and her rider took off from the other corner and sped toward them by the straightest course.

Elaina angled Tiercel away from the hefty griffin, but the opposition countered and continued on his direct path.

Jousting, is it? Elaina unhitched one of her wooden, padded tournament spears. "Race the wind, Tiercel. *Maisvolay!*"

She hugged his neck as he lowered his head and tucked in his legs. His wingbeats increased speed and power. Air whipped past her. As they came into range, Elaina changed her grip on the spear, raised up, and threw it with all the muscle in her upper body. The spear struck the trailing edge of the female griffin's wing, eliciting an aggravated gronk.

Elaina frowned. *I forgot to time her wingbeats*! *Stupid*! *I could have had him.*

Tiercel banked around for another try, but the other griffin was already setting up for her rider's spear throw. He hurled the weapon at her.

"*Seyaratay!*" Elaina ordered.

Tiercel's wings snapped tight against Elaina's legs. They dropped several feet as the tournament spear zoomed over their heads, nearly taking off strands of Elaina's hair.

She leaned back in the saddle. "*Abretay!*"

He unfurled his wings and climbed with an elated shriek.

"Good boy!" she praised, patting Tiercel's neck.

Elaina twisted around. Her opponent veered away from his failed effort. Elaina sent Tiercel into pursuit. He closed the gap with the enemy's bulky hen, taking tighter corners and gaining advantage with his sleeker form. She unhitched her second spear. Just a few more yards and she'd be close enough for a good throw.

Ahead of her, the other contestant tugged something off his belt and threw it. A cloth flicked open, spreading a black cloud into the air.

Coal dust!

Elaina gasped and leaned hard to the right. Tiercel squawked an alarm and dove, rolling hard enough over to go nearly sideways. Elaina fell from the saddle. When the tether snapped taut, the harness pulled hard across her back and chest.

Elaina dropped the spear and grabbed the leather strap with both hands. "Tiercel, down to land! *Desenyay!*"

Her opponent arced and raced toward her. Hanging from the tether, she lacked offensive and defensive abilities, and Tiercel couldn't maneuver fast enough to dodge.

The gray griffin closed in.

She looked down. Fifteen feet separated her from the ground. Close enough to unhook from the saddle and drop the remaining distance. That would free Tiercel to evade.

Clinging to the tether with her left hand, she fumbled with the clasp. The sudden pull of her weight had warped the catch. Sunlight reflected off metal. A real knife, not a wooden tournament one, sailed past about an arm's length above her. The tether vibrated like a lute's string and tore. A collective gasp and a chorus of boos echoed from the stands.

Elaina smacked into the ground like a discarded saddlebag, jarring every bone in her body. A sharp, burning pain screamed from her left arm louder than Tiercel's angry shriek.

She rolled onto her back and found him banking to give chase. Elaina tucked her injured arm against her body. Drawing a deep breath, she yelled, "*Nidavay*, Tiercel! *Nidavay!*"

He aborted pursuit and dove. But their enemy wasn't going to let them escape that easily; he headed for Elaina. Tiercel landed and interposed himself between her and the approaching griffin. He fluffed out his feathers, raised his wings a few inches, and growled.

"Easy, Tiercel." Elaina rose to a crouch. "This isn't supposed to be real combat."

She started to stand until the terrain whirled around her. She stumbled, falling back to her knees.

Tiercel looked at her.

"*Nidavay*, Tiercel! We're not done yet, but I need you here."

He pinned his eyes on the approaching griffin hen and her rider, armed now with the second of his three tournament spears. Elaina gripped the handle of her wooden dagger in its sheath.

Their opponent hovered nearby at an angle that would temporarily blind him every time the female griffin's wings went up.

"Bad gerfin! Bad! Stupid popinjay!" Tiercel shrieked.

"In your opinion." The rider smirked. "Surrender, Your Highness, please. You've lost."

Elaina watched the female griffin's wingbeats. "By the rules, I'm not dead yet, and no hold has been called."

"Please, I have to—"

When the gray's wings swept downward, Elaina hurled the dagger sidelong. It flew past the wing and whapped her opponent in the chest, releasing a thin cloud of chalk and leaving a white blotch on his doublet.

The crowd cheered.

That takes out the rider. Now for the griffin.

Although "dead" by the rules, the rider hurled his spear anyway, getting another round of boos.

Elaina fell to the right, the spear hitting the brush right behind her. "*Batallyay*, Tiercel!"

Tiercel launched at the other griffin and swiped his padded foreclaw, getting a burst of chalk from the padding and leaving a white mark on the huge hen's neck. She squawked and retreated.

The horn sounded, signaling the end of the match.

"About time." Elaina flopped on her rear and inspected her arm. Her riding doublet was torn. Blood stained the padded cloth. "What did I hit?" She glanced around and found a broken branch on a nearby shrub sporting a tuft of stuffing from her jacket. "That would do it."

"Ellie?" Tiercel landed and trotted back to her. "Ow, Ellie?"

Elaina fumbled with the buttons on the front of her doublet. "Yes, sweetie. Ow."

He laid on his belly next to her. "Up, Ellie! Fly, Tiercel."

"Rules say I have to stay where I go down if I'm safe." She leaned against him and showed her griffin the cut safety line. "Besides, you know who would have both our hides if we tried flying without a proper tether."

Elaina unfastened the last button and slid her uninjured arm out then winced as she peeled the doublet's left sleeve off. Elaina pried open the tear in her shirt, expecting to see a deep gash. For all that it hurt, the cut was the length of her hand but shallow.

Tiercel rested his beak on her other shoulder and whined. "Poor gerfin. Poor gerfin!"

"I'll be fine, Tiercel." She wrapped her right hand around the bleeding wound and rubbed her cheek against his soft feathers. "Lyssa will bind it when she gets here, and that'll hold until I get to the physician's tent."

Tiercel's head snapped up. "Elaiya Costas Akilay!"

His favorite announcement for her maid was a poor butchery of Elaina's full name. Lyssa was the only one to ever use it.

Elaina followed Tiercel's eyeline to a group of people coming across the roped off section of grassland serving as the spring griffin games field. The Griffin Master led the way, his sweeping green and gold cape declaring his position as head marshal.

Lyssa followed half a step behind, wisps of gray hair flying loose from her braid. She had hold of the marshal's arm. Eyes narrowed, she gestured wildly with her free hand. The school physician and her apprentice followed.

"Forgetting the coal dust, live steel, and severed tether, she was wounded." Lyssa gripped his arm tighter and whipped him around to face her. "When were you going to call a hold? Once he'd killed her?"

"I do have the experience and the authority to marshal these games, madam." He wrenched his arm away from Lyssa.

"Then you should try exercising it!"

"She won, didn't she?" he asked.

Lyssa pointed a tense, trembling hand skyward as if she meant to deliver a whack to the marshal. "Not the point!"

The marshal sighed. "They're both advanced students, and this is the gold feather bout. I can't have an ambiguous ending."

Lyssa rolled her eyes. "Oh, yes, and the cheater gets silver now. That's an equitable solution." She gave him a shove and jogged the rest of the way, crouching at Elaina's side when she arrived. "How bad is it?"

Elaina lifted her hand away from the injury. "It probably hurts worse than it is."

Lyssa peeked through the opening and nodded before yielding her place to the school physician.

Tiercel leaned closer. "Good gerfin?"

"You did a fine job." Lyssa ruffled his head feathers. "Good griffin."

"Good gerfin! Nice gerfin!" He straightened and whistled.

The physician untied the cuff of Elaina's shirt and lifted it out of the way. "What did you hit?"

"That shrub back there." Elaina glanced over her shoulder, sending a glower at the offending branch.

Lyssa nodded. "You very nearly landed in that shrub."

The physician shook her head and muttered, "Should've called 'Hold,' Marshal. Could've restarted once I'd tended this."

She used a piece of white muslin to clean away the blood then bound the injury. Elaina grimaced as the healer tied off the bandage.

The apprentice put the rest of the roll away.

"Now, that does it for the obvious injury." The physician looked closely at Elaina's eyes. "You had trouble coming to your feet after the fall."

Elaina shook her head. "I was knocked silly for a moment. I just needed to catch my wind."

"Umhm. I've heard that from other competitors seconds before they passed out." She stood and offered her hand.

Elaina clasped the physician's wrist, and the woman yanked her to her feet. The spinning sensation passed in moments. Tiercel hopped up and trotted around behind Elaina.

"Good?" The physician kept her grip on Elaina's arm.

"Good." Elaina nodded.

Lyssa frowned. "No bravado now. You hit awfully hard."

Elaina clasped Lyssa's shoulder. "I'm fine, really."

The marshal stepped forward. "Can you complete the award ceremony, Your Highness?"

She picked up the severed end of her tether. "I'll need to claim my respite to get my tether exchanged, but I can participate."

"Very good. I'll inform the headmistress."

The physician took a step back. "See me again after the award ceremony, Your Highness."

Elaina nodded in thanks. "I will."

Lyssa picked up Elaina's doublet and inspected the hole in the sleeve. "It'll do for the awards, I suppose."

Tiercel leaned his head between them. "Fly, Tiercel?"

Elaina smiled and hugged his neck. "Soon! Are you ready to grab our trophy?"

"Good gerfin. Yeah!"

"Then let's get our tether switched out."

Lyssa tugged on the safety harness.

A shock of pain flared along Elaina's ribs, nearly doubling her over. "Ow! Lyssa!"

"Umhm. Bruised at the very least." Lyssa checked the seams and stitching. "But the harness is good. Let's go. Your respite will end soon enough."

"Come on, Tiercel." Elaina hissed in mild pain under her breath and waved him along.

He walked next to her to their pavilion and whistled while she pulled her doublet back on. The pavilion was black, white, and blue striped, the colors of her native Corby. Her coat of arms decorated a banner on a pole in front. In the nearby pavilions, children of the local Sonjikstani nobility milled around. Some acknowledged her with a bow or curtsey, others with a scowl.

Elaina hid a frown. *My Sonjikstani mother and attendance in a Sonjikstani school isn't enough for you?*

Lyssa patted her arm. "Leave them to their grumpiness, dear. You earned your feather fairly, which is more than I can say for the silver feather this time." She dug through a box of spare gear and came up with an extra tether.

Elaina detached the torn one and let Lyssa hook up the replacement.

"All right. Off you go!" Lyssa gave her a push.

When Elaina grabbed the saddle handholds and pulled, her injured arm protested. She frowned. *The modern way this time.* She stuck her foot in the stirrup and swung up into the saddle as if mounting a horse. "Fly, Tiercel!"

He reared and leapt into the air. She directed him to the wooden stands decorated in the school's green and gold where the silver and bronze contestants were already perched. Tiercel landed in position easily.

The marshal stood in front of them. "You know which reward you received. Do not dishonor yourself, your family, or the school by trying to collect the wrong one." His stern eye pierced each of them but rested longest on the cheater.

Elaina looked at him from the corner of her eye. *You would try to claim the gold after losing in front of everyone?* She leaned closer to Tiercel's head and whispered, "We have to be quick."

"Go, gerfin!" His padded talons thudded on the wooden deck and released a sparse cloud of chalk as he pranced in place.

The marshal walked to the horn on the edge of the platform and blew a long note.

Tiercel took off like an arrow from a bow. Launchers atop the stands made a loud pop as the feathers were shot out over the playing field from three different directions. Gold was always the furthest. Cloth parachutes unfurled to slow and steady the descent of the feathers. The yellowish glint at the far end of the field caught Elaina's eye. She directed Tiercel toward the gold-laced griffin quill. He blazed on ahead, leaving the second and third place winners in his wake. Tiercel made the end of the field in good time and dove under the falling feather. Elaina reached up and snatched it from the air. The gold lining the shaft had stiffened the feather and dramatically increased its weight. She adjusted her hold on it and quickly pinned it across her lap with her injured arm. The assembled crowd cheered, and Elaina could swear she heard Lyssa above all.

"I have it, Tiercel! Let's return to the platform."

Tiercel slowed and circled around. The bronze winner was already back to the wooden deck, and the silver winner was not far behind. Tiercel made good time and added his own clucks and whistles to the crowd's adulations. When he touched down on the platform, Elaina rose up in the saddle, holding her trophy high. Her abused ribs drove a sharp pain through her back and chest, and her arm burned, but she gritted her teeth and honored the crowd.

Origin:
In 2020, Bear Publications released *Worlds of Weinbaum*, a collection of public domain short stories that were tweaked to fix the science and some very not-modern attitudes about women and persons of color.

This story was written for a follow-up anthology to be set in the same universe but was shelved because of the severe differences in writing style. The current version of "One with Nature" has been tweaked to take it out of Weinbaum's universe so it'll stand on its own feet.

One with Nature

Al closed his copy of *The Collected Works of Henry David Thoreau*. He'd probably finish "Walden" on the return trip. For now, he fished the fat rubber band out of his pocket and wrapped it around the book a couple of times. The spine had permanent white creases that obscured the title and author. Before too long, pages would start falling out. He sighed. Time to order his fifth copy.

"I see a landing spot." In spite of the over-the-ear headphones, the noise of the helicopter's rotors and the constant low-level vibration of the engine all but drowned out the pilot's voice over the comm line. "That beach is plenty wide enough."

Propping his elbow on the arm of the chair, Al looked out the window at an island paradise. The spinning blades over his head cut the sunlight into a fast flicker, like watching an old motion picture. Tall trees resembling multi-tiered palms with huge leaves waved in the breeze. Vines with clusters of brilliant red, orange, yellow, and purple flowers festooned the canopy like holiday garland.

The pilot brought the helicopter in for a flawless landing on the beach.

After stowing his book in his backpack, Al shouldered the bag, slid the door open, then leaned toward the pilot. "Coming?"

"No," the pilot said, shaking his head. "I'll stay with this ol' bird."

Al winced and glanced toward the opposite side of the island where they'd spotted civilization. "I might be a while."

"Quite all right." The pilot flicked switches and the rotors whined as they slowed. "Take your time. Just remember that the captain wants us back onboard by sunset. I don't think we should leave our ride unattended."

More likely, the pilot simply didn't want to meet the locals and deal with the unknown.

"I'm sure the natives are perfectly harmless," Al said.

"I'm sure, but curiosity can do more damage than malice." The pilot opened the door and stepped out.

Al took off the headset and left it on the seat. "Suit yourself." He hopped out, keeping his head down. Intellectually, he knew he wasn't nearly tall enough to give himself a helicopter haircut, but standing upright courted fate.

He ducked until he was well away from the helicopter. The vibration so constant during the flight left his legs tingling even now on solid ground.

On a wide-open part of the beach, Al stood still and took in the surroundings. He inhaled deeply and closed his eyes for a moment. Saltwater and sweet nectar, not smog and trash bins. The sun warmed his face without the shadows of skyscrapers. Birds chirped and wind rustled through the trees. No horns honking. No loud music. This was nature as God had intended it, at least here on Neoterra. The terraformed world had much in common with Old Earth, but not nearly the same. After reading the historical accounts of Old Earth and exploring large parts of Neoterra, Al preferred his current home world. Much more to see and do here.

The island would be perfect if he hadn't been dressed in long pants and a button up shirt as required by the Academy's dress code. Sweat beaded on his brow, and he headed for the nearest shade.

As he approached the tree line, winds blew in from the ocean, but high overhead the massive leaves moved the opposite direction, which provided relief from the sun. Peculiar, but then maybe the wind was the opposite direction at that height? However it happened, the shade and breeze were better than air conditioning.

"Thanks!" He smiled up at the canopy.

A path nearly the width of a city sidewalk opened through the undergrowth. Although strangely hidden in the distance, with every step, the nearest few feet opened as if the greenery moved out of his way of its own accord.

He smiled. What an interesting plant! Al knelt and slowly reached for the nearest leaf. When he came within a few inches, the leaf withdrew.

"No need to be afraid. I won't hurt you." He moved a little faster, and the vegetation cleared a bigger space around his hand.

The renowned explorer, Michel Cuvier, had discovered a plant that reacted to proximity by curling up its leaves. He'd theorized that the plant could detect body heat or perhaps vibration. This one might be a distant cousin. A few more experiments showed that the distance required to make the plant retreat depended largely on how fast he moved.

Al slipped his backpack off his shoulder and rooted around for a pen and notepad. After flipping to a blank page, he jotted notes about his find and sketched a few pictures. Maybe Cuvier would be willing to compare discoveries.

Keeping his notebook and pen in hand, Al followed along the strange path until he neared a white, sandy beach populated with a few dozen people. He crouched behind a leafy shrub and observed through a gap in the foliage.

The islanders had a coppery complexion and shiny black hair. Men wore loin cloths and shawls, and women wore sarongs, but instead of patterned material, their clothing was made of large leaves. The women decorated their hair with flowers, and everyone had rope-like jewelry made of twisted vines wound around their arms and legs.

The official records suggested Polynesian descent for this colony, Hawaii in particular. If this had started out a Hawaiian group, it had since diverged.

Unlike the traditional Hawaiian culture, men and women worked side-by-side. Some were doing the typical chores needed on an isolated island community. They tended the garden, mended nets, sharpened knives, and prepared food. Good for them! They were being productive in a way that didn't harm the environment. Doing everything the old-fashioned way meant they could sustain their community and the environment at once. On such a confined island, that sort of stewardship was essential. His own hometown of Little New York could learn a few things from these people.

A second group sat facing the sun with their arms spread wide. He smiled and nodded. They took care of their mental health, too. Modern medical science had provided evidence that even a quarter hour of meditating did wonders to improve emotional state, cardiovascular health, stress tolerance, and a host of other ailments. While these islanders might not have access to the latest medical research, they obviously had the kind of instinctual knowledge that came from a thorough understanding of nature.

A third group stood nearer a rubbish heap, or maybe it was a compost pile—the faint unpleasantness of decay carried on the wind—with their feet buried in the sand. Odd, perhaps, but then sand in full sunlight could get rather warm on bare feet. They were most likely taking a break from turning over the compost pile, a necessary function for proper nutrient development. Their efforts would result in the best fertilizer for their gardens. No tools were visible, but using their hands ensured that they knew how their compost was developing. These were clearly people not afraid to get their hands a little dirty, unlike the prissy fellows he worked with who required everything to be nearly hospital-sterile.

Al spent a few minutes taking notes—both subjective and objective—and making quick sketches. Using these islanders as a prime example, perhaps he could finally gain some ground on encouraging people to take better care of their environment. They needed to get closer to nature. Technology had its place, sure, but pollution of the modern industrial age would ruin everything in only so many years. Balance. That's what they needed to strive for.

When he'd learned all he could from basic observation, he stepped out into the open and moseyed toward a few people mending nets. The group meditating in the sunlight shifted slightly, all in the same direction. Curious, but harmless. One of the men near the compost pile whistled. When he had the eye of the net menders, he pointed in Al's direction.

Al kept his pace slow and his hands visible as one of the net menders snatched up a spear and jogged partway before slowing.

"Hello." Al stopped well outside the reach of the spear. "My name is Doctor Albert Simmons. Call me 'Al.' I'm an anthropologist with the Western Academy of Natural Sciences. I mean you no harm. I just want to talk and observe." He held up his notepad. "Can you spare the time?"

The man aimed the point of the spear at Al's chest. "Stay." He jogged back to his fellows.

Al kept a smile firmly in place. He didn't much care for being treated like a trained hound, but he was an intruder, so he stayed.

After a conference with a few of the others, the spear-wielder returned. "Follow, please." He led the way back into the tree line, angled away from the helicopter. As before, the path through the underbrush cleared for them.

They walked deeper into the jungle, and Al looked over his shoulder. There was no sign of the path, and yet when he looked straight down, the ground at his feet was clear of plant life. Truly fascinating how it did that! He'd have to retrieve sample containers from the helicopter and do some collecting before he left. He knew a few botanists at the Academy who'd be enraptured by plant life that didn't care for being stepped on and did something about it.

More to the point, if they could grow it where the usual sidewalks were, they could increase the green space even in the heart of major cities. The plants would simply move out of the way as people passed and close back in when there were no feet to trample them. Increasing the plant life would reduce the effects of pollution, increase the general mental health of the population, and beautify what was rapidly turning into a concrete jungle.

Movement to his left caught his eye. A young woman stood among a cluster of open-topped boxes made of large leaves and vines. Each held a baby sleeping peacefully. Al smiled, thinking of his own wife and child. Such precious little ones, and the locals were introducing their children to nature as early as possible. How much more perfect could that be? From their earliest experiences, those babies would know what nature was all about. They would grow up comfortable with the world around them. So much healthier than the stainless steel and stark white environment that had greeted his own son.

His guide stepped into a wider clearing partially shaded by the tree canopy. An elderly man wrapped in undulating vines dotted with fist-sized yellow and red flowers approached and perched on a leaf and vine hammock at the edge of the clearing. He had hair whiter than the sand on the beach. Was he *ali'i*? Royalty?

The guide approached the elder and spoke in a language with minimal consonants. Definitely a Polynesian language, but he couldn't say for sure which one. Too bad foreign words were out of bounds in Scrabble. This language would be handy when his tray held all vowels.

The elder nodded and waved the guide to one side. The vines on his arm writhed like snakes, sending an unnatural chill down Al's spine.

"Come, Al Simmons of the Western Academy of Natural Sciences. Be seated, and we shall talk." The elder pointed to a collection of vines and leaves weaving themselves into a chair as he spoke. "This one is Kauri. He once lived among your people, which makes the language easier. What brings you to our island?"

Al crossed to the newly formed chair and gingerly perched on the edge. Surely, it wouldn't hold his full weight. "I'm an anthropologist, a scientist who studies cultures and civilizations, and I'm compiling a comprehensive work comparing the civilizations our ancestors came from to the civilizations they developed after our arrival. The colonization records show that the people who settled here were Polynesian. Is that correct?"

"Yes. This one and all those who arrived with him are Polynesian. This particular one is Hawaiian."

Curious the way Kauri referred to himself as "this one." That wasn't a Hawaiian trait. Al made a note and starred it as something to ask about later.

Best not to get too personal too early in the interview. "That's interesting, Kauri. Can you tell me about how the island was colonized? It's pretty far off the beaten path."

The elderly fellow nodded, sending a ripple through the vines wrapped around him. "This one was still a child when the first colonists arrived, but because of him, the civilization exists."

Al flipped his pen into writing position and waited for the old man to continue.

"This one set off from the mainland with his parents and nearly all of the Polynesian arrivals on Neoterra. Following schools of fish, they found many small islands. None were large enough to sustain a population." Kauri settled against a wall of vines which stiffened and became a chair back. "Our group left the islands in search of one that could sustain us."

Al paused and looked up. "They didn't head out across open water, not in those tiny sailboats."

"So they did." Kauri blinked slowly. "So they did. No schools of fish to follow, and just the blessed sun and stars as guides. What better guide could they want?"

A sun-worship religion? Why would the colonizing Polynesians be polytheistic? Christian missionaries had arrived in Hawai'i around 1820, Old Earth calendar. By 1900, Christianity was the dominant religion. Could they have reverted to polytheism after arrival? That would be a first among all the cultures Al had studied so far.

Well, if they had reverted to their polytheistic traditions, that still posed a problem. Although traditional Hawaiian beliefs boasted of an impressive assortment of gods and goddesses, Al didn't recall one for the sun. The sky, yes. That would be Wakea, but not the sun.

Kauri struck his palm with his fist. "A storm came up. No doubt sent by Kaha'i."

Al nodded. He knew about the thunder god.

"The boats were driven here to this island." He made a sweeping motion with his hands as if gathering something to himself. "They broke apart on the reefs, but their job was done, and the people made their way to shore.

"The trees of the island took care of them, providing fruit within reach for food, collecting rain in leaves for water, and sheltering from sun and rain under their canopy." Kauri raised his hands and looked up through the branches. "Were the people grateful?" He dropped his hands into his lap and scowled. "No, they were not, and so they had to be taught their lessons."

Al glanced at Kauri. "Lessons? What happened?"

"The people were not content with the trees' provision." His brow furrowed, and he made an abrupt slicing motion with his hand. "They chopped trees down! The traitors! After all the trees had done for them! Did they use deadwood already fallen? No. Driftwood washed up on the shore? Certainly not. Young, healthy trees felt the bite of steel."

"Curious. I saw no artificial structures as I walked here." Al glanced back the way he'd come. Maybe he should skip sample collecting, given how totally worked up the old boy was getting.

"Of course, not!" Kauri took a deep breath, and the tension in his face abated. "The lessons were learned, but I'll come to that in due time." He shifted position in his hammock-turned-chair, which sent vines into motion to accommodate him. "The trees, of course, defended themselves."

Al continued writing. "Defended themselves?"

"Of course. They grew sharp spines, retracted their leaves to remove protection from the elements, and hid away their fruit."

An anthropomorphism, surely, but Al dutifully wrote it down. Ground cover plants moving out the way could be reacting to proximity or vibration, but selectively growing spines, curling up leaves, and hiding fruit? He'd like to think such things were possible, but that sounded like science fiction.

"The sun beat down on the people, and the fruit they had harvested began to rot. Just payment for their brutality. One boy, this young boy—recall I told you this one was very young when the people arrived—declared to the elders that the trees were angry. The elders didn't believe this one. They laughed and bid him be gone from their sight. But the boy was right. He took a piece of fruit and a leftover piece of fish and buried them together."

Al nodded, and if he was now the leader of the people, that would explain their affinity for nature. He'd led them well. "Smart kid. Did his effort appease the trees?"

"They graciously honored this one's offer. The nearest tree unfurled its leaves to shelter this one from the sun and lowered fruit within this one's reach. The other people noticed. Each buried a seed and a fish. So, the pact was sealed. People and trees became one and now live in harmony."

A quaint story, but definitely a myth. Myths could be helpful, though. They were good teaching tools, and Kauri must be using this one, and ones like it, to show his people how important good stewardship of the environment was to their survival.

"Thank you for the story." Al flipped his notebook to a new page. "Do you mind if I ask you a few questions?"

Kauri steepled his fingers. "You may ask."

"Has your culture changed significantly since your arrival on the island?" He already knew the answer. The change from Christianity to a polytheistic religion was a huge shift by itself, but the Academy insisted on getting the truth from the horse's mouth.

"Only for the better. All live in perfect harmony with the trees. The people—" Kauri pointed toward the coast, "—gain food, shelter, clothing, longevity, and other gifts in exchange for nurturing the trees and providing nourishment for them. In the end, both are stronger for it. A noble partnership, wouldn't you say?"

Indeed, it was a noble partnership. Before today, Al hadn't seen a society so well-tuned to nature, an admirable goal for the entire planet to adopt. He nodded toward the beach. "And the people I saw on the beach? There were three groups, two tending to chores and the third at rest. Can you tell me about their work?"

"Each takes a turn at each task, depending on what is most needed." Kauri shrugged. "Surely, in your society, people do various tasks."

"They do, of course, but we haven't achieved nearly the same affinity with nature as you have." In fact, anyone who even suggested such a path was declared a "tree hugger." Tragic, really. There was so much to be learned from the environment. "But, some of us strive to create more parks and gardens. Increasing the green space around us, we hope to develop more of a love for nature. There's a long way to go. Perhaps if I can encourage people to meditate on nature as I saw your people doing, they'll learn that having a peaceful spirit is better than the stress of their normal lives."

Kauri frowned. "I see you still don't understand. The people and the trees are one."

As he stood, the vines around him shifted, revealing more of his skin. His complexion had a greenish hue, and tendrils from the vines appeared to end in perfect alignment to bulges in his skin.

Al did a double-take. That couldn't be right. Kauri showed no pain in his movements. In fact, he moved more fluidly than any octogenarian Al could think of. He'd said that the people and trees were one. Surely, he didn't mean literally. That was a figurative statement, wasn't it?

After speaking to the guide in their vowel-heavy language, Kauri gestured toward the beach. "Let's return to the others."

He led the way and the guard followed. As before, the ground cover cleared a path as they approached and closed behind them as they passed.

When they reached the nursery, the caretaker laid a baby in one of the leaf cribs. At that moment, another baby cut loose with a cry that might wake the neighbors on the next nearest island. A vine stretched out from near the woman and rocked the leaf cradle. He'd swear the vine had extended from the woman, and as his angle changed, he became more convinced. The vine came from her hip, not just nearby.

That had to be an optical illusion. Surely, like Kauri, she was simply wrapped in vines. The vine didn't come from the woman so much as it was entwined around her, reacting to the sound of the child crying.

Al wrenched his gaze away from the woman. "Kauri, the vines your people wear as adornment—"

"They are not adornment." Kauri continued walking without looking back. "We do not wear them as you wear your clothes. We can no more put them aside than you could remove your hand."

Al stopped short. He looked from Kauri to the guide to the woman then back to Kauri. That "one with the trees" assertion was literal. They really were some sort of what? Parasite? Hybrid? Brand new life form? Chimera?

Kauri looked back over his shoulder and smiled. "Ah, now you begin to understand."

The guide nudged Al with the butt of the spear. He followed the old man, but at a greater distance.

They emerged onto the beach. The net-mending crowd had set their work aside and hurried to hammocks descending on vines from the canopy.

The group meditating turned, facing directly into the sun. Phototropism. They weren't simply meditating on the virtues of natural living. They were turning with the movement of the sun, just as many plants did. A woman who was now in the shade of a tree picked herself up from the sand and darted to a smallish tree under the canopy. She embraced it, and tendrils from the tree burrowed under her skin while she smiled contentedly and sighed.

Al stared, slack-jawed.

The men standing near the compost pile stepped high, bringing their knees nearly to their chests. A collection of roots dangled from the soles of their feet. As Al watched, the roots shrank up, not winding around the foot, but disappearing into it. That was not just an illusion, bad lighting, or a weird angle.

A hard shiver rattled Al as he backed several steps away and crashed into the guide. Al spun. "I-I-I'm-I'm sorry. I'm so sorry!"

Al's heart beat like the rotors on the helicopter. Bile rose in his throat, and he swallowed hard.

"Now you fully understand." Kauri took in the whole island with a sweep of his arms.

"I-I must be going." Al backed in the direction of the helicopter and spoke faster than a jet aircraft flew. "Expected back at the ship soon. Captain gave me a strict time table. Mustn't be late."

"You can't leave here." Kauri scowled. "You should not have come, but now that you're here, you will be joining us one way or another."

Al spun and stumbled a few steps before he built up into a solid sprint. A spear flew past him and landed in a shrub.

Kauri yelled orders to his people.

The groundcover opened before him and closed behind him, but the path was narrower. No longer a city sidewalk, but less than two feet. He jumped over vines stretched across the gap at knee-height to trip him and ducked others pulled chest-high to clothesline him. As the path narrowed to barely wide enough to plant his foot, the ground cover caught at his shoes and pants. Behind him, the clamor of people running after him grew louder. Something bounced off his backpack. Another spear raced past his shoulder as he twisted and slapped away a vine with a noose at the end.

He burst onto the beach where the helicopter waited. The pilot was untying a cord that stretched between the helicopter's nose and a sleeve over the end of a rotor blade.

Al fell against the side of the helicopter. "Let's go! We have to go. Right now!" he said between gasps.

"Upset the natives?" The pilot smirked.

"Something like that." Al glanced over his shoulder.

"I'll take care of the bird. You get settled inside."

Al tossed his backpack and notebook into the helicopter and scrambled up after them while the pilot finished with the straps on the rotor blades. Slapping the headset off the chair, Al sat and cinched the seatbelt around his hips with adrenalin-borne speed.

He watched the tree line, expecting Kauri's angry mob to explode onto the beach any second. With any luck, the trees' efforts to slow him impeded them, too.

Finally, after most of eternity, the pilot climbed into the front seat and flipped switches.

The guide ran onto the beach with his spear ready. Staring wide-eyed, Al gripped the arm of the seat hard enough to turn his knuckles white. The rest couldn't be far behind. The guide threw the spear, but it landed short.

The rotors whirred up to speed, but the copter stayed on the ground as a flock of large-billed, green birds passed. The vines raced toward them. Al's breath caught.

Once the brilliant green birds were gone, the helicopter lifted off. More of the natives ran onto the beach. Below, the vines fell short and retracted into the forest.

Al blew out a breath and leaned back against the headrest. He closed his eyes.

The pilot's voice was faint, but the tone indicated a question. Al used the cord to reel the headset back to him and slipped it on. "Sorry, again?"

"I said, 'Where to?'" the pilot asked.

"Home." Al clasped his shaking hands in his lap. "Fastest way there."

"You got it. Come back tomorrow?"

"No!" he said a little too quickly. "No. I learned all I needed."

"Fair enough. You sit back and enjoy the scenery, Doc. We'll be on the carrier in thirty."

Origin:
That old fanfic of an obscure TV series I
mentioned? This is it. It's been tweaked to take it
out of that universe, of course, but I'm sure if
you've seen the series yourself, you'll figure it out.

This one is also the only not-speculative fiction tale
in the set and the longest one.

Worst Kept Secret

More than anything about this trip, Ron liked
the feel of the wind through his hair as he drove his
Royal Red Metallic 1961 Lincoln Continental down
the road. There was a sense of freedom that was the
chocolate cake of life. Having a buddy like Gil along
would be a very generous helping of icing.

At his next stop in Xylon, Texas, Ron would pick
up Gil for their summer-long sight-seeing tour, the
last bit of random freedom before both of them
returned to East Texas to go to work in Dad's oil
business. Gil would be driving trucks, and Ron was
going to start in accounting. Just like Dad had done
when Grandpa had owned the business.

Someday, Ron supposed they'd each find a
home and maybe even a girl to settle with. In the

meantime, there was nothing better than traveling the open road with his pal.

There was only one hitch. Gil didn't want to leave the company he worked for without giving proper notice. Decent of him, but he had two more weeks to go there. Xylon wasn't exactly a hopping metropolis. Ron would have to find something to do with himself for a couple of weeks.

Roslyn, the town he'd stopped in for gas, had displayed a "help wanted" board. The sawmill where Gil worked in Xylon requested skilled and unskilled labor. They paid between $0.85 and a dollar and a half per hour, temporary and permanent positions.

Some of the other guys checking out the board hadn't cared for the listing, complaining it was too vague. For that reason alone, Ron planned to check it out. There'd be less competition that way. He'd never worked at a mill, but whatever the work was, he was up to it. He just needed to fill his time for a week or two. Earning a little pocket money would be a nice bonus.

The speed limit signs gradually dropped from highway speeds to 30 mph. He entered the town from the north on Highway 75.

Xylon was quaint, but not unlike any of the other little bergs he'd seen. East Texas was polka-dotted with these tiny towns spaced some thirty miles apart. They'd started out life as water stops for the railroads. Most of them still existed in some form but had lost their old glory.

As he entered the town, Ron checked out the environment. Some of the houses were rather nice and well-kept while others only a few streets over would be better off leveled and rebuilt. Businesses were mostly mom-and-pop establishments along with the necessary department store any self-respecting town needed to be able to hold its head up among its peers. The City Hall was old and ornate, decorated with spires, rockwork, and statuary.

He'd almost made it to the far side of Xylon before he spotted the café where he'd be meeting Gil.

Ron pulled into a parking space. The time was too late for breakfast and too early for lunch, but the café in most places was a quick, simple way to get a feel for the people of the town.

Pocketing the car keys, Ron strode through a door with a bell hung just above it to herald his arrival. Just inside, a sign with movable letters welcomed him and invited him to find a spot to sit. Gil waved from the end of the counter. Ron headed over and hopped up on the next stool.

A very--"homely" was too kind a word--well, a waitress came over to take their orders. "Kathy," as her name badge read, would have been better off with a lot less war paint and a few more trips to the orthodontist.

"What'll it be, boys?" Kathy's nasal voice made a buzzsaw sound appealing.

"Coffee, black." Ron tried on a smile and just felt that much more awkward for it.

"A big glass of buttermilk, if you have it." Gil didn't even bother with the barest grin.

Kathy bobbed her head. "Coming right up." She winked and walked away.

Ron winced. "I hope she's not par for the course around here. Is she a transplant?"

He looked around. All the other female patrons were old enough to be his grandmother, but in spite of their age, many had the shades of faded beauty.

"You wish. Slim pickin's around here." Gil shook his head.

Kathy returned with a steaming cup of joe and a tall glass of buttermilk. How Gil could drink that stuff Ron would never know.

"What will you have to eat?" Kathy spun her pen into writing position and stood poised to jot another order.

"Coffee is fine for me, thanks." Ron blew across the top and took a tentative sip. Not the worst he'd ever had, but far from the best. It was hot, anyway.

"I'm all set here." Gil raised his glass.

She tore the ticket off her book and put it face down between them then turned to Ron. "You new in town?"

Ron could already envision Gil's wild rejoinder. *"No, I've been hiding him in the back forty for twenty-five years."* But Ron suspected the effort would be wasted.

"I just came in from Roslyn." Ron twitched his head toward the north. "I heard they needed help here at the mill."

"They just might at that. Mr. Colby, he's the one that owns the place, hasn't been his self since the last illness laid him up for a bit last December." Kathy clicked her tongue against her twisted teeth and shook her head. "Sad affair, that. And you'll want to watch yourself with the missus. You've known more cordial crocodiles, I'm sure."

Ron had hoped Kathy would wander off, but she leaned on the counter and just stared.

"So, you planning on staying?"

Gil smiled. "Funny, I was about to ask you the same thing."

"Me? Sure. I grew up here." Kathy shrugged. "Got nowhere else to go."

Ron feigned a sip of coffee to avoid laughing. He had been right. Gil's one-liners didn't even get caught on the tip of the waitress's huge nose before zooming over her head.

Kathy looked past them as the door opened then left to greet the newest arrival.

"Wow." Ron watched her go. "Any denser than that and she'd be her own black hole. What do you say we finish up here and split while we still can?"

Gil nodded, but they needn't have worried. Kathy's MO appeared to be to attach herself to the most recent customer.

Once finished, Ron left enough to cover the bill and a fair tip then led the way back to the car.

"South to Highway 12 then east." Gil pointed.

Ron pulled out and followed Gil's directions. Crossing Main Street brought a change as sudden as flipping a light switch. They went from middle class to affluent in less than two intersections. South of the highway was definitely the preferred neighborhood. Houses were elaborate and lawns were immaculately manicured. North of Highway 12 was only slightly less desirable. Yards were still beautiful and conspicuous consumption was still obvious, but the decimal was moved back a step.

Xylon ended abruptly, as if a wall prevented any easterly growth. Fences along each side of the road sported signs that read, "No Trespassing – Private Property."

Five miles down, the signs looked the same. The owner of the land had quite a spread, especially if the holdings went back from the highway some distance.

"Just up ahead on the right." Gil pointed.

A sign for the "Xylon Sawmill" aimed them down a gravel side street to the right.

The sound of a massive, industrial saw split the air and grew louder as they got closer. Finally, the road ended in a large, paved lot. To the left stood a single-story building marked "Office." To the right, a pavilion held a few picnic tables. Straight ahead was the large building housing the saw itself and everything else it took to turn a tree into lumber.

Ron parked the car and hopped out. Aware of eyes on him, he turned and saw three guys about his and Gil's age staring like predatory animals. He waved then jogged to catch up with Gil.

Ron leaned toward Gil. "What's with the unwelcoming committee?"

Gil sighed. "You showed up with me, and I speak two languages."

"I speak two languages." Ron cast a quick glance back over his shoulder.

"Yeah, but your English doesn't have that special Mexican cadence to it."

Ron rolled his eyes. "You put up with that all the time?"

"That's why I drive the truck. I only get to deal with that between runs." Gil opened the door to the office. "Two more weeks. Then it's you and me and the open road."

The inside of the office was like no mill Ron had ever been in. Flowered wallpaper graced the walls, and lace curtains hung in the windows. A girl, who didn't look old enough to be out of high school yet, sat at an ornately carved desk. A matching wardrobe took the place of a supply cabinet. Two well-padded wingback chairs sat with their sister table bearing a Tiffany-stained glass lamp with dragonflies buzzing across a blue field. The girl, pretty but not gorgeous, looked out of place in a simple blue calico dress. As they walked in, she quickly slid something into a desk drawer.

"Good morning!" She beamed a congenial smile, but she kept her seat.

That felt odd, but Ron let it go.

"Hey, Liesel. This is my friend Ronald Moore." Gil patted Ron on the back.

"Hi." Ron stepped forward. "I understand that you're seeking skilled and unskilled labor."

"Oh, yes, yes. There are a few permanent positions and a couple temporary ones." Liesel opened a side drawer on the desk and withdrew a clipboard.

"I'm only in town for a couple of weeks," Ron said.

She looked to Gil. "Oh! This is the friend you're traveling with?"

"Yeah! Can't wait to get started."

She added a pen to the clipboard and held it out. Gil darted forward and collected it before they retreated to the wing backs. The application was pretty straightforward, so Ron filled it out while Liesel busied herself with correspondence.

The main door creaked open.

"Say, Liesel, do you—" The gray-haired 60-ish man saw them and stopped short. "Later. It'll keep until later."

"Wait, Mr. Langston." Liesel fished a paper out of her desk. "The schedule was just approved for next week."

"Great." Langston crossed to the desk. "Exactly what I came in for."

Again, it seemed odd that Liesel kept her seat. Ron had expected her to meet Langston partway or at least rise. Whatever the cause, Langston didn't seem bothered by the breach of etiquette.

"Thanks, Liesel. Sorry to interrupt." Langston left with the paper in hand.

Ron returned the clipboard to Liesel.

She looked through the application, nodding. "Very good. So, you've never had experience with mills, but you've done accounting."

"I've been training to take over the accounting department in the family business."

"That's perfect. And two weeks should give me enough time to get caught up on the-the special project." Liesel returned the pen to the intricately carved cannister on her desk. "Oh, I think you'll do fine. It's father's decision, of course."

She pulled out a file folder and slipped the application in. Then, keeping the folder in her lap, she jotted something on the paper. When she set the folder aside and reached under the desk, Ron wasn't sure what to think until she came up with a pair of metal crutches. Sliding her arms into the cuffs, she grabbed the handholds and pushed herself to her feet with a bit of a grimace. The file folder went into the large pouch on the apron tied around her waist. If her legs were deformed in any way, he couldn't tell. The calico dress flared down to her ankles, and she wore normal shoes. Suddenly, her refusal to rise and greet guests and Langston made total sense. Standing was a significant effort.

Ron quickly schooled the surprise out of his features. If Liesel noticed anything amiss in his expression, she didn't let on, but Ron suspected that she was very familiar with people being awkward around her.

"Come with me, please." She led him toward the door behind the desk.

Ron quickly stepped ahead and opened the door for her.

The office was as strangely incongruent as the antechamber although the details varied somewhat. Pink satin decorated the windows and covered the sofa and chairs in the corner and the two chairs at the desk. The desk and its chair had spindly legs and delicately carved cherubim.

Behind the desk sat a graying middle-aged man perusing a newspaper. His eyelid and jowls drooped on the left side and his hand on that side seemed heavy.

"Dad? Mr. Moore is here about the temporary accounting position." She hobbled to the desk.

"Certainly, dear." Mr. Colby rose.

His left arm hung awkwardly, not entirely paralyzed, but not altogether functional either. When Mr. Colby went to shake Ron's hand, he missed on the first try. His grip had a lot in common with wet noodles.

"Please, have a seat." Mr. Colby's left hand flopped in the general direction of one of the chairs.

Liesel handed him the folder then turned to go. Mr. Colby looked at the paper for only a couple seconds before setting it aside.

"Well, tell me. How was the drive in?" Mr. Colby asked.

Weird way to start an interview, but he could handle small talk. "It was fine. A really pretty drive out this way. I came in from Roslyn."

"Umhm. Nice scenery up that way." Mr. Colby shifted in his seat. "Did the weather hold for you?"

"Yes, sir. Very pleasant." *OK, so that takes care of the weather report. On to accounting?*

"Which way did you come in?" Mr. Colby asked.

"Roslyn." Ron kept a well-practiced "polite face" firmly in place.

"Nice drive up that way, especially if the weather holds," Mr. Colby tried to fold his hands on the desk, but the left one wouldn't interlace with the right, so he just ended up stacking his hands. "So, what can I do for you?"

I think his saw blade is a little dull. "I'm here about the temporary accounting job, Mr. Colby."

"Oh, right, right. Sorry. You'll have to forgive me. I've been ill recently." Mr. Colby glanced in the folder again then stood. "Pleasure to meet you. Just see Liesel for the current job postings. She'll get you set up."

"Thank you, sir." Ron shook Mr. Colby's hand and left.

Liesel was still handling the correspondence. Gil left his perch at the wingbacks and joined him.

"Mr. Colby said to see you about the current job postings." Ron stepped around to the front of Liesel's desk.

Liesel smiled. "Oh, good. I just knew he'd like you." She pulled a paper out of the desk drawer and opened it flat. "We have jobs for a bookkeeper, a truck driver, and a couple long-term jobs around the mill itself. The bookkeeper pays a dollar and a half per hour. Hours are 7:30 to 4:30. Lunch from noon to one. I'm usually here 7 to 430, but we can get you a key if you want a different schedule. You'll handle payroll and timesheets and help me with tracking charts for the government."

Ron nodded. "When do I start?"

"Have you found a place to stay?" She crossed the accounting job off the list.

Ron cast a glance back at Gil. There was barely enough room in his parents' house for them. Better if he got his own space.

"Not yet. Is there a boarding house?"

"Two, actually." Liesel looked up at the corner of the room. "There's Peachtree Arms at 2nd and Laurel, and Ellis House at 8th and Oak. Not to tell you your business, of course, but I'd recommend Ellis House. The police are out at Peachtree often, and not without cause. I don't know what Mrs. Ellis charges these days or if she has vacancies."

"Thanks. I'll check into it." Ron smiled.

"Once you're situated, come on back if you want to start today. Otherwise, I'll see you in the morning." Liesel tucked the paper back into her desk.

"We'll be back. Thanks again." Ron waved and left. He turned to Gil. "You have time to come along, or is it time to get to work?"

Gil checked his watch, a worn out affair with a scratched face and a cloth band starting to fray at the edges. "I'll go with you. I took off until lunch."

He and Gil hopped into the Continental and headed back out to the highway.

Ron shifted into the next gear as the engine revved. "I got the definite impression—"

"That it's Liesel running the show not the old man?" Gil grimaced. "Yeah. Mr. Colby's 'illness'? A stroke. He survived it, but he's been a little soft in the head since."

"What about Liesel? Polio, you think?"

"The official story is 'birth injury,' but something about it doesn't ring right."

Ron thought back to the gal and wondered how he could solve that mystery without prying into her personal life like some nosy jerk. Maybe something would present itself. "Cute kid, though."

"Yeah, in a kid-sister kind of way." Gil snorted. "She's only just out of high school."

"And what was up with hiding the account book?" Ron turned onto Oak Street.

Gil shrugged his shoulders. "Not entirely sure, but there's some kind of secret project the missus wants her to do."

Ahead, a sign in front of a two-story house with attic dormers announced their arrival at Ellis House.

"I'll probably find out this afternoon." Ron pulled up to the curb and parked.

Ellis House looked like any normal but relatively large house rather than an apartment or hotel. Steps led up to a wrap-around porch that sported a collection of wooden rocking chairs. The white paint and gray trim could use a bit of touching up to cover the flaking areas. He supposed it might be a bit more cozy inside, but if not, this would only need to last the fortnight.

They approached the house and rang the bell.

A severe-looking woman in a plain gray dress and hair piled up into a tight bun answered the door.

Ron smiled. "Mrs. Ellis, please."

"You're wanting rooms, I presume." She stared at him with a critical eye.

"Yes, ma'am, just one for me if you have any vacancies."

She gestured for them to go into a comfortable but utilitarian sitting room. Unlike the office at the mill, this room had been decorated in durable materials that were old enough to look as weathered as the exterior paint.

Ron waited for Mrs. Ellis to find a seat before he took one. Gil stayed standing nearby.

"There is no smoking in the house. Women's rooms are on the first floor. Men's on the second. No men allowed in the women's rooms and vice versa." Mrs. Ellis numbered her points on her fingers. "Come and go as you like. Rooms are $4.25 per day or $27 for the week, paid in advance. That gets you the room, clean linens once per week, coffee and rolls for breakfast, and whatever I've made for supper. Breakfast is available between 6:00 and 8:00 in the morning. Supper is served at 6:00 PM. If you want a brown bag lunch of a sandwich, fruit, and chips, that's another $3 per week. All payable in advance."

"Fair enough," Ron agreed.

He withdrew his wallet from his back pocket and paid Mrs. Ellis $30. After tucking the money into her apron, she led them upstairs to a plain room with a bunk bed, a simple dresser, and a desk stocked with pens, paper, and an envelope.

"Will this do?" She crossed her arms over her chest.

He stepped into the room and turned a complete circle to give the space a perfunctory look. "Yes, ma'am. Thank you."

Mrs. Ellis turned to go. "I'll have your lunch ready shortly."

She left without any further benediction.

Gil watched her go. "I hope the blankets are warm enough. A person could get frostbite around here."

"I know what you mean." Ron blew out a breath.

They went down to the car to get his things. He was traveling light with just a suitcase and a shaving kit. By the time they had finished running everything up to the room, Mrs. Ellis had returned with his brown bag lunch. The two of them drove back to the sawmill.

📖

Liesel was going to go cross-eyed. She could understand why father hadn't kept up with the

133

books after the fourth quarter of last year, but why had he left them undone for three whole years? Now their records were being demanded and with father out of sorts, organizing all the data fell to Liesel. Jeffrey was too young, and Mother could hardly add a column of numbers. She sighed. She shouldn't think like that, even if it were true.

The doors started to open, and Liesel quickly slid the ledger into a drawer of the desk. All this hiding and sneaking was silly, but as was true with so many things, it was easier to just do things the way Mother wanted them done.

Speak of the devil and she appears.

Mother walked in with Jeffrey.

"I saw that." Mother shook her finger. "Really, Liesel, you must be quicker than that when it comes to getting the books out of sight."

Liesel huffed. "If you'd let me work on this at home—"

"Work stays at work. Home stays at home." Mother arranged the pencils in the can to form a neat ring around the edge.

Jeffrey flopped into one of the wingback chairs and crossed his arms over his chest. If his lower lip hung any further, he'd walk on it. There was no telling what he was in a snit about this time, and she didn't care to find out.

Liesel brushed an errant hair away from her face. "Well, we hired a temporary bookkeeper this morning. That should help. He'll start this afternoon or tomorrow morning. He'll take care of the payroll and daily records, and I'll take care of the books."

Mother shifted the stained-glass lamp a quarter of an inch to the left. "Who is it?"

"Ron Moore. He's a friend of Gil Soto and will be in town for this week and next."

Mother moved Liesel's desk blotter a half inch to the right. "So, no one of importance, then."

That translated roughly to, "No one wealthy enough to consider seriously."

Feeling a spurt of mischief, Liesel smirked. "Oh, I don't know. I thought Mr. Moore was very handsome."

"Looks mean nothing. You need a man who can provide for you." Mother crossed her arms and glared. "And in your case, you'll need one who will even look at you."

As often as she heard those cracks against her, they still cut her every time.

Mother pulled Liesel's crutches out from under the desk.

"I need those." Liesel reached for them and missed.

"And they're right over here when you do." Mother put them in the cabinet across the room.

They might as well be in the next town. "Why can't we keep them over here where they're more useful?"

"Clutter, dear." Mother ran her finger along the top of the cabinet then checked for dust. "They clash outrageously with the brass fixtures. We must present a professional appearance. Come along, Jeffrey."

"I want an ice cream." Jeffrey stomped his foot.

"After your father's luncheon appointment and not a moment sooner." Mother waved him forward. "Come along, now."

Still glaring at Mother, he stalked after her into Father's office. For a twelve-year-old, Jeffrey acted like he was still four, and yet Mother raved about how clever he was and went on about how he was destined for greatness. Someone needed to take that boy over a knee and soon, if it hadn't already become too late.

Less than two minutes later, Mother and Jeffrey led Father out. This "luncheon" was just a fancy cover-up for his physical therapy appointment. The stroke had left his one side all but paralyzed, but the doctors had kept him alive. Now he was mentally addled, unable to dress and feed himself adequately, and completely incapable of running the mill. At times, Liesel wondered if the doctors might have been kinder to let him die. Sure, he was young, not even fifty yet, but a lifetime of abusing his body daily with alcohol and cigars had caught up with him. If anything good had come of it, he had a kinder disposition most of the time. Now and again, his old self re-emerged, particularly if he'd been drinking, but she suspected he took his cues from Mother.

Once they were gone, Liesel pulled out the ledger again and continued to check the third quarter figures from two years ago. She'd only finished half the column when she looked up at the clock. Lunchtime would be starting in five minutes, but she might need that long to get to the cabinet. She looked at the converted wardrobe.

"Professional appearance." She rolled her eyes. "Of course, it's much more professional for someone to come in and find me sprawled on the floor."

Using the desk for support, Liesel pushed herself up. The joints in both legs protested loudly, but she grimaced and persisted. She held on to the desk and made her way around to the other side. Then came the hard part. Fifteen feet with nothing to hang on to separated her from the cabinet, but the distance might as well have been fifteen miles. Liesel took one step then another. Without the crutches to transfer some of the stress to her arms and shoulders, each step shot a lance of pain up her legs. Third step, fourth, but the distance seemed no less. On the next step her right leg buckled. Liesel tried to shift her weight, but her left leg failed, too.

As she fell, the door opened, and Gil and Ron walked in. Both rushed toward her, but she hit the ground before either could get to her.

Ron crouched next to her. "Are you all right?"

She felt her cheeks color and couldn't meet his eyes. "Yes, I'm-I'm fine."

Gil went to her desk. "Where are your crutches?"

She pointed. "There, in the cabinet."

Ron lifted her to her feet and supported her. "What are they doing over there?"

Gil retrieved them.

"Mother puts them there." She tried to stand on her own, but her right leg buckled again.

"Why?" Ron caught her.

"They clutter up the place."

Gil looked ready to say something, but he held his tongue. shaking his head.

"Why didn't you follow the wall around?" Ron asked.

Liesel pointed to each side wall and the short run of steps leading up to the daises that Mother had someone build to give the room more character.

"I can hardly navigate stairs with my crutches. Without them?" She shook her head.

Ron flushed. "I'm sorry. I didn't notice that when I was here earlier, and I had to climb up them to get to the chairs."

With Ron keeping her steady and Gil helping her get the crutches situated, she was soon ready to travel again.

"Thank you." She tried to smile. "You're just in time. I was on my way to blow the horn for lunch. All the guys will meet at the pavilion, and I'll introduce you to everyone."

Mother, of course, would be incensed that she hadn't let Gil handle introducing Ron to the others, but there were times when she hated being so isolated. Some of the guys, at least, were nice.

She went to the door and gave the chain nearby one long tug. The air horn blasted a single, prolonged note. When she started for the cabinet again, Gil rushed ahead of her and pulled out a brown bag.

"Yours, I presume."

"Yes, thank you." She wrapped the open end of the bag around the handle of her crutch.

"Will Mr. Colby be joining us?" Ron looked back at the door to the inner office.

Liesel shook her head. "No, he had an appointment for lunch."

This time, Ron looked ready to say something but stopped himself.

Ron opened the door for her, and she led the way to the pavilion. They walked with her, keeping her pace rather than setting their own and demanding that she keep up. By the time she reached the pavilion, all the workers were there.

She made the rounds, introducing Ron to Cliff Langston, the foreman; Willie Simpson, a crane operator; Hugh Johnson, the other truck driver; Darren Barkley, Lane Pierce, and Billy Langston, and the other thirty or so men who did various jobs around the inside of the mill as needed.

"Mr. Moore will be helping me with the payroll and other records." Liesel sat on one of the open benches.

Hugh stared hard at Ron. "Unless you want to see the hospital from the inside, you keep away from Liesel. She's my girl."

Liesel scowled. "Hugh, I'm not now, nor have I ever been, or ever will be your girl. Get that through that dense rock you have for a brain."

"Only a matter of time, honey." Hugh winked. "You'll come around. It's only natural for the two wealthiest families in Xylon to be joined in marriage."

She knew better than to expect any of the other guys to come to her defense. Gil tried whenever he wasn't on the road, but all Hugh saw was a poor Mexican who wasn't worth hearing. Ron started to say something, but he hadn't managed the first word when Wally cut in.

"Two more months." Wally spoke around a bite of his sandwich. "That's all I'll need."

"And you'll have enough for the truck?" Billy asked.

"Umhm! I'll be able to start up that catering business."

"Are you sure there is enough business around Xylon to keep it afloat?" Billy chugged a swallow of his soda.

Wally nodded. "Ralph and Marge did it for years."

"No problem." Hugh waved his hand dismissively. "The business from the Colbys and my uncle alone will keep any catering business going."

"Oh, yeah, the all-potent Colbys and the ever-powerful Aldus Rodman," Billy sneered. "How could I forget?"

Mr. Langston cuffed his son alongside the head. "Keep a civil tongue in your head, boy."

"Yes, sir," Billy mumbled.

He was half again Liesel's age, and seeing Billy bow to his father's wishes gave her a painful realization that she would never be out from under her mother's rod and whip, not as long as she remained in Xylon anyway.

Liesel finished her peanut butter sandwich and started in on the nectarine.

"So, what does a guy do for fun around here?" Ron took a bite of an apple.

"Oh, depends on what you like." Darren looked past them. "You can go tubing down Livingston River on weekends, if we've had enough rain."

"Which hasn't happened in months." Billy rolled his eyes.

"There's a park." Liesel conjured a mental picture of the flower gardens in full bloom.

"Yeah, if you're into being bored looking at flowers." Hugh snorted.

"And there are some good places on 1st and 2nd Streets where a guy can get a beer and a gal." Lane exchanged nods with a couple other guys.

"Friday nights, there is a dance at the VFW hall." Billy leaned closer. "There's no admission, but it's not bad, and there's live music. Most of the town shows."

"Yeah, but they cut you off at two drinks, and those are mostly water," Lane complained.

Ron gestured to his glass. "Well, drinks are nice, but congenial company is often better."

"I prefer a little of both," Gil said.

A vehicle pulled into the lot. Liesel saw the family car and steeled herself. She started collecting her lunch trash.

"Liesel Colby, you get over here this instant!" Mother shrieked.

"If you gentlemen will excuse me." Liesel pitched her trash in the nearest bin.

As she pushed herself to her feet, Gil, Ron, Wally, Mr. Langston, and—after his father's encouragement—Billy also rose. Liesel headed, not for the car where Mother stood, but toward the office door. Not about to be deprived of an opportunity to chastise, Mother met her. Jeffrey had half an ice cream cone in his hand and apparently the rest on his face.

"Honestly, Liesel, eating with men. What goes through your mind?" Mother scolded.

"Introducing Mr. Moore to the others."

"And once introductions were made you should have returned to the office." Mother huffed. "It's not like you haven't anything to do."

Liesel suppressed a sigh and headed inside. Someday, sooner than later if all went as planned, she'd leave this place.

📖

Ron parked in the mill lot and stepped out of the car. Friday had come at last. The week had quickly settled into a routine. Arrive at 7:30, handle the general accounting and daily reports while Liesel sorted out the tangled mess of a financial statement no one was supposed to know she was working on, eat lunch with the guys while Liesel had a working lunch alone in the office, then back to the bookwork until quitting time. On Wednesday, Gil and Ron had tried eating lunch with Liesel just to keep her company. They'd had a grand time until Mrs. Colby had arrived to get Mr. Colby for an appointment. Mrs. Colby had soundly berated the poor girl in front of them for shirking her responsibilities. Protests had been categorically ignored. The next day, Mr. Langston had told them to eat with the guys and let Liesel work in peace. It wasn't right, but Ron had seen the poor girl's mother turn a stray pencil shaving into a tirade.

"See you later." Gil hopped out of the car.

"Careful out there."

Gil turned and walked backward a few steps. "Me? You're the one on the battlefield."

"With exactly one casualty." Ron held up one finger.

"Yeah. Poor kid." Gil turned and jogged to the truck.

Ron headed for the office and passed the Colby family car. The car was brilliant blue, the latest model with all the bells and whistles. Looking around, he found Mr. and Mrs. Colby talking to Mr. Langston; or at least, Mrs. Colby was talking, and the two gents couldn't slip a word in edgewise. That meant Liesel should be alone in the office. This would be a good time to inject a little levity into her otherwise dreary day.

As Ron approached the door, he heard a clatter then a thud.

"Leave me alone!" Liesel yelled.

Ron burst into the room. Hugh Johnson had Liesel pushed up against the wall. One crutch lay in the middle of the room, and he was trying to wrestle the other one away from her while he kept her free hand pinned.

Ron slammed the door. "Let her go, Johnson!"

He started across the room to pull Hugh off Liesel. Hugh spun, pushing Liesel away. She steadied herself with her remaining crutch and the back of the desk chair.

"Miss Colby, are you all right?" Ron kept his eyes squarely fixed on Hugh.

"Yes, thank you," she replied.

The tears threatening to spill out of her eyes and the pain etched on her face as she flopped into the chair conspired to call her a liar.

"Mr. Johnson came in to get his pay, and that's all he's going to get." There was a surprising amount of growl in her voice.

Ron went to the safe and pulled out the cashbox and the payroll book. He opened to Hugh's page and counted out his wages, only handing them over after Hugh signed off on the receipt.

"You'd better steer clear, Moore." Hugh made a fist.

"If you need to learn how to treat girls with respect, I know where you can get lessons free of charge." Ron stood up straighter and matched Johnson's tone.

Hugh snorted, pocketed his money, and left.

Ron retrieved Liesel's other crutch and brought it back to her as she tugged the sleeve of her dress down over the welts on her wrist.

"I think you have grounds for assault." He propped the crutch on the side of the desk.

She sighed. "Calling the police won't do anything useful."

"Have you tried?" he asked.

She shook her head. "Not me, but Carolyn."

"Carolyn?"

"Carolyn Everson. She used to live around here. Beautiful girl. A couple years older than me. Hugh pursued her relentlessly, but she wouldn't have anything to do with him. He slapped her around once, bloodied her lip. Her father called the police and filed charges. Hugh's uncle bribed all the judges in the nearby circuits, and Hugh's friends perjured themselves, claiming Carolyn fell. The charges were dropped."

Is that what had happened to all the pretty girls in this town? Hugh scared them off? And what in blazes was wrong with all the guys in town? Not one of them had tried to give Hugh some free lessons on proper respect for girls? Or maybe Hugh was just too dense to get the point.

"And what became of Carolyn?" Ron asked.

"Graduated high school and moved away for college." Liesel let out a breath. "Now, the police chief, Mr. Knowles, is happy to arrest Hugh, but then Hugh's uncle just buys off whoever needs to be bought. Can't have his only heir in jail, you see."

"And I suppose telling your parents is no good." Ron glanced to where he'd last seen them.

Liesel sat up straighter and adopted a reasonable match for her mother's nasally whine. "Well, it's about time somebody took an interest in you. If you wouldn't play so hard to get, he wouldn't have to try so hard to get you. You're not a nun, you know." She dropped the accent. "Don't think taking the habit hasn't occurred to me, but I'd be doing it for all the wrong reasons. Well, if all goes according to Hoyle—"

Mrs. Colby's voice, harping at someone of course, drew inexorably closer. Ron quickly stowed the second crutch under Liesel's desk then darted to his own seat and made like he was recording something in the payroll ledger. Liesel opened the desk drawer that contained the financial reports no one was supposed to know about. As Mrs. Colby opened the door, Liesel quickly shut the desk drawer.

"Not fast enough," Mrs. Colby scolded. "Honestly, Liesel, it's a wonder the whole town doesn't know."

Bold of her to think no one else did. They might not know exactly what she was working on, but people sure knew she was up to something.

Mr. Colby continued on to his office, and Jeffrey flopped into one of the wingbacks and gnawed on a licorice stick. As often as Ron saw the kid eating sweets, it was a miracle Jeffrey wasn't a toothless blimp.

"Oh, and of course, it's Friday. Every man who works here will be in to collect his pay, and naturally, you wear the frumpiest dress you own." Mrs. Colby shook her head.

"It's comfortable," Liesel replied.

"High collar, long sleeves, how will you ever attract a man like that?" Mrs. Colby went on.

"You know, Mrs. Colby, as a card-carrying male member of the species, I can tell you that some of us like to dream, and a girl who shows all leaves nothing to dream about," Ron chimed in.

Mrs. Colby scowled. "Don't encourage her."

Ron shrugged. "Somebody should."

"Cheeky." Mrs. Colby reorganized the pencils in the can. "I'll thank you to mind your own business, Mr. Moore."

The diversion worked. Mrs. Colby left off chastising Liesel and went on a tirade about strangers interfering with the disciplining of children. All the while, she attended to needless tidying, scooting various objects half an inch this way or that. Ron knew the lecture was winding down when Mrs. Colby put Liesel's crutches in the cabinet.

Mrs. Colby looked at her diamond-studded watch. "Look at the time! Where does it all go? Come along, Jeffrey. It's time for your swimming lessons. Liesel, I expect you to get more done today than you did yesterday."

The mother and her impish son left.

Liesel sighed and pulled out the financial statement. "How does she expect me to accomplish anything when she's in here for half an hour at a time?"

Before Mrs. Colby had come in, Liesel had been about to say something. He'd guessed it had to do with future plans, but before he could prompt her about it, she became deeply engrossed in her work. Ron busied himself with the daily records of the trees cut down and board feet of lumber prepared.

They'd been at it for an hour when Liesel groaned and put her head down on the desk.

"I can't get this column to add right." She erased something toward the bottom of the ledger. "I'm sure I'm doing the math correctly, but I'm getting the wrong number. It doesn't make sense when I do the checksum."

Ron joined her and looked over the work. "Let's see what another set of eyes can do."

Her entries were meticulously detailed. He didn't have to ask for an explanation of any of her terms. He flipped back a few pages to track some of the old figures she had to carry forward and noticed something peculiar. The mill had steadily lost ground over the last couple of years and finally went into the red at the end of last summer. Then this past January, there had been an abrupt about-face. Costs had decreased resulting in an increase of profits. Within the last month, profit margins had exceeded what they'd been before the decline.

Something else strange occurred to Ron.

The waitress at the cafe had mentioned that Mr. Colby's illness had been last December. If that illness had been the stroke Gil had mentioned, then Liesel—still in high school at the time—was responsible for the sawmill's recovery. Mr. Colby didn't seem to be all there, and Mrs. Colby never did anything but berate people. The foreman only did what he was told and hadn't once shown initiative. How many other people knew about Liesel's work?

As Ron continued toward the current work, he found the problem. "Here. This entry shows $720.81, but when you moved it over you wrote $702.81."

"Ugh. You're right. That was stupid of me. I should have seen that." She rewrote the number. "Thank you."

He gave her a light pat on the back. "No problem. It's an easy mistake to make."

Ron returned to his own work.

Pity that the town let Hugh get away with mistreating women. The mill would lose an able and skilled manager at this rate.

📖

Gil watched Wally load the flatbed truck with pallets of lumber. From here, Gil would drive the finished lumber to Roslyn's train depot then, on the return trip, stop at the site where the guys were chopping more trees to pick up the next load before returning here to start again. It was a pretty slick system. Gil was setting up for his third run of the day. This would be the last before lunch.

As he waited, well out of the crane's way, the other truck drove up and parked. Hugh climbed down from the cab and made his way over. He

147

looked ready for a fight, and after hearing the latest outrage Hugh had committed, Gil had a knuckle sandwich with his name on it.

Hugh squared his shoulders and clenched fists. "You better tell your buddy to stay out of my business, or he'll get what's coming to him."

"This business my pal stuck his nose into, it wouldn't happen to have something to do with those three red scratches on your neck, would it? See, 'cause if it does, you should probably know that me and Ron, we believe there's a right way to treat a girl, and we also believe that there's a right way to treat slobs who don't treat a girl the right way. Y'dig?"

"Stay away from my girl." Hugh squinted and gritted his teeth.

"See, now there's another problem. We all heard the girl say she doesn't dig you, man. Maybe you better be the one who backs away from her." Gil shifted his foot back in case Hugh turned all this bluster into action.

Wally whistled a shrill note. "All right, Gil, you're all set."

Gil snugged on his gloves, gave Wally a wave, and climbed into the cab. As he backed up the rig, he made a mental note to get the whole story from Ron later.

Gil took the Highway 215 bypass up to 75 then headed north into Roslyn. He passed the haul road to the cutting site along the way and made the railway in decent time. Gil helped himself to the coffee the station provided for workers and drivers while the crane operator unloaded the lumber. After collecting the necessary paperwork and signatures, Gil headed back into town, passing Hugh on the way out of Roslyn. He was halfway to the 215 turn off when he came across a gorgeous redhead in a green miniskirt, heels, and a white blouse heading toward Xylon from a disabled car. Well, he couldn't leave a damsel in distress, could he? It just wouldn't be right.

Gil pulled onto the shoulder and stopped behind the disabled car, a green Ford leaning toward the right front. The girl turned then ran back to him.

"Need a lift?" Gil asked.

She smiled, flashing a perfect set of pure, white teeth. "What I need is a tire change."

"I can do that."

"Oh, would you?"

"My pleasure."

She gave him the trunk key, and he dug out the spare, wrench, and jack.

"I'm Eve Barclay." She studied him for a moment. "I've seen you around town, haven't I?"

"Gil Soto. I'm working out at the sawmill for a couple more weeks. Barclay, so are you related to—"

"Darren Barclay, yes. He's my kid brother." She dropped her voice to a whisper. "He's a complete clod, but what can you do?"

"There's no accounting for kid brothers." Gil smiled. He'd know. He had three.

He had the tire changed and the flattened one in the trunk in short order.

"Are you going to the VFW dance tonight?" Gil asked.

"Wouldn't miss it. Pick me up at 8." She beamed a terrific smile.

"I'll be there."

Once he had her address jotted on the back of a receipt, Gil waited until she was under way before he headed out, feeling a thousand feet tall and as light as a feather.

At 4:30, a flood of loggers, drivers, and mill workers descended on the main office to collect their pay for the week. With Liesel's help, Ron paid them all their wages. It was nearly five o'clock before they finished, but surprisingly, no one seemed bothered by the wait. Perhaps it was just old hat by then, or maybe with two of them working at it, they were moving just a little faster than usual.

Once the queue had cleared, Gil left his perch near the wall and came to collect his pay. Then Ron paid Liesel, and she paid him and her father. Ron picked up the ledger and Mr. Colby's salary, more than all the rest of the workers together, and knocked on the office door.

"Yes, come in," Mr. Colby called.

Ron stepped inside. "You need to sign the ledger for your pay."

"Oh, right, right." Mr. Colby fumbled with a pen. "Certainly."

Ron brought the ledger to him. Mr. Colby stared at his pen. He blinked a few times, his brow furrowing.

"Sign your name, right here, sir," Ron prompted, pointing to the next line on the ledger.

"Oh, yes, right," he said.

As he signed, Ron compared the other signatures on the page. Mr Colby had had a strong hand for a long time then a very sudden degradation back around last December with a gradual improvement since then.

Ron left the stack of money on Mr. Colby's desk.

"Friday already?" he asked.

"Yes, sir."

The main door opened.

"What are you doing in here?" Mrs. Colby demanded.

"Waiting for my ride," Gil replied.

"Oh, well, fine. B-but be quick 'bout it," she said, her words slurring a bit. "P-places to go and things to do this evening."

Ron left Mr. Colby's office in time to see Mrs. Colby make an unnecessary adjustment to the Tiffany lamp. As Ron walked past her, he got a definite whiff of alcohol.

"Let's go, Thomas." Mrs. Colby took a few steps toward the inner office.

"Coming, dear," Mr. Colby replied.

After locking the cashbox and ledger in the safe, Ron took his leave of Liesel and followed Gil out.

Gil sucked in a breath of fresh air. "Wow. A guy could get almost tipsy just standing near the missus."

"And the night's still young."

"In its infancy," Gil added.

They arrived at the car about the time Mr. Langston reached his in the next space over. The Colbys came out of the office at that moment.

"Hurry up, Liesel!" Mrs. Colby snapped. "You can do better than that, and stand up straight. You're all slouched over. B-bad enough that you do nothing with your hair or your face, and you wear dresses that make nuns look underdressed. Must you have b-bad posture as well?"

The tirade continued well after the Colbys were in the car. Liesel had just barely gotten situated and closed the door when Mrs. Colby threw the car into reverse and sped off.

Mr. Langston watched them go then turned. "I know what you two boys are thinking. I can see it in your eyes. You're wondering how a wrinkled old prune like Winnifred ever produced a darling angel like Liesel."

Gil scratched his cheek. "Something like that."

"You might wonder, but the solution's quite simple, really." Mr. Langston smirked.

"Stepmother?" Ron guessed.

"Oh, no, no. Thomas only married the one time." Mr. Langston edged closer. "But with the one he picked, that's more than any man needs."

"Adopted?" Gil asked.

"Winnifred would've liked to have been able to claim that, but too many know she was pregnant and carried to term," Mr. Langston said.

Ron's next thought was illegitimate, but he didn't dare say that out loud.

"I give." Gil said, flipping his hand in the air.

"Stork got confused. Delivered the baby to the wrong place." Mr. Langston nodded once, sagely. "Somewhere out there, there is a sweet, gentle-hearted family wondering how they got such a brat for a daughter."

Ron smiled, but it faded as another question sprang up. "Mr. Langston, what happened to Liesel's legs? Polio?"

"Naw, nothing like that. The official records say congenital defect." Mr. Langston put air quotes around "official."

"What about the unofficial records?" Ron asked.

"Oh, well, you undoubtedly got your first hint already if Winnifred was true to form this evening and you came anywhere near her." Mr. Langston winced. "Just for a little while this evening, watch Winnifred. You're both pretty smart. No doubt you'll figure it out. See you this evening, lads." He hopped into his car and left.

"Something about Mrs. Colby drinking?" Gil asked.

Ron held up his hands. "Apparently. Maybe something to do with how she acts when drunk."

"I guess we'll see tonight." Gil slid into the shotgun seat of the Continental.

They were the last ones out of the lot.

📖

Ron sat at a table near the dance floor in the VFW hall. Much of the town appeared to be in attendance, so he would have thought there'd be some cute gal for him to ask to dance. To his amazement, there wasn't even one. Instead, he drowned in a sea of gray hair, married folks, a few obvious couples, and kids Liesel's age or younger. Aside from Gil's date, there didn't seem to be girls both his age and unattached. That just wasn't natural, and Ron wondered how many Hugh had scared off.

Ron took a sip of his drink and glanced at Mr. and Mrs. Colby and Liesel. Mr. Colby had downed two vodka-and-sodas in the first ten minutes, which had only made him loopier than usual, if that were possible. Ron couldn't hear their conversations, but Mr. Colby would start talking, then stop, develop a blank stare, and stay that way for a long time.

Mrs. Colby, although more lively, wasn't much better. She took a sip of her own martini, waited a bit, then drank from the martini in front of Liesel, who hadn't touched anything to eat or drink since arriving. Once Mrs. Colby finished both drinks, she stood and took her handbag before promptly dropping it. Mrs. Colby hadn't made it two steps before she dropped it again. By actual count, Mrs.

Colby lost her grip on the handbag eight times between the table and the restroom then another five times on the way back.

Ron shook his head and looked back at Liesel as he put all the pieces together. He felt a firm touch on his shoulder as Mr. Langston slid into the seat next to him.

"Figure it out?" he asked.

Ron frowned deeply. "Yeah. Just now. She dropped Liesel as a baby and injured her."

"Down a flight of stairs." He clicked his tongue against his teeth. "Didn't get her to the doctor until the bruises had faded. Back and leg injuries. Doctor said she'd never walk. That she gets around on crutches is a testament to her own persistence."

"And Mrs. Colby is so rough on Liesel because—"

"—The poor girl's a constant reminder of the town's worst-kept secret," Mr. Langston finished. "There are four people who saw the accident. The Colbys offered us each $1000 for our silence. To my shame, I took the money and didn't say otherwise when the Colbys insisted the girl had been born that way."

"So why tell me now?" Ron asked.

"When a man gets to be my age, he realizes he has more years behind him than ahead of him." Mr. Langston drew a deep breath, held it for a moment, then blew it out. "As they say, confession is good for the soul."

Mr. Langston rose and slapped Ron on the back before he left.

Ron looked over to the Colbys' table. Mrs. Colby was now working on a pair of scotches, neat. Mr. Colby was headed for the buffet. Liesel, staring at the wood grain of the table, couldn't be more bored if she tried. Ron was starting to feel the same. All the kids Liesel's age had paired off, so there was little chance of someone coming to relieve the tedious evening for her. Asking Liesel to dance would feel like dating his kid sister, but he could rescue her from boredom and have some cordial company for the evening.

He walked over and offered Liesel his hand. "Miss Colby, would you like to dance?"

Mrs. Colby snickered. "She can't d-dance."

"How would you know? You've never let me try." Liesel reached for her crutches leaning on the next chair over.

"You can't even walk," Mrs. Colby insisted.

"Well, we won't likely be doing the jitterbug or the Charleston, but maybe a nice waltz or foxtrot will do." Ron held the crutches while Liesel got the cuffs situated on her arms.

"He's only asking out of pity for you or d-desperation for himself," Mrs. Colby sneered.

"On the contrary, ma'am. If we were only a few years closer in age, I'd be saving up for a ring," Ron replied.

He helped Liesel to her feet, noting the smile on her face and the glare on her mother's.

Liesel had changed from the puritan-like gray, long sleeved, high collared, ankle length dress she had worn to work into a navy-blue satin with long gauzy sleeves and a white lace collar. It was still very modest but pretty.

"You look lovely," he said.

"Thank you." She blushed and looked down.

He led her back to the table he and Gil had staked out just as the current song ended. Gil, half-winded, returned without his date.

"Eve's off powdering her nose," he explained.

Ron helped Liesel into a chair then sat.

Gil leaned close. "Rescuing a beautiful girl from an ogre?"

Ron nodded.

"Good man." Gil sat and took a swig of his beer.

"Hey, this band isn't half bad," Ron said.

"They play a bit of everything." Liesel smiled and looked across the dance floor. "Like Texas weather. If you don't like it, wait a few minutes and it'll change."

Eve returned and looked Liesel up and down. "Who invited the kid?"

"I asked her to join us," Ron said.

Eve snickered behind her hand. "Oh, poor Ron. Fishing from the kiddie pool?"

"Abraham was ten years older than Sarah, and Boaz was a generation older than Ruth."

Eve glanced around then murmured to Liesel. "Don't feel bad, dear. Everyone likes the cute ones, not the smart ones."

"Some guys prefer a girl who can keep up with a meaningful conversation," Ron said.

Eve crossed her arms. "Well with her—"

"Hey, ease up, huh, Eve?" Gil held up a hand between Eve and Liesel. "Let's keep it light, yeah?"

Eve shrugged. "Whatever you say."

The current song ended and a slow waltz started.

Ron turned to Liesel. "Do you want to try?"

Liesel smiled. "Sure."

He considered some logistics. "Leave the crutches here. I'll support you."

"OK."

He helped her stand and led her to the dance floor. After a little instruction, they started off. He had to hold her up but not quite as much as he'd expected. Her right leg seemed weaker than the left, but he shifted the arm around her back to support her a little better. The biggest adjustment he had to make was remembering to take smaller steps. They wouldn't win any dance marathons anytime soon, but she did better than he'd hoped. When the song ended, something more energetic started up, and Ron led Liesel back to her seat. On the way, Gil got up and took Eve to the dance floor. Eve leaned toward Ron as they passed.

"She didn't do half bad for a cripple," Eve said.

Gil rolled his eyes and mouthed, "Sorry."

Fortunately, Liesel either didn't hear the snipe or chose to ignore it.

"Would you like something to drink?" Ron asked.

"Yes, please. Iced tea if it's available still."

He grinned and offered a tiny bow. "Coming right up."

When he got to the very well-stocked bar, he signaled the bartender.

"Two iced teas, please." He held up two fingers.

The bartender nodded and turned away.

A loud slap was heard over the music followed by a clatter. Ron whirled around and saw Hugh push Liesel. She landed on the floor next to a toppled chair. The music stopped. Gil was between them a heartbeat later. As Ron rushed back as quickly as the stunned crowd would allow, Hugh took two swings at Gil. Gil ducked the first and blocked the second then returned fire with a fist to the jaw, which rocked Hugh's head back. A second to the gut left Hugh on his knees gasping for air.

Gil slid back a pace and shook out his hand. "That's your first lesson, and if you keep harassing girls, I got another one for you."

Behind him, Hugh's two pals, Darren Barclay and Lane Pierce, were getting ready to jump Gil.

"Gil, behind you!" Ron pushed his way through the last two stunned dancers.

By the time Ron reached his buddy's side, Liesel had used one of her crutches to trip Lane. He sprawled face down. Darren held his hands up and stepped back. Lane scrambled to his feet and advanced on Liesel.

"Don't." Gil darted between them. "I got a lesson for you, too, if you need one."

"Hugh Johnson, you stay right where you are," a man ordered.

Leaving Lane and Darren to Gil, Ron turned. A heavy-set man with graying brown hair burst through the crowd. Hugh, in a crouch, looked ready to spring. Ron prepared himself to protect Gil's back, but no one made a move.

The people cleared a path for the man. He stood between Ron and Hugh and put a hand on Gil's shoulder.

"It's Chief Knowles. I'll take it from here. Will you two stay with the young lady until I get back?"

"Yes, sir," Ron said.

"You'd have a fight on your hands if you told us not to," Gil added.

"Thank you." He pointed at Lane, Hugh, and Darren. "You, you, and you. Come with me." He led them away. "I ought to whip your hides. Lane, Darren, when your daddies hear you stood by and let--"

The music started back up, drowning out the rest of the threat.

While Gil righted chairs, Ron picked Liesel up and settled her in one then retrieved her crutches.

He sat down beside her. Just like that morning, she fought for composure and won the battle.

"I'm sorry," Liesel said.

"Exactly what part of that was your fault, huh?" Gil flopped into a chair next to her. "You shouldn't put up with that. He had that slap coming and more besides."

"How'd that get started?" Ron asked.

"After you went for our drinks, Hugh sat down and drank the rest of Gil's beer," Liesel began.

Gil looked at his empty glass. "Son of a gun. So he did."

"Then he tried to kiss me. I pushed him away. Then he wanted to dance, and I said no. He pulled me up anyway and-and—"

"I saw that part." Gil glared in the direction Hugh had gone. "He was all hands. She slapped him, and he threw her down."

"I saw the rest." Ron wrinkled his nose in disgust. "Right here in public? Out in the open?"

"With his uncle's money backing him up, he doesn't care." Liesel took in the room with the sweep of her hand. "You'll note how many people stepped in to stop him: Gil, you, and Mr. Knowles. No one else."

"Yeah, yeah. Gil is right, Liesel." Ron patted her shoulder. "You had no fault in any of this. You've been real clear about telling him to back off."

Mr. Knowles rejoined them with a clipboard in hand. "Well, I've got one of my boys sitting on Hugh. The other two are just guilty of bad judgment and poor taste in friends. I gave them stern warnings, and I'll talk to their daddies in the morning. Not much else to be done with either at this point, but Hugh...That may be a whole other kettle of fish. I saw enough to fill in the gaps for what I didn't. How about it, Liesel? You've got ample grounds for charges."

What seemed like an obvious choice gave her pause.

"I'd do it, if I were you," Gil said.

Ron nodded in agreement. "It's twice in one day."

"Twice?" Mr. Knowles asked.

"Yeah, when I walked into the office this morning, Hugh had Liesel pinned to the wall. I'd only be guessing at what he had in mind, but I'd bet it's not in her best interests," Ron said.

Liesel unbuttoned the cuff of her sleeve and showed Mr. Knowles the bruises on her arm.

Mr. Knowles scowled. "That boy, if he were mine...."

Liesel sighed. "What good will it do? Filing a charge was no help at all for Carolyn."

"Well, maybe it'll help, and maybe it won't, but unless you file the charges, all I can do is give him a stern talking to." Mr. Knowles' jaw clenched for a moment. "With your cooperation, I can arrest him, give him a stern talking to, and put him in jail until his uncle posts bail."

She stared at the table for a moment. "The way I've been dealing with it has been pretty useless. Might as well do something different. All right." Liesel looked back at her parents, who were deeply engrossed in plates of hors d'oeuvres. "Mother won't be thrilled, but I'm about to a point where I don't care about that anymore, either."

"Good. You've made the right choice." Mr. Knowles took up his pen. "You two boys excuse us for a few minutes. Stay near at hand, though. I'll want your statements shortly."

Ron and Gil nodded and stepped away.

"So, here's a question for you." Gil twitched his head toward the Colbys "What kind of father keeps a jerk like Johnson on the payroll with his own daughter around the place?"

"Better question. What kind of parents sit there stuffing themselves and do nothing when their daughter is being assaulted by a jerk like Johnson in plain view."

Gil grunted. "Yep. That's a better question."

"Where'd you lose Eve?" Ron asked.

Gil looked around and shrugged. "Easy come, easy go."

"You don't sound too heartbroken."

"Yeah, well, easy on the eyes, hard on the ears." Gil put his finger in his ear and jiggled it.

Ron couldn't say he was too depressed to lose Darren Barclay's sister for the evening, either.

While he waited for his turn to talk to Mr. Knowles, Ron wondered how long it would take for Hugh's uncle to post the bail. He suspected Hugh wouldn't wait much longer than that before he pestered Liesel again.

Aldus Rodman pushed his nephew toward the car. "Get in."

"What are you so mad about?" Hugh stumbled a step and caught himself. "I'm the one who got hurt."

"And whose fault was that?" Aldus demanded as he got in. "Molesting an underage girl, in public no less. I only hope that split lip and pain in your gut taught you something, because this is the last time I clean up your mess."

"Uncle, I—"

"When your mother sent you down here after your little indiscretion up north, I cleaned it up for her sake." Aldus slammed the car door. "In her delicate condition, the scandal would have killed her as surely as a bullet. Then you got into exactly the same mess down here with another girl, and I cleaned that up for you, too. Bonnie McLeod, Carolyn Everson, now Liesel Colby. Liesel Colby? What the devil do you see in her? An easy target with those crutches? Such a scrawny little wretch isn't hardly worth a second look."

"I can't help—"

"You interrupted my negotiations with foreign investors." Aldus shifted into drive and pulled away from the curb. "Worse, with so many witnesses this time, it'll cost me plenty to shut them all up. You've become a bigger liability than an asset, so as I say, dear nephew, I hope that boy who hit you knocked some sense into that dense skull of yours because the very next time you louse everything up, I'll leave you to rot in that jail cell. Do you understand me, boy? The very next time."

Hugh deflated. "Yes, sir."

Aldus turned onto the highway. "Liesel Colby. In public, no less. Idiot."

He growled and drove his idiot nephew back to the VFW hall to pick up his car.

📖

While Gil waited for Wally to load the truck early Monday morning, a familiar car drove onto the lot. Hugh hopped out and bee-lined to Mr. Langston. How could he possibly be back so soon?

Gil looked up at Wally. "Back in a sec."

Wally nodded, and Gil jogged to the office. He walked in and found Ron sorting papers but no sign of Liesel.

"Where is—" he began.

"Powder room." Ron twitched his head in the direction of the restroom facility.

"Hugh's back."

Ron frowned. "That didn't last long."

"Uncle's pockets must be pretty deep." Gil gestured toward the door to Mr. Colby's office. "What do you say?"

Ron blew out a breath. "I don't think he'll get it."

"Maybe if we use small words." Gil winced and shook his head. "We gotta try."

"Yeah, I guess we do. The missus is useless."

Gil followed Ron to the door and hung back. Ron knew how to handle these corporate types. Ron knocked and waited for Mr. Colby to invite them in.

"Mr. Colby, do you have a minute? Gil and I would like to talk to you if you can spare the time." Ron stepped far enough into the room to give Gil space, but no further.

"Certainly, boys." Mr. Colby gestured to the chairs across from his desk. "Come on in. Have a seat. What can I do for you?"

"Well, sir, what it is—" Gil ran out of words. How did you tell a guy who wasn't entirely there that one of his workers was a hazard for his daughter?

"Hugh Johnson." Ron took over. "Mr. Colby, on Friday, I came in and found Hugh pinning Liesel to the wall. Then again, on Friday night, he got more than a little fresh with her. Honestly, Mr. Colby, we're afraid that if Hugh keeps working here near Liesel, he's going to keep after her, and she's going to get hurt."

Thank God Ron had a way with words. Gil preferred actions.

"Oh, Hugh." Mr. Colby chuckled. "He's kind of sweet on Liesel. If she wouldn't play so hard to get, he wouldn't have to try so hard to get her. Why I remember a time when I was courting Winnifred..." He trailed off and went blank.

"It's not just a little dating game that he was playing, Mr. Colby," Gil insisted, leaning forward. "There are marks on her arm where he grabbed her."

Mr. Colby shook his head quickly. "Oh, terribly sorry, boys. Did you need to see me about something?"

Gil blanched. He had to be kidding. Or was he really that scattered?

"No, sir." Ron stood. "That was all we had. Thank you for your time."

Gil begrudgingly followed Ron out.

After the door closed, Gil frowned. "Too far gone to even realize what's happening."

"Yeah, and that bit about playing hard to get? Direct quote of Mrs. Colby," Ron said.

"Now what?"

The other door opened, and Liesel returned with her mother and Jeffrey in tow. Jeffrey flopped into one of the wing backs and blew a gum bubble as big as his head. Mrs. Colby was looking the shade of green usually reserved for hangovers. Liesel sat down and slid her crutches under the desk.

"You, Moore." Mrs. Colby jabbed her finger at Ron. "I have another engagement and can't make the bank deposit for last week. It's in the safe. Take it to the East Texas bank in Roslyn and make the deposit. Because of liability issues, you'll have to ride up with your friend's next delivery or Hugh's, I suppose. It's all the same to me."

"I'll take care of it." Ron went to the safe.

"And no lollygagging." Mrs. Colby put enough growl in her voice to impress a grizzly. "There's plenty to do here."

As Ron got the deposit from the safe and checked it over, Mrs. Colby rearranged the lay of the curtains then put Liesel's crutches in the cabinet.

"Come along, Jeffrey." She strutted to the door.

Jeffrey blew another gum bubble then followed his mother out. Once Gil heard the car drive off, he retrieved Liesel's crutches.

She smiled. "Thank you."

"Sure thing." Gil glanced toward the mill. "You're going to be OK here?"

"With you both gone?" She looked away from him. "I hope so. If it means anything, Darren came by yesterday after church. He apologized and said he'd keep an eye on the office."

"Well, we'll hope that was real repentance and not just the remorse of getting the law in his business." Ron slid the deposit into a bank bag. "I'll be back as soon as I can."

"I'll be fine." Liesel's smile didn't make it to her eyes.

Gil led the way back to the truck and found one gone and Wally finishing up the second. He looked around the lot. "Where's the other truck?"

Wally motioned ahead of him. "I finished it before you finished with the missus. Langston told Hugh to get on the road."

Gil turned to Ron. "Great. He'll be back before us."

Ron set his jaw grimly. "Let's close the gap as much as we can."

They both climbed up into the cab, and Gil pulled out onto the road.

Ron felt like he'd been bounced half to pieces. The suspension system on the truck wasn't anything like the Continental to begin with, but Gil had pushed the far edge of the speed limit as much as they dared to close the gap with Hugh. Maybe Darren had been serious about keeping an eye on Liesel, and maybe he hadn't.

When Gil stopped at an intersection near the East Texas bank, Ron hopped out.

"Back as soon as I can," Gil promised.

Ron closed the door and walked past a mechanic shop to get to the bank. Making the deposit should have taken only a couple minutes, but the line was long. As often as Ron checked his watch, he didn't get to the front any faster. Twenty minutes later, he arrived at the teller and completed the transaction in no time.

As he headed for the door, a man in a tailored gray suit intercepted him.

"Excuse me, young man." The man's accent was definitely from the other side of the pond. "My name is David Aarons."

Ron shook the man's hand. "Ron Moore."

"A pleasure, Mr. Moore. Do you work for the sawmill in Xylon?" Mr. Aarons asked.

"Yes, sir"

"Excellent. Excellent." Mr. Aarons' poker face gave no hint to the man's actual emotions. "If I might trouble you to deliver a message for me?"

"No trouble at all, sir," Ron said.

"Good. This is for Miss Liesel Colby only." He paused and drilled the point home with a stern look.

"Please tell Miss Colby that I received what she sent me, and the answer is two weeks from today."

Ron nodded once. "Mr. David Aarons received what she sent, and the answer is two weeks from today."

"Exactly. I know it's a bit cryptic, but she'll understand."

"I'll see that she gets the word." Ron tipped his head with a smile.

"Thank you," Mr. Aarons said and promptly left.

Ron shrugged and departed the bank in time to see the mill's other truck head back out of town. The sense of urgency was acid on Ron's nerves. He heaved a breath and headed for the corner.

"Wait, mister," a voice called.

Gil would be a few minutes yet, so Ron squelched his aggravation and turned. A kid not long out of high school jogged over from the mechanic. He offered his hand then looked at the grease on it and thought better.

"Sorry. I saw you get out of the sawmill's other truck." The boy wiped his hands on a soiled rag hanging from his belt. "Do you know Liesel Colby?"

Ron arched an eyebrow. *Another errand to run?* "Sure. I work in the office with her, temporary bookkeeping help."

"Would you do me a favor and tell her 'Happy birthday?'" The boy's smiled turned a little mischievous.

"It's her birthday?" Ron asked.

"Yeah. Mailman accidentally delivered an application for Mr. Aarons' to dad, and we opened it before realizing it wasn't ours. Anyway, if I'm doing my math right, Liesel... err, Miss Colby is eighteen today." His smile soured. "It's a cinch she won't hear boo from that family of hers, and I just want to be sure she hears it from somebody."

Ron chuckled. "You've got a deal. Who should I say sent the birthday wishes?"

The boy looked away. "Well, let it be from you. You work with her and all, and I don't want to cause her any trouble with her boyfriend."

"There is no boyfriend."

"Really? I thought–that other truck driver for the mill, the one who just went by, Henry or Huey or—"

"Hugh Johnson. Hugh's dreaming. Four times that I personally witnessed, Miss Colby has emphatically told Hugh to buzz off." Ron mimed swatting something away from him.

"Seriously? Do you think she'd date a grease monkey?" The kid's smile returned.

"If you treat her like a lady, I don't see how you can miss." Ron offered the ghost of a grin. "So, who do I tell her sent the birthday wishes?"

"Albert. Albert Swanson."

"Well, Albert Swanson, I'll pass it along," Ron said. He made to go.

"Wait," Albert called.

Ron sighed and turned back.

"You said she's had to tell this Johnson guy to split four times. Is he not getting the message?" Albert asked.

Ron almost smiled, seeing a hint of Gil in the kid's body language.

He took a step closer to Albert. "He's a slow learner, but the other truck driver explained it to where even Johnson will get the message."

"Good. Well, thanks," Albert said.

Ron crossed over to the opposite corner and read the bills posted on the community bulletin board while he waited. Gil pulled up a few minutes later, and they were on the way to the next stop.

Gil waited next to the Continental. It was quitting time, and as usual, he had to wait while Ron fought his way past the ogre as they'd come to call Mrs. Colby.

Finally, the door opened and the ogre's shrill nagging followed Ron out. He quickly walked over.

Moments later, the ogre led the rest of the family out.

"—and you'll dress appropriately this evening." The ogre scowled as she looked Liesel from head to toe. "Not for a nunnery. Is that clear?"

"Yes, Mother," Liesel replied.

"The red formal will do or the ivory, I suppose." The ogre squared her shoulders. "And stand up straight. There will be plenty of eligible bachelors there, and you'll want to make a good impression, so do something reasonable with your hair, will you? And make up."

She was still harping as they drove away.

"She's in rare form," Ron said.

"Can you imagine living with that?" Gil asked.

"Not me. How'd it to go with Langston?" Ron slid into the Continental's driver's seat.

Gil rolled his eyes. "It didn't. He's going to retire soon and doesn't want to cross Rodman."

"Meaning, he's also willing to stand by while Hugh keeps harassing Liesel," Ron said in disgust.

"That's the size of it." Gil sighed. "So, how many people told Liesel happy birthday yesterday?"

"That Albert kid just about called it. You, me, Albert, and Police Chief Knowles."

Gil scoffed. "Even six brothers and sisters, we got a cake, ice cream, and a piñata. What do you wanna bet that Jeffrey kid gets all the trimmings?"

"And then some. No bet," Ron replied.

They drove back to the boarding house and parked.

"Look at that," Ron said, gesturing.

Gil followed his buddy's eye line to a black and gray Rolls-Royce. "Nice. Mrs. Ellis must be attracting better clientele."

They headed up the walk and entered. Mrs. Ellis was in the parlor with a tall, thin, gray-haired man wearing a very well-tailored suit.

"Well, the boarding house wasn't my original retirement plan, but with Teddy's funeral putting me back so far, I'm getting along." Mrs. Ellis looked past her guest. "Oh, Mr. Moore, Mr. Soto. There's someone here to see you."

Gil let Ron lead the way.

"This is Mr. Aldus Rodman. Mr. Rodman, Mr. Ron Moore and Mr. Gil Soto." Mrs. Ellis pointed to them each in turn. "If you gentlemen will excuse me, I must see to the evening's supper." With a polite bob of her head, she left. "Gentlemen, I'll be brief." Mr. Rodman turned to face them directly, hands at his sides. "I have a business proposition for you both. We can discuss it over dinner. Shall we say 8:00 o'clock?"

Gil exchanged a look with Ron.

Ron straightened his shoulders. "Actually, Mr. Rodman, we weren't planning to stay in town more than another week or two at the most."

"Perhaps I can change your minds." Mr. Rodman's smile reminded Gil of a great white. "Certainly no harm in listening."

"All right, sure," Gil said.

"Splendid."

He pulled a card out of the inside jacket pocket with his name printed on one side, and a map from Xylon to his house on the other.

"8:00 o'clock, gentlemen." Mr. Rodman stepped past them and left.

Ron inspected the card, frowning. "What did you just get us into?"

"The opportunity to reject an offer we're not supposed to be able to refuse," Gil replied.

"Do you suppose this is how it always starts?" Ron asked.

"You mean the big buy off?"

"Yeah. You know, I'll pay you so much if you lay off my nephew."

"Maybe." Gil arched an eyebrow. "Maybe Rodman just needs a lesson on how to treat girls."

"Well, come on. Let's get ready," Ron said.

Yeah, Gil thought as Ron jogged off to freshen up first. *Don't want to keep the great white shark waiting.*

📖

The house of Mr. Aldus Rodman would compare favorably with the circles Dad traveled in, Ron decided. In spite of the hot summer, the lawn was still a lush green, and flowers not meant for the harsh climate of Texas still bloomed. The water needed to accomplish such a feat was itself a show of conspicuous consumption on par with the Rolls-Royce.

Ron parked his car and stepped out. As usual, when dealing with high society, Gil hung back a step. Ron didn't mind. He returned the favor whenever they went into the gun-and-knife section of town.

171

Surviving in both places took a unique skill set that one of them had and the other didn't.

A wide granite walkway led to the front door, which had been neatly carved with an intricate pattern of trees and flowers.

"Knuckle buster." Gil smirked.

Ron smiled and rang the doorbell.

A half-bald man in a gray vest and starched white shirt with black trousers opened the door.

Ron stood up straighter. "Mr. Moore and Mr. Soto to see Mr. Rodman."

"Of course, sirs. Mr. Rodman is expecting you in the parlor." The butler bowed them through. "This way, please."

They followed the older fellow down a short hall and found Rodman in a room that had been decorated in a wildlife kind of scheme. Hunting rifles and shotguns were displayed in an ornate, velvet-lined cabinet. Taxidermied specimens littered the walls and every flat surface, including a sizable display in one corner featuring a doe with a pair of fawns. As he continued to take in the room, he spotted other "mother and offspring" arrangements, and that chased a shiver down his spine. There was something just wrong about killing such vulnerable creatures. Suddenly, Hugh chasing Liesel made more sense. His uncle had trained him to pursue the weak.

Ron tore his attention away from the décor and found the man himself reading a book.

"Oh, gentleman. So good of you to come." Rodman put his book aside. "Please, be seated. Dinner shall be ready shortly, I'm sure."

Gil sank down on a couch, and Ron took the adjacent chair.

"I trust you had a pleasant drive." Rodman steepled his fingers in front of his chest.

"Yes, sir. Beautiful countryside," Ron said.

"Indeed. I don't permit logging within one hundred yards of the road. I may have to change that someday, but for now, it'll do." Rodman spread his hands. "Well, let's get down to business so we can enjoy the rest of the evening, shall we?"

Ron smiled. "As you say."

"Well, Mr. Moore, what are your intentions toward Liesel Colby?" Rodman asked.

Ron stiffened. "Mr. Rodman, unless you are the legal guardian for Miss Colby, I don't see how that's your business."

"Ah, discretion. I like that in a business partner." Rodman's grin carried no mirth and didn't reflect in his eyes. "So, gentlemen are we agreed? Fifty-fifty profit split, and you can divide your half however you see fit."

Gil cleared his throat. "Now, Mr. Rodman, Ron here's the college man, so maybe I missed it somewhere, but you haven't told us what this proposition is yet."

Rodman smiled. "Observant, too. This gets better all the time. Gentlemen, I've made my fortune investing in start-up businesses. I supply the ideas and the starting capital and leave it to my partners to handle running the actual business. I maintain ownership, of course, but my partners may call themselves owners, presidents, chairmen, emperors, whatever they like for all I care. My involvement remains undiscovered."

Ron crossed his legs and laced his fingers over his knee. "I gather Xylon sawmill runs that way."

"Exactly." Rodman's smile faded. "In fact, I had Colby pegged for this next venture, but with his

173

unfortunate collapse last winter, I've had to make other arrangements. I have in mind a textile factory. With cotton being grown across central and southern Texas, I have an ideal place in mind. Naturally, it will take a few months to build, but that will give you some time to work in another of my textile factories to learn the business."

"OK, so why the interest in my intentions toward Miss Colby?" Ron asked.

"The girl's got a head for numbers and no denying it." Rodman glanced at one of the mounted heads on his wall. "Naturally, I expected she would come along with her father on the new venture, but even if Colby hadn't taken ill, that social klutz my sister reared has all but guaranteed Liesel's departure to seek other fortunes."

"That doesn't explain it," Gil said. "Offer her the position outright."

"That will never do." Rodman furrowed his brow. "I prefer the behind-the-scenes approach. Capital and ideas are mine. Personnel issues and day-to-day running are for someone else."

"So, the deal is contingent on keeping your name hidden and employing Miss Colby." A lead weight formed in Ron's gut. Even if he didn't have a job waiting for him with Dad's company at the end of the summer, there was no way he'd work for this pompous, conniving jerk.

"Exactly. Marriage, coercion, share of the profits, or whatever fits your personal idiom. Just secure her involvement."

The butler came to the door. "Dinner is served."

"Very good, Roberts. We shall be along directly." Rodman stood. "Well, Mr. Moore, Mr. Soto, that's my proposal. Give it some consideration and let me know by, say, Friday."

Ron nodded, but he could already answer the man right then. There was an undeniable mercenary quality about securing Liesel's participation by any means necessary. Gil, no doubt, felt the same.

After taking leave of their host, Gil followed Ron back to the car. They climbed in and started off. Gil counted to ten on his fingers.

"What are you doing?" Ron asked.

"Making sure all ten are still there. I shook Rodman's hand." Gil tilted his head toward Ron. "So did you. Have you checked?"

Ron chuckled. "He did kind of give me that impression, too."

"Can you believe that guy?" Gil affected Rodman's accent. "'Marriage, coercion, share of the profits, or whatever else fits your personal idiom.' It's no wonder he's got a nephew like Hugh."

"The nut sure didn't roll far from that tree." Ron glanced over then pulled onto the highway. "Dad has a name for guys who do business like Rodman. It's not very polite."

"I'm sure. Any question what we're going to tell that nut tree on Friday?"

"Not at all." Ron shifted into another gear. "People are tools to him. Nothing more. His bank account is all that matters."

Gil scowled while he thought about that. "I don't know. If that's it, why bail out Hugh? Why bribe judges and witnesses?"

"I suspect Rodman has no kids. It may be a matter of protecting his inheritor," Ron suggested.

"Grooming his replacement?"

"Something like that, yeah," Ron said.

"Huh, makes sense."

They reached the next intersection and turned west toward Xylon. They'd gone not quite halfway when they caught up to a car weaving all over the road.

Gil squinted. "Hey, isn't that the Colbys' car?"

Ron grimaced. "I think you're right."

"Tie a ball of yarn on the bumper, and she'll knit us both scarves." Gil braced himself as Ron had to brake suddenly.

"She's smashed. Let's follow and make sure they get home OK."

"Definitely."

Twice, the car started off the road. Liesel leaned up over the back seat, grabbed the wheel, and righted the car. Both times, Gil's guts knotted. A steep ditch slid into darkness on either side of the road. Any car headed into that would become an accordion. Ron tried honking to get the ogre to pull over, but she just waved them around, as if they could've gotten past her weaving.

As they started over the Livingston River bridge, the Colby car drifted into the oncoming lane. A car came around the corner the other way. Brakes squealed. Horns honked. Mrs. Colby wrenched the wheel back to the right and overcorrected. Gil tensed and gripped the armrest on the door as the car crashed through the guardrail. Sparks flew as the metal shrieked. Bits of shattered glass and plastic erupted from the various lights. The car plummeted nose-first into the Livingston River.

Gil hopped out before Ron had the car fully stopped. He expected to see a raging river threatening to carry the car downstream, but he'd forgotten where he was. This was Texas, where wet-weather creeks were very generously named rivers.

The inch-deep trickle of water in the middle of the riverbed wouldn't hardly carry off a leaf let alone a car. In fact, the car was more likely to catch fire.

Ron joined him. "The other driver raced off soon as I started toward him."

"Nice. We could've used the help." Gil glanced back over his shoulder at Ron. "I don't see any movement."

He headed for the near end of the bridge and started down the embankment. Ron was right behind him.

The front half of the car looked like a kid's paper fan, but the back was fairly intact. There was no chance of getting the front doors open. Gil grabbed the nearest back door and gave it a yank, but it hardly moved. He tried twice more before he got it open. Jeffrey was slumped sideways on the back seat, the broken wing of a kid's toy airplane impaled in his gut.

Ron managed to get the driver's side rear door ajar. Gil rushed around to that side to help him shove it open the rest of the way.

"The kids got an airplane wing in the belly." Gil glanced toward the kid. "Do we pull it out or –"

"Leave it." Ron shook his head. "Otherwise, he could bleed to death before we get him to the hospital."

Gil sniffed the air and smelled smoke.

"I smell it, too," Ron said. "Let's get them out if we can."

Gil went around and lifted the boy out, careful not to dislodge the plane piece. He placed kid near the edge of the riverbed then hurried back to the car. Ron was carrying Liesel.

"You got her?" Gil asked.

"Yeah, see about the parents," Ron said.

Gil crawled into the back and leaned over the seat. He felt for a pulse in Mr. Colby's throat and got nothing. When he turned to Mrs. Colby, he had to fight down his dinner. Blood didn't usually turn his stomach, but there was no way she was still alive.

He slipped out of the car as Ron returned.

Gil waved him off. "Don't ... just ..."

"Oh." Ron bowed his head. "Well, let's get the kids to the hospital, and then we'll call the police to deal with the car...and the Colbys."

"Yeah," Gil said, still trying to shake off the queasiness.

"You OK?" Ron asked.

"I will be." Gil swallowed hard. "Come on. Before this thing catches fire or blows up or something."

"We'll have to put Liesel between us and stretch the kid across the back seat." Ron scooped Liesel into his arms.

Gil gingerly lifted Jeffrey and headed to their car in the blinking red light of the hazards. He slid Jeffrey into the back seat then helped Ron get Liesel situated between them.

The trip into town took an eternity. In the dim moonlight, Gil looked Liesel over. She was wearing a bright red dress that was cut shorter and lower than anything she might have picked out. On just about any other girl, it would have been dazzling, but on Liesel, it didn't flatter her at all. It was artificial, cheap, almost obscene.

Blood was caked on Liesel's face, and Gil traced it back up to a cut above her eyebrow. He didn't see anything else, but there was no telling what kind of injuries she had that weren't visible.

As they finally passed the turn off to the sawmill, Liesel moaned and shifted. Gil wrapped his arm around her to steady her when she started to flop forward.

"Hey, hey, take it easy, Liesel." Gil gently rubbed her arm. "Don't try to move much, yeah?"

"What? Where? Gil?" She slurred terribly and feebly tried to push away.

"Yeah, yeah, right here. Ron, too, and Jeffrey." Gil tightened his hold on her. "You were in a car wreck. We're on the way to the hospital, but you gotta stay still, yeah? We don't know how bad you're hurt."

"OK."

"You're going to be okay, Liesel. We're almost there." Ron slowed into the next turn. "Just take it easy. Everything's going to be fine."

She nodded slowly then went out again.

The only sight more encouraging than the "Welcome to Xylon" sign was the driveway of the hospital itself. Ron pulled up to the emergency room doors.

"Stay here. I'll get help." Ron parked and slid out.

Gil steadied Liesel as she started to move again.

Moments later, nurses, orderlies, a doctor, and two gurneys followed Ron to the car.

The doctor looked in through the window. "Get the boy to OR, stat. Get the girl into a treatment room. You two, any of that blood on you belong to you?"

"No," Ron said.

"Got it carrying the kids out of the ditch." Gil looked down at his stained shirt.

"OK. Stick around. I may need to talk to you," the doctor said.

Gil let the experts get Liesel and Jeffery. After they were rushed away, Gil went inside and flopped into a waiting room chair while Ron went to a pay phone. Ron was still describing the wreck to the police when the doctor returned. Gil met him part way.

"How are they, doc?" Gil asked.

"I'm sorry, but Jeffrey didn't make it," the doctor said.

Gil groaned and ran his hands through his hair.

"Nothing you could have done differently. A major artery was severed by that broken toy," the doctor said as Ron hung up.

"Liesel?" Ron asked.

"We're waiting on X-rays, but offhand, I'd say it's a concussion." The doctor looked from Ron to Gil and back again. "Has she been unconscious the whole time?"

"No." Gil shook his head. "We were just at the turn off to the sawmill when she came around a little."

"Not for long, though. She blacked out after a minute or two." Ron looked at Gil. "She started to stir just as we pulled into the parking lot, didn't she?"

"Yeah, but I wouldn't say she was coherent, and she didn't stick around."

"She was alert, aware of her surroundings?" the doctor asked.

"No, not really," Ron said.

"Well, she recognized my voice and called me by name when I talked to her," Gil said. "She didn't really open her eyes, and she wasn't all there."

"Her speech was slurred," Ron added.

The doctor looked thoughtful for a moment. "Alright. Thank you. I'll be back when I know more."

"Thanks, doc," Gil said.

The doctor left again, and Gil sank into the chair.

Ron squeezed his shoulder before settling down beside him. "Mr. Knowles will be by later to get a statement about the wreck and the driver who left the scene."

Gil shrugged. "The wreck I can tell him about, but the other driver? All I saw were headlights."

Ron looked away for a moment. "I didn't get a clear look, but I'm almost sure it was Billy Langston."

"If it was Billy, why didn't he stop?" Gil asked.

"Who knows," Ron replied quietly.

Gil looked up at the clock. Almost 1:00 AM. This was going to be a long night.

📖

Liesel lay awake in the hospital. She'd had a lot of time to think over the last couple days and a lot of time to grieve. Finding sadness over the death of people who'd only treated her with contempt felt odd, but they had been the only family she'd had, and now they were gone.

Father's lawyer had been by. As expected, her family's whole estate was hers, and the funds had been transferred into her name already. She'd inherited more than even she had expected.

Mrs. Langston had visited with a change of sensible, decent clothes.

Then the funeral director had been in to go over the arrangements with her. Mother had already set everything in order just after father's stroke. Only after that meeting had Liesel felt the loss of her family.

Many of the men from the mill had stopped in to pay their respects.

181

Gil and Ron, bless them, came by every evening after work just to chat, play a few rounds of rummy, and pass the time.

They or Mr. Knowles must have warned the nursing staff about Hugh and his cronies. The two times Hugh, Lane, and Darren had shown up, a nurse had practically followed them into the room and stayed until a security officer had arrived to escort them out.

Liesel had spent most of the day trying to stay too distracted to think about Jeffrey and her parents. She must have played a couple thousand rounds of solitaire and memory and read every magazine in the hospital cover to cover. Ron had refused to bring her any of the bookkeeping to do, but he had brought her a puzzle book from the five and dime down the street.

Liesel had just decided to solve another cryptogram from the book when the door opened. Mr. Rodman entered with a smile like a Trojan horse.

"Oh, Liesel, darling. How are you feeling?" He deposited a half-dozen daisies in the pitcher the nurses had left for her to get drinking water from.

"Better, thank you," she replied.

"Good, good. Terrible tragedy about your parents and Jeffrey." A built-in sneer meant his sincerity needed a little work.

She nodded, and the corners of her eyes burned, but she determined not to have a breakdown in his presence.

"Well, since you're feeling better, we need to conduct a little business," Mr. Rodman said.

Liesel had no doubt he would have conducted the business even if she had been comatose.

"I'm closing the mill," he said as casually as if announcing steak and potatoes for dinner.

"What? Why?" She struggled to sit up, alarmed.

"Textiles, my dear. We're just at the edge of cotton country." He mimed pinching something small. "With the mill losing money now—"

"Hold on." She held her hand palm out. "The mill has made a profit since January."

"Yes, when you took over after your father's illness. I know." His exaggerated shrug did nothing to improve his sincerity. "Too little, too late, dear. The arrangements were already made."

"Mr. Rodman, over half of the men in Xylon work at that mill," she reminded him.

"Well, yes, but they can all have jobs in the factory once it's running. You have my word."

And what good was his word? "And how long will that take?" Liesel asked. Months, she guessed.

"Conservative estimates put it at six months," he replied.

"Six months? Mr. Rodman, some of the loggers are in bad straits when they can't get work a couple days on account of the weather. Six months might as well be six decades!"

He brushed away her concerns with the back of his hand. "Bad stewardship of money on their part is not my concern."

"You'll lose your workers," Liesel argued as her chest tightened with anger. "This town will dwindle to nothing."

"When the factory is finished, they'll return or new blood will move in," he replied.

"But there is no need to close the mill at all before the factory is running." She envisioned the aerial view of the mill site. "There's plenty of usable land. You could build the factory then raze the mill."

"To be financially feasible in the short term, the actual building will be gutted and retooled and the contents will be sold for the capital." He tilted his head and spoke as if to a child. "Liesel, you don't understand. I didn't come here to get advice or opinions. I came to inform you of decisions already made. Langston will be informing the men today."

"Mr. Langston, not you?" she asked.

"Precisely."

"The town will conclude that closing the mill is my idea." She glared at him, catching on to his corrupt plan.

"Likely, but that's not my concern." He waved his hand dismissively and started for the door but returned. "Oh, and since Mr. Moore and Mr. Soto turned down my offer to become managers of the new factory, I've had to call in my own man from another textile factory. He's going to be taking over the house your family has been renting." He pulled out a thick roll of bills and counted off a couple. "Here you are. That should cover the prorated remains of the rent your father paid for this month. The new occupants will arrive by Sunday evening, so you'll need to vacate the premises by Saturday evening at the latest. That includes all the office furniture your mother installed at the mill. Good afternoon, Miss Colby." He dropped the bills on her bedside table and left.

Liesel clenched her jaw and glowered at the payment. She didn't want his money. It was as dirty as he was. As she thought about it, she realized it was all his money. The inheritance, the physical property at the house and the mill, and the money in her parents' bank accounts. Every penny of it was tainted by crooked dealings and underhanded practices. She'd sooner give it all to charity and start again in Roslyn. A good-paying job waited for her. She could easily live within her means. The rest of Xylon, however, would be destitute within a few months, weeks even. What better charity than the locals?

Liesel rang the nurse to ask for paper. If she planned everything right, Rodman's ill-gotten money would go for supporting those his plans would have destroyed.

Ron had never seen so many stunned, angry men. At lunch time, Langston had gotten the crew together and given them the news. The mill and logging operations were closing, effective immediately. No reason was given, but they would all be paid for a full week's work. No one could believe that they were suddenly out of a job. For most, the mill had been the only source of income for years.

Many, assuming Liesel had taken ownership with her father's death, blamed her. Ron, with a lot of help from Gil, had tried to set the record straight and pinned the responsibility for calling the shots onto Rodman. So the guys, instead, blamed Liesel for selling out to Rodman. Same old story played again. Blame the crippled girl because the rich man made things difficult. It was truly sickening.

Ron paid the last employee, Liesel, and put her money in an envelope. The cashbox, ledger, and all other official paperwork went into the safe. He tucked Liesel's envelope into his pocket then left with Gil. They found Mr. Langston waiting for them at the car.

"That was a foolish thing you did," Mr. Langston scolded.

"What?" Ron asked.

"Telling folks it was Rodman's decision, not Liesel's," he replied.

Ron rolled his eyes. "What is this town's aversion to telling the truth?"

"You don't know how rough he can make things."

Gil scowled. "Ron might not know, but I've seen what happens when he throws his weight around. I have half a mind to go out to his house right now and tell him in terms even he'll understand just what kind of coward he is. Hiding behind a girl's skirts so he doesn't have to face the results of his decisions, and I'm sorry, Mr. Langston, but you're not much better. You were willing to stand by and let Hugh molest an innocent girl, and now you're willing to let that same innocent girl get crucified for a decision she had no part in."

Ron remembered Friday night's encounter with Mr. Langston recounting the bribe he took to cover up Mrs. Colby's drunken blunder that had left Liesel injured for life.

"You said Friday that confession is good for the soul." Ron took a step closer. "That may be, but what good is confession without repentance? You're doing the same thing now that you did years ago."

Mr. Langston backed up a pace. "You- you just don't understand."

Gil folded his arms. "You're right. We don't. We don't see how a man can just stand there and watch a little girl suffer over and over when the only wrong I've ever seen her commit is taking more guff from people than she should."

Ron got in the car and waited for Gil. They left Mr. Langston stunned and drove to the hospital. The antiseptic smell blasted him in the face as they walked in.

They took the elevator to the next floor. When they stepped off, the nurse on duty waved them over.

"Are you here to see Miss Colby?" she asked.

"If it's OK," Ron said.

The nurse stood and leaned over the counter. "You've got to talk her out of leaving. She's not well."

"Where is she going?" Gil asked.

"I don't know. All she'll say is that she has too much to do," she replied.

Ron grimaced and shared a look with Gil. "We'll see what we can do."

As they headed down the hall to Liesel's room, the voices carried.

"This isn't a jail cell," Liesel insisted.

"You're not well," a nurse replied.

"I'm well enough!"

Ron hustled faster and entered the room. Liesel was fully dressed in a tan dress with blue flowers and trying to get past an older nurse.

"Let us take care of it." Ron placed his hand on the nurse's arm.

"Maybe you can talk sense into her," the nurse muttered as she left.

"We'll try," Gil said.

Liesel sighed. "I thought you guys would be headed out."

"I'm paid up through the end of the week at the boarding house. Might as well stick around at least that long," Ron explained.

"Come on. Sit down and tell us why you're in such a hurry to leave," Gil pointed to the bed.

Ron pulled a chair closer. "If the food's that lousy, maybe we can sneak in better."

She looked ready to push her way past them both and leave.

"Look, if you can convince us that you're right and the nurse is wrong, we'll help you go. Deal?" Gil rested against the nearest wall.

After a tense moment, Liesel dropped onto the end of the bed and set the crutches aside. "I have too much to do. The doctor wants me here until Friday because of my 'special condition,' and that only leaves me Saturday to get everything done. That's not enough time. Yes, I'm dizzy when I move around, but I'll be fine."

"I've had a concussion." Gil winced. "They don't improve much unless you rest."

"It's not the funeral, is it?" Ron asked. "You said your mother made all the arrangements back in December. It's all set for Saturday at sunset, isn't it?"

"That's all taken care of."

"Then what is it?" Ron asked.

"Mr. Rodman was here." Liesel looked away from them. "He informed me about the mill closing and gave me until Saturday evening to clear out the house and the office. I tried to talk him into keeping the mill at least, but he wouldn't hear me. He's already got the house rented."

"If it's just a matter of packing, that's easy. Ron and I—" Gil started.

"It's not just the packing." Liesel blew out a breath. "The mill closing is going to hit the entire town like a cannonball. Half the families pull their only income from the mill. When they lose that, they lose their only prospects. The factory won't be ready for six months. Some of the families can hardly last six days of the seven between Fridays."

She pulled a few sheets of paper out of her purse and flattened them. Ron and Gil gathered where they could see. She'd set up a sort of ledger sheet. Accounts receivable showed her inheritance, which was a whopping six-figure amount, and something marked "prorated rent refund." For accounts payable, she listed each of the 60-odd men who worked for the mill. For most she had a real name, but for a few there was only a job title and description. Next to each name, she listed an approximation of their rent or mortgage payments and other major bills. For one fellow, she listed an amount annotated "medical bill," and for another "funeral," and for Wally, "catering truck." The far-right column was marked "Total."

Gil pointed. "These totals over here don't add right. They're all too high."

Ron looked at them closer and everything clicked. "You're planning to use your inheritance to pay off the millworkers' major debts, set Wally's catering business off, and pay their mortgages for six months."

"Yeah?" Gil turned the paper toward him for a closer look.

"How do you know these figures are right?" Ron asked.

"They're close, but they aren't just vague approximations. I helped most of the guys with figuring out their taxes last spring." She shrugged. "I saw their bank statements. I don't have the real numbers, but most of them were matching or nearly so in most bills. I remembered as close as I could and padded the amount. Anything left over when everyone's taken care of will be evenly split among the various churches and earmarked for charity."

"Are you sure you want to do this?" Gil settled against the wall again. "After everything that's happened, you don't owe these guys a dime."

"They have kids and wives who had nothing to do with it." She pointed to the accounts receivable. "And more to the point, all this and all the proceeds that I can get from selling off the furniture and Mother's jewelry and furs and all the rest of it, it's all Rodman's money, and I don't think he's ever made an honest penny in his life. I meant to give it all to charity. A good use for tainted money. Why not keep the citizens of Xylon afloat until that factory is up and running? I wanted to take care of this on my own, which I can't do on Saturday, because I don't want the town to know where the money came from. Too many wealthy people have bought people off for favors or silence. I don't want anyone to even think that I'm playing that game."

"If you're going to give the whole shebang to the people of Xylon—and it's yours to do with as you wish—what are you living on?" Ron asked.

"I accepted the accounting job with Mr. Aarons' Fine Jewelry store." Liesel set her papers aside.

"That's a week-and-a-half away." Gil counted off the time on his fingers. "And you'll be another week or two until your first paycheck. That's almost a month on pocket lint. It's no good for a guy and worse for a girl."

She smiled. "It's not that bad. Last spring, when I helped the guys sort out their taxes, I charged them five percent of their refund. For some, it wasn't much. A few dimes, maybe. There were a couple I did for free because they had to pay in, but there were some that came to quite a bit. Between all of them, I made about $500 of honest money from people who are generally decent, if maybe a little scared. $500 should be enough to put me up in a hotel until I can find a room in a decent boarding house or locate a small apartment or a house to rent. It'll hold me until that first paycheck if I mind my purse right."

Ron looked past her. "So, you need to go to the bank and set up all these payments. Pack up the house and office. Sell off the contents of both, less your own clothing and personal property. Divvy up the remaining proceeds among the four churches. Find a boarding house or a small house or apartment in a part of Roslyn safe for a young lady, and... does that cover everything?"

"That's about the beginning and the end." Liesel took a deep breath as if to center herself. "Too much to do Friday night and Saturday morning. That's why I have to go now."

"With written permission from you, Gil and I can do all of that, and you can stay here in bed, where you belong, until the doctor says you're safe to move around," Ron offered.

"I couldn't ask you to do all of that."

"You didn't. We offered." Gil smiled. "We needed something to do with the rest of the week, anyway. So, what do you say? Yeah?"

She paused then slowly smiled. "Yeah."

"All right." Gil clapped his hands and rubbed them together.

"So how do we set things up so you two can act on my behalf?" Liesel asked.

Ron grabbed the pad of paper from the bedside table. "You'll need to write a letter giving us permission to access your accounts, make payments on your behalf, and have possession and control of your property. We'll take your ledger with us, and we'll need a list from you of the things in your house that you want to keep. That should do it."

"And it might be a good idea to let the police chief know that we're helping you out." Gil moved closer to look over Ron's shoulder.

Liesel tapped the pen against her chin thoughtfully. "Both here and in Roslyn."

Ron helped her with the wording, and they had everything they needed before the end of the hour.

"Now, while we take care of this, you're going to get back into that hospital gown and do what the doctors tell you, right?" Ron pointed to the discarded gown on the bed.

"Right. Thank you. That doesn't seem like enough for everything you've done, but I really do appreciate it." Liesel stared at the floor.

Gil smiled. "That covers it just fine."

"We'll be back to check in with you," Ron said.

They left and went down to the nurse's station.

"All taken care of," Ron said.

"How did you ever convince her?" the older nurse who had been arguing with Liesel asked.

"Well, she really did have a pile of things that has to be done by Saturday." Gil leaned closer and whispered, "So, we're going to do them."

"That's good of you," the younger nurse said.

"She's kind of been our kid sister lately." Ron looked around for signage to point the way. "Where can we find the billing department?"

"First floor." The older nurse pointed to the elevator. "As you exit the elevator, turn left, and go to the end of the hall. You can't miss it."

"Thanks," Gil said.

They started off for the elevator.

The younger nurse reached after them. "This business she's so anxious to get to, does it have to do with Mr. Rodman's visit? That's when she seemed to get more agitated."

Ron nodded. "He's giving her until Saturday to get out of the house."

"He evicted her? Before the funeral?" she asked in horror.

"Nice guy," Gil said in parting.

Ron led them to the elevator. On the way down, Gil snapped his fingers then hit the stop button.

"What?" Ron asked.

"She forgot something." Gil pointed to the papers Ron was holding. "There's another mill employee with a hospital bill for emergency room services, operating room services, and a nearly week-long hospital stay."

Ron caught on. "Her own medical bill."

"Yeah, and if she's blowing her whole inheritance on these bums, she's not going to get the clean start like she thinks," Gil said.

"So, we pay hers first. This letter gives us permission to act on her behalf."

Gil started the elevator going again. "Yeah, and if that means some of these other jokers don't get six months' rent free, then maybe they should be grateful enough that they're not listed as accomplices on a police report."

With pep in their stride, they stepped off the elevator and turned left.

📖

Gil backed the moving truck up to the Colby house. They'd rented the truck from Roslyn the night before after leaving Liesel at the hospital. The house was as amazingly huge now as it had looked last night. The two-story spanned half a city block, and the grounds, immaculate and well-fortified with flowers and shrubs, took the rest.

When the truck was as close as possible to the entryway, Gil opened the rear while Ron unlocked the house's front door.

After clearing out the mill's office yesterday, Gil and Ron had been in and out of the house several times. They'd taken the food stored in the pantry and refrigerator to the charity pantry. Then they'd taken all of Mr. and Mrs. Colby's clothes and shoes to a church's clothing closet. Jeffrey's clothes, along with the things Liesel had told them to get rid of from her own closet, had all gone to the children's home.

As often as they'd been in and out of the house yesterday, Gil was still stunned by the marble floors and mahogany woodwork and the arched staircase leading up to the master bedroom and Jeffrey's room. Liesel's bedroom, the only lower-level one, was off the kitchen. Ron had called it the servants' quarters.

The house Gil had grown up in with six other siblings could have fit three times in the ground floor with some space to spare.

A tap on the shoulder from Ron broke Gil out of his wool gathering. They did have an awful lot to do today. Between them, they systematically packed the furniture onto the truck, using the linens to wrap some things and drawers as boxes to pack smaller items. They lacked only a few things from the ground floor when they had the truck stuffed. Until they knew if Liesel needed furniture, they left the bedroom set in her room. After securing the house, they took off for Roslyn.

"So, now that we have all this, where's it going?" Gil asked.

"I've been thinking about that." Ron twisted toward him. "There may be a consignment store in Roslyn. It's a pretty big town. Otherwise, I saw a flyer for a community wide flea market in the park on Saturday. We could rent another truck, park this one, load the rest of the stuff in the second truck—"

"And unload it all at the flea market on Saturday," Gil finished. "Sounds good to me."

"Let's make our first stop at the mechanic," Ron suggested.

Gil smiled. "Playing matchmaker?"

Ron snorted. "He seemed like a nice kid. Besides, a local might tell us where we can unload the back of this truck."

Gil grinned knowingly at his friend. "Uh-huh."

When they reached Roslyn, Gil pulled up to the mechanic and followed Ron toward the garage.

A heavy-set man looked up from the engine he was working on. "Can I help you?"

Ron stepped forward. "We're looking for a kid who works here. Albert Swanson."

"He's not here, but I'm his father, Al Senior. What do you need?" The man grabbed a grubby towel to wipe his hands.

"Well, we're friends of Liesel Colby." Ron glanced toward Xylon. "Albert asked me to deliver a message to her earlier this week, and I wanted to bring back word to him about how it was received."

"Liesel Colby? Oh, yeah, I read about her misfortune in last night's paper." He shook his head. "Albert was pretty upset. He wanted to cancel his trip, but I had to convince him that he'd given his word and had better honor it. Any girl worth looking at would respect him more for being honorable than for pestering her in a hospital when she's resting. A girl wants to look her best when first meeting a guy, you know?"

"When is Albert due back?" Gil asked.

"Sunday night. He's up in Dallas at a car show. He restored an old 1930 Plymouth for a guy who's going to meet him there and take the delivery. Left this morning, early."

"If all goes well, Miss Colby will be here in Roslyn by Monday," Ron said.

"I'll let him know you were by," Al replied.

Two steps toward the truck, Gil turned back. "Oh, Mr. Swanson, is there a consignment store or something like that in this town?"

"Not really. What are you trying to unload?" Al asked.

"Furniture." Gil patted the side of the truck. "A lot of it."

"When Miss Colby's folks died, she was left with a mountain of debts," Ron explained. "Then the landlord gave her until tomorrow night to clear out of the house, but she won't be released from the hospital until late this evening or early tomorrow morning. So, we're helping her get squared away."

"Good of you." Al craned his head. "What kind of furniture? Wouldn't happen to be antiques, would it?"

"I don't know if they're all that old, but definitely that style." Ron looked back at the truck.

Al shrugged. "Well, worth a try. Go up to the next stop light and hang a right. Go 5 miles out of town. You'll find a new bed and breakfast, Livingston View or something similar. Just finished construction. The owner, a Mrs.-Mrs. Jan? No. Mrs. Guinevere Hart-something." He snapped his fingers. "Hartley. Guinevere Hartley. She took out an ad in last night's paper promising top dollar for antiques in good repair."

"Thank you, Mr. Swanson. We'll try it." Ron stepped up into the passenger seat of the cab.

After Gil was situated, they headed out according to Mr. Swanson's directions. At the city's edge, Gil noted the number on the odometer and counted off the miles. Just over four miles out, a blue and white sign marking the Livingston Vista Bed and Breakfast pointed the way down a gravel driveway. Gil followed it up to an enormous place with massive two-story columns holding up the roof over a wide porch that ringed half the building.

As they got out, a gray-haired woman with a wide smile came to greet them. Gil hung back to let his more eloquent buddy do the talking.

"Gentlemen, welcome, but I'm afraid we're not quite open for business yet," the woman said.

"Mrs. Hartley?" Ron asked.

"Yes."

He produced the letter from Liesel giving them permission to sell the house's contents. "We were told in town that you were seeking antiques." He handed her the inventory they'd written out in the wee hours of last night. "Here's what we have."

She returned the letter but kept hold of the inventory. "Let's see a sample of it."

"Of course."

Gil opened the back door and pulled out the loading ramp. Mrs. Hartley walked up as Gil uncovered the easiest pieces to get to. She gave the ones she could reach a thorough inspection.

"And it's all similar?" she asked.

"The styles vary from one set to the next, but the quality is the same," Gil said.

She looked at the inventory. "This isn't all of it here."

"No, only the ground floor, minus the China hutch. We couldn't fit it in this load." Ron traced his finger down the inventory to where they'd stopped.

"Provided I like the look of the rest of the pieces, I'll pay you $3000 for this load and the same for the rest."

Gil brightened. "Where would you like us to unload it?"

"Put it in the foyer." She pointed toward the house. "I'll sort it into the various rooms once I see exactly what we have. I'll get the rest of the men to help you with it."

"Thank you," Ron said.

She nodded and left.

"How big is this foyer that we can fit two truckloads of stuff into it?" Gil asked.

"You saw the foyers at the Colby place and at Rodman's," Ron reminded him.

"Yep, that'd do it."

With the help of the other workers, the truck was unloaded in no time. In fact, they almost tripped over each other coming through the door. Mrs. Hartley supervised about the last half of the project and inspected each piece.

"Reasonable replicas." She ran her hand along the detailed scrollwork on a glass-fronted bookcase. "And in good condition, too. Very good, gentlemen. Here is your money. I've written up another copy of your inventory and signed it if you'll sign mine."

Ron took care of that.

"Now, when should I expect the other half?" she asked.

Gil looked up at the corner. "Well, it's an hour driving time to get to and from the Colby house. A couple hours to load."

"You'll be in time for lunch. I do hope you'll join us."

"Yes, ma'am. Thank you," Ron said.

Gil led the way back to the truck, and they were soon on the way.

Ron was stuffed. Mrs. Hartley had prepared some of the dishes she planned to serve her guests, and the food had been excellent. If Livingston Vista failed, it wouldn't be on account of the cooking.

With the furniture delivery dealt with, the house was empty except for Liesel's personal things and her mother's furs. After some thought, they'd taken the bedroom furniture, too. Keeping the truck an extra day would have been expensive, and they couldn't count on borrowing a van or pickup, and the Continental sure wouldn't haul it off. If they did have to get an unfurnished space for Liesel, they'd use some of the $6000 from the bed and breakfast to purchase furniture and have it delivered.

After dropping off the truck and getting the car back, Ron drove to the jewelers. He felt exposed carrying a shoe box full of jewelry, but he hoped to be rid of it soon enough.

They walked into a very neat, tidy shop. Display cases lined the room and another occupied the center.

"Can I help you?" A middle-aged woman approached them.

Ron handed the box to Gil and pulled out Liesel's letter.

"Oh, yes. Mr. Moore and Mr. Soto. Mr. Aarons is expecting you." She gave the letter back. "One moment please."

She went through a door marked "Employees only" and returned shortly with Mr. Aarons, who had a neatly tailored navy-blue suit today. He met them and shook their hands.

"Gentlemen. Miss Colby phoned to tell me to expect you." Mr. Aarons waved for them to follow him. "She has explained the whole situation to me. Honestly, it's refreshing to see generosity in her generation. What with so many rebelling against the establishment, and it's good of you to lend your hand. Come back to my office, if you please, and we'll have a look at what you've brought."

They followed him back to a well-appointed but still very functional office. The walls, painted a flat tan color, were decorated with images of natural rock formations. The desk and matching chairs were strictly business without any of the gaudy adornments of the mill office's furniture.

Gil handed Mr. Aarons the box.

"Please, have a seat, gentleman. Can I get you anything?" he asked.

"No, sir. I'm fine, thank you." Ron sat in one of the two open seats.

"No, thanks," Gil said.

Mr. Aarons pulled out a jeweler's loupe and inspected each piece in the box. Some hardly warranted a cursory glance, but others took considerable care. He sorted the full box into three piles, the one on the far right growing faster than the others. The largest pile consisted of what Dad called "Eye-grabbers." They were gaudy, and far too large to be real gems. Most likely, they were glass. The middle pile had an assortment of garnets, tiger eye, turquoise, and the like along with what Ron would have thought were legitimate precious stones, even diamonds, rubies, and sapphires. The left pile, the smallest, was clearly better quality than the other extreme. Mr. Aarons finished his sorting.

Gil pointed at each pile from right to left. "Fake. Not so good. Better stuff."

Mr. Aarons smiled. "A reasonable deduction, Mr. Soto. Yes. This collection here is costume jewelry. I'm afraid I have no use for it. You might try giving it to one of the clothing closets at the churches in Xylon or perhaps the orphanage. The children could use it to play dress up, I suppose. This middle collection here consists of semi-precious or poor-quality stones. I do have a few stores that do significant business in such things. These I can use. The pieces over here are the quality of the set. I shall take those as well. I was instructed to pay you directly rather than pay Miss Colby in her first check."

"Yes, sir." Ron tapped the letter in his pocket. "We were given instructions on how to dispose of the funds."

Mr. Aarons waved his hand. "Fine, fine. Well, shall we say $400 for the semi-precious and damaged, and $1800 for the better pieces?"

"That will be agreeable, sir," Ron said.

"Splendid." Mr. Aarons stood. "I'll return directly."

Once he'd left, Gil pointed to the costume jewelry.

"All show, no substance," he said.

Ron nodded. "What do you think? The clothing closet won't find a home for some of those things. They're pretty outrageous."

"Well, those really gaudy ones, give those to the kids." Gil mimed showing off a huge eye-grabbing ring. "The girls will play dress up, and the boys will have treasure to bury."

Ron chuckled.

Mr. Aarons returned and sat down. "Sorry to keep you waiting." He counted out $2200 and handed over a receipt. "There you are. As agreed." He swept the costume jewelry back into the box and gave it to Gil. "Is there anything else I can help you with, gentlemen?"

"Yes, sir. Is there a furrier in town?" Ron asked.

"Indeed, there are two. You'll want Katz's. Two blocks north and four blocks west," Mr. Aarons said. "I do business with him now and again. Shall I phone to tell him to expect you?"

"If it's no trouble," Ron said.

"None at all. What else can I do?"

"I realize this is a little out of your line, but we are not real sure where to start." Gil rubbed his chin. "We need to find a boarding house or apartment where Miss Colby can live within her salary."

Mr. Aarons thought a moment and picked up the phone. "Send Mrs. Chambers in, please."

Shortly after, there was a light knock on the door, and the middle-aged woman from the front counter came in. Ron and Gil rose.

She closed the door and held a small notepad and a pencil at the ready. "Yes, sir?"

"Mrs. Chambers, Mr. Moore and Mr. Soto are helping young Miss Colby settle the family affairs. One of their tasks is to find a room in a boarding house or a flat suitable for the young lady. Of course, given Miss Colby's condition, the room will need to be on the ground floor or have a lift. Do you know of anything appropriate?"

"Well, there is... no, no, that's an attic loft. What about, oh, yes, of course." She looked at Ron and smiled. "There is a boarding house four doors down. Grace Hall. It only rents to unmarried or widowed women, but I don't know what they have for vacancies."

"Thank you. We'll check into it," Ron said.

"That will be all, Mrs. Chambers." Mr. Aarons replied.

Ron shook Mr. Aarons' hand. "Thank you, sir. You've been a great help to us."

"My pleasure, gentleman." Mr. Aarons shook Gil's next.

He escorted them to the showroom and bid them a good day.

Gil checked his watch. "You know, it's 2:30 already."

 "Wow. Where did the day go?"

"How about I leave you at the bank and then go get the furs. Then I'll deal with Katz and Grace Hall and pick you up again."

Ron handed Gil the keys.

Mrs. Chambers caught them on the way out. "I won't keep you, since the bank closes at three on Fridays, but I thought you should know. Liesel almost didn't get the job. She wasn't dressed professionally enough for Mr. Aarons. He is very strict about always looking and acting like a professional. Mr. Cairns, the vice president, convinced Mr. Aarons to hire her because she does handle the books well. Mr. Cairns said that her very casual dress was appropriate for the sawmill, and naturally, Miss Colby would have the sense to dress for the job."

Ron sighed. "She doesn't have anything like business attire. Her closet had a handful of the casual ones and a few formals, most of which didn't leave much to the imagination. She had us get rid of most of the formals. She'll be here a week before the new job starts. Could you take her shopping one day and show her what she'll need to meet Mr. Aarons' standards?"

"Certainly. I have Wednesday off next week. If she can be available, we'll do it then," Mrs. Chambers said.

Ron smiled. "Perfect. I'll let her know she has an appointment with you."

They left, and Gil dropped Ron at the bank. As he walked in, he pulled out the authorization letter and the list of men from the sawmill.

Gil left Grace Hall after securing a downstairs room for Liesel and paying her rent a few months ahead. It was only fair that she be afforded the same courtesy she was giving everyone else. The room wouldn't be available until Sunday night, but the landlady had agreed to store Liesel's things until then. Liesel had her overnight bag for tonight and tomorrow night, and he'd brought her the gray dress for the funeral. Everything was set.

When Gil pulled into the bank's parking lot, Ron wasn't in sight, but the sign in the bank window read "Closed." Gil parked and waited. Almost 45 minutes later, Ron and an old guy in a jet-black suit walked out together. Both were all smiles, so Gil supposed all had gone well.

Leaving the keys in the ignition, Gil slid over as Ron got in.

"Were you victorious?" Gil asked.

"Mission accomplished. It was close though. Only $52 left in the account to spare. We moved that into Liesel's personal account. We still have the B&B money. How did you make out?"

"The furs were like the jewelry. There were a few fakes. 'Dog hair,' Katz called them, but I don't think he meant that literally. A couple were poor quality. The last was actually pretty good. He gave me $750 for the lot. The other errand went better. Grace Hall had only a second-floor room, but while I was explaining the problem to the landlady, another gal overheard and offered to vacate her ground floor room to take the second floor. The landlady agreed and made the room available for Sunday night. She even offered to store Liesel's things until then."

"So, you went ahead and packed her stuff." Ron glanced over.

"Yeah. Rodman showed up while I was there to get the furs. Just let himself into the house without so much as a knock." Gil rolled his eyes. "He didn't say two words to me, but I thought it best to clear out everything that was left."

"Good idea. That guy makes my teeth itch."

"Yeah, and who wants itchy teeth?" Gil snickered. "Anyway, the rent's a little steep—$6.50 a night for a bed, clean linens, and three squares—but it's walking distance to work for Liesel. I used the fur money to pay Liesel up as far as I could, just short of four months. I say we stop by there and pay up the whole six months. What's fair is fair, yeah?"

"Absolutely," Ron said.

They stopped at the boarding house, and Gil led the way to the door. He rang the bell and waited for Mrs. Poole to answer.

"Oh, Mr. Soto," she said.

"Yes, ma'am. Mrs. Poole, this is my friend Ron Moore." Gil looked over at Ron. "He's got the rest of Miss Colby's money. We wanted to pay her up a total of six months."

"Of course. I'll be right back with my receipt book."

Within minutes, paper of different sorts changed hands. Then Ron put up the Continental's top, and they were on the way back to Xylon. While Ron drove, Gil sorted what was left of the money into four even amounts, keeping some aside for Liesel to buy the clothes that she would need to keep her job.

They stopped at each of the four churches and left the money where the priests or minister would find it then quickly made an escape. It became something of a game to get in and out of the church unnoticed.

With the last of the errands completed, they went to the hospital then up to the second floor.

The nurse at the desk waved them over. "I'm afraid you can't take her with you tonight."

"Oh, something wrong?" Ron asked.

"She woke up at 2:30 this morning with a terrific headache again." The nurse frowned and shook her head. "The doctor ordered another test and should have the results back in the morning. That's the soonest he'll consider releasing her."

"Can we see her?" Gil asked.

"Sure."

They went to her room, and Gil knocked before stepping in. Liesel was playing solitaire, though she pushed the cards aside the moment she saw them.

"Oh, hi!" She beamed a smile guaranteed to melt the hardest heart.

"We heard you had a rough night," Ron said.

"Yes, but I'm feeling better now." She frowned and looked away. "The doctor won't let me out until tomorrow afternoon, though."

Gil shrugged. "Yeah, but you wouldn't want to stay in an empty old house anyway. It's kind of creepy."

"We finished all the errands." Ron handed her the receipts. "The furniture went to a new B&B opening just outside Roslyn. The jewelry went to Mr. Aarons, except for the costume jewelry. Some of that went to the clothing closet. The rest went to the orphans. The clothing went to the community closet and the orphanage. The furs went to a furrier Mr. Aarons recommended. Food went to the charity pantries. The bank took care of setting up mortgage payments and will mail the rent to the renter's landlords, and we found a boarding house four doors down from the jewelry store. They only rent to women, and a first-floor room will be ready for you Sunday night. You get breakfast, a bag lunch for work, dinner, and clean linens."

"It's a little pricy, $6.50 a night, but you're paid up six months. That should give you time to find another place if this one won't work out." Gil gave her the money he'd set aside. "You'll need this before you start work."

"Why?" she asked.

"We were stopped by a worker in the store and warned. Mr. Aarons runs a tight ship. He wants all his people dressed professionally." Ron winced. "Nothing in your wardrobe passes muster. It's all too formal or too casual."

Liesel shook her head. "Then I don't know what he wants."

"That's why you have an appointment with Mrs. Chambers. She has Wednesday off and offered to take you shopping to show you the ropes."

Gil pointed to the bills they'd given her. "You'll need that money to get properly outfitted."

"Thank you." She stuttered through a few useless syllables. "I-I can't – that was just so much that you accomplished in almost no time at all." She set the money on the bedside table. "Even if I hadn't been stuck here, I don't think I could have done half as much. I really appreciate your help."

"No problem at all," Ron said.

"How about a few hands of rummy before dinner?" Gil asked.

Liesel gathered up the cards and shuffled.

Standing at the graveside, Liesel felt drained. She hadn't much cared for her family, and there certainly wasn't much love lost, but the funeral had sapped her strength. She really just wanted some food and rest, and in the morning, Ron and Gil would drive her to Roslyn on their way out of town, and she'd be rid of this place for good.

As the funeral ended, folks headed for their cars. Only a few—Gil, Ron, Mr. Knowles, and a couple people from Roslyn—actually bothered to stop by and offer their condolences. The rest had come either for the sake of appearances or out of respect for her parents. She didn't care. She'd rather sincerity than forced kindness.

Ron and Gil stood off to the side, probably waiting to give her a ride to the hotel, and she was grateful for their help. All of it. She never would have made it through this weekend without them.

Mr. Knowles walked over to them. "I'll get her to the hotel. She has some business with a funeral director."

"Is that OK with you, Liesel?" Ron lightly gripped her arm. "We don't mind waiting."

"It's OK," she said.

She'd presumed enough on their kindness already this week.

"We'll see you in the morning, then." Gil waved.

Liesel nodded. "I'll be ready. Thank you."

They left, and Liesel took care of the last paperwork with the funeral director. Then Mr. Knowles walked with her to his car. The ride to Xylon's only hotel was thankfully short.

When he parked at the hotel, the sign read, "Vacancy."

Liesel followed him into the lobby. Luke Maddox, the owner, pushed his glasses up on his head.

"A room for the lady." Mr. Knowles handed her a pen and pushed the guestbook toward her.

Mr. Maddox took the pen and the book away. "No vacancy just now."

"Your sign says otherwise." Mr. Knowles hooked his thumb toward the sign.

"I just rented the last room a few minutes ago." Mr. Maddox reached under the counter and flipped a switch. "I must have forgotten to change the sign."

"Maddox, you haven't had a full house since the day you opened." Mr. Knowles scowled.

"Must be a lot of folks here for the funeral," Mr. Maddox said.

"Uh-huh," Mr. Knowles put his arm around Liesel's shoulder. "Wasn't born last night, you know. Come on, Liesel. There are other places." At the door, Mr. Knowles stopped and looked back at the desk. "Known you your whole life, Luke. Never would have figured you for another man's dog."

As Mr. Maddox stuttered through a protest, Liesel hobbled back to Mr. Knowles's car.

"If my wife weren't out of town, I'd just take you home with me." Mr. Knowles put the car in gear. "Let's try Mrs. Ellis. If that's no good, we'll try the rectories of the married ministers in town."

When they arrived at Mrs. Ellis's boarding house, Liesel hoped to see the Continental, but it wasn't there. Disappointing, but Ron and Gil had a right to be out doing something more interesting than running her errands and taking care of her.

"You wait here. I'll go check things out." Mr. Knowles stepped out of the car.

"Yes, sir."

Once he was gone, she absently rubbed her sore legs. She couldn't wait until tomorrow when she could go somewhere that might not have been purchased lock, stock, and barrel by one of Satan's own minions.

After a few minutes, Mr. Knowles returned and got her overnight bag and dress. "Alright. It's all set up. She had two rooms left and agreed to put you up in one of them."

Liesel followed him up to the house.

He set her things in the parlor. "She's off preparing a room, but she'll be back in a few minutes. Will you be alright?"

"Yes, sir," She managed a smile. "Thank you."

"You're welcome. Call me at the station tonight if you need something, OK?" he said.

"Yes, sir," she replied and watched him leave. Liesel parked herself on a chair and waited. When Mrs. Ellis came down the stairs, Liesel pushed herself back up to her feet.

"The only space I have for a girl is the attic loft. The charge is $5 per night," Mrs. Ellis said.

Liesel paid out of the money Gil had set aside for her shopping. When Mrs. Ellis didn't come forward to take it Liesel went to her.

"The room is prepared. You may go up when ready." Mrs. Ellis pointed to the stairs.

Without another word, she turned abruptly and strode toward the kitchen.

Returning to the parlor, Liesel put the overnight bag on the floor and draped the dress over her shoulder. Pushing the bag in front of her, she began the trek to the stairs then the longer one to the attic.

After a couple refreshing adult beverages and some lively music, even if it was just a jukebox, Ron felt better. Funerals always left him feeling a little blue even when the subject of the event wasn't anyone he cared for. When Mr. Knowles had offered to give Liesel a ride, Ron had been happier than he would have liked to admit. It wasn't that he minded helping the poor girl out. He just needed some time to put his head back on straight. Gil's suggestion of a couple drinks and some tunes had done the job well.

Before the funeral, Mrs. Ellis had declared a late supper time at 7:00 PM, and it was nearing that time now. Gil had even bought in for dinner at Mrs. Ellis' since his family would have already eaten by now. Ron was ready for something solid followed by a peaceful evening. He wasn't ready for what he found when he walked in.

Liesel was halfway up the steps to the second floor. She moved her bag up a step then adjusted the dress over her shoulder and moved up, slowly and obviously with a lot of pain.

"Liesel?" Gil called.

When she turned, her foot slipped. Ron bolted forward and caught her before she fell far.

"I've got you," he said.

She shook like a leaf in a thunderstorm, and he had to wonder if that near fall made her remember some part of that first fall down the stairs, the one caused by her drunken mother's clumsiness.

While Ron held on to her, Gil disentangled the crutches, the extra dress, and the overnight bag. Ron carried her back to the parlor and set her on the couch.

"I thought you were going to the hotel," Gil said.

"The last available room was rented just before I arrived." Liesel sniffled and brushed her eyes with her fingers.

"And probably went vacant the moment you left again." Ron looked at Gil. "Stay with her while I get to the bottom of this."

Ron walked into the kitchen and found Mrs. Ellis setting the table. The other guests were already gathered. He counted the place settings and came up one short. With a grunt, he went to the cupboard to help with the last one.

"What are you doing?" Mrs. Ellis asked.

"You missed a spot." He opened a drawer in search of silverware.

She snatched the dishes away from him. "I forgot nothing."

Ron pointed to each place. "Me, Gil, you, Frank, Bud, Kathy... where's Liesel?"

He already knew, but before he landed on the older woman with both feet, he wanted to give her a chance to redeem herself.

"She has her space in the attic. She'll take that and be grateful." Mrs. Ellis crossed her arms over her chest.

"The attic? You didn't just put her in the empty second-floor room? You put her in the loft?" Ron stared at her, wide-eyed.

"Wouldn't be proper to house her on the men's floor."

"Oh, no, but perfectly proper to starve her and put a kid who can't hardly maneuver on level ground all the way up in the attic." Ron pointed at the ceiling. "Why not put a ladder to the side of the house and tell her to sleep on the roof?"

"Knowles tricked me. He asked if I had space left before telling me who it was for," Mrs. Ellis said.

"Oh, the horror." Ron pressed his hand to his chest. "When Gil and I came in, we were just in time to catch her as she fell on the stairs. Why can't you put her up on the parlor couch for tonight, or why can't one of you more able-bodied ladies take the loft and let Liesel sleep down here for one night?"

Mrs. Ellis glared. "Absolutely not. And I'll thank you to stop trying to tell me how to run my business."

"I wouldn't have figured you for being on Rodman's payroll, too,"

"You don't understand." Mrs. Ellis put the extra place setting away. "It's easy for you, being an out of towner, a drifter."

"Easy? Easy? I don't think Gil and I have ever worked as hard as we have in the last few days, but you know what? We didn't mind it in the least because it was the right thing to do. We saw a good kid getting a raw deal from virtually this whole town because you were all terrified that some rich tyrant would frown if you did the decent thing. Rodman has played you all for suckers, and the saddest thing about it is that you'll have to someday stand before a righteous God and explain to him why you couldn't see your way clear to help a girl who has done no harm to you and has lost more in the past week than you'll ever know. My conscience is clear. How's yours?"

Ron gathered two of the place settings and put them away.

"Now what are you doing?" Mrs. Ellis asked.

"Mrs. Ellis, I don't have an appetite anymore." Ron paused at the kitchen door. "When I tell Gil about the way you do business, if I know my buddy, he won't either. I'm leaving in the morning." He left the kitchen without a backward glance and returned to the parlor.

When Gil saw the look on his face, he stood and offered Liesel his hand. "Say, why don't we have a picnic in the park?"

"After dark?" Lisa asked.

"Sure. We can check out the stars." Gil shrugged. "Park curfew isn't until 10:00 PM."

"Why not?" Ron added. "We can grab sandwiches from the diner or maybe a pizza to go."

Liesel managed to smile. "OK, sure."

"Alright. I'll take these up to your room, then we'll go get the fixings and head on over." Gil gathered up her dress and overnight bag.

Ron walked with Liesel down to the car.

The attic loft itself had no electricity, and the stairs were steep and unlit. The only light came from the open doorway to Ron's room. So, as Ron backed down the stairs with Liesel in his arms, Gil stayed a step or two below with a hand on his buddy's back to support him. How Mrs. Ellis had expected Liesel to get up and down these attic stairs... It was more than Gil could figure. The cruelty floored him.

"Last step," Gil said.

He backed out of the way so Ron could turn around in the narrow space.

"I'll bring her out to the car," Ron said.

Liesel's things were already stowed.

Gil returned to Ron's room and paused, looking at the writing kit on the table. Gil had half a mind to give Mrs. Ellis a piece of his. He'd had it with secrets and wanted to fill the old hag in on who really owned the mill, how Liesel had been crippled, who'd actually closed the mill, and exactly where the windfall blessing for over half the town's households was about to come from. The truth was, however, that the only one of those secrets that wasn't already public knowledge was the last one, and no doubt when it became public knowledge, everyone in town would find some way to color it against Liesel. Ron had said it best last night. This town would be held accountable by God sooner or later. He'd set things right again, and probably more efficiently and completely than anything Gil could come up with.

After making sure they had everything, Gil picked up Ron's suitcase and headed downstairs. He expected to find Ron and Liesel waiting by the car, but there was no sign of either one. The passenger door on the Continental stood open.

Gil rushed to the car, looking both ways down the street. The tail end of a red car disappeared around a corner. As Gil tossed the suitcase into the passenger seat, something gold caught his eye. He bent down and found Ron's watch on the floorboards, a graduation gift from a grandparent. The band was broken. A thorough understanding of his buddy and a faint blood smear on the watch's face told Gil that Ron hadn't gone willingly.

Gil didn't have the keys to the Continental. He closed the door and ran back up to the house. In the kitchen, he put a dime on the counter and called the police.

Ron had only just set Liesel down in the car when she'd seen Hugh and some of the younger men from the mill racing forward. She'd managed a monosyllabic warning, but that was enough for Ron to duck the fist swinging at his head. With five opponents, Ron's valiant effort hadn't lasted long or gotten far. She'd never felt so completely useless. Once Hugh's gang had subdued Ron, they'd packed both of them into two cars and had driven away. Liesel, in the front car with Hugh, Lane, and Darren, craned around to try to see Ron in the red car with Billy and a logger named Clyde. She couldn't see her companion. He had been on the near edge of unconsciousness when the guys had made an end to pummeling him.

"Oh, don't you worry none. Y'all are gonna get what's coming to you," Lane sneered. "Then we're going to go find Gil and do him the same."

"Leave Gil and Ron out of this." Liesel glared.

"Shut up." Darren looked at her in the rearview mirror. "If they're in this, it's their own fault or yours."

The cars pulled onto the sawmill road and broke through the chain blocking the way. Liesel tried to banish the gruesome mental images that came into her mind. They stopped at the main building. Lane pulled her out of the car and slung her over his shoulder. Clyde and Billy dragged Ron out of the back of the other car. Blood covered his face, and when he got his feet under him, Billy twisted Ron's arm behind his back and shoved him forward. He was able to move under his own power, which relieved her fears greatly.

The inside of the old sawmill smelled of gasoline. The sawdust, usually swept and bagged for removal, had been strewn on the floor a couple inches deep. She didn't need a college degree to see where this was going.

"Hugh's uncle won't like this." Liesel speared Darren with a look. "He has plans for these buildings."

"Our plans are more important," Lane said.

As he sat her down in the corner farthest from the door, she could already smell the smoke.

📖

Blood spots on the sidewalk outside Mrs. Ellis's and the broken watch had convinced the police that foul play was involved. A little logical reasoning had come up with Hugh as a likely suspect and smoke rising from the area of the mill suggested a place.

As they turned down the gravel road into the mill, the broken chain convinced Gil that they'd figured right. They neared the parking lot when a couple cars came up from that way.

"That's the red car I saw." Gil pointed.

"Stay here and stay down until we know if they're armed." Mr. Knowles twisted around to look at Gil.

Gil would have rather bashed heads but did as told.

217

The two officers bailed out, one armed with a pistol, the other with a shotgun, and crouched behind the car doors.

The officers from the second car took positions behind large trees off to the side.

"Give it up, boys. It's no good," Knowles yelled.

Billy Langston, Darren Barclay, and a logger Gil recognized but didn't know by name stepped out of the car with their hands raised and came forward.

"Hugh, Lane, don't make me come in after you," Knowles said.

Lane threw in the towel next, but Hugh ran for it. Before Gil could take off after him, one of the younger officers sprinted, closed the distance like a cheetah out for a kill, and brought Hugh down. Gil stepped out of the car as the police cuffed and searched the members of Hugh's gang.

"How about it, Lane." Mr. Knowles stood over Lane and rested his hand on his sidearm. "Where are Moore and the girl?"

Lane threw a glance at the burning mill. "Guess."

Gil ran flat out. He got through the main door and found Ron tightly bound on the floor. Pulling out a pocketknife, Gil freed his buddy's hands.

Ron coughed and pulled out his own pocketknife. "She's in the back corner. Go on. I'll be alright. Go on."

Gil left Ron and tried to make his way toward the back. The air was hot and full of heavy smoke. Breathing through his handkerchief didn't do much to help. Twice the path he picked was barred by flaming parts of walls or the roof.

"Liesel!" he called then coughed heavily.

"Gil!" she cried. "Get out of here, Gil."

"Not without you!"

He found a way back and saw her struggling to her feet. Gil swept her up in his arms and picked a way out through smoke that he could cut with a chainsaw. By the time he staggered into fresh air, soot filled his eyes, and they teared so badly he couldn't see straight. Someone took Liesel from him, and someone else got him far enough away that the heat wasn't noticeable.

"Ron?" Gil called.

"Here," he replied. "You OK?"

"Yeah, yeah." Gil coughed like he'd gotten pneumonia. "Got crud in my eyes, and I feel like I've been chain smoking tires. You good?"

"Yeah. I'll be all right," Ron said.

"Liesel?" Gil asked.

"Talking to an officer. She doesn't look hurt." Ron said.

"Get all three of them to the hospital then bring them to the station," Mr. Knowles ordered from nearby. "I want them under protective custody until the judge gets to town in the morning."

"So much for getting on the road today." Gil sighed.

"Tomorrow's good," Ron said.

Someone helped Gil into a car, and Ron climbed in next to him.

A very feminine-sounding cough came from the front seat, so Liesel was also with them. Soon afterward, they were off.

📖

Aldus surveyed the damage. He could just about wring the neck of that idiot nephew of his. The sawmill proper and the pavilion were a total loss. Fortunately, there hadn't been much wind yesterday, so the fire hadn't jumped to the nearby stands of timber.

In one stupid move, Hugh had all but ruined Aldus's plans. To get the textile factory open on time, he would need an increased initial cash input. Construction workers would have to be paid overtime. Simply stalling the start date wasn't an option. He'd made deals with powerful clients. His other factories were already operating at maximum efficiency, so he couldn't meet his obligations by using existing facilities. He'd have to clear the site and start building from the dirt up.

After such a colossal blunder, Hugh had actually called after seeing the judge this morning and begged for the money to pay the fine. Aldus had kept his word. He would not pay for any more of Hugh's indiscretions. Perhaps sitting in jail for a long time would teach him some sense.

Aldus took one last look around the burnt wreckage and left. New plans had to be made to get the factory operational in time.

📖

Ron was sore in places he hadn't previously known about. After taking a beating and being trapped in a burning building, he felt lucky enough to be alive.

He stood in Aarons's Fine Jewelry store and waited for the watch repair. After hearing about yesterday's trouble, Mr. Aarons himself had offered to do the work.

Mr. Aarons returned with Ron's watch, now intact. "That'll be $2."

Ron pulled out his wallet and paid for the work. "I'd expected a bit more."

"I'm a veteran of two wars, Mr. Moore. When I meet a fellow veteran, I try to do him a good turn." Mr. Aarons wrote out a receipt.

"I was never in the military," Ron said.

"Perhaps not, but you and Mr. Soto went toe-to-toe with a whole town and a man who is little more than an affluent bully. You rescued a prisoner of war and acquitted yourselves quite admirably. Not all battle fronts are on foreign soil with conventional weapons, you know."

Ron smiled and put his watch on. "Thank you, sir. It was a pleasure meeting you."

"The pleasure is mine, Mr. Moore. Do stop by for tea if you're ever back this way."

"I'll do that."

Ron left and found Gil waiting in the car.

"Everything all set?" Gil asked.

"Ready when you are." Ron looked toward Grace Hall. "Liesel's all taken care of?"

"Yeah, I've even introduced her to Albert." Gil nodded toward the mechanic's shop.

Ron slid into the front seat behind the wheel. "How? You've never met him."

"How many 19-year-old grease monkeys two doors down from the jewelry store are there?" Gil asked.

"Right."

"Anyway, Mr. Swanson gave Albert an hour for lunch, so they're at that little cafe a block over." Gil smiled. "You're right. He seems like a good kid."

Ron pulled away from the curb. "I think she'll be OK now."

"Yeah. Where to next?"

Ron pointed. "That way."

A summer of adventure awaited them wherever the road led.

Origin:
In the anthology *Hero's Best Friend*, there's a tale called "The Hat" about a cockatoo who needs to snitch the hat of a spy to get the evidence they need to stop the guy.

This story is set in the same universe starring a secondary character from "The Hat", a white-capped pionus named Cappie.

The Antidote

No one needed him.

Cappie grumbled as he finished preening and looked around the empty aviary. The cockatiel flock in the big cage across from him had been summoned to entertain the queen and her guests. The falcons in the far corner were off hunting with the king. Mick had Cloud on one mission, and Frank had Ash on another. Even the messenger pigeons were off delivering messages. No one, it seemed, needed a trained white-capped pionus.

At least with everyone gone, and the drapes pulled, the light level in the room was a nice, comfortable twilight. Perfect for not blinding his eyes.

He ruffled his tail feathers to get them all to lay right, then grabbed the cage bar with his beak. He swung around to grip another with his feet as he made his way to the food bowl.

After rooting through the peas and corn, he shook his feathers in frustration. He'd meant to save some chili peppers for a snack later, but they'd been so good, he'd eaten every bit right away. He snatched a pea and set to work shelling it, which could be almost as much fun.

The fluttering of many bird wings came closer, muffled by the aviary door. He paused with the half-shelled pea in his beak and tilted his head to one side. The pitch of the sound suggested tiny birds.

They couldn't be the messenger pigeons—they'd use the bird flap on the wall to his left so they could ring the bell to let Ingrid know they were home—which left the cockatiel flock.

Even as Cappie thought it, a yellow and gray blur of cockatiels flew in through the window above the door and zipped around the room. A couple circuits later, they landed on top of their cage and burst out with a chirpy cacophony that was sure to bring Ingrid.

Footsteps preceded the click of the door latch, and as he'd predicted, his favorite human strode in.

The green gown she wore was a perfect match for the deep green feathers on his back, and her yellow hair resembled the lutino cockatiel in the flock across from him.

Cappie dropped the pea and scrambled back up to his perch to squawk, "Hi, Ingrid! Hi, Ingrid!"

"Hello, Cappie." She closed the door behind her then glided across to the window above the bird flap and drew back the drapes.

Brilliant afternoon sunlight poured in through the window, turning a patch of the floor golden. He squinted until his eyes adjusted.

She spent a few moments staring out the window before she went to the table in the middle of the room and tapped on the red oak surface.

The entire cockatiel flock fluttered over to her and crowded around. Well, the whole flock except for Spinner, who landed on Ingrid's shoulder instead. Smiling, Ingrid tapped twice, paused, and then tapped twice again. This time, Spinner joined the others. Silly bird was always doing crazy things like that.

Cappie danced from foot to foot, whistling. Ingrid had been playing with the cockatiels all afternoon. When did he get a turn with his favorite human?

Reaching under the table, Ingrid pulled out a couple sticks with seed clusters attached and set them on the table. The cockatiels wasted no time digging in.

"Guard! Over here! Whoa!" came a muffled voice through the closed door.

The door latch clicked, and Frank walked in with Ash perched on his hand.

The maroon-tailed, gray parrot lifted one foot. "Hi! Guard! Over here, good bird!"

Ash was so good with voices. As hard as he tried, Cappie never managed to sound even remotely correct.

"Wow, he sounds perfect." Ingrid offered Ash her hand and waited until the bird stepped over.

"And he picked it up fast. You just have to get him to say it on command." Frank nodded and leaned on the table, adding, "And nothing else but that."

"There's time. I'll link it to a finger snap." Ingrid set Ash in his cage and closed the door.

"How did the cockatiels do?" Frank admired the little flock as they finished up their snack and returned to their cage while Ingrid dropped a few pistachios in Ash's bowl between the bars of the cage.

"They were a hit, as always."

"That's great. And how's Cappie's training coming?" Frank asked as he walked over.

"Oh, he's trained. He can retrieve, follow in-air commands, and backtrack a course to come home."

Yeah! *I've been working hard on my skills.*

"It's a pity he couldn't help with the hat retrieval. It worked out fine in the end, but Gregory spotted Cloud too soon, and Cappie would be easier to hide than Ash will be in this other matter."

Cappie cocked his head. *The hat matter, huh*?

He remembered that incident like yesterday. They'd wanted Cappie to be able to grab a hat from some guy's head and fly with it. No problem, except that it weighed more than a house.

Cappie fluffed up his head feathers and squinted. *Could Frank pick up a house and fly with it*?

"Oh, Frank, you're expecting the wrong things from the little guy." She dropped a few pistachios in Cappie's bowl. "He's a pionus. He might weigh half a pound. Maybe. With the coins and papers tucked into the hat, it probably outweighed him. Even Cloud struggled with it, and she's an easy two and a half times his size. And, he'll never speak as clearly as Ash, no matter how hard we train. Each of my birds has things they're good at. When the right mission comes along, he'll be the perfect bird for it.

You'll see. We don't take the pigeons out to hunt rabbits, you know."

"Fair enough." Frank took a step back. "Well, thanks for letting me borrow Ash."

After making sure the cages were secured, the humans left. Cappie stayed perched where he was. He wasn't strong like Cloud. He wasn't an excellent talker like Ash. He wasn't even as entertaining as the cockatiels.

No one needed him.

📖

Cappie was awake before the sun. He preferred it that way. Dawn was a perfect time.

The evening before, after spending some time being grumpy about Frank, Cappie had played with his toys for a while, eaten a pistachio, and then gone to sleep as soon as the aviary was too dark to see. Today was a new day, and he was going to work hard.

But first, breakfast.

Cappie climbed down to his food bowl and almost shrieked his joy.

Four whole pistachios for breakfast!

Ingrid had left him five pistachios, one of which he'd eaten last night. Although not nearly as good as chili peppers, pistachios made such a fun noise when he opened them. He grabbed the first one and held it with his foot while he pried it apart with the point of his beak. The nut made a satisfying crack, and he discarded the shell to enjoy the rest. Before he knew it, he was out of pistachios and had nothing but corn and peas left. Those were okay, too, he supposed.

The day went on in a typical fashion. After the sun was up, Ingrid arrived to clean cages and give everyone clean food and water, and then came training. The cockatiels worked on their newest trick, while Ash practiced saying his new phrase whenever Ingrid snapped her fingers. As usual, Spinner got different directions than the rest of the flock. By the end of practice, Ash made fewer extra comments and sound effects when Ingrid snapped her fingers.

Then, it was lunchtime, and everyone got some good, grainy bread. Cappie shredded the bread to dig the seeds out before moving on to eat the crumbs.

After lunch, Cappie waited on his perch. It was his turn for training, and he meant to prove himself a useful bird. Whatever skill she wanted him to practice, he'd be the best. Then, someone would need him.

As Ingrid approached, Cappie raced to the door and perched there, waiting as she swung the the bars open.

"Your turn, Cappie."

She offered her hand.

He stepped out, fluttering his wings. "Hi, Ingrid. Hi!"

"Hi, Cappie. Today, we are going to work on your endurance. I might need you to fly a long way."

He waited for her hand signal then launched himself airborne, flapping hard to come up to speed. In his peripheral vision, he watched her for new hand signals. After three circuits of the room at full speed, she still hadn't given him the landing command.

His breathing grew harder and his chest muscles burned with exertion. When he could, Cappie changed tactics to glide and flap now and then to regain speed. Those brief rests on the wing helped.

At some point, he lost track of the number of laps he'd taken around the room.

In the distance a clock chimed, and at long last, Ingrid held out her arm.

The exhausted bird pulled a tighter turn and dove lower than the height of Ingrid's arm before he swooped back up to shed his speed and land on her wrist.

"Very good, Cappie." Ingrid held him up at her eye level. "That's your longest flight yet."

His breathing whistled through his nares. "Goo' 'ird."

"Yes. Good bird."

Footsteps running down the hall preceded the door bursting open. Frank bent over with his hands on his knees, panting like he'd flown several laps around the room himself.

Cappie jumped halfway to the clouds and trilled his flock alarm, which sounded like one of Cloud's giggles.

"Easy, Cappie. Easy. It's okay." She petted his head as he crouched a bit in case he needed to fly. "What's wrong?" Ingrid asked their visitor.

Frank stood straighter and blew out a breath. "The prince was poisoned. Tainted darts hit him and both of his bodyguards when they were out riding. The guards only just got him home before they collapsed."

Ingrid gasped. "Oh, heavens. Do we know what it was? Is there an antidote?"

Frank nodded. "The herbalist narrowed it down to one of three. She has the ingredients for two antidotes and has a colleague who can supply the missing ingredient for the third."

"We're talking about the prince's life here. Can we trust this other herbalist?" Ingrid scowled.

"She thinks so. The missing herb has many functions. Only one is for this antidote, so the request will look innocent enough." Frank braced himself on the table. "Trouble is, this colleague is in Avengarde. I'm to ride out there, collect the antidote, and bring it back."

"You'll never get into Avengarde." Ingrid shook her head. "The word is they've become paranoid about visitors, and they've never liked us much to begin with."

Cappie bobbed his head. *This sounds like a retrieval job. I'm good at retrieving.*

"Right. That's why I need to borrow Ash. He can fly in, exchange the gold for the ingredient, and fly out." Frank mimed the actions with his hands.

Ash. Of course. Everyone needs Ash. Cappie grumbled.

Ingrid shook her head emphatically. "No, not Ash. He hates wearing a backpack. Getting it on him is a four-handed operation while he spends the whole time shrieking loud enough to impress Cloud." Ingrid reached under the table and slipped a bird backpack with torn straps and gaping holes off one of the shelves. "This is what's left after the last time we put it on him. That's five minutes of no supervision."

Frank sighed. "Then—"

"That's not all." Ingrid held up a hand to pause him. "Even assuming you leave immediately, and run into no soldiers on the way, it could be late afternoon when you get there. Ash doesn't see well in dim light. Certainly not enough to identify a blue herbalist flag."

Dim light? I see perfectly in dim light. I love the twilight!

Frank pinched his eyes shut. "And Mick won't be back with Cloud for a few more days."

"Cloud's not stealthy enough." Ingrid held Cappie closer to Frank. "This is the bird you need. Cappie does great in low light, and as long as you have him out where he can see, he can backtrack on his own if you run into trouble."

Yeah! I can do it!

"Is he strong enough?" Frank asked, eying Cappie.

"What's the cargo?"

Frank plopped a couple coins on the table. "Two gold coins and a short note on the way out, and a thumb-sized glass vial with a cork stopper and possibly a note on the way back."

"As long as it fits in his backpack, the weight's no problem." She retrieved his pack from the shelf under the table. "Let's get this on him and run a quick test."

Cappie hopped down to the table and stood still while Ingrid slipped on his pack. He had a job to do. A real job!

Cappie clung to his perch with one foot while gripping the bars of the carrier cage with the other. At first, the horse's galloping gait had tossed him around in the carrier strapped behind the saddle, but now, a few hours into the trip, he'd gotten used to the rhythm. Even when Frank had switched horses to the riderless one, and then switched to a different pair of horses, Cappie kept his balance.

Without any toys to play with or snacks to chew on, Cappie had watched the terrain zipping by just like he'd been taught. After all, he might have to find his own way back.

The galloping and horse-switching had ended a while ago. Now, they alternated between a fast and a slow walk. As the sun sank toward the horizon, Frank veered off the road, which was when Cappie got a good look at a tall stone wall. It looked like home, except for the different colored rock and the red-and-gold flags hanging from the edges.

Behind a shrub taller and wider than the horses, Frank stopped and stepped down, then unhitched the straps keeping Cappie in place. Cappie tightened his grip as Frank crouched in the grass. Once his carrier stopped moving, Cappie stepped off the perch and waited. As soon as the door was open, he hopped out onto Frank's hand.

Frank fished a blue herbalist flag out of a pouch on his belt. "Cappie, herbalist." He held up the flag. "Cappie, herbalist. Herbalist. Go."

Cappie crouched then launched off Frank's hand, flapping hard to come up to speed. He looped around and soared over the wall into the city.

This version of home had the buildings in all the wrong places, so, the herbalist could be in the wrong place, too. When he spotted a flash of blue like the flag Frank had shown him, he wheeled around and descended. A blast of wind caught the blue cloth and flicked it out straight, A white bowl with a stick on it came into view, matching the symbol he needed.

Cappie angled his wings to slow down. Flying past the flag, looking for a bird-friendly entrance, he located the platform for a bird door. He turned a tight circle and landed on the platform then walked through the curtain into the herbalist shop.

This place looked different, too. The shelves with all the jars were to his left and the bench with all the tools was on the right. Backwards. He looked for a bell to ring but found none.

"Hi! Hi!" Cappie called. "Goo' 'ird. Hi!"

"All right, all right. I'm coming." A woman's muffled voice came through a door to the right.

"Hi!" Cappie called again.

The door swung open and a woman in a faded blue herbalist dress stepped out, wiping her hands on a stained gray apron.

"Well, aren't you a cutie." She waddled over. "Now, hold still so I can see what's in this backpack."

To give her easier access to the pack, Cappie turned away from her but watched her in his peripheral vision.

She fumbled with the catch for a moment then flipped it open, withdrawing two gold coins and a note.

"Greetings, Della. This is Cappie. I've sent him to retrieve a half ounce of..." Della's voice dwindled to unclear mutterings. "Oh. That's easy. Someone must have a bit of a tummy ache. You wait here."

Della rooted through the jars and grabbed an opaque one along with a small glass vial. She carried both to her workbench, but Cappie couldn't see what she did with them. He thought about flying over to look from her shoulder, but if she liked bird observers as much as the herbalist at home, he'd get in trouble and lose his snack for today. Ingrid had promised him a chili pepper tonight, and no way he'd forfeit that. Instead, Cappie passed the time preening.

After forever, Della returned with a glass vial full of a pale gray-green powder and a note. Cappie stayed still while she loaded his backpack and secured it.

"There you go, Cappie. Return. Cappie, return."

He stepped out to the bird landing platform, crouched, and leapt into the air. After spiraling up to altitude, Cappie spotted the sun low on the horizon and banked the proper direction.

Frank waited, still perched with the horses behind the shrubbery.

Cappie passed the man, then came in for a landing on top of his carrier cage. "Hi, Fwank! Hi!"

"Cappie. That was quick. Did she give you the medicine?" Frank checked the backpack and pulled out the slip of paper and the vial for a moment, then slid them back again and secured the strap. "Good. Let's get moving."

The bird stepped onto Frank's hand then hopped into his carrier. He clambered up to his perch and hung on tight as Frank tethered him to the horse's saddle. Then, Frank climbed up onto the horse's back. He led the extra horse by the reins.

They returned to the road and headed east, toward home.

They'd passed the corner of the city wall when the main gate creaked open and five men on horses rode out onto the road. Each one wore a tabard with the symbol matching the flags on the wall. They turned to Frank.

"You there! Halt! Identify yourself."

Frank looked over his shoulder. "Hold on, Cappie. This is where the going gets rough." He urged the horse into a gallop.

The guards followed.

Soon, the bird settled into the rhythm of the horse's gallop. One foot gripped the perch, the other held the side of the cage. Behind them, their pursuers drew smaller versions of the noise-and-smoke makers. Five loud pops were followed by five loud bangs and billows of gray smoke.

Cappie squawked his protest to the noise as Frank ducked lower in the saddle then turned off the road and into the brush.

Trees and shrubs zoomed by, some scraping against the side of the carrier and stinging Cappie's toes. He hissed and scooted toward the center. He'd have a harder time holding on, but at least he wouldn't have to worry about tree parts.

Still, the five men followed.

Frank glanced back and muttered. Guiding the horses forward, Frank groped for the carrier cage door latch. Once he found it, he dropped it open, and ordered, "Cappie, fly home. Cappie, fly home. Fly home."

From the back of a moving horse? Are you crazy?

Frank repeated the command urgently, adding, "I'll meet you there."

When Cappie left his perch, the horse's gait bounced him around a bit. Twice he was almost to the door when he stumbled sideways. At last, Cappie erupted from the cage and flapped hard, aiming for the tree canopy where his feathers, except for his white forehead and rose-pink undertail, would blend in.

"Catch that bird!" one of the pursuers ordered when Cappie passed over them.

Two of the men veered off as Cappie reached the road and turned to put the setting sun at his tail.

He made for the opposite tree line and paralleled the road with at least one tree in the way. Dodging branches and brush slowed him down some, but the extra cover, he hoped, would shield him from their eyes. Their horses would get tired before he did.

The sun had already set, but Cappie had no trouble navigating. The moon was approaching full and gave him enough light to see by. After outflying the horses, Cappie extended his endurance by gliding when he could. He stopped a couple times to rest and to get a sip of water from a horse trough at the station where Frank had swapped equines on the way out, and then a quick snack from a birdfeeder at a farmhouse. In spite of these rests, his muscles ached, and his breathing whistled through his nares.

At last, he saw the walls of home ahead. He flapped harder to get enough altitude and zipped over the top then wove his way among the familiar buildings to the landing platform outside the aviary. He reared back to shed speed then dropped onto the platform hard enough to jar every bone in his body.

Sloppy. He'd do better next time.

Cappie pushed through the curtain to go inside and nudged the bell hanging there with his beak. The chirps of a half-dozen cockatiels almost hid Ash's growl. The aviary was darker than outside, but Cappie knew everyone's voice. The aviary door opened, and Ingrid glided in with a lantern casting its yellow glow.

She gasped. "Cappie!"

"Hi, Ingrid. Hi."

"Did Frank send you back alone?" She set the lantern down on the table and hurried over. "You poor bird. You must be exhausted. Let's get this backpack off and let you get some rest."

Tired, he sat still while she removed the pack. When she offered her hand, he stepped on and accepted the ride to the perch in his cage.

"I need to deliver this to the herbalist right away, but I'll be back with a snack for you. You earned it."

Cappie settled on his perch and rubbed his lower beak against the top one. Try as he might, he couldn't stay awake for his special treat. As his eyes closed, he ground his beak happily.

He loved being needed.

Origin:

The next several stories (all the way through "The Bust") are the offspring of *Remnant in the Stars* and *The Loudest Actions*. To help you keep the order settled, here's how they land.

1. Waffles – A couple hundred years before *Remnant in the Stars*
2. Mr. Octopus and the Shellfish – A few years before *Remnant in the Stars*
3. Buying the Dream – Shortly after Mr. Octopus and the Shellfish
4. Freak Occurrence – Just before *Remnant in the Stars*
5. (*Remnant in the Stars* would go here).
6. Terms of Service – Between *Remnant in the Stars* and *The Loudest Actions*
7. (*The Loudest Actions* would go here).
8. Big Enough – Shortly after *The Loudest Actions*
9. The Marksman – Shortly after *The Loudest Actions*
10. The Model – Shortly after *The Loudest Actions*
11. The Bust – Shortly after *The Loudest Actions*
12. (The untitled Book 3 that's in planning stages will go here).

Waffles

Sora sat in the middle of the huge, elevated pillow the aliens had given him. The silver rails wouldn't be effective at keeping him penned if he really wanted to get loose, but the last time he'd slipped off his cushion to go explore the area, a bunch of tall aliens in their pale-colored lab coats had charged in. Their intense worry had made his head hurt, and he'd cried for Mommy before he remembered that she had died not long after their scoutship had crashed. Daddy had died in the crash even before the tall aliens arrived to help, and now Sora had to wait until Uncle and Auntie could catch up with the rest of the ships.

It just wasn't the same.

The aliens were nice enough, and Mommy had said it would be okay for him to trust them. They really had done lots of doctor stuff to help her and Daddy, but they had been too hurt to save.

Tears burned in Sora's eyes as he remembered Mommy's thoughts fading away even as the aliens fought to keep her alive. Sora brushed his damp cheeks with the hand that wasn't wrapped up in a heavy, white case. He stared at the ceiling for a moment and hissed, tired of crying, tired of boredom, tired of playing memory and number games alone.

A soft tap on the door heralded a female alien, one of the doctors, before she stepped into the room. She was impossibly tall, like all the aliens. Sora barely came up to her knees. And she had no scales. Instead, her arms, face, and lower legs were all smooth and an odd pinkish-tan kind of color. Her clothes hid everything else, but he supposed the rest of her was the same. After all, he had scales everywhere except the frill on his head, which was a membrane between spines that moved with his feelings. None of the aliens, even the boy ones, had a frill like his. Instead, most of them had fluffy stuff that sprouted from the top of the head and from a ridge just above their eyes. Some of the boy aliens had fluffy stuff around their jaws, too.

Sora fluttered his frill up and down and made his eyes wider to show the alien doctor that he was happy to have a visitor. Maybe she would play number games with him? As old as she was, she was probably lots better than him, but someone to play with would be less boring. Much, much less boring.

Sora set his list of prime numbers on the edge of the bed nearest to her. She spoke, but her words still did not mean much. He picked out "feel" and recognized the way the words changed pitch as a question. The warm kindness in her thoughts chased his cold sadness into a black hole, at least for now.

She picked up his list and compared it to the paper he had written the spiraling sequence on yesterday. Someone had added other symbols squashed into the spaces between his writing. He stood on top of the cushion and looked over her arm. The alien symbols repeated their forms just like his own writing. Alien numbers?

After studying the similarities for a moment, Sora darted to the head of the bed, which bounced a little with his movement. There, he snatched a paper from the table within arm's reach and wrote prime numbers again. Then he added the alien numbers above his own. She smiled and compared the sets. Her eyes grew much wider. She spoke again, and he recognized the words "pattern" and "numbers." Then she wrote another list.

Sora took the paper from her and wrote the numbers in his own figures. One, two, four, eight, sixteen, thirty-two, ____, ____, ____, ____. Easy. That was a simple doubling pattern. He wrote sixty-four, one hundred twenty-eight, two hundred fifty-six, and five hundred twelve. As he handed the paper back, his tummy rumbled. He looked up at the ceiling and wished he could disappear. He'd eaten and still his tummy made all the noise because there hadn't been enough.

He looked at the tray of food someone had brought him earlier. The weird meat stuff was the only thing left. Mommy had said that eating meat would make him sick no matter how hungry he got, so he didn't touch it. The rest—eggs, grainy stuff, and red triangle-shaped plant pieces with teeny seeds on the outside—he had devoured in no time, which had done almost nothing about his hunger.

Doctor smiled again and spoke about food. He blinked once. He could definitely use some. She lowered the rail on her side of the big, stiff pillow. When she reached her hands toward him, he ducked under them and slid off the edge of the pillow, landing easily on his feet. Doctor reached for Sora's hand, but he pulled away. She was nice, but she wasn't Mommy, and girls had girl germs. Alien girls probably had even worse girl germs.

For the first time since Mommy died, Sora got to leave the room. He had to jog to keep up as Doctor led him down a long corridor with lots of little doors. She looked back at him and smiled then slowed her steps. As they walked, a sugary smell became stronger. He sniffed the air as his tummy rumbled again.

Doctor led him into a wide, open room. People sat at tables alone or in small groups, chatting while they ate. They didn't seem to be playing number games or memory games, though. Food time was practice time. Even he knew that.

Sora followed Doctor over to a wall with a bunch of buttons. She stared at him for a few moments, which made his scales crawl. Was he supposed to do something? Before he could figure out what, she clicked a combination. A plate with some kind of bread marked with square holes all over the top slid out of an opening. Melting yellow stuff filled in some of the holes, and thick syrup overflowed the rest. Doctor got a second plate with the same kind of stuff and went to the nearest table. Sora climbed into the chair. Doctor sat next to him and put one plate in front of him and one in front of herself.

Sora looked at the weird bread. How could he eat this? If he picked it up, his fingers would get all messy. He hated dirty hands, and he hadn't seen spoonsticks since he'd arrived here. The nearest thing they had was too short-handled to use properly.

Doctor took a plastic-wrapped bundle out of a cup in the middle of the table. Inside was a short, sharp-handled spoonstick with a few prongs on the end. She used that to carve off a piece of sticky bread, which she stabbed with the prongs to lift it into her mouth. Weird, but Sora tried to mimic her. His first bite fell off the prongs. He tried again and got the piece into his mouth. It was sweet like candy and a little chewy like the donuts Mommy used to make. The corners of his eyes burned with tears again, but he made his eyes wider. He was tired of crying, and he didn't want Doctor to think he was sad about the food. He took another big bite and then another until it was gone.

He pointed to the sweet, square-marked bread. "Can I have another? Please?"

Fizzy amusement bubbled from Doctor's thoughts. She asked a question. He made out the word "another."

What did that mean? He leaned away from her and narrowed his eyes.

She pointed to her sticky bread with the mutated spoonstick. "Waffle."

"Waffle?" He pointed the weird spoonstick at his plate. "Waffle, waffle?"

"Very good!" She smiled. When she continued talking, he understood nothing for a moment then he picked out, "One ... waffle ... you, and ...."

"Yes, yes!" Sora cried.

Leaving the table for a moment, she went back to the wall and returned with another sticky waffle on a plate and a bowl full of pale, green, oval-shaped plant stuff. He'd had those before. They had a sort of skin around sweet, squishy mush. Biting into them to make them pop open was kind of fun. Sora tore into the second waffle with the same speed as the first, but he slowed as he started to get full. He could really learn to like these waffles.

Maybe staying with these aliens until Uncle and Auntie caught up wasn't so bad.

Mr. Octopus and the Shellfish

Janice paused at the mirror to check her hair and make-up. She hardly recognized herself. Her usual hairdo was no more complicated than a ponytail and a couple clips. Her sister had spent the afternoon here armed with a curling iron and makeup kit. With so much hairspray keeping her hair in place, she practically had a curly helmet piled on her head. And make-up? Wow, did circus clowns wear this much? She had half a mind to run a brush through her hair and a washcloth over her face, but there wasn't time for that. She'd no sooner wet the washcloth than her date would ring the bell.

Between fancy hair, make-up she didn't normally wear, and a sequined formal, she'd be self-conscious all night. Rather than agreeing to this dinner and opera, she should have insisted this first date be pizza and a show at the dollar theater. That was more her speed.

The doorbell rang.

Janice darted away from the mirror, if "dart" could work with her high heels. She blew out a breath and plastered a not entirely genuine smile on her face before opening the door.

Bob Hamilton stood there with a bouquet of exotic flowers, the sort that looked more like geometric shapes rather than actual flowers. They probably cost enough to feed a family of six for a month, but really, she'd've been thrilled with a carnation. His gray tuxedo exactly matched the gray accents in her dress, which seemed just about creepy. She hadn't discussed her clothing choices with anyone except her sister, and Emily didn't know Bob from the Easter Bunny. How had he gotten the color so perfectly? Coincidence? No such thing existed.

Bob stepped across the threshold and offered the flowers. "For you."

Janice accepted them with fumbling hands. "Um, thanks! Come in. I'll go put these in water."

She walked to the kitchen and opened one cabinet after another. There had to be a vase in here somewhere.

"You don't get flowers often," Bob said from the kitchen door.

Janice jumped, startled, and turned toward him. "No, not too often."

"That's a pity. We'll have to remedy that."

She gave up the search and grabbed the huge plastic mug she drank her soda from while she worked on tough maintenance jobs. The flowers went in with the plastic wrapper still intact. Water from the tap splashed off the leaves and the wrapper, pooling in puddles on the counter.

"I'll find a real vase and clean that mess later."

Bob's smile went a little tense.

"Ready?" Janice asked.

He stayed in the doorway and pulled her into a tight embrace, upsetting her balance as he leaned in for a kiss.

Janice pushed away from him. "Hey, easy there, Casanova. I thought we had reservations to get to."

His tense smile turned humorous, almost mocking. He led her out to a hovercar, a recent model with sleek lines, a gold-accented interior, real wood, and leather.

Michi 2P. Old-style combustion engine. The maintenance bills on this one are almost as bad as the original price. What does this guy do for money? Even CEO of Hoverworld doesn't cover this.

Bob opened the door for her. Once she settled into a seat that seemed only millimeters above the pavement, the door closed with a squeak and a bang.

Need a bit of oil there, Bob.

He strutted around the front of the hovercar and swooped into the pilot's seat like a bird after its prey. When he powered up, the engine whine indicated a miscalibrated injector. Not the end of the world, but not an efficient configuration, either.

Okay, that's enough grease monkey analysis for tonight.

Bob gunned the throttle, and the G-forces shoved Janice back into the seat. She folded her hands in her lap and plastered on a polite smile. The tight corners at two to three times the recommended speeds and sudden accelerations would cost him big if he mistimed the gear shifts, but if he wanted to increase his already impressive maintenance costs on his 2P, who was she to complain?

Turn down the testosterone, pal. I've been chief engineer for a race team. You think squealing around corners is going to impress me? Really?

Bob finally decelerated as he turned into a long driveway leading through gardens and vineyards to Mario's, an Italian place with prices ranging in dollars per noodle. He parked in the nearest spot and powered down.

"Nice car, isn't it?" Bob patted the dashboard.

"Not bad. I prefer the Michi 4S. Less flashy than the 2P, but better handling on the curves, lower on the maintenance, and better aerodynamics." She opened the door and stepped out then leaned in to look at him again. "Better get your mechanic to check the calibration on the third injector. It's misfiring now and then, especially in a left turn. Ten degrees to the right should do it." She caught his wide-eyed stare for a moment before she closed the door.

He stepped out and secured the hovercar with a key fob. "You're a mechanic?"

Did you even read my profile, buddy? "Engineer. Formerly of the Titan IV race team."

"Formerly?"

"Got tired of living out of a suitcase eleven months of the year. I'm taking a break, and then I'll find a nice ship to crew on. Still get the change of scenery, but my suitcase stays in one room for more than a long weekend."

He met her at the rear bumper of the Michi and wrapped an arm around her waist. His hand drifted downward.

Janice stepped away and shot him a look to communicate her displeasure. "Let's keep it light tonight, huh?"

His smile belonged on a Great White. "If that's what you want." He gestured her on ahead.

I guess staring at my big booty is slightly better than grabbing it.

The outside of Mario's was done in brick and stucco. The trellis overhead held fake vines with lighted grapes in green, red, and purple. The rustic look ended at the door. Inside, gold-gilt wallpaper glittered in the guttering light of fake LED candles. Red upholstered chairs picked up the color of the background pattern in the wallpaper and contrasted with the white travertine tile.

The maître d', wearing a black and gold tux, stepped forward and spread his arms wide before clasping his hands in front of his chest. "Robert! So good to see you again. I did not expect you so soon. This way, please."

Didn't expect you? Didn't you say you had reservations for this joint?

Janice followed the maître d' through the restaurant to a distant corner far enough away from the next nearest patron to have its own postal code. She sat in a spot that gave her a good view of the rest of the room. Bob took the seat next to her and scooted it closer as he sat.

"You'll get my elbow up your nose if you sit that close." Janice shifted her chair away from him.

Bob grinned at their host. "The usual."

"Of course." He bowed and left.

As he went, Janice scanned the table. Origami napkins, enough silverware to melt down into the armor plating of a Class 5 Scout, tablecloth, crystal cruse of olive oil... "Menu?"

"Already taken care of." Bob smiled.

"Oh? What are we having?"

"Focaccia with cheese and sundried tomatoes, fettuccine with marinara sauce, an excellent red wine, and a sorbet for dessert."

Pizza appetizer, spaghetti for dinner, and ice cream for dessert, more or less. "Sounds good, but I'll pass on the wine."

He frowned. "It's an excellent vintage."

"I've been sober for five years. Shootin' for ten."

"This is a special occasion, and I'm buying."

First date arranged by a dating service is not a "special occasion." "Bob, not even for a wedding. The only alcohol I ever use these days is involved in cleaning solvents."

His eyes narrowed. "We'll see."

Yeah, you sure will, jerk. Keep this up, and you're about to be eating this dinner by yourself. "So, when's the show?"

"Eight o'clock, so we have plenty of time to enjoy dinner." He leaned closer and winked. "And company."

Well, one out of two maybe. "So, your profile said you spend your holidays traveling to exotic places. Where was your last trip?"

He launched into an epic-length tale of his hunting escapades in a Martian preserve. He chattered on and on, laughing at his own jokes and describing his amazing hunting prowess against animals that were effectively caged. Janice surreptitiously checked the time on his watch: a half-hour into dinner and counting. Their appetizer arrived, but even a mouthful of fancy pizza didn't curb his bardic tendencies. Janice nibbled on focaccia while Bob wolfed it down between and among his unending description of a gazelle hunt that ended badly for the gazelle.

As dinner arrived, he finally took a breath long enough for her to interject. "So, I've never had gazelle. What's it taste like?"

"Taste like?"

"Sure. You killed it. You ate it, right? Responsible hunters use their kill." Janice moved her plate aside as the waiter deposited a huge bowl of flat noodles in tomato sauce.

Bob waved his hand dismissively. "I have no need for that. I hunt for the thrill, not the food."

The waiter set another bowl in front of Bob then showed him the label of a dark green wine bottle. After the waiter poured a couple swallows in Bob's glass, Bob made a grand show sniffing it and swirling it before he swallowed.

What? No gargling?

The smell was strong and fruity. In the back of her awareness, the old craving reached out to her like a drowning child. Just a little wouldn't hurt. One glass, nothing more. She could stop at just one. It'd be the polite thing to do.

Bob nodded to the waiter and flipped Janice's wine glass right side up.

Just one glass wouldn't hurt. Surely her willpower was that strong.

Yeah, that's what you thought last time you fell off the wagon.

As the waiter finished pouring Bob's second serving, Janice covered her glass with her hand.

Bob frowned.

"I said 'no' on the wine." She turned her glass upside down again.

He sighed. "You don't know what you're missing."

"Maybe, but I know what I want."

He flicked his napkin out across the table before tucking it into his shirt. Janice chose the more refined option of unfolding hers under the table and draping it across her lap.

The dinner itself was excellent. The marinara reminded her of a little mom-and-pop restaurant she'd frequented whenever the race team was in Italy. Just the right combination of spices and a hint of fire. The noodles were fresh, not the boxed, dried out variety, and the flavor complimented the sauce nicely.

As good as the food was, the company left something to be desired as Bob continued regaling her with hunting trip adventures. She needed a crowbar to get a word in crossways, and she must've left that in her other purse.

He finished his meal first, surprisingly. A mouthful of food continued to be no impediment to his tales.

Good food shouldn't be rushed.

Bob paused and checked his watch. "We do need to make it to the show. Unless—." He gripped her knee. "You just want to skip the show."

Janice picked up the dessert fork and admired the tines. "If you want to keep it, remove it."

He jerked his hand back. "You could be friendlier."

"I agreed to dinner and a show, nothing more. Pizza, root beer, and the discount theater would have done fine by me." She glared.

"And I improved upon your suggestions. You could match my effort. I'm certainly doing my part to show you a good time."

"Oh, you think a ride in a fancy car, a hoity-toity restaurant, and an opera are payment in full for a little sack time?"

"A little reciprocity wouldn't hurt. I've dated plenty of girls who thought that was more than enough."

Janice tossed the napkin on the table before she stood and pulled her wallet from her purse. "There's a term for girls who sell themselves." She fished out a couple hundred in credit chips and tossed them one at a time onto his plate. "That'll cover dinner and the ticket to the show." She shrugged and pulled out a five. "And fuel money. Forget I exist, Bob." She slipped around the other side of the table and headed for the door, aware of other patrons' eyes on her. *Yep, I just created a miniature scene. Go back to your overpriced food and drink. Enjoy. Really.*

The maître d' moved to intercept her.

She speared him with a glare. "Robert's got the bill. I have to go. Great food, but the company? Eh."

When she stepped to one side, he moved to counter, so she hustled the other way to get around.

Once in the parking lot, she frowned. This overgrown spaghetti shack was surrounded by vineyards and gardens. The main road was a good kilometer away.

Well, burn some of those pasta calories.

Her shoes crunched on the rustic gravel and gave her a stern reminder of why she usually wore more sensible attire. Had it been real pavement, she would have hazarded removing her shoes and continuing barefoot. She reached the end of the driveway and looked both ways down the row of restaurants, some obviously for higher brow clientele than others. All she needed was somewhere to sit and wait for Emily. The fish-and-chips shop two doors down would serve fine.

She made a click with her tongue to engage her implant comm. "Hey, Em, you around?"

"Yeah, yeah, I'm here. How'd it–uh-oh. Nowhere near long enough for dinner and a show."

"Great dinner. Company not worth hanging around. Meet me at the fish place near Mario's."

"On the way, sis. Sorry it didn't work."

The connection dropped.

Well behind her, an engine revved, a Michi 2P needing some general maintenance by the sound of it.

Her pulse throttled up. In a perfect world, Bob would behave himself and honor her request to be left alone, but he hadn't behaved himself all evening. Why start now?

Janice growled and walked toward the fish-and-chips joint as fast as she could manage in heels. The engine roared closer. She looked back over her shoulder at Bob's car as it turned toward her. She collided with someone much taller. He caught her and steadied her as she turned toward him. He was a tall, thin guy with blond hair a touch too long for military but shorter than the current fashion. His blue plaid shirt hadn't seen an iron since its original construction.

"Hey, you okay?" the guy asked.

She nodded. "Yeah. Date gone all wrong. I'm going to park it in there for a bit." She hooked a thumb toward the fish place.

He looked past her. "Share a cab? I'll see you home and make sure whoever bozo is gets the clue."

Thanks, but I've had enough of the males of the species tonight. "Nah, I got this. Already called my sister for a ride. We arranged it ahead in case the date turned out to be octopus rather than human."

He smirked. "If you're sure."

"Yeah. I appreciate the offer, but the guys I crewed with taught me a thing or three."

"Okay."

She watched him start off down the street toward a cab before she headed for the shop. The Michi 2P pulled up behind her and powered down.

"Janice!" Bob called.

She glowered over her shoulder. "Go away, Bob. Totally not interested."

As she reached for the door, he grabbed her arm and pulled her away toward the corner of the building. "Look, I just want to talk."

She jerked free of his grip. "All you've done is talk and talk and talk and make moves I told you I wasn't interested in." She drew a breath and hollered with her best pit crew voice, the one that could be heard over race engines. "Now bug off!"

One step closer to the door, he snatched her arm again. She jerked loose and spun, swinging her sequined purse at him. He leaned away, but the trailing edge clipped his chin.

A brilliant yellow taxi pulled up and the tall blond hopped out. "Hey!"

As Bob cocked back for a punch, the blond rushed forward and caught his arm.

"Leave her alone. Even I heard her tell you she wasn't interested."

Bob pulled free and threw a punch the blond wasn't ready for. The block missed, and Bob's fist caught the blond square in the jaw. Bob grabbed the guy's wrinkled shirt, swung him around, and shoved him into the alley.

So, what, everyone else enjoying the show or just can't be bothered to get involved, Janice thought bitterly. She had to get help somehow.

Janice stepped into the alley where Bob had the blond pinned to a wall. He continued throwing punches while the blond tried unsuccessfully to protect himself. She drew in a deep breath and screamed like a girl. That'd take a minute or two to do anything, if it worked at all.

A nearby trash bin smelling of dead fish gave her an idea.

If you can't fight 'em, gross 'em out.

She lifted the lid and grabbed the first bag she came across. "Get off 'im, punk!" She swung the bag, hitting Bob across the shoulders.

He stumbled and turned toward her, growling, fancy gray tux in disarray and torn at the shoulder seam. When he rushed her, she swung the bag again, and it tore, showering shellfish parts all over Bob and the alley. Bob staggered and looked himself over. Face pale, he stumbled toward the street, coughing. His breath wheezed as he clawed at his throat and fell.

Wouldn't've happened to a nicer guy, Janice simpered.

She crouched near the blond.

He bled from a pressure cut over his eye, his nose, and the corner of his mouth. Sirens closed in as the blond groaned and lifted his hand partway to his head before it dropped to his side.

"Take it easy, mister. Help's coming." *You should've stayed out of it, but thanks for trying. Else it'd be me lying there.* She frowned. *Nice thinkin' there, Janice. The guy saves your butt and you're thinking "Better you than me?" Nice. Real nice.*

Red and blue twirling lights reflected off the walls as the police hovercar landed.

"You stay right here, mister, while I go fill in the authorities." She gripped the blond's shoulder then stood and waved the police over.

📖

Janice sat next to the blond, Derek Eaton according to his ID. The concussion he'd gotten for being a knight without armor had kept him wobbling in and out of awareness while the ER docs took care of the damage and then left him under observation for the last couple hours.

Derek squeezed his eyes closed then opened them.

Maybe a little more coherent this time? "Hi there."

"Hi there." His voice was raspy, like someone just waking up in the morning. "You're the-the-"

"The gal you rescued from the nut, right. Name's Janice Nili."

"Derek Eaton. You okay?"

"Me? Peachy. You, however, ended up with a concussion and a fascinating collection of bruises." She winced. "I feel bad about that."

"Don't. I chose to step in. What happened to that guy?"

"Allergy attack. I whacked him a couple times with a bag of shellfish parts. It broke and doused him in shrimp guts. Apparently, he's allergic to seafood. Paramedics and police showed up right after he collapsed, choking and gagging." She shrugged. "Who knew? They tell me he'll be okay."

Derek studied her face. "I recognize you from somewhere."

"Do you watch racing much? I was an engineer for the Titan IV team for the last few years."

His eyes lit up. "That's it. My brother's on the pit crew for the Enceladus team."

"Not a bad crew, Enceladus." She leaned a little closer and whispered. "Their pilot plays it a little loose with the rules, though."

"That's what I—"

A light knock on the door preceded the nurse. "Visiting hours are ending in a few minutes." She left again.

Janice frowned as the door closed. "Well, that's annoying. Guess I'd better go rescue my little sister from the waiting room and head for the homestead. They'll probably let you go home soon, though, now that you're up. Thanks for the help."

"Glad you're okay."

She stood and fidgeted for a moment. *So, what else do you say to a guy who took a beating for you?* "See ya 'round, maybe?"

"Sure."

The nurse returned a few minutes later and ordered Janice out. Janice collected Emily from the waiting room and headed for home, where the first order of business would be canceling her membership to the dating service. There had to be a better way to find a good guy.

The ghost of a smile tugged at her lips as she got into her sister's car. She glanced back at the hospital. *Then again, maybe I did find one.*

Buying the Dream

Janice waited until the pops were a couple seconds apart before she pulled her popcorn out of the heater. A bit of lemon-ginger-garlic salt, and she was ready for an evening full of movies and snacks. She put the popcorn on her coffee table and darted back to the kitchen for a couple napkins, a peanut-butter-and-chocolate candy bar, and a bottle of apple juice. Not the dinner of champions, sure, but this rare splurge gave her something to look forward to after a contract job ended.

This time, she had nothing lined up for her next job. Something would come along, and in the meantime, she still had over half of her severance package from the race team she used to engineer for.

Seconds after she'd settled on the couch, the communication system played her ringtone, an ominous-sounding march from an old science fiction movie she liked.

She tapped her implant comm to initiate the relay between the implant and the house system. "Hello, who're you?"

"Janice Nili?" a familiar-sounding man said.

Why do I know your voice? "You can't be. I'm Janice Nili."

He chuckled. "Derek Eaton."

"That's a lot more likely." *Name rings a bell, too.* "Whatcha need?"

"You may not remember me, but I'm the guy who tried to help—"

The voice and name brought up the face of a blond in wrinkled clothes. "You got Bob the Octopus

257

off me when that date went all wrong. My knight without armor. How're you doing?"

"A lot better for sure."

Considering our last meeting, you sound pretty chipper.

"I'm glad to hear it. What's up?" She sorted through the available movies to find a good one.

"No strings attached, nothing funny, and 'no' is a perfectly acceptable answer, but I just came into an inheritance, and I've wanted to get my own cargo ship. I just don't want to get a lemon. Would you be willing to come along as an expert opinion? Make sure I'm not getting scammed or something? I'd pay for your time."

Janice stopped scrolling. He said "no strings attached" but was that for real, or would he be like Bob the Octopus and turn into all hands once they were together?

Eh, he seemed like a nice guy, and he got the stuffing knocked out of him to get Bob off me. "When d'you have in mind?"

He hesitated. "Is Saturday good? We could meet at the hangar downtown. They're having an auction, and there were a couple prospects I liked in the list."

Janice nodded. "Sounds good. When do they start pre-inspection?"

"7 am." The cringe came through his voice.

"See ya there, and I'll check out the listings online. We can compare notes."

"Great! Thanks."

The connection broke, and Janice disengaged her implant comm. She picked a movie and tossed a handful of popcorn in her mouth.

📖

Derek paid the cab driver and hopped out. His watch showed a few minutes before seven, and a crowd of rough-looking sorts had already gathered outside the hangar entrance. He scanned the faces for the slightly overweight engineer he'd met outside the fish place a while back. Would he even recognize her without all the sequins and hairspray?

A shrill whistle came from a gal perched on the low rail fence surrounding a pay-by-the-minute parking lot. Her jeans and T-shirt were a size too small, but a fuzzy neon green jacket discouraged gawking.

She waved him over.

He jogged to the fence. "Good morning!"

"Hi there! How in the world are you?" she asked.

"Great. Thanks for coming."

Behind him, the crowd noise grew. He looked over his shoulder as the group herded through the doors and into the hangar complex.

Janice cupped her hands around her mouth. "Mooo!"

Only a couple people turned, but they continued going through the gate.

Derek chuckled. "What do you say we wait for the cattle to thin some."

"Works for me." She pulled a handheld tablet from her jacket's inside pocket. "So, in a perfect world, what does success today look like?"

He leaned on the fence next to her. "Well, I want to go into business for myself, and I need a ship."

"What kinds of runs? Cargo, spy missions for police or military, transporting people? What?"

"That might depend on the crew I recruit." He shrugged. "I haven't thought that far ahead."

"Well, this all affects the kind of ship we look for." She opened the auction page on her tablet. "What size crew do you want?"

"Four, maybe five."

"Good choice. When you get over six, you get extra paperwork for the government." She shuddered. "Next question: do you want pretty, fast, or pretty fast?"

He stared up at the clouds for a moment. "I don't need a race machine, but I don't want a rust bucket."

"Fair enough. Hyperspace-capable or solar system only?"

"Many of the jobs I see on the boards need hyperspace-ready."

"Atmosphere-capable or space only?

"Atmosphere."

Janice grinned. "Good choice. Otherwise, you have to pay local couriers if the delivery or pick-up is planet-side." She held the tablet closer to him. "All right, let's narrow the field. We only have a couple hours until the auction starts."

Her screen showed many of the ships in thumbnail images. Some of them already had big red Xs drawn on them.

"What's wrong with those?" He pointed to one of the marked-out ones.

"Major structural damage, missing key systems, starting bid high enough you could get a new one, so why bother with someone else's junk heap. Stuff like that."

Even with her deletions, there were still some fifteen ships on the list.

"How many do you think we can check out?" he asked.

"Three or four if we're thorough. All fifteen if we hustle." She filtered the list first by crew size then by atmospheric capability.

That left four for them to look at.

Derek pointed at the third one. "Looks like a bird."

Janice smiled, her eyes sparkling. "Ooo. The fun you could have with that paint job."

She switched her tablet to 3D mode and tapped the third image. The current body was red in front, mutating to orange and white in the back. Black scorch marks scarred the surface.

Derek traced one of the lines. "It's been in combat."

"Yes, it has." Janice called up the description. "But she survived. That counts for something. Well, we have a Class Five scout, two light cargo ships, and a gunship to check out." She looked toward the gate then hopped down from the fence. "I think we can get through without risking a stampede now."

Derek followed her to the tail end of the mob trying to get in. A kid at the door gave him a map of the hangar showing where all the different auction lots were. Comparing the lot numbers to Janice's list, Derek marked the ones they wanted and led the way through the hangar to the nearest one, the gunship.

The crowd gathered around the ship looked more street gang than businessman. A man in a leather jacket, jeans, and a white shirt stood at the bottom of a two-man hydraulic lift. "—has a Quasar III reactor and an Aphelion engine," he was saying.

"Wow." Janice drew a deep breath. "And how much space does that leave for crew and cargo?"

"This ain't no smuggler ship, sister." The spokesman smirked.

A wave of snickers rolled through the crowd.

Janice propped her hands on her hips. "Hey! I prefer the term 'creative cargo hauler'."

Louder laughter erupted from the group.

Janice tapped his arm. "This one's a bust."

He followed her away. "What's the problem with that engine?"

"Nothing. Great combo, if you're powering a small colony ship. I'm sure it's got power to spare and a glorious weapon system, but a power plant and engine that size on a Class Two gunship? You get a crew of three, maybe, if they're real cozy and everyone takes a shower every day."

"Which means zero cargo space," he concluded.

She nodded quickly. "That or you're tripping over it. So, what's next?"

Derek looked at the map again. "Class Four cargo ship. Requires a crew of five, so it's at the upper limit, but roomy."

Unlike the gunship, the Class Four's hangar bay was empty except for an old guy in coveralls sitting on the loading ramp. The ship itself was pristine and smelled of recent paint. The ovoid shape was blunted at the tail where the engines were, and the wings seemed out of place.

"Howdy, folks. Go on up and check 'er out." The man in coveralls aimed a thumb up the ramp.

"Thanks." Derek let Janice lead the way. "So, wings were a late addition?"

The ramp ended in a huge cargo bay with one corridor leading forward and a ladder leading up.

Janice took the corridor. "Yeah, that was real common about ten years ago. Planetary couriers went on strike, so lots of cargo ships were retrofitted. Not a big deal. If it's been in service for the last ten years, they did it right."

The corridor led past crew quarters and various common areas including a rec room, mess hall, and medical. Each looked utilitarian.

When they reached the bridge, Derek counted four stations. "Command, tactical, pilot, and astrogator."

"Yep. Standard configuration." Janice stopped at a system. "The tactical may need an upgrade depending on how much trouble you get into. All it has is CIWS—um, that's close-in weapon system—and front-firing missiles. Shield rating is a little light but not bad." She toured the other stations. "The rest looks pretty standard. Let's head to the engine room."

On the way back to the cargo hold, they paused to check out crew quarters. The rooms were hardly bigger than the bed, closet, and computer required, and each pair of rooms shared a bathroom. Functional, as long as no one was claustrophobic. The mess hall was a couple decades behind modern equipment, but it was clean. Half-expecting twenty-year-old medical gear, Derek stepped into the infirmary. He was no specialist, but everything looked recent.

Back in the cargo bay, Derek climbed the ladder first. Years ago, Dad had drilled it through his head that he should never follow a lady up a ladder. Sure, Janice was wearing pants, but some lessons never went away.

Derek stepped away from the ladder and offered Janice a hand, but she kept her eyes on the rungs and never noticed.

The engine room had all the charm of a blank wall, but the reactor readout showed nominal, and Janice pulled up the service log on the computer.

She scrolled through entries. "Not exactly on time with basic maintenance, but not bad, really. I think you may have a winner. It needs an interior decorator in the worst way, but the bones are good. Cosmetics are easy. Let's go check out the other two."

He followed her to the next one, the Class Five scout with the bird-like form. Repainting this to some kind of exotic bird would be fun.

A man built like a bar bouncer and dressed in a suit and a snarl descended the ship's boarding ramp. He crossed his arms over his chest. "Move along. This ain't the ship for you."

"Why not?" Derek asked.

"Mister, you deaf or just lookin' for a hospital." He slid his jacket aside to reveal a pistol.

Derek glanced at Janice. If she'd been a guy, he might have made a bigger stink with the punk, but if he started something, what would happen to her?

Derek glared at the punk then ushered Janice away. "We'll skip that one."

"Good plan."

"What's the last on our list?" He glanced back to make sure the guy in the suit stayed put.

She checked the map. "Class Three cargo ship." She pointed to the next bay. "Right there."

This one had sleek lines, like a sideways teardrop with wings. Several people outside it oohed and aahed, checking over every inch of the ship.

"Yes, very pretty, but does it have it where it counts?" Janice waved for him to follow her up the ramp.

Inside, a low thrum rattled the ship every few seconds.

Derek scowled. "What's that?"

"A sound you don't want your reactor to make." She headed starboard into the engine room. Here, the thrum was joined by a barely audible whistle.

"How high do they have that thing cranked?" She ran over to the control panel on the wall. "Seventy-nine percent? It makes that noise at seventy-nine percent? Looking for a meltdown, are we?"

Derek checked the reactor access port and called up the specs on a small screen set into the wall. "Fusiks Two-Fifty?"

"Fusiks—" She grabbed his arm and pulled him toward the door. "Out! Out, out, out, out, out!"

He stumbled the first few steps then got his feet under him "That bad?"

"Not if you don't mind going bald, developing cancer, wearing a radiation monitor, or glowing in the dark." She didn't stop until they were well away from the ship. "Fusiks Two hundred series is the reactor equivalent of Hoverworld Romp."

Derek winced. The early version of the hovercar with a combustion engine had tended to catch fire at inopportune moments.

"They leak radiation when pushed over their limits," Janice continued.

"And they're still in use?" Derek asked.

"Well, the Two-fifty was supposed to fix that problem, but—," she twirled her ponytail around her fingers, "I like my hair too much to find out. If they were running that thing at seventy-nine percent dead standstill and it sounded like that, what do you have to crank it to for flying?"

Derek ran his fingers through his hair. "And replacing the reactor is cost prohibitive."

"Even if you can find one that'll fit in the hole of a Fusik." She leaned toward him and whispered conspiratorially. "And that's a big 'if.'"

"So, that leaves the other cargo hauler, the Class Four in need of a decorator."

Janice nodded. "Unless Mr. Universe is finished with guard duty."

He checked his watch. "We've got a little time left. Let's check."

As they wove their way back to the right bay, Derek peered through the crowd. The punk bouncer grabbed a guy by the shoulder and gave him a shove.

He frowned. "Nope. Okay, well, on to the auction hall."

At the door, an usher handed people a brochure. "Have a seat. We'll start in thirty minutes. Have a seat."

Derek studied the guy as they approached. *Why do I know you?*

When he reached the usher, the man pulled a slip of paper out of a pocket and slid it into the brochure. "Have a seat. We'll—"

"—Be starting in thirty minutes," Janice recited in a butchered attempt at the man's tone. "Thanks. We heard."

As Derek moved away from the door, he fished out the inserted paper and unfolded it. "*I need to speak with you. Alone. Front right corner. Mom.*"

His guts sank. Now he knew why the usher looked familiar. He was one of Mom's agents. While he hadn't seen Mom since Christmas dinner, this would be work-related, and he'd deliberately stayed out of his mother's line of work.

"Great," he muttered.

"Problem?" Janice asked.

"Don't know yet. Find a spot. I'll join you in a minute!" Derek jogged off to the front and hooked a right.

Mom, with neon pink hair and a mini skirt, sat in the furthest seat.

Derek flopped into the chair next to her. "Business or pleasure?"

"Would I be dressed like this for fun?" She looked down at her skirt.

"Right. So, what's the caper?"

"Busting a thief. I need your help."

"I suppose we can skip all the usual arguments about how I don't work for the department." Derek sighed. "So, what do you need?"

"Lot Twenty-seven." She showed him a copy of the map. "That's the bird-shaped Class Five you tried to look at. We're sure there are stolen artifacts stashed onboard. I need you to buy it and give us permission to search it before you take possession. Keeps you out of trouble, and we get our proof."

"And I get a ship I know nothing about." He crossed his right ankle over his left knee. "They're not all winners here, y' know."

Mom handed him a data chip. "The specs. Show them to your engineer friend. I can personally vouch for its defensive ability."

"And if the bid exceeds my available resources?" Derek asked.

"I'll cover the excess."

Derek ran his fingers through his hair. "All right. If Janice approves the specs, I'm in, but you do actually have agents for this sort of thing."

"Legal issues that way. As a private citizen, you have leeway my agents don't. Thanks, Derek."

He nodded and stood, scanning the crowd for Janice's green jacket. He found her and headed over.

"That looked tense," Janice remarked.

He handed her the chip as he sat. "Yeah. Stats on the Class Five scout we were interested in. Whaddya think?"

She plugged the chip into the bottom of her tablet and called up the data. He looked over her arm as she scrolled through it too fast for him to make sense of. "Well, if your source is good, this thing is not bad. Power plant is a bit light, and engine could use tweaking, but it's all very doable."

Almost wish you'd said it was a hunk of junk. "Okay, that's the one I'm getting."

She shrugged and gave him back the chip. "Wanna fill me in?"

"Can't. Not here, but how about over beer and pizza tonight?"

"You make that a root beer and you're on." She edged closer and spoke behind her hand. "Matter of national security?"

He smirked. "Something like that."

She nodded once. "Here's hoping it stays under budget."

"Seriously."

They chatted about harmless stuff until the lights dimmed. The auctioneer stepped up to the podium and waited until all conversation died off. He projected the first lot and started taking bids. Derek left the bid button on the arm of his chair alone until the gunship came up. He put in a couple low bids but ducked out of the bidding war as soon as the number of bidders shown on the projection dropped to three. He let them battle it out to the end.

When the Class Four cargo hauler came up, he repeated his gambit.

You'd better be right about that scout ship, Mom, or you're going to hear about it.

He stayed in that bidding war longer than he probably should have, and when someone else got it, he frowned and heaved a sigh.

Janice leaned closer. "If it lives up to its specs, the Class Five scout's a better ship. It's got better defensive and offensive ability, and it's faster."

He nodded. "Thanks."

"No problem, but I'm dying to find out what's going on."

He smiled. "Be thinking about your favorite pizza joint."

"Ooo." She stared up at the corner of the room. "Tough call. There are so many!"

When Lot Twenty-Seven came up, the projected image changed to the red, bird-shaped scout. The opening bid of fifty-thousand showed, and immediately a new bid of seventy-five thousand came up. Derek tapped in a bid for one more thousand, the minimum increment. The next bid was eighty thousand, so Derek bid eighty-one thousand. And so it continued. The other guy bid eighty-four thousand, and Derek bid an extra one.

When the bid reached ninety-five thousand, someone in the front center yelled, "Ah, quit playin' around!"

"Quiet in the gallery, please," the auctioneer said in an emotionless tone. "Current bid is ninety-six thousand."

Janice covered her mouth with her hand. "How far can you go?"

"I have a backer, so, however far I need to," Derek whispered.

"Go, man, go!"

The bid crept upward, past what Derek's loan would cover even if he used all his inheritance for the downpayment. Finally at one hundred fifty-one thousand, the other bidder dropped out.

"When I find out—" a guy from the back started.

"Quiet in the gallery," the auctioneer interrupted.

Derek's implant com beeped.

"Thank you, Derek. I already transferred the excess to your account." Mom's voice was totally deadpan.

"Any advice on how to avoid getting my head bashed in by your target's allies?"

"Security forces are already moving in. Sit tight until the end of the auction. Everything will be wrapped up by then."

"You got it, Mom."

"I love you, Son." Only the barest hint of emotion entered her voice.

"Love you, too."

Janice whispered, "Mom? Now, really, what's the story?"

"How about pizza, root beer, test flight, and a story?" Derek asked.

"You're on!" She started to stand.

Derek caught her arm. "Give security a chance to collect the goon squad."

She did a double-take. "Oh, I can't wait to hear this one."

Derek smiled.

Freak Occurrence

Derek ushered Janice and Vincent up the ramp while Peter took cover underneath it and watched for the wetware-enabled thugs chasing them.

"Did we lose them somewhere?" Derek asked.

Peter snorted. "Not likely. Be ready for company when we take off."

"Come on. The sooner we're in friendly territory, the better I'll like it." Derek started up for the ship and waved for Peter to follow him.

Peter backed up the ramp and triggered the hydraulics to button up the hatches. The engines whined through emergency startup as Derek ran down the central corridor to the bridge. Vincent was already there, powering up systems. Derek paused at astrogation. With a few key taps, he called up the astrogation presets and sent the outbound jump coordinates to the pilot's station before he slid into that seat. Peter came in and took his usual spot at tactical. Derek engaged the antigravs and lifted off, exiting the hangar and gaining some distance from the Martian colony's surface before eyeballing a course to dodge the lopsided moon in front of him.

The loud whine preceded a flare of light that shot past *Gyrfalcon's* starboard wing. The ship pitched toward port, and Derek leveled her out before standing her on her tail.

"What was that?" Janice demanded over the implant comm.

Derek leveled the ship out again and headed for space. "They've got a gunnery station. Janice, put all shields aft."

"Recharge rate on that will be about ten seconds, so don't keep a straight path." Peter tapped his screen. "And, we've got mechs coming for us."

"*Samurai* or *Dervishes?*" Derek asked.

"You wish." Peter shook his head. "The computer is labeling them 'experimental.' No telling what we're up against."

Vincent chuckled. "If they're as badly cobbled together as the last bunch, we can hope they'll fall apart."

"Yeah, maybe." Peter opened up the turret hatch behind him. "Doc, you up to manning the starboard turret?"

"We never got to those lessons. Is it point and shoot?" Vincent glanced starboard then back at Peter.

"Not exactly. Skip it until we can get that lesson in." Peter climbed into the port turret.

Derek set the targeting system to the nearest experimental mech. "Missile range in ten seconds."

Another blast from the station gun zipped just over *Gyrfalcon's* head. Turbulence from the thin Martian atmosphere swayed the ship.

"How long until we hit the coordinates?" Janice asked over the comm.

Derek checked the preset and frowned. "A while. A couple, three minutes. We have to get out of Mars' gravity well."

"Faster is better. Can't get a clear reading on those mechs. No telling what's coming at us." Switches snapped at Janice's end of the connection.

"Keep our shields aft at full until they overtake us."

"Okay. That'll be in about a minute unless Pete can discourage them."

Derek winced. "Course is set already."

The missile warning on the console lit bright red and an electronic tone sounded. Derek turned off the alert and checked the radar. Heat seekers. No problem. Once they got close enough, a couple flares would take care of that. He set the targeting system to the missile and watched the range counter dwindle. At five hundred meters, he tapped the flare release twice. The radar showed the missile taking the bait.

A moment later, *Gyrfalcon* bucked as a missile shockwave hit the tail.

The tracking computer defaulted to the next nearest unfriendly ship, a huge shape marked "experimental mech."

Gyrfalcon lurched hard and sparks flew from the astrogation station. The blue haze of the shields winked out.

"Shields are down!" Janice yelled. Her voice echoed faintly from engineering and louder over the implant comm. "Astrogation computer went with 'em. Please tell me your course is set already."

A pink glitter filled the screen. *Gyrfalcon* jolted, and the engine whine spun up while speed wound down. Derek pushed the throttle to full. The deck plates rattled, but their speed continued to drop. *Gyrfalcon* throttled down without Derek's input.

"You won't be able to break free of the tractor beam that way. That only happens in old movies," Janice said.

"Suggestions?" Derek asked.

"Turn into it and shove a missile down their throat?" she suggested.

"Might work, actually," Peter chimed in.

Derek yawed the ship one hundred eighty degrees. Sudden acceleration shoved him into his seat before the inertial dampening system took over.

He locked the targeting system on the mech with the tractor beam as *Gyrfalcon* accelerated, crossing its usual maximum speed by half as the engine and tractor beam cooperated. The missile fired with a whoosh.

"Missile away," Peter announced.

The missile sped toward the target. The pink haze vanished. Derek switched targets to the station itself and fired another missile as the opposition scattered. The repetitive thud of the rail gun echoed through the ship. Derek strained to pull the ship around to a new course. The inertial dampeners whined in protest until he had *Gyrfalcon* back on its outbound course, still going a third faster than their usual atmospheric maximum. The experimental mechs reorganized and came after them again.

Derek checked the countdown timer to the outbound jump point. "Here they come."

Hazy blue shields flickered back on.

"Persistent, aren't they? They act like we deleted the classified information they stole." Janice snickered.

"Funny that," Peter's voice echoed weirdly from the turret and the implant comm.

Derek checked the radar. "Looks like we're outracing the rest of them. We hit our coordinates in ten seconds."

"Well, we can thank that guy with the tractor beam. Turning into it gave us the advantage."

When the astrogation readout lit up, Derek engaged the hyperdrive. Space turned red for the outgoing portal then gray for hyperspace.

Sighing in relief, he sank back into his chair.

Terms of Service

The shuttle landed on the space station with a thud that resurrected memories of the crash Sora had barely survived as a child. Eyes artificially widened, Sora paid the pilot and led Pashan out to the hangar. He kept his pace slow for her little legs and joined the end of the security line. He would have rather had the forthcoming meeting without her in tow, but his time to teach her mental control had come. Pashan was still learning English, so he could talk to Kirsten and Pete in a language she didn't fully comprehend. That was good enough.

The hangar was a huge, box-like structure decorated with safety and instruction signs in English and Aolanian. He'd read each one in both languages twelve times before they reached the halfway point in the line.

A man in a dark gray suit with maroon pinstripes rushed past them and squeezed into line ahead.

Pashan's eyes narrowed, and she spoke Aolanian. "Daddy! Why does he get to squash us out of line like that?"

He squeezed her hand. His paler yellow scales had faint striping that looked weird compared to her darker yellow. "He has poor manners, and if we try to educate him, we probably fail. Such a conversation delays us, and we are late to meet with our friends."

By the time the man reached the security personnel, he had checked his watch five times, looked at the clock on the wall three times, and straightened his black-and-red tie at least six times.

As he arrived at the security scanner, he fumbled with his ID and dropped it.

Pashan rushed forward, scooped up the ID, and held it up to him. "Here you are, rude human who has no manners."

"Thanks, kid." The man spoke English and managed a smile as he took the ID.

Sora squinted at Pashan. "Do not match his rudeness with your own."

"He does not even know what I say." Pashan glanced at the man. "He only knows that I give him back what he drops."

"You assume he does not know what you say. Some humans do speak Aolanian." He narrowed his eyes further. "Can you tell which by looking?"

Pashan's gaze wandered to the rafters. "No, Daddy."

The scanner flashed green, and the man hurried through.

Sora swallowed hard as he approached the security console with its scanner port and screen.

After a soft chime, a hyper-polite female voice came on. "Please hold your ID card in front of the scanner." The instructions repeated in Aolanian.

Sora pulled out his ID and followed the directions. A red light passed over the card.

"Thank you." The voice spoke Aolanian only now. "Please select the reason and duration of your visit from the list. If your reason and duration are not available, select 'Other' and a security agent will be with you shortly."

Probably not. They are human, so they are tall.

The screen showed two columns. The left gave times ranging from less than an hour to over a year. Sora selected four hours or fewer. If they stayed any longer than that, Pirien would have his scales for missing dinner. The right column gave a list of reasons for the trip. He tapped on the one marked, "I visit a friend."

"Thank you. Enjoy your stay," the system said.

The green light turned on, and Sora helped Pashan present her ID card. Once she was allowed through, he guided them down the winding corridors. As they neared Kirsten's quarters, his stomach went into a flat spin and his hands shook.

He took a deep breath and blew it out. The last time he'd felt like this, he'd been trying to glue together the courage to ask Pirien's family if they would consent to him being her husband. He could only hope this meeting turned out as well.

One hundred twelve point six two meters from the checkpoint, marking the beginning of the military sector, Sora reached Kirsten's door and stopped.

"—Any idea what this is about?" Peter's deep baritone came through the door.

"None." Kirsten's voice was harder to make out. "He just asked if—"

Pashan jumped up and triggered the door chime. "They are easier to hear if we are inside."

"Yes, little one." Sora managed to widen his eyes for her sake. *But then I have to be brave, and I do not wish to be.*

The door opened. Kirsten stood in front of them, wearing slacks and a buttoned shirt that was practically her uniform when off duty.

She smiled and stepped back. "Come in. Can I get you anything?"

Sora gestured Pashan in ahead of him. He mentally swapped languages to English for Peter's sake. "No, no, we eat before we come over." *Besides, if I put anything in my stomach right now, I guarantee it does not stay there.*

Pashan raced into Kirsten's apartment and went straight to the cardboard toy box Kirsten had stocked with puzzle books and pencils.

She is happy for hours.

Sora climbed up onto Kirsten's solid blue fabric couch and looked up at the far corner of the room. Meeting the eyes of his friends was too hard. He waited for Kirsten to settle at the other end of the couch and turn to face him more directly.

"You're the one who brought the agenda, Sora." Peter, in his own uniform of tan cargo pants and a green t-shirt, sat in a squashy armchair and sipped a fizzy, purple soda. "What's up?"

Sora wrung his hands a little. "I do not know how to ask."

"Just go for it." Kirsten's smile melted some of the ice lining his intestines.

"How do I get into the military?" His words tumbled out as if in a race.

Kirsten exchanged a look with Peter before she leaned toward him. "Why would you want to do that?"

"Yeah, I can't think of anyone less suited." Peter set his drink on the end table next to him. "You can't join and then refuse to pick up or handle weaponry, y'know. And you sure can't bring squirt with you." He twitched his head toward Pashan.

"To be Christian, I must, yes?" Sora glanced at each of them.

Peter planted his elbows on his knees. "What gave you that idea?"

"Well, I go to the church Kirsten tells me about, the one that meets on the freighter near my home ship." Sora clasped his hands in his lap to hide their shaking. "They are very nice people. When the service starts, they sing 'Onward Christian Soldier' and 'Battle Hymn of the Republic.'"

Peter looked at Kirsten. "I'm terrible at those patriotic songs. 'Battle Hymn?'"

Kirsten twisted his direction. "'Mine eyes have seen the glory—'"

"'—Of the coming of the Lord.' Got it." Peter nodded. "Go on, Sora."

"Yes, yes, and then the preacher speaks of David, a great warrior, and God says David is a man after His own heart."

"And so, you concluded that—" Peter laughed.

Sora narrowed his eyes. *You think this is a humorous thing*? He turned to Kirsten. "I am wrong?"

She chuckled. "You are confused, my very good friend. When a church puts together a worship service, they sometimes align the music and the preacher's message on the same theme."

"Yeah, and David was described as a man after God's own heart, but not because he was a warrior." Peter took another sip of his soda. "Whenever David messed up—and he did a phenomenal job of messing up now and then—he sought God's forgiveness and put his trust in God in some really dark times."

Kirsten braced her elbow on the back of the couch and rested her head on her hand. "In fact, David wanted to build a temple for God, and God sent a prophet to tell David to back away from that plan because he had been a warrior. Instead, his son Solomon built the temple. He was no warrior."

"So, Christians do not have to be in the military?" Sora asked.

Peter shook his head. "Nope. In fact, I didn't become a believer until after I was discharged."

Sora looked up at the ceiling. "My two greatest teachers are in the military, so when the preacher speaks of David, I think this is a requirement."

He sighed. All the tension building up since church that morning drained away.

Big Enough

Pashan followed Mommy, Daddy, and five of her siblings into an arboretum on the human space station where Kirsten lived. The trees and grass in here were pretty, almost like the forest on the bug planet she'd visited with Daddy a few weeks ago for the dumb negotiations but with many fewer bugs here. The air smelled more like dirt than the ship they lived on.

Once inside, Daddy waved Pashan forward. "Use your mind to find Kirsten then lead us to her."

Ugh! Training. Still all the training. Even more so now that she had control of her telepathy without Daddy's help. Maybe she could make a game of it.

"The fastest way?" Pashan's eyes widened.

"Any way you want," Mommy said.

She could make this training fun. Pashan hooted and turned in a circle. She closed her eyes and reached out. Lots of humans were in the arboretum today, but after being close to Kirsten for the whole trip to the bug world and really, really close to her mind during the last battle, Pashan knew the pilot well. She telepathically sorted through all the people and found Kirsten in no time.

Instead of going straight to their very good friend, Pashan ran the other way. She looped big trees, ran up the slide, walked across the balance beam, took a spin on the merry-go-round, and then ran all the way around the park to the picnic table where Kirsten waited for them.

Kirsten still wore bandages on her arm, but the crutch and the sling were gone. When Pashan had quiet moments at night, she could still hear and see the missile attack Kirsten had barely dodged. The explosion had pitched their badly damaged mech into the dirt. Although Pashan had been safe enough in the cargo netting Kirsten had rigged to protect her, Kirsten herself had been badly wounded when the mech's complex control system came apart and slashed her.

Pashan skidded to a stop. "Hello, Abbott Jade Kirsten Pilot!"

"Hello Hadesha Calonti Pashan Targeting Computer." She pressed her hand to her heart and showed everyone her palm.

Pashan looked up at the artificial sky. Her ability to keep up with vector changes without using math had allowed her to replace the damaged targeting system in the banged-up mech. Daddy said she would be a great astrogator someday, but she dearly hoped she would never have to be a targeting computer for a combat pilot again. "Is it okay if I do not wish to be a targeting computer?"

Kirsten smiled. "I hope that our trip to Monta is the only time you have to be one for a pilot."

"I hope you do not have to fly a ship that is broken again." Tears burned in the corners of her eyes as she remembered that battle. *No brain. You do not get to think of that more.* She spun to Mommy. "I go draw now?"

Mommy blinked once. "Go ahead. I call for you when it is time to eat."

Daddy took her tablet out of the bag he carried and gave it to her.

"What do I draw today?" Pashan looked around for a suitable model.

She'd drawn all the trees, flowers, and fern spheres she wanted on the bug world, and people were still very hard. Maybe if she got to see Cerise

Allan Vincent Doctor again, he would show her more about people drawing. For now, she would start with something easier.

The slide sparkled in the distance.

Pashan ran to the playground and crawled up onto one of the benches there for mommies and daddies to watch their kids play.

She turned on her tablet and launched the drawing program. It came up in flat picture mode. Perfect. Just like Cerise Allan Vincent Doctor had shown her, Pashan made quick, short, overlapping lines to create the general shape of the slide. Her first effort came out all wrong. The slide was not that fat or that curvy. She erased the bad lines and tried again.

An orange-speckled yellow hand grabbed the edge of her tablet and yanked it out of her grasp.

Seca darted away singing. "I get your tablet! I get your tablet!"

Pashan jumped down from the bench and chased after him. "Give it back, Seca!"

"Okay. I give it back." He stopped and held the tablet out to her. "Here it is."

As soon as she reached for it, he yanked his hand back and held the tablet over his head. "Pashan is too short!"

"Give it back, Seca!" She jumped for it, but she wasn't as tall as his shoulder, so even with her best jump, she couldn't get as high as his hand stretched over his head.

Seca laughed, holding it lower but still out of her reach.

"*Seca! Enough! Do not antagonize your sister!*" Mommy's thought voice swatted at him like a blunt stick. "*Give her the tablet!*"

He kept dancing around with the device just out of reach.

Tears burned in Pashan's eyes. "You are too mean."

"*Seca! Your mother tells you to stop. She does not mean when you feel like it!*" Daddy's too-loud mental voice was even louder when he was mad. "*You come here right now! I start counting primes. I stop when you arrive. The number I stop on is the number of minutes you have discipline. 2... 3 ... 5 ...*"

Seca tossed the tablet at Pashan and ran. She caught it and jogged back to the bench then crawled up. Her picture now had a big black stripe from the stylus dragging across when Seca pulled it out of her hand. She erased the stripe and repaired the drawing. After finishing the sketch of the slide, she started on the merry-go-round.

"Hey, kid, do you speak English?"

Pashan looked up at a big human girl with yellow hair and blue eyes, "Yes, yes. I do not say it good, but I say it."

"Can you help us?" The girl crouched in front of Pashan.

Pashan sniffled. "I draw now. I do not want to play."

The girl shook her head. "Not playing. My kid brother threw his puppy's ball into a hollow log. The puppy went in after it and won't come out. You look small enough to fit. Mom will kill us both if something happens to that puppy."

"You do not play a mean joke to me?" Pashan squinted and reached out with her mind. The human's was all slippery but full of spiky worry.

"No. Come see if you don't believe me." She stood up and pointed.

Pashan hissed. "I follow."

The human girl led her to a bunch of trees. A pipe decorated like a hollow log had a sign nearby that forbade crawling into the hole. A mangled piece of wire mesh hung useless from one screw at the end of the log. A human boy leaned over with his head near the hole.

"Come on! Get out of there!" He slapped the pipe with his hand.

A small animal whined inside.

Are all brothers mean?

"Jace, quit it! You're just going to scare him worse," the girl scolded.

Jace huffed and stood. "He won't come out!"

"If you yell at me and make very much nose, I do not come out, either, if I am a puppy." Pashan looked inside the dark tube.

Green dots of light shined back at her.

"Nose?" The boy laughed and pointed at Pashan. "You said 'nose' instead of 'noise.'"

Pashan squinted up at the human boy. *Let us hear you speak Aolanian.*

"Leave her alone. She's going to help us." The girl propped one hand on her hip and shook a finger at the boy.

Pashan sat back. "I do not fit with the hole."

"You'd fit. You're little enough," the girl insisted.

"No, no. I do not fit. The hole is twenty-six-point-four centimeters across. I am thirty-point-nine centimeters across."

"You said you'd help." Jace crossed his arms over his chest. "You look little enough to me."

"I do help, but I am big enough so I not do something dumb like get stuck in a hole. I am back soon!" Pashan ran back to the picnic table.

She found Seca staring up at the treetops. He sat at the table with a computer tablet in front of him. He hissed. "Dad, can I be done yet?"

"Are your lists finished?" Daddy asked.

"One. The other is too hard!"

Daddy looked over Seca's shoulder. "You do not finish yet. I give you the choice of discipline. You choose lists. Finish please."

Seca hissed again.

Pashan ran up to Kirsten. "Kirsten!"

"Pashan!" Kirsten mirrored Pashan's tone.

"What do puppies eat?" She crawled up onto the bench next to her and spoke Aolanian now because Kirsten was good at it.

"Whatever food-like thing they get their little teeth on. Why?"

"There is a puppy stuck in a hole after a dumb boy throws a ball inside. They want me to crawl in to get the puppy, but the hole is littler than me, and the puppy is scared, so I think I get the puppy to come out if he can have food."

"Good idea! Much better than getting stuck in a hole." Kirsten went over to a little basket on the table and took out a sandwich in a clear plastic box. She opened it and took out one of the flat, wiggly pieces of meat. "Here you go. You might get him to come out for a piece of ham."

The ham was cold and a little slimy, but Pashan took it and ran back to the pipe.

"Meat?" the girl squinted at her. "Aolanians eat meat?"

"No, no, silly. Humans do." Pashan held the meat as far into the pipe as she could. "I tell my very good friend Kirsten what is wrong, and she give me a part of her lunch. Come on, puppy. I have food for you!"

The green lights of the puppy's eyes walked forward slowly, only a few steps at a time. As the green eyes came closer, Pashan backed away until the puppy ran out and snapped at the meat. Pashan dropped it and jumped back. The little brown ball of fluff gobbled the ham without chewing it.

"You did it!" The girl scooped up the puppy and swung it around in a circle. "Thanks!"

Jace leaned over and looked into the pipe. "What about the ball?"

"Balls do not eat snacks, so I do not think of how to get it." Pashan found a long, skinny stick and handed it to him. "Maybe you get it with this. Maybe next time you do not throw a ball in a pipe that says do not go in here."

"*Pashan, time for lunch!*" Mommy called.

"I must go now!" With a wave, she ran back to the table to enjoy food with Mommy, Daddy, rude Seca, and her very good friend, Kristen.

The Marksman

Peter stood in the waiting room, the last of ten contestants. The cheers and jeers of the audience gave him a good idea of how the current competitor was doing. He'd given up trying to gather hints about the course by listening to the crowd's reaction. He'd even tried timing the distance between the reactions and judging the severity of the response. Nothing matched up consistently, so all he knew was that some people did better than others, and some never made it to the end. What else was new?

A huge roar of applause told Peter the gal currently on the course had completed her run through the gauntlet. He blew out a breath in an effort to quell the tension in his stomach.

The waiting room door opened, and one of the judges leaned in. "Quinian, you're up."

Peter smiled. If Janice were with him, she would've come back with, "That's 'You're up,' not 'Europe.'"

The judge's exhausted expression suggested she wasn't in a mood for one of Janice's goofy jokes, so Peter nodded once and grabbed his rifle, keeping the barrel aimed at the ground as automatically as breathing. Most folks got jittery when they were keyed up, but his hands were rock steady. His guts on the other hand...if they turned any further, he'd puke.

After opening the door at the end of the long hall, the judge gestured Peter through first. She pointed to the broad, white tape tacked to the ground by U-shaped staples. The middle of the tape was scuffed up and twisted from so many competitors launching themselves from that spot.

Peter took his place but stood easy with his gun cradled in a safe direction.

"You have sixty seconds before the starting buzzer." The judge clapped a thin, long-fingered hand on Peter's shoulder. "Time to beat is 4:13, and top accuracy is 72%. Good luck."

"Thanks."

Peter surveyed the course from the slightly raised starting point. The trail wove a wide S-curve through a forested patch and then increasingly dense urban areas. Judging from the course length of some five hundred meters or so—and the number of apparent obstacles—there was no way he would complete the course in 4:13. That was the bigger of the two purses available for this contest, and the 72% accuracy spoke volumes of what the other competitors had gone for. The smaller purse for accuracy was well within reach.

The buzzer blared. Peter swallowed hard and started down the incline to the main level of the course. He kept his pace measured and deliberate, scanning from side to side for the first pop-up target. By the end of that incline, he'd found nothing to challenge.

Uh-huh. Trying to psych me out, lull me into complacency. I'm not that dumb. He smirked.

A vague, thin sparkle drew his attention to a shrub on the left. Peter brought his rifle to his shoulder and slowed his pace by half. A servo whined behind his right shoulder. Peter spun back that way as a silhouette jumped up. Before it had fully settled, Pete took quick aim and fired. The humanoid figure dropped as the beam hit dead center on the white spot marking the target's full-points zone.

By the time the target was down, Pete refocused on the first sparkle that had drawn his eye. It might be nothing more than an intended distraction, but until he confirmed that, it was a potential threat. The lack of crowd reaction hinted toward something more serious. The reflective screen surrounding the course deflected errant shots away from the crowd and into safe directions, and though it blocked his view of the bystanders, he could still hear the crowd noise.

A soft click and the bush sprang open like a double door. A white dot gleamed on the black shape inside. As the target's gun rose, Peter pegged the reticle and the shrub snapped closed. Polite applause from the crowd beyond the one-way barrier told him he'd passed the first, and probably the easiest, of the challenges.

The queasy feeling in his gut faded some as he continued down the course. He reached the first bend in the S when movement caught his eye. He turned as a target slid from behind a tree. The white dot was smack in the middle of the forehead of the gray image of a girl and her dog. Peter dropped his aim. Hitting the wrong target would wreck his score.

No applause. He must have missed something critical.

As he turned, keeping his gun aligned with where he was looking, a servo whine drew him back to the kid and her pooch. A silhouette slipped out from behind the girl. The white dot was centimeters above the kid's ponytail. The gun came up faster this time, but Peter pegged the baddie long before the other weapon locked into place. Both images slid behind the tree. Applause echoed in the auditorium.

He continued down the track through the middle of the S. Shrubs were joined by mockup buildings. Keeping an eye on the doors and windows, Peter walked slowly. Movement in his peripheral vision turned out to be a gray cut-out of an Aolanian child behind a fake hovercar. The target dot was right between the eyes.

Two servos whined from the left. Peter turned to a silhouette appearing in a ground-level window. He aimed and pulled the trigger, but instead of the low power pulse beam he'd expected, a shower of sparks erupted from the gun above the trigger. His hand stung as the sparks zipped past his thumb and index finger. Peter dropped the gun and hit the dirt, the target's beam firing over his head. A collective gasp came from the crowd. Grabbing his rifle, he darted under the cover of a shrub at the edge of the path in front of the mockup house.

He glanced at the burns stinging his right hand. Nothing major. Just an annoyance, but he shook his hand a couple times and flexed his fingers. Peter pulled the multitool from its case on his belt and flipped the screwdriver open. The side panel screws were tight, but he had them off in moments while staying too still to activate any other targets. When the last screw came away, Peter used a flat screwdriver to pry off the panel. No smoke. No flames. Just the smell of ozone and burnt electronics. A short wire had snapped close to a connector. Peter gave the wire a little tug. There was still plenty of give to reconnect it.

Something heavy moved in the brush.

Great. That'd have to be one of the roving targets. Probably a heat seeker.

Peter gathered a handful of dry leaves from the edge of a nearby yard and plopped them on the sidewalk. He flipped the magnifying glass out of his multitool and focused the overhead sun on the leaves. Within moments, there was smoke followed by fire. He fed a few more leaves into the flames then added some twigs before he ran up the path back the way he'd come. The crowd booed. He rolled his eyes and ducked behind one of the targets he'd already disabled. His stomach turned as he loosened the connector then stripped a centimeter of insulation off the end of the wire. Crunching gravel warned him of the approaching target.

Well, that didn't last long.

Pete resisted the urge to look up and stayed focused on reconnecting the trigger. His screwdriver slipped, scraping a cut along his other hand. He twitched but lined up the screwdriver again. The leaves crunched, only a few steps away now, urging him to finish.

He checked the connector, dropped the multitool, and brought the gun up.

The roving target had a vaguely humanoid form. Red eyes on the ovoid head shined at him. The droid brought its gun to bear. Peter snapped up and took quick aim at the dot on its chest before he squeezed the trigger. The gun whined then fired a pulse that struck true. The droid dropped flat.

Peter folded up his multitool and put it away as he sighed in relief. Somewhere along the way, he'd lost the cover plate for the panel he'd removed. The gun would do fine for the last few shots without it as long as he kept water and excess dust out of the way.

When Peter stepped back onto the path, the crowd cheered. He waved at the invisible audience and ran down the trail to the last place he'd been. The little fire he'd set had burned itself out, leaving scorched cement. The first-floor target still lingered.

It turned to get a bead on him. Peter pegged the white dot easily then continued. The applause from the crowd sounded polite at best. Sure, that hit wasn't as exciting as the last.

As he neared the second bend in the S-shaped path, machine servos whirred from two directions. He turned toward one, stepped back, and dropped into a crouch. A purple bolt flew over his shoulder and hit the building façade in front of him. Peter flinched and found the white circle on the first target. He took rough aim and fired. Before he knew if his shot landed, he whirled and looked into the barrel of the other target's gun. Peter ducked the next bolt then popped back up and pegged the white circle just a hair left of center. The crowd's applause crescendoed.

Turning back to the first target, he confirmed the result of his hasty shot and frowned. He'd hit the white spot, but only on the outside edge. That counted, but it'd cost him some accuracy points. He wrinkled his nose and checked the repair on his gun. The screw was still pinching the wire in the connection like it should. If it could hold for a handful more shots, it could then fall apart all it wanted.

Peter rounded the last curve. The exit was directly ahead, through fifty meters of manufactured building façades. He could sprint it in seconds if he were stupid. Instead, he crept along, staying nearer to the structures on his left. Wind blew leaves across the street, but the lack of bird and bug noises ratcheted up the churning in his gut. He strained to hear the little motors of his targets drawing down on him or the snap of one popping up.

Halfway to the exit and still nothing.

Even the crowd noise had gone silent. Had he somehow disqualified himself and disabled the rest of the course? Disqualification was supposed to be announced with a buzzer. There hadn't been one, had there? Had he been too focused on his task to notice it?

Oh, quit being paranoid. If I'd done something that dumb, I'd've known about it by now.

Peter neared the end of the course. At ten meters to the exit, a soft whirring noise drew his attention to the edge of the last building. A robotic arm took aim at him, but the rest of the target stayed behind the corner. Shooting anything but the white circle would cost him accuracy points. He darted across the street in hopes that he could see enough to shoot the circle.

He'd no sooner settled than the whirring of another small motor heralded a second droid setting up opposite the first. He ran along the wall until he was too near the second one for it to aim. The first tracked him still and fired shots that struck the wall behind him. When he reached the corner, Peter pinned the second target's arm against the wall with his shoulder and turned, firing point blank into the white dot on its chest.

As it crumpled, he spun and dropped to his knee. A bolt flew over his shoulder. Peter took quick aim at the white dot on the remaining droid and fired. The target toppled.

The crowd erupted into applause. Peter stayed still, listening for the next threat. Only a few steps separated him from the exit. The buildings stopped. Not even a scraggly patch of grass grew near the path. That wouldn't rule out a pop-up target.

The crowd noise died down again. He moved along the building and listened. Nothing. He pushed off from the wall and jogged the last few meters then stepped through the exit and was greeted by a cheering crowd. A digital scoreboard showed his time at 12:47, which was abysmal compared to the rest of the field, but his accuracy score glowed 93%, good enough to secure the purse by some 20%.

Peter punched the air.

The Model

Vincent sat at a table at an outdoor cafe where he had an excellent view of a collection of brilliantly colored hibiscus plants. The stunning blooms were the size of a dinner plate in shades of red, purple, yellow, variegated, and even a fantastic blend of blue. He didn't typically do florals, but how could he pass these up?

The touchscreen menu slid up from the middle of the table. He scanned through the options. Coffee, his usual drink of choice, had less flavor than hot water here. He went with his second choice. Hot Irish breakfast tea with a bit of milk and sugar. As for lunch, a Cobb salad would do fine. Once he had tapped his order in, the menu retracted into the table. Vincent turned his chair toward the row of flowers. He sat with his right ankle on his left knee and propped his drawing tablet on his lap. When he flipped it open, the three-dimensional canvas took shape above the screen. Vincent switched it to two-dimensional mode. He just needed the basic image now. Conversion to 3-D would wait.

Stylus in hand, he quickly sketched in the basic shape of the hedge and the location of the flowers. Then he started on the background. The waiter arrived and set his salad and tea on the table. Vincent thanked the young man and continued.

He'd just finished the basic skeletal structures when a lady in a wide-brimmed blue hat sat at the one table between Vincent and his model. She tossed her keys and purse on the surface as the menu slid up. After jabbing in a few food entries, she huffed and drummed her fingers.

Perhaps he could ask her to sit somewhere else or at least remove her hat, but he wasn't here for a confrontation. She seemed to be in a hurry, so he could work on other parts of the image while she sped through her meal.

Vincent switched his stylus to color mode and started filling in the background with darker colors, extrapolating the part he couldn't see. He sipped his tea, better than this joint's coffee but not by much, and nibbled at his salad while he worked.

The impatient young lady's food arrived, and she gobbled it down while casting glares his way. Vincent put the grouchy woman out of mind. If she was looking for a fight, she could find it somewhere else.

By the time he'd finished the building behind the plants and the darker greens of the hibiscus bushes, the woman finished her meal. She threw her napkin on the table and snatched her keys and purse.

He checked the background he hadn't been able to see and made sure the speculations of color and form were adequate, then he zoomed in on a flower.

The lady strutted over, heels click-clicking on the pavement. "Look, Grampa, it's customary to ask someone before you use them as a model."

Vincent arched an eyebrow. He rose slowly and turned his tablet toward her. "Young lady, I have been an accomplished artist since before you were born. In all that time, I have never known a plant to object. You sat down after I'd started drawing if you must know."

"Oh." Her cheeks reddened. "Sorry. I-I thought—Never mind." She fumbled with her purse and hurried away.

He watched her go then sat and continued shading in his far more pleasant model.

The Bust

Derek blew out a breath as *Gyrfalcon* settled on her landing gear. His hands shook and tension across his forehead threatened to ignite a headache later.

Calm down, already. We've been over the plan a million times, and this isn't that different from the last six of these we've done.

Cloak-and-dagger runs like this one paid well, sure, but they'd give him ulcers someday.

Leaving the engines in standby, he rose and patted the pulse pistol hidden under his loose, wrinkled, Hawaiian shirt. He shouldn't need it, but having his sidearm handy took the edge off the jitters.

Derek followed Peter down *Gyrfalcon's* main central corridor and stopped at the cargo hold long enough to knock on the nearest crate. "We're here."

"Right!" Sergeant Florakis's baritone voice coming from inside evidenced none of the heavy tremor Derek felt.

As Peter keyed the ramp, Derek's implant comm chimed.

"Yeah?"

"I'll keep the engines warm," Janice said.

Derek smirked. "You do that, Chief Engineer."

"Only engineer," she muttered.

Peter turned away from the ramp controls and looked down the corridor toward engineering. "Hey! What am I?"

"A very skilled apprentice?" Derek asked.

Janice laughed. "A model-builder, full scale models."

"Yeah, I guess." Peter slapped the release mechanism, and the ramp lowered.

Derek followed his gunner down into a nondescript hangar. Repair equipment lined two walls. Plastic crates stacked directly ahead had to be the "farm equipment" he was supposed to collect.

"Okay, so where's our contact?" Peter rested his hand on his holstered pulse pistol.

Derek took a few steps out of *Gyrfalcon's* shadow and looked down the long axis of the ship. Strange for the goods to be here without someone to keep an eye on them. Could that be part of the camouflage? Why would a shipment of farm tools need an armed guard? Then again, those tools could be worth a planet.

A buzz came from the crates.

"Good afternoon, Mr. Eaton. Leave the money and pack up the crates on your ship. You may leave when you're ready."

The accented voice was clearly their contact. Derek would recognize that breathy bass anywhere.

His implant comm beeped. "No good," Florakis said to him. "If he's not present to make the exchange, we have no case against him. He could claim that voice was computer generated."

Derek nodded. *Knew that without your help.* "Nothin' doin'. I don't do business with a speaker in a crate."

"You do this time," the contact insisted.

"No, I don't, pal. Face to face or not at all." Derek patted his pocket, not the one the money was in, but the contact wouldn't know that. "I can take this money and go buy another cargo, and then you're just sitting here with your 'farm equipment' lookin' for something to do. You want to do business, show up."

"Don't be stupid, Mr. Eaton. You stand to make more from this run than any five other runs together," the speaker insisted.

"Yeah, and my daddy didn't raise an idiot." Derek ran his fingers through his hair. That tension headache was getting closer. "Face to face or we're done, and don't bother calling me again."

No response came as seconds ticked closer to minutes.

"You've scared him off," Florakis admonished.

Maybe, but if it was no good without the contact present then scaring him off neither gained nor lost anything.

The main hangar door slid open, admitting four guys easily Peter's size. Each held a pulse rifle and swept the business end back and forth through a wide arc, frequently crossing their rifles through the space occupied by the guy next to them.

Peter snickered and covered his mouth with his hand. "Amateurs."

"That is kind of surprising. I thought we were dealing with pros," Derek whispered. "Maybe just an act?"

"Wishful thinking."

The goon on the left pressed his fingers over the red LED on the side of his head. When he pulled his hand away, the light had turned green indicating his implant comm was now active. He spoke too softly to hear.

Seconds later, the door opened again, and a man strutted in. His brilliant green shirt blazed against the austere black of his suit and tie. The angle of his nose and his dark tan complexion suggested Aztec in his genealogy, and his thin physique almost looked sickly.

"Yep, that's our guy," Florakis said through the implant comm. "Remember, he's gotta lay a hand on the money personally."

"So you told us." Peter rolled his eyes. "We have done this once or twice."

"Sorry. Just don't want anything to go wrong. We've been trying to get this guy for a long time."

The contact stepped forward and spread his arms wide. "Satisfied, Mr. Eaton?"

"Much better," Derek replied, nodding. "I like knowing who I'm doing business with."

The contact shoved the nearest guard on the shoulder. "Go get my money."

Derek forced a smile as he fished credit chips from his pocket, leaving one behind. Peter had already predicted this possibility and devised a way to fix the problem. If only it were foolproof.

The goon stopped too close for comfort and held out a hand. Derek handed over the chips, expecting the guy to count them. After a quick once-over, he hefted the coins in his palm and walked back to the contact. Derek slid his hand back into his pocket and gripped the remaining chip tightly enough to press the edge into his palm. Timing mattered, so he made himself breathe easily.

The contact sent three of his goons out ahead of him to check the corridor. The fourth stood next to the door and faced into the hangar.

"Now," Peter whispered.

Derek pulled out the last chip. "Hey, pal!" He tossed it. "Missed one!"

The contact turned and snatched the chip out of the air then continued toward the door.

The door opened and security forces entered while the men who'd been hiding in the crates rushed out of *Gyrfalcon's* cargo hold. Derek reached for his hidden pistol but left it in the holster. The contact was outgunned and surrounded. Turning this into a firefight would be stupid, but he'd met dumber criminals.

The armed goon at the door snapped the gun to his shoulder and caught a stun beam from one of the security officers. His eyes rolled back in his head as he sank to the ground.

As one of the security agents stepped forward with handcuffs, the contact sent an armor-melting glare Derek's way.

Derek smirked and shrugged.

Peter patted Derek's shoulder. "That'll do it."

Casting a final glance at their contact, Derek followed Peter up the ramp.

At last, his tension headache eased.

Origin:
I had an idea for a group of gamers who do problem solving missions for the admins. They deal with an assortment of mishaps ranging from cheat codes to belligerent jerks causing customer service issues.

What started out to be a story about a rescue mission turned into a collection of stories that appear in each of several anthologies. These two were in the *Rise and Rescue* anthologies, which were charity projects to support the recovery efforts after the raging fires in Australia. They're now out of print.

Feeling Swamped

Leif E'tree stood on the top of the guild tower looking out over Tocksiturdle Swamp. The few minutes he took every evening to enjoy the expanse of greenery and the distant waterfall stripped away the stress of his real-world life. Pressure faded with each moment of simply savoring the view. Family drama, gone. Work tension, history. Health concerns, goodbye. Good riddance to all for the next few hours.

The in-game timer buzzed in his ear to remind him that he was here for another purpose.

Leif glanced up and into the left corner of his vision where he'd set the system clock. As if out of thin air, a faint digital readout showed 6:55. Time for some long-distance recon of Tocksiturdle before meeting his group in the main hall.

"Farsight," Leif whispered as he squinted to engage one of the traits granted to elves.

A two-minute countdown next to an eye icon appeared in his peripheral vision above and to the right of his head. All the fine details in the world sharpened like applying the proper filter to a graphic image. The veins on leaves and the texture of the tree bark stood out for him. The stones making up the walkway were so detailed, he could make out individual grains and small cracks.

He located the Tocksiturdle Swamp level warden, a tall, bar bouncer sort of brute whose entire purpose in life was to turn away people who were below level 5 or too ill-equipped to stand much of a chance of surviving the region. He was decked out in spotless plate armor and carried a glowing, two-handed sword capable of bisecting even the most robust opponents in a single swipe.

Behind the warden, the main path wound into the swamp. Leif traced it with his newly enhanced eyesight, scanning five meters on either side. The brush was too dense for him to see much deeper than that.

The massive turtles the swamp was named after were scattered everywhere. The further reaches of the path were practically paved with the beasts, ranging from pug- to elephant-sized.

Over their heads, tiny globes of light called wisps zipped around like technicolor fireflies. They were harmless balls of energy until riled up. His last encounter with them still sent a chill down his spine. Angry bees were friendlier.

The turtles and wisps had other company. Venus flytraps the size of a small car lined the path in the distance. Supposedly harmless frogs parked on lily pads. After surveying as much of the region as he could, Leif traced the path back to the warden in time to see a party of scraggly-looking adventurers entering the swamp. What had they been spending their coins on? Surely not armor and equipment. He'd seen total noobs with better gear.

"Wait just a minute." Leif focused his attention on them.

Identifiers floated over their heads. Yeah, Level 1s, all of them. Two warriors, a tinkerer, and an acrobat. Their names were a mess of alternating upper- and lower-case letters, numbers, and symbols that Leif had neither time nor inclination to figure out. Level 1s in a Level 5 area? They were going to get their butts handed to them.

Leif frowned. "Come on, Warden. You're only supposed to let Level 5 and up into that area."

He blinked twice to disengage Farsight and darted to the stairs as the countdown and eyeball icon vanished. Leif tapped his leg twice and whispered, "Superior balance," to engage another trait. A new two-minute timer appeared next to a stick figure on a line.

He sat sidesaddle on the banister and slid down, tweaking his balance with micro-shifts of his weight. Gravity increased his momentum, and the ground floor charged up at him seconds later.

Moments before smacking the decorations at the end of the banister, Leif pushed off from the rail, flipped once, and landed. He jogged several steps before colliding with the wall. Certainly not gold medalist material, but he was an herbalist, not an acrobat. His team did have an acrobat, a sprite named Gemina Stex, who could've earned perfect marks in last year's Olympics.

Leif high-tailed it to the entrance of Tocksiturdle Swamp.

The warden stepped into the path. The blue title floating over his head marked him as a Level 20 NPC, which would keep most players in Newburgh from doing something stupid, like challenging him to a duel. Close up, he was even more impressive than he'd seemed from the tower. The warden was built like a tank and tall enough to look Leif straight in the face, a feat no human players could manage.

"Entering this area alone is ill-advised." The artificial inflections in his speech gave away that the computer controlled this character. "You would do best to recruit a party at the Adventurers' Guildhall."

"You just allowed a party of Level 1 noobs in there!" Leif leaned aside to catch a glimpse of the other party, but they were too far down the path.

"Level 1 players are not permitted in this area." The warden's perpetually stern look shuddered then glazed over. "You're wrong, pal. There weren't any Level 1 players here. Now go away." Atypical wording and the suddenly nasal voice screamed that something was already amiss with the AI. After another shudder, the stern look returned.

Leif frowned. One of those noobs had cheat codes. His guts still did backflips when he recalled the last time someone had tried that. The freaked-out AI had gone on a Halloween kick that was a long way from the fun costumes and trick-or-treat adventures Leif would have preferred.

"Hey! Leif! You don't wait for us anymore?" The squeaky voice could only be Gemina.

As he turned, Leif's peripheral vision found her hovering at his eye-level. She floated in midair. Her butterfly wings flapped lazily, as if that motion alone could keep a four-foot tall sprite off the ground. Her sapphire blue, leather armor—built for protection, not eye candy—matched the color of her wings.

Behind her, at the edge of the guild's garden, Morgrim Thanyu and Angie Neer were jogging as fast as Morgrim's bulky dwarven physique would allow.

Armor hampered Morgrim further. Since he was the team's only warrior, they'd pooled funds to get Morgrim decked out in previously owned plate. It still sported an appreciable number of bangs and dents even after Angie's latest repairs. He carried his warhammer by the shaft close to the business end.

Next to him, Angie, a tinkerer, looked like she'd blow away in a stiff breeze, but that was an illusion. Her chainmail weighed a ton.

"So, what gives?" Gemina floated midair with her hands on her hips and a squint-eyed glare.

He aimed his thumb over his shoulder. "Bunch of Level 1s got past the warden."

"No way." She shook her head and wagged her finger back and forth. "The warden's whole job is to stop noobs."

"Yeah, well, you ask him."

"Step aside, elf." She rolled her eyes and pushed past him. "Hey, Warden, did you see any noobs pass this way?"

When she got exactly the same response he had, Leif crossed his arms over his chest. "See?"

"Yep. That's weirder than a left-handed, glow-in-the-dark biscuit." She shrugged. "Still, if they want to use cheats, they deserve to become roadkill in there. Y'know?"

Leif thought back to the day Morgrim had rescued him after some twit named Fritz had tried using cheat codes. Sure, the twit had bypassed the leveling system all right, but he'd turned into a psychotic skeleton along the way. "Already forgot what happened the last time some goofball used cheats?"

She squinted and looked past him then frowned. "Yeah, I remember. Glitchy AI wouldn't let anyone log out and then decided we needed to be spooked. Not good. Nope. Not good at all."

He shook his head. "No. So maybe we should go fetch them before they mess up the AI or turn into a grease spot."

Gemina blew out a deep breath. "All right. Let's see what Morgrim and Angie have to say. Morgrim might have to put on his developer hat."

Still waiting for the other half of the party to catch up, Leif glanced at the digital clock and sighed. What was taking them so long? Morgrim's encumbrance due to his physical bulk and armor choices meant he wasn't the quickest thing on two feet, but they should have arrived by now.

Leif used both hands to shield his eyes from the fiercely bright artificial sun. The downside of being an elf was that those extra snazzy senses sometimes got overwhelmed. Morgrim and Angie were talking to a group of players. Two of them were in shirt sleeves. One had leather greaves and vambraces that were a hiccup away from becoming scrap. The other had a dented helmet and a chainmail shirt with holes he could throw a cat through.

Without engaging Farsight, Leif couldn't make out their names and level tags, but the state of their gear declared their status as one step out of character generation. Had they even finished the tutorial yet?

After a few words and some emphatic gesturing, the ragtag party stormed off. Morgrim mimed applying the toe of his boot to a tender area.

Leif gestured for Gemina to follow, and they met the other two halfway.

Morgrim waved his hand in the direction of the departing players. "Get a load of this. Some dope at The Tern Inn is handing out 'secret quests' to Level 1s. Says it's a magic phrase that will give access to Tocksiturdle Swamp to go collect a prize in the middle."

Leif nodded. "Yeah, there's another party in there now. I didn't get here fast enough to stop them. What say we go do our good deed for the day and escort them out?"

"We're gonna have to." Morgrim sighed. "Otherwise the AI is going to get so bugged, it'll blow a fuse that'll make Mt. Vesuvius look like a firecracker. It'll be weeks before we can get the game online again if that happens."

"What about the twerp who's pranking the noobs?" Gemina asked as she led them back toward the warden.

"I'll send a signal flare to the tech on call." Morgrim grumbled and kicked a rock with some gusto. "So much for a nice, normal evening." As they neared the warden, Morgrim pushed past Leif. "Let me by, bud." He drew himself up to his full height, which wasn't quite up to the belt of the warden. "Warden, voice recognition: Morgrim, developer access number '2 for 6 or 1.'"

The warden cocked his head to the left and scowled then straightened again. "Recognize developer code '2 for 6 or 1.' Welcome, Morgrim Thanyu."

"Howdy. How many players in the swamp?"

The warden blurred at the edges for a moment then sneered. "Wouldn't you like to know?"

Leif rolled his eyes. If the nutcase at the inn could get the AI to snark at recognized developers, they could be in for a wild time. Was this a coding problem or an active hacker?

"Cheeky." Angie glared at the warden.

Morgrim growled. "Answer the question, Warden, or I'll blast you down to pixels in the morning."

The warden's upper body convulsed then straightened. "There is one group of four, no, three."

If the AI was still trying to fight the malware, they might have a chance.

"Freeze the monsters in the swamp." Morgrim pointed down the path.

The warden shook his head. "Unable to freeze an active battle."

"Then freeze everything else currently in there." Morgrim spoke through his clenched jaw.

"Done."

"Who's on call?" Morgrim asked.

The warden squinted. "That'd be Sal Imander."

"Send Sal a note to check for trolls at Tern Inn and search Level 1 inventories for cheat codes."

A wave of distortion made the warden look like a fun-house mirror reflection. "What if I don't wanna?"

"You want to be pixels?" Morgrim hissed. "I'm about to clear everything else off my to do list in the morning so I can turn you into coded dust."

The warden frowned. "You're such a grouch."

"More than you know. Now, listen. I'm on a rescue mission, so after my party enters, allow no other entries until I return."

The warden slumped and stuck out his lower lip. "That's no fun."

Morgrim hefted his hammer.

A twitch that encompassed most of the warden's body caused him to step back to keep his balance. "Message received. No one else enters after you."

"Thank you. Once I return, you can reboot and resume normal operation. Signoff developer access '2 for 6 or 1.'" Morgrim waved for everyone to follow. "Look alive. No tellin' what's in there now."

The warden resumed his stoic demeanor.

A dozen steps past the warden, the terrain changed from a fantasy town to a gloomy swamp. The stone-paved walkway quickly degenerated into a muddy path. Although Leif's VR rig didn't give him access to smells, he imagined the odor mutating from the fairly neutral smell of the town to the musty funk he expected for this environment.

In scattered clusters, small points of colored light hung suspended in midair. As he watched, they formed different emojis. One group of wisps outlined a smiley. Another set did a hand pointing at them. Another bunch made a skull.

Leif pointed. "So much for being frozen."

Morgrim rolled his eyes. "As long as they don't mess with us, I don't care."

"All right, so which way from here?" Angie asked.

Gemina fluttered higher. "I see footie-prints!"

"Lead on, sprite." Morgrim pointed with his hammer.

Leif let the pair lead the way while he stayed back with Angie. The monster freeze was obviously not as advertised, and if the AI turned mean, she was not the best fighter in the group. Sure, she was Level 5 like the rest of them, but tinkerers gained terrific crafting skills at the expense of combat ability. Alongside the path, a couple of frogs kept pace with them by hopping over each other. Leif smirked.

"They got pretty far." Angie looked back the way they'd come. "Are you sure they were noobs?"

"I saw their tags." Leif shrugged. "If whoever's passing out codes is going for the extra points on dastardly, he'd have rigged it so they wouldn't get attacked until too far in to escape."

When they came to a fork in the path, Leif expected to see the appropriate piece of silverware sticking out of the ground. After all, the AI seemed to be in goofball mode. Instead, the two frogs pacing them pulled a top hat, cane, and tuxedo coat out of the mud and danced their way into the dense plant life.

At least the struggling AI had a sense of humor this time.

Gemina stopped. "Ah, nuts. No more footie-prints. Want me to scout ahead? Should be safe enough with all the monsters on pause, which is not the same as them being on paws." She snickered.

Morgrim shook his head. "Puns are the lowest form of humor."

"Except when I'm flying above you." She tapped his helmet.

Leif joined Gemina up front. The path to the right looked exactly like the one they'd followed to this point. The squashy ground would keep footprints. To the left, the path was visible only as a narrow space through swamp muck. He called up his skills list then selected "Perception" from the transparent heads-up display. A red neon arrow pointed down the swampy path. That was clear enough.

He smiled and pointed left. "They went this way."

"How do you know?" Gemina propped her hands on her hips.

"He's got it figured." Morgrim pointed down the right path. "If they went this way, there'd be footprints to follow. There aren't, so…"

Leif leaned closer. "Actually, I engaged Perception, and there's a literal arrow pointing that way."

"Subtle!" Gemina chuckled. "I knew there was a reason we kept you around."

They took the left fork.

Wisps gathered along the side of the path and lined up to spell out words. "Got the hacker and codes. Can't reboot until you and the noobs clear. System unstable. Be quick. – Sal."

Morgrim looked up at the heavy foliage overhead. "On it, Sal."

Voices carried on the still air. Morgrim held up a hand to pause the group.

"It's going to knock the tree down."

"Kill it!"

"You kill it."

"You really think that pebble's going to do anything?"

"You got a better idea?"

There were three voices, one female and two males. A loud smack punctuated their conversation periodically.

"That has to be them." Gemina flew a few yards ahead then looked back.

"Yep, so let's move." Morgrim motioned for them to follow then took off in a splashy jog.

Leif was able to speed walk and keep the pace, but the swamp muck threatened to pull his shoes off unless he walked on his toes.

He stumbled to a stop when a conga line of small turtles crossed the path. They stood on their hind legs with their forelegs holding the shell of the turtle in front of them. Leif shared a sidelong look with Angie.

"Beats the horror plotline it chose for us last time," Angie whispered.

"By miles!" Leif chuckled.

The path took a sharp bend and opened into circular patch of solid ground. A padlocked treasure chest as big as a smart car stood in the middle. Beside the chest, a pile of bones topped with a skull sat next to worn-out leather gloves, a junkpile-worthy mace, and a horned helmet.

The eyes of the bone pile's skull glowed yellow and the bones reorganized into a figure. The skeleton donned the helmet and strapped it tight then slid on the gloves, sat cross-legged, and tapped its fingers on its knee.

Leif shuddered. He was four levels higher than the last time he'd encountered a cheat code-generated skeleton, but skeletons still turned his insides wobbly.

At the edge of the clearing, two elves and a dwarf had managed to get up to the lowest limbs of a cypress tree. A toxic turtle bigger than the chest bashed its head into the tree trunk. The bony ridges on the top of its head left indentations in the bark. The dwarf threw a sling stone at the turtle but it bounced off the shell without doing any damage.

The female elf pointed at Morgrim. "Look!"

"About time!" The dwarf paused mid-throw.

Leif looked more closely at the statuses and identifications floating over their heads. The two elves were down to a couple health points apiece, and the dwarf was only slightly better at twice that. None of them were poisoned.

They needed names. As a matter of principle, he refused to sort out the gobbledygook they'd chosen.

He pointed at the female elf. "Thing 1." Then at the male elf. "Thing 2." Last, at the dwarf. "Thing 3."

"Got it." Angie clapped him on the shoulder. "Theodore Geisel would approve."

The skeleton's ID was simpler: Fritz, Level ???

Hoo boy. The skeleton that had wiped out his first party had been named Fritz. That battle had not gone well. Not at all. A chunk of lead settled in his gut.

"Help!" Thing 1 hollered.

The tree cracked with the toxic turtle's next head bash.

Leif looked up at Gemina. She had a knack for strategy that he could only dream about.

"All bets are off for whether turtles play by the rules, so watch yourself." Gemina floated above them. "Normally, these things breathe poison gas, so keep your distance from the bitey end until we know. Morgrim, smack it to next Tuesday with your whammer. Leif see what you can do with your bow. Angie, you got any grenades left, or at least the parts to do your engineer thing?"

Angie pointed to two metal spheres on her utility belt. "A couple, but I'm not keen on a turtle gut shower."

Leif nodded. He liked turtles, but he didn't want to wear one.

Gemina shook her head. "If I can get it under the turtle, the shell will take care of that." She looked at the turtle for a moment. "I think. Maybe hold onto that until we see if Morgrim's whammer does the trick."

Another head bash made the tree crack again.

"Can you talk yourselves to death later?" Thing 2 threw a piece of cypress bark their way. It twisted and spun before falling straight down.

Leif glared at the trio. They'd caused this mess in the first place!

"Watch your mouth, or we'll let you be turtle chow." Morgrim aimed his warhammer at them.

"Yeah!" Gemina pivoted mid-air and jabbed her fingers at the noobs. "You're just lucky we came along."

Leif slipped his bow from his shoulder.

Morgrim glanced back at them. "Let's do this."

He charged at the toxic turtle. The impact of the warhammer against the turtle shell rang through the forest like a bell.

As Leif circled to flank the turtle, Fritz bolted to its feet and darted into his path. "Remember me?" The voice sounded like Fritz had enjoyed a lovely bowl of gravel for breakfast.

Leif tossed his bow aside and drew his staff. "Yeah, yeah I do, but I'm stronger now." He twirled the staff around his hand and struck a pose.

Fritz's eyes turned red, and it charged, rusted mace raised over his head. Leif held his staff at the ready. As soon as Fritz was in range, Leif stepped forward and twisted, bringing the bottom of the staff up and around in an arc that connected with Fritz's descending forearm. Bones from elbow to fingertips flew ten feet then boomeranged back and reattached as good as new.

The mace attack continued, and Leif jumped aside. The head of the mace tugged at the leather sleeve of his armor but missed him.

"Morgrim!" Leif hit Fritz's femur.

The bones separated and reconnected.

"It ain't a normal skeleton. Go for the skull." Morgrim slammed his hammer into the turtle's shell.

Leif hopped backward to dodge another mace swipe. He stepped in and drove the end of the staff between Fritz's eyes. It staggered back as its health bar lost a handful of points.

Time to use the environment. Leif ran past Fritz, delivering another whack to the face. He put the treasure chest behind him. If Fritz charged him again, maybe a good shove into a wooden chest would do some damage.

Fritz waded into range. Leif brought the staff up for another headache-inducing hit. Fritz deflected with the mace, which broke on impact. The head of the mace thudded into the dirt.

Leif pivoted, bringing the other end of the staff around. Fritz ducked and picked up the mace remnant. It hurled the broken mace at him. Leif leaned aside, and the metal ball skimmed his upper arm. He winced and drew a breath through his teeth. Before he could set up for another attack, Fritz charged, helmet first. Leif dove aside, letting Fritz smash into the chest.

"Olé!" Gemina shouted from somewhere above him.

He scrambled back to his feet. Fritz twisted and jerked but couldn't get the horned helmet loose. When it fiddled with the chinstrap, Leif rained blows on the base of Fritz's skull, visible below the bottom of the helmet.

Fritz's health bar dropped with each strike, changing color from yellow to red. Before Leif could deliver the final blow, the helmet shattered like glass, and Fritz staggered back. Leif didn't give it time to get its bearings. He gave it one last crack upside the head. The health bar zeroed out, and Fritz collapsed into a pile of dissociated bones.

Brilliant blue movement drew his attention into the tree canopy. Gemina was looping a rope around Thing 3. Using a creatively engineered double pulley, Thing 3 descended to mud-level while Gemina carried Thing 1.

Leif leaned on his staff, panting, and glanced at Morgrim.

The turtle was down less than a quarter of its health, and Morgrim's armor sported a couple new scratch marks. His health was in somewhat better shape than his armor, but that wouldn't last if his armor failed.

Leif shook his head. "Gotta help him."

"Wait!" Gemina flew in from the opposite side of the clearing. "Got a heal elixir for the Things?"

He fished out a mid-range elixir, one of his last two. "They can split this. Bring back the empty."

"Thanks." She squinted toward Morgrim. "He's not doing as well as I'd hoped."

Leif glanced up. "That's a big turtle. I'll get in there with my staff."

She shook her head. "If his steel-headed whammer isn't getting the job done, your staff'll break before it does any appreciable damage. Think you can hit the less armored parts with arrows?"

Leif studied the turtle. Heavy scales covered its legs and head. That left the neck, a relatively small target.

"If I manage some good hit numbers."

"Try. If that's no good, I'll get Angie's grenade under it." Gemina flew off.

Leif slid his staff into its sheath and retrieved his bow. "Joining the fray, Morgrim."

"Fine, fine, just stay away from the turtle's face, and don't aim toward me." He delivered another resounding blow to the turtle's shell.

As the creature pivoted, Morgrim circled with it, staying directly behind its stubby tail to avoid the beak on the other end.

Leif drew a red-feathered arrow. Those had steel arrowheads, which might have a chance of doing damage. Using the marks on the arm of the bow to help his aim, he lined up for a shot at the narrow gap in the armor between where the main shell ended and the head scales started. With bated breath, Leif released the arrow. It flew true and pierced the turtle's neck.

The toxic turtle roared, a sound that belonged in a dinosaur movie, and rushed toward Leif. Well, as close to a rush as a massive turtle could manage. Morgrim ran up behind it and delivered another hammer blow. The status bar above its head turned yellow.

While Leif nocked another arrow, he darted to the left. There wasn't enough time to aim, and when he let loose, the arrow bounced off the front edge of the shell.

Angie knelt at the edge of the clearing and readied her double-decker crossbow. Her first shot ricocheted and missed Morgrim by inches.

Morgrim ducked. "Hey! Friendly fire ain't friendly!"

Angie winced. "Sorry! Sorry. It's still jumping when I pull the trigger."

The turtle sucked in a breath and exhaled an expanding green cloud of bubbles.

Angie giggled. "Cute."

"Get outta there, Leif!" Morgrim waved.

Holding his breath, Leif ran toward Morgrim. The edge of the cloud overtook him, and his eyes teared and burned. A crossbow bolt whistled past his ear.

"Sorry! I was sure I had that fixed last night," Angie hollered.

A firm, calloused hand caught Leif by the wrist and pulled him.

"You're in clean air." Morgrim released him. "Well, clean as a swamp gets, anyway. Leaving you with Angie."

Leif nodded and expelled the stale air from his lungs then sucked down a few good breaths. His eyes burned, and when he opened them, everything blurred.

Chainmail clattered as Angie wrapped her arm around Leif's shoulders. "Come on. Let's get the gunk out of your eyes."

"I've got water in my bag." Leif patted the bag hanging cross-belted over his shoulder.

"Me, too, but let's get out of the clearing first. You're down a third of your health, so you'll need a healing elixir, too."

"There's only one left."

"One's enough." After several quick steps, she slowed. "Leaving dirt for swamp."

His next step squished in the mud. A few moments later, they stopped.

"Gimme that grenade." Gemina's wings flapped as she flew closer.

A soft click from Angie preceded Gemina's departure.

"Grenade?" Thing 3 asked.

"Yep. Now what did I tell you about shutting up and staying still?" Light pressure from Angie's hand tipped Leif's head down. "Lean forward, Leif."

Cold water washed across one eye then the other, and the burning stopped.

Leif blinked several times, clearing his vision. "Oh, loads better."

"Your status bar isn't showing poison, so I think you just need that heal and you'll be good."

"Thanks."

Before he could get the elixir out of his bag, something splashed nearby. Leif reached for an arrow as Angie prepped her crossbow.

"It's me! It's me! Hold your fire!" Morgrim yelled.

He ran toward them with Gemina trailing behind but gaining fast. A firecracker boom echoed from the clearing.

A blast of hot air whooshed past, carrying glitter and streamers.

Angie snorted. "Better than turtle guts."

Morgrim joined them. "Wasn't a bad idea, but I don't want to do it that way all the time."

"Let's go look in the chest." Thing 2 slipped past Leif and headed toward the clearing.

Gemina shook her head and blocked the way. "Nope. You didn't earn it."

"We are on a quest!" Thing 3 tried—and failed— to match Morgrim's permanent scowl.

"No real quest uses cheat codes, which are a violation of the user agreement." Morgrim jabbed his finger at the noobs.

Angie hid her mouth with her hand. "Which they probably didn't read."

Leif shrugged. Did anybody outside the company's legal department ever read those?

"Move while we talk. Sal can't reset the region 'til we're clear." Morgrim took the lead and stepped over a group of synchronized swimming frogs forming an asterisk with their outstretched legs.

When the muck threatened to pull his shoes off, Leif walked on his toes again.

Gemina fluttered closer to the noobs. "You got the quest from some guy at an inn?"

Thing 1 pulled a paper out of a belt pouch and offered it. "Yeah, this hooded guy named Connar."

"Betcha a root beer float his last name sounds like 'test.'" Angie waggled her eyebrows.

Leif put the two together. *Connar Test? Ah. Yes, Con artist handing out fake quests.* He smirked. "No bet."

Gemina flew ahead and handed the paper to Morgrim. He looked it over then wadded it up. "Doesn't follow the format for a legit code."

"And how would you know?" Thing 2 propped his hands on his hips.

"Because he's one of the programmers." Leif shrugged. "Sorry, kids, but you've been had, so if that skeleton was a pal of yours, he won't respawn at the guildhall. The AI isn't fond of cheats."

Thing 1's eyes grew as big as the dilapidated buckler on her arm. "We didn't know!"

"Ever hear the adage 'If it sounds too good to be true, it probably is?'" Gemina ran her fingers through her hair. "We'll get you out, and then you go quick-like-bunny to the constable. If you're lucky he'll give you chores to do, and you'll be good to go. If not, well, you're Level 1. You're not losing much."

"What about that guy–" Thing 3 snapped his fingers several times. "Um, hooded freak at the inn?"

"Connar," Thing 2 said.

"Yeah, what about him?"

Morgrim's eyes narrowed. "Another developer already gave him the divine boot to the keister. Permanently. Now hustle."

"You're not going to go look in the chest?" Thing 1 asked.

Morgrim glanced back. "Nope. Didn't earn it."

Thing 2 stopped and pointed back toward the clearing. "You killed that turtle."

"Yeah, but we didn't get to that point honestly." Leif grabbed Thing 2 by the shoulders to steer him down the path again. "Morgrim used codes to freeze all but your battle so we could get to you in time."

Thing 1 tensed until she shook. "Wait, wait, wait! You can use codes, but we can't?"

"I'm authorized in special situations. You ain't." Morgrim glowered. "Now keep moving."

Morgrim and Gemina led the way, and Leif stayed back with Angie, keeping the surviving noobs in the middle.

"You still haven't downed that healing elixir," Angie said.

Leif looked at everyone's status bar. He and Morgrim were the only ones showing injury. His own health bar was down by a third. Morgrim, though, was south of half.

He rushed ahead and handed the elixir to Morgrim. "You need this more than I do."

Morgrim flipped the lid off the beaker. "Thanks, elf, but be sure you make one for yourself once we're clear." He chugged the elixir then gave the empty beaker back and belched. "That hit the spot."

Leif put the beaker in his bag and checked Morgrim's status bar. Full and green again. He waited for Angie.

As they backtracked, the scenery shuddered and parts blackened. A high-pitched whistle built up.

"Move it!" Morgrim ran.

After half a minute of backtracking, they returned to solid ground. Half a minute after that, they passed the warden.

Morgrim waited until they were all clear. "Rescue mission complete."

The warden snapped to attention. "Rebooting region. Standby."

The noobs ran off without so much as a farewell.

Gemina planted her hands on her hips and scowled. "Ingrates. They didn't even say goodbye."

Leif shrugged as the swamp winked out of existence and a huge loading bar hovered midair. They didn't do it for the kudos anyway.

Up a Tree

The system teleported Gemina Stex into the main room of the Guildhall. Humans, dwarves, elves, and sprites milled around her. Nametags and health bars over their heads showed who was who and how they were doing health wise. Normally, she didn't mind all the floating monikers, but in a crowd this dense? Visual overload!

The Adventurers' Guildhall was decorated with ample amounts of dark wood and paintings of the game designers and playtesters. Morgrim Thanyu, one of Gemina's teammates, was in a few different pics, some as his current character, and some as his alternate persona, a much higher-level dwarf tinkerer.

Once she'd oriented herself, Gemina wove her way through the crowd. For a brief moment, she looked up and considered taking to her wings, but the low ceilings and tall elves meant she'd still have cramped traveling.

After a few million rounds of "excuse me," she made it into the corridor. She made a quick jog to the room Morgrim reserved for them to gather before they set out on the evening adventure, unless Leif had spotted another problem and took off without them like last time.

When Gemina walked into their room and found the rest of the gang gathered, she glanced to the left of her vision to check the system clock. No, she wasn't late. Barely. She smiled and perched on the "sprite chair," a glorified stool with no back so it wouldn't interfere with her wings. Unlike the hunting cabin-styled main room, this meeting space was done in wrought iron furniture and simple chairs with puffy steel gray cushions. On the walls, silly paintings showed the company's employees posing with their characters. Morgrim posed as his real self—a middle-aged gent in western wear and a cowboy hat—with both of his characters beside him.

"Well, hello, all you fine folks." She nodded toward the main room. "It's crazy out there."

Morgrim snorted. "It's that time. Everyone's off work, and dinner's et by now."

His plate armor sported fewer dents. Even the scratches from yesterday's toxic turtle adventure were gone.

"Whoo, Angie! You gain a level?" Gemina turned toward their human tinkerer.

Angie Neer nodded. "When you used my grenade on that turtle, that pushed me over the limit. I put my points into armory so I can take care of our stuff."

Gemina high-fived her. "Suh-weet!" She turned to Leif, who usually got there early to make elixirs and do a bit of recon with his elf eyesight advantage. "How's Tocksiturdle looking today?"

"Back to normal, or as normal as a swamp with car-sized turtles can get." Leif smirked.

Gemina thought back through last night's adventure when the hacker had bugged the AI so badly that it had turned comedian on them. "No dancing frogs, no wisps mocking us with their emojis, no turtle conga lines?"

"No synchronized swimming frogs. The reboot reestablished situation normal."

"Took some doing with the cleanup today, but it's all good." Morgrim stood. "Well, before everything hit the fan yesterday, we were on our way to rescue a damsel in distress."

Angie popped up. "No time like the present."

As usual, Morgrim led the way, and Leif and Angie followed behind. They'd make a cute couple except that Angie was played by a middle-aged housewife with three kids under ten years old, and Leif was actually a teenage girl. That left poor Morgrim as the only real guy in the group. He didn't seem to mind.

As soon as they were outside, Gemina kicked off the ground and flew over their heads. Walking actually drained her stamina. Sprites were meant to fly.

Now that she had space to move, Gemina pulled a few aerial loops to stretch out. She came to the end of the last one and looked down at the empty street. Where did everyone go?

When she turned back to the way she'd come, the others were gathered in front of a fencepost. Morgrim carried on a conversation with it. The scowl on his usual frowny face meant trouble. The sort of thing that guaranteed to ruin their evening.

Gemina slumped, sighing, as she flew back to the others.

"And there's no one else who can take this?" Morgrim asked the fencepost.

"I'm sorry. I know your group got to field yesterday's mess. I tried everyone else. They're all in other sectors or off-line." The voice coming from the fence post was a woman. "Maybe it'll be a quick fix."

"Yeah, and maybe it'll take us all evening." Morgrim growled and looked at each of them. "What do you say?"

"Let's check it out," Angie said.

Leif nodded. "It's not what we had planned, but it still gives us XP and loot."

Morgrim looked up. "How about you, sprite?"

She wanted to give him a resounding, "No!" since they'd just spent last night sorting out Tocksiturdle's AI glitch, and all the paperwork that went with that, but they'd all known that signing up on a game developer's team meant they might have to help with admin duties. That balanced out the perks: no respawn penalties, sneak peeks at new features and areas, and occasional gifts of gold or equipment.

Gemina shrugged. "I'm with you guys."

Morgrim turned back to the fence post. "All right, Ellie. We're on it."

"Thanks, Morgrim. I've told the warden to admit only you and your group. I'll be keeping my eye on you from here. Just say the word if you need an access node."

"Right." He turned away from the fence post.

"So, what's the hubbub, bub?" Gemina asked.

"Customer service complaint. Some idjit is sniping people on the path through Trierluk Forest." Morgrim jerked his thumb toward the Guildhall tower. "Let's see if you can spot them, Leif. Maybe we can get the drop on the ambush."

"See you up there!" Gemina waved and flew for the tower balcony. The wind blowing through her hair and along her wings was the whipped cream on her coffee.

She intentionally overshot the top of the tower, practiced a few aerial maneuvers, then landed on the balcony rail in a perfect handstand before starting on one of her balance beam routines. These were so much easier as a sprite than as a wingless human, but things she learned in the real world she could do here, after she adjusted for being half the mass of her real-life human self.

As she finished the routine, Leif reached the balcony with Angie not far behind. Morgrim? He'd be a while, unless he'd opted to wait for them downstairs. Climbing all the way up here was taxing for dwarves in plate armor.

Gemina executed a perfect dismount and landed in the air before settling on the tower next to Angie.

"Morgrim will wait for us downstairs," Angie said.

"Figured." Gemina nodded. "By the time he gets all the way up here, Leif will be finished with snooping."

Leif tapped next to his eye to engage his ability, whispering, "Farsight."

Nothing visibly changed as Leif looked along the road that connected Trierluk Forest to Tern Inn and then to Tocksiturdle Swamp.

"Got 'em. There's a team of four in Trierluk hiding in trees. One of each race. Two fighters, an herbalist, and a thief." He gasped. "Three level 7s and an 8."

Angie grimaced. "That's going to be tough."

"Maybe we can just ask them nicely to stop being jerks." Gemina leaned closer and whispered, "You know how convincing Morgrim can be."

Leif snorted. "We'll be fighting them for sure."

"How far in are they?" Angie squinted into the distance, but there was no way she'd see anything this far away.

"You know that massive oak halfway to the castle? They're about fifty yards short of it on the right side of the trail." He winced. "Ow. They just wasted a group of level 2s. They must've gotten in before Ellie locked it down."

Angie clenched her jaw and growled. "Well, let's not give them any more opportunities to snipe at other folks."

Leif blinked a few times to disengage Farsight. "Let's get to it."

"I'll meet you down there." Gemina kicked off from the balcony and did a couple somersaults midair before heading downward.

Naturally, her more direct route had her on the ground well ahead of her team. The fence rail became her next balance beam while she thought about their problem.

Clearly, going straight down the road would just turn them into targets. These knuckleheads weren't likely to hold their fire just because Morgrim was a developer, if they even recognized him from the photos in the Guildhall. Their best bet was to circle around and use the trees for cover. That would take longer, of course, but if her team was going to tackle a group two levels up, they'd need all the advantages they could gather.

She had no real confidence that they'd get through this without a fight. The sort of folks who'd ambush players five levels lower than them weren't usually the reasonable type.

So, they'd need to make sure Leif had restocked his potions after last night. He was usually pretty good about that, but checking never hurt.

After finishing her routine, she perched on a fence post until her team caught up. They started for the forest at twice their usual traveling speed.

"Three level 7s and an 8. What do you suggest?" Morgrim adjusted his grip on his warhammer.

"Seriously? Get your pal Ellie to pull the plug on these morons." Gemina shrugged. "But I'm guessing it's not that easy, or she'd have done it already."

"Yep, as long as they're in Trierluk, she can't oust 'em without confusing the AI. If we can get 'em back into this neutral zone then—" In an abrupt gesture, Morgrim aimed his thumb over his shoulder.

"Yeah. I like those prospects." She rubbed her chin. "You know they won't listen if we ask them to knock it off as nicely as we can."

"No, but we gotta try anyhow. Protocol." Morgrim rolled his eyes.

"So we ask, they tell us to take a long walk on the sun, then what? Repeat the request with more force?" Leif mimed punching someone.

"That, or see if we can get them to play a game of tag." Gemina waggled her eyebrows.

"Right!" Angie nodded. "If Ellie's watching, she could drop the admin hammer on them once we clear the forest."

Morgrim stroked his beard. "That just might do it as long as they don't know that it's the forest protecting them. I like how you think, sprite."

Gemina smiled and drifted back to fly next to Leif. "What you got for elixirs?"

He flipped open his bag as they passed Tern Inn. "I've got five heals and four antitoxins."

"Good." She gave him a thumbs-up. "Then let's loop around behind them and use the trees for sneaking up. Morgrim gives his 'stop being a dork' ultimatum. They laugh and call us names that trip the prude filter, and then we either fight it out or play tag."

A large crowd of low-level players congregated around the entrance of Trierluk Forest. The artists for this region had given the entrance to the forest a beautiful arboretum decked out with dark green vines bearing purple flowers. The flowers hissed at anyone who came close. A warden stood in the way. Like the warden guarding the entrance to Tocksiturdle, this one stood as tall as Leif and was as heavily muscled as Morgrim—and high enough level to discourage anyone who thought about battling past him.

"All right, make a space." Morgrim started pushing past the crowd. "Let us through."

Angie and Leif followed in Morgrim's wake as Gemina zoomed overhead.

Once they were in front of the warden, Morgrim faced the crowd and cleared his throat while flowers hissed their displeasure. "Listen up, folks. It ain't good just hangin' out here. No telling how long it'll take to find and oust the vermin takin' shots at y'all. As soon as we get the problem taken care of, a system announcement will go out. Thank you."

When he turned back to the warden, the huge NPC stepped aside long enough to let their party pass. The rest of the gathered crowd broke into a roar of complaints when the warden blocked the way again.

The forest, for all the dense trees, had a cheery disposition. Flowers grew in vibrant clusters. Butterflies fluttered by. Birds sang sweetly in the trees, and cute bunny rabbits hopped along.

All that beauty hid the threats. Spear grass launched real mini spears, squirrels tossed golf-ball sized acorns, and mushrooms spewed laughing gas. Fun times.

When they were a couple hundred feet down the path, Morgrim guided the group to the right off the beaten path and into the rest of the forest. They hadn't gone twenty feet before the first acorn zoomed in and bounced off Morgrim's metal helmet. A chucking squirrel chattered in a nearby tree.

Morgrim frowned and scooped up the golf ball-sized acorn. "Really?" He flung it sidelong and whapped the squirrel on the head.

It took far more damage from the acorn and fell over dead.

"Whoa! Critical hit on the critter!" Gemina applauded.

"Yep. Not likely to get a real challenge this close to the edge. If we get past the oak tree, then we'll find trouble." Morgrim hefted his massive hammer and turned the group east again, paralleling the road. "Can you get a bead on them, Leif?"

The elf shook his head. "Farsight's on cool down for another minute. Soon as I get it back, I'll snoop again."

"Definitely." Gemina nodded. "It would totally stink if they ambushed our ambush of their ambush."

A telltale swish of spear grass came from the right.

"Down!" Angie warned.

Gemina dove and crouched behind Morgrim. The barrage of spear grass zoomed past, each spear as long as her hand but only as wide as a soda straw.

Morgrim twisted around and rubbed his knuckles on her bare head.

She flinched away. "Hey! Not my fault if you're big enough to hide behind."

"Uh-huh. Some reason you don't think your helmet is a good idea just now?" he teased.

She patted her head with one hand and rolled her eyes. "Forgot all about it." Gemina reached into her bottomless belt pouch and thought about her helmet. It appeared in her hand, and she got it situated. "Better?"

"Better," Angie said.

Gemina turned toward Angie. The tinkerer usually reminded everyone about dumb things like helmets and armor lacings.

"You told me not to nag you anymore." Angie held both hands palm out.

Gemina sighed. "You're right. I did." Her cheeks grew warm. She mimed pinching something small. "Maybe you should nag me just a little?"

Angie nodded. "I'll do that."

"Uh-oh. They've abandoned their place." Leif squinted and slowly turned his head side to side. To their left, a flock of brightly colored birds flushed from the trees and grouched about being disturbed.

Leif turned that way. "There they—Morgrim, look out!" He tackled the dwarf as Gemina launched into the nearest treetop.

An arrow with black fletching thumped into the side of the tree Gemina stood in, making her jump. "Get a tree between you and them."

Angie, Leif, and Morgrim each scrambled to a different tree and crouched.

"Leif, the name of the level 8?" Morgrim asked.

"Ruth Less. Level 8 fighter, female human." Leif slid his bow off his shoulder and nocked an arrow.

"Got it." Morgrim drew a deep breath. "Listen up, Ruth. I'm Morg-"

"I know who you are. I just don't care."

"Yep, that's Ruth talking." Leif sighted along his bow. "I'll lose Farsight in about half a minute."

"Listen up. This ain't the player-versus-player zone." Morgrim put some extra growl into his voice. "You want to fight other players, go do it there."

Ruth laughed. "I don't think so. That's too boring. I'd rather watch all the kiddies try to run. Makes the target practice more fun."

Gemina clenched her fists and stomped her foot. *What a total jerk!*

"Kid, I ain't askin'. I'm tellin'. Clear out right now or get cleared out." Morgrim took one of his hatchets off his utility belt.

"Don't make me laugh. Even your highest levels are below ours." Ruth chuckled. "We won't hardly break a sweat."

"Battle don't always go to the strong or the race to the swift," Morgrim yelled. "Now, give this up and take it to the player versus player zone."

Ruth's response was rendered into goose honks.

Gemina snickered. "Well, the prude filter works. Leif, are they grouped together?"

"I've lost Farsight, but I think I can see them from this angle. They're not camouflaged. So, unless there are orange, purple, turquoise, and blue-gray trees out there, they're in a line."

"Angie, get ready with that grenade." Gemina tapped her chest corresponding to where Angie's bandoleer was.

Angie nodded.

Movement and bright colors drew Gemina's eye. The quartet ran toward them and no longer bothering with concealment. Her guts rumbled a bit, same as they always did in a lopsided fight. Silly, really. First, she couldn't actually get hurt. Second, one of the perks of being on Morgrim's team was that if they died, there were no respawn penalties. Still, her guts got growly every stupid time.

Leif shot an arrow, hitting Nick Yerstuf, an elf, in the leg an inch below the bottom of the ring mail doublet he wore. Nick stumbled and yanked the arrow out just in time to get nailed by another one. If Leif could keep that up, they were golden.

Angie popped up and threw her grenade like a fast-pitch baseball. Ruth caught it. It blew up before she could throw it again. Her health dropped to a quarter.

"Wow! Ground zero!" Gemina smiled.

Nick and Gunnar Killya, a dwarf, both took a third of the damage. The sprite, Kell D'Baddies escaped by flying up. Nick went down and vanished. Ruth and Gunnar quaffed healing elixirs and returned to full strength.

"Ruth's mine." Morgrim threw the last of his hatchets and readied his warhammer. "You two get the dwarf. Gemina?"

"I get the flying chick. Gotcha." Gemina kicked off from the tree a moment before a mini crossbow bolt thumped into the branch. "Hey!" She zipped out of the canopy to find a turquoise-armored sprite with a smirk that begged to be slapped off.

Kell wore a mix of plate and chainmail. She must've put some major points into Strength to still be able to fly. Acrobat against fighter? This wouldn't go well, not with a straight fight anyway, but Gemina had no plans to meet her adversary in battle for long.

Gemina drew her daggers, one in each hand.

After hooking the crossbow to her belt, Kell drew a knobby club from a bottomless bag. "Let's see what you've got, kid."

Before she could reply with her snappiest one-liner, Kell raised her weapon and charged. Gemina waited and dodged up and over, slicing with both daggers at the last second and scoring a couple hits. She spun midair and looked at the health bar over her opponent's head.

Gemina snorted. *Just gotta do that forty-eight more times.* Still, if she could keep dodging that club, that just might work.

Kell laughed. "That's it?"

"Would you like to know what these blades are coated with?" Gemina held up both daggers.

Absolutely nothing, of course. Playing with Morgrim meant playing squeaky clean. Tranq darts for her blowgun, no problem. Poison-coated blades? Absolutely not. Maybe Kell didn't know that. Psychological warfare could even the odds.

Kell growled and charged again. This time, Gemina dove under the attack. She slashed with both daggers. One skipped off the breastplate, and the other scored a very minor hit under Kell's arm.

Gemina blew a raspberry at the other sprite. "Catch me if you can!" Twirling midair, Gemina wiggled her nose and whispered, "Improved velocity."

She shot off toward the edge of the forest. Kell, of course, had the same trait and two extra levels of points to maybe bolster the skill, but this was the only chance Gemina had to beat a level 7 fighter. Maybe all that armor would slow Kell down some.

Gemina stole a look back at Kell in hot pursuit, club at the ready, and gaining fast. Too fast for all that armor she wore. Her equipment must be giving her some nice bonuses. The end of the forest was coming up, but could Gemina lead Kell over the border in time? More importantly, was Ellie-the-admin paying attention?

Yards short of the forest edge, a hard whack on the back of Gemina's thigh cost her nearly a third of her health and sent her careening toward the trees below. Her heart thudded in her ears as she twisted around and dove through a gap in the canopy to land in a wobbly handstand on a narrow branch. She bent her elbows and pushed off, zooming back through the same spot in the canopy. She spun, looking for turquoise and not seeing it anywhere.

"Now where in the orange, polka-dotted elephant did she go?" Gemina muttered.

A tiny paper with a folded corner, the system notification icon, appeared in the upper left corner of Gemina's vision. She focused on it, and a transparent scroll opened in front of her, floating on air.

System notification: Trierluk Forest has been removed from quarantine. All players can continue quests in that sector. We apologize for any inconvenience.

The scroll faded.

Gemina punched the air. Kell must have crossed the line while looping around to come back. Ellie-the-admin *had* been paying attention.

She made her way back to where she'd left her party. Morgrim was talking to a tree trunk while Leif helped Angie chug an antitoxin elixir.

"—Think they deserve the ban hammer, personally." Morgrim leaned his warhammer on the tree.

"I'll present the case, but I'll need statements from your entire party," Ellie said.

Morgrim glanced over their group. "Once we get everyone healed up, we'll go to Tern Inn and tell our tales."

"I'll have the recorder going, and thank your team for me. Second night in a row they gave up for admin duties."

"Yep. Just recruit someone else tomorrow."

"Let's hope there's no need. Signing off, Ellie Vater."

"Hi, guys, miss me?" Gemina asked.

Angie looked up and winced. "Apparently Kell didn't."

Leif fished a healing elixir out of his bag. "One for you."

Gemina swooped down and grabbed it. She slurped it down one swallow at a time until her health bar was full. She capped the bottle and tossed it back.

A wooden treasure chest wrapped in gold bands appeared in their midst, payment from the admins for taking care of another hassle.

Maybe this wasn't a total waste of a session. Gemina smiled.

Origin:
This is another case of "I can't figure out where to start this thing." When I was drafting *Urushalon 1: Like Herding the Wind*, "Seek and Find" was the first chapter. Then it was the prologue. Then it became the prologue for *Urushalon 2:Into the Open*. No matter where I put it, it didn't seem to fit. I needed the *U1* prologue to provide some history for folks since the setting is a bit peculiar. Although *U2* doesn't have a prologue, "Seek and Find" doesn't relate to the plot directly. It's just a nifty bit of backstory. Finally, I found a place to put it. It takes place long before *U1*.

Seek and Find

Amaya Ulonya perched on a knee-high stool next to the low-slung hammock where her patient rested. She pressed two fingers behind Adri's ear to count her pulse and then lightly rested a hand on her chest to count breaths. A pulse of one hundred and a respiration of twenty per minute were both a little slower than average but reasonable considering the circumstances.

Garbled yelling in a man's voice came through the door. Amaya turned that way and strained to make out the words. Nothing registered. She shrugged. Her staff would either handle the problem or summon her if she was needed.

The visible bruises on Adri's thin, pale face hadn't changed much since midnight, but then the regenerative salve had been applied to the long gash above her sparse left eyebrow, not to superficial bruises. Today's dose would take care of another bad laceration on her arm. Maybe the bruises would get taken care of the day after that.

Amaya had just begun to unwind the bandage on Adri's head when the clinic door slipped open with a wood-on-wood scrape.

"*Kiand*," Talin Elka said.

Three years after first earning the title, Amaya hadn't gotten used to hearing it applied to her.

She looked back over her shoulder at the *kiandara*.

"There's a human couple in the foyer." He came closer and fixed his eyes on his injured partner while addressing Amaya. "They're in a panic about something and talking so quickly I can't understand most of the words. When I asked the man to speak slowly, he just got louder. The woman is so distraught, her words are unclear. There's something about their son and the Marquette police department."

After discarding the used bandage in the orange biohazard container, Amaya gave Adri's head injury a quick inspection. Only a thin, reddish line remained of the wound that had bled freely only a few hours ago. The regenerative salve had performed its duty well.

Amaya relinquished her place to Talin. "Take over for me here. The scalp laceration has healed adequately for now. Change the rest of the bandages and apply the day's dose of regenerative to the cut on her arm. I'll deal with the humans."

Talin sat next to Adri and seemed to deflate as he considered her. "I should have helped her. She's no combat specialist."

Amaya crouched next to him and rested her hand on his shoulder. "You carry no fault in this, Talin. Nothing about this job is safe. You had your time more than occupied with the other two, and if you'd waited for reinforcements, the suspects would have likely escaped. Both of you were out of darts. Adri knew her limitations and chose to step into the fight. She will recover."

He covered her hand with his. "I will, too. Go on. They need you up front."

She squeezed his shoulder then walked away, pausing at the door to glance back. Talin was unwrapping his partner's bandages. He'd be fine.

The door slid closed behind her, and she made her way down the long hallway to the entry.

In the foyer, Amaya found one of her staff comforting a crying human woman slumped on the tan couch while a man paced the length of the room. His khaki shorts, blue flannel shirt, and heavy-soled boots labeled him a hiker, at least for the time being. The woman wore a blue denim dress that came down past her knees and boots that were similar to the man's. Both looked a little disheveled, and the man hadn't shaved but didn't have the degree of growth that suggested skipping the razor was his habit.

"I am Amaya Ulonya Kiand. Can I help in some way?" she asked in English.

The man turned to the counter and slammed both palms on it. "Do you speak English?"

That wasn't obvious from my greeting? "Yes, fluently."

"Finally. We're camping near here." He pointed toward the campgrounds a few miles to the east. "During the night, our son got past us and out of the tent. We can't find him. When we went to the Marquette police, they sent us here. They said you people know the terrain better."

Amaya came closer. "How old is your son?"

"Four." The man held up fingers to match his answer.

"Three," the woman said through her sobs.

The man looked back at her with a scowl. "He'll be four next month, Anna. Let's not mince."

"I'll get my medical kit in case he's gotten into some mischief. Then I want you to take me to your campsite." Amaya spun away from them.

She darted down the hall to the briefing room and picked up the dark gray backpack with her insignia on it. Slinging it over one shoulder, she returned to the entryway and followed the couple out to 1925 Ford Model T Fordor, black like all human vehicles of the type. The first of those had only been released a couple months ago, so whatever this man did for his wages, income was not a problem.

He opened the passenger door for his wife then started the car and closed his own door. Amaya attributed his rudeness to anxiety and let herself in the back seat.

The gears in the transmission complained loudly as the man shifted without quite pushing in the clutch. Amaya considered offering to drive, or even better, taking one of the kiandarai avicopters, but she held her peace. The humans might not be able to find their way from the air, and men of the species didn't have much regard for women of their own race behind the controls of their cars. An

Eshuvani woman? Amaya suspected he wouldn't even dream she knew how to drive.

In spite of the rough start, the man impressed her by driving in a reasonable fashion. Only his white-knuckled grip on the steering wheel spoke of his impatience.

Upon leaving the edge of the Eshuvani enclave, the road went from smooth to a collection of potholes that had only gotten worse with the recent onset of spring. The winter ice had, if nothing else, temporarily leveled out the roads. The car bounced her around the back seat, and more than once, she ducked before her head could collide with the roof.

They soon reached a small campground and wove their way among the sites to a tan canvas tent pitched between a line of trees and a ring of scorched stones where a fire had recently burned.

Amaya stepped out of the car before the man had a chance to demonstrate any lack of consideration. She surveyed the immediate area and suppressed a frown. Whatever clues the boy had left in his departure had been obliterated by the frantic parents. She could hardly blame them when she'd breached all spoken and unspoken protocol the day her own husband and child had died.

Her hand trembled. Amaya forcefully shoved thoughts of her slain family out of her head. She'd been through the Rite of Final Memorial. That had supposedly been the end of all the pain, and she couldn't afford to become an emotional wreck now when these parents needed her.

"When will the others arrive?" the man asked.

Amaya turned toward him. "Others?"

"Yes, others. The ones who will help us with the search." He gestured to the surrounding forest with abrupt arm motions.

"Mr.–"

"Osborn. Charles Osborn."

"Mr. Osborn, *kiandarai* are the Eshuvani police and emergency medical force. I am highly rated in search and rescue protocols, and I'll do everything I can to find your son."

"I want–"

Amaya came up to her full height, almost a hand-length greater than him, to show in body language he would be familiar with that she would not be cowed. "I understand your concerns, but your bursts of temper will not help. There is no one else available, and even if there were, twenty people trampling around the site would only obliterate any trail we might find. Now, I need information. What is your son's name?"

"Edward." Mrs. Osborn sniffled and dabbed her eyes with an embroidered handkerchief. "We call him Eddie."

"When did you see him last?" Amaya asked.

"I put him to bed at sundown." Mrs. Osborn pointed to the tent. "He was so tired I didn't even change him into his pajamas. When we went to bed ourselves a few hours later, I'm sure he was still there."

"But did you actually see him there?" Amaya asked.

"Well, no, he'd made a little tent out of blankets within our bigger tent, and I didn't want to disturb him," she said.

"So, at some point after nightfall, he slipped away. How was he dressed?"

"Denim overalls and a red, striped shirt, long sleeves," Mr. Osborn said.

"And sneakers. He has red sneakers." Mrs. Osborn brushed at her eyes. "And he's a redhead, cut short, of course, and he has freckles."

Amaya built the mental picture as well as she could, leaving the unknown features blurred. "When you were out hiking yesterday, did you see anything that particularly fascinated him?"

Mr. Osborn rolled his eyes. "The usual things that a boy his size would like. Rocks, twigs, the odd rabbit or bird."

"Which way did you go on your walk?" She prayed they'd stayed to known paths, but that wouldn't preclude Eddie wandering off at random.

"We took one of the marked hiking trails." Mrs. Osborn pointed back the way they'd come. "The entrance is a little ways down the road."

Amaya nodded. "I understand. Remain at the camp. Should he wander back this way, it will do no good for him to find the camp abandoned."

She went to the entrance of the tent and crouched. The hard-packed ground had been swept clear of needles, leaves, and debris before the tent had gone up. Nothing useful would be learned there. Standing again, she adjusted her backpack across her shoulders and began walking in an expanding spiral around the tent.

Mr. Osborn growled. "Now what are you doing?"

"Trying to pick up your son's trail." Amaya kept her eyes on the ground.

"I'm coming with you." He reached for a walking stick.

Amaya stopped and met his stare. "No, you will not. You will remain here with your wife. Once I locate his trail, I'll be traveling at a speed that would not be comfortable for you. I will do everything I can to find your son and return him to you."

He turned red in the face. "Now see here!"

"Charles! Enough! Let her work." Mrs. Osborn grabbed her husband's arm with both trembling hands.

Amaya returned to her search.

"I don't trust her," Mr. Osborn whispered.

"She can still hear you," Mrs. Osborn said.

"I don't care."

"She introduced herself as *kiand*. That means she's a police captain and a doctor," Mrs. Osborn said.

"Not exactly." Amaya projected loudly enough to be heard across the distance. "A *kiat* is a doctor. *Kiandai* have a medical rank above nurse but below doctor. There is no equivalent in your culture. The nearest translation is 'practitioner.'"

"She's Eshuvani. They can't be trusted," Mr. Osborn whispered.

"Grandpa always spoke well of the Eshuvani." Mrs. Osborn said at a normal volume. "All that talk about magic and mental powers is nonsense."

"He said that because one of them adopted him."

"Yes, Grandpa was an *urushon*, but that had nothing to do with it," Mrs. Osborn said.

"*Urushalon*." Amaya completed another circuit. "It means, 'beloved.'"

"Yes, exactly. Besides, I've seen their machines. It's no magic," Mrs. Osborn said.

Mr. Osborn sighed. "We'll see."

When Amaya came around for the fourth time, he leaned on the picnic table with his arms crossed in front of his chest. Mrs. Osborn busied herself with unnecessary tidying.

The next round of the spiral took Amaya into the tree line and under the picnic table. The one after that yielded a result. In the damp leaf litter, two full strides inside the tree line, the soft dirt bore the distinct imprint of a child's sneaker bisected by a deeper stripe. The boy's shoes were on but untied.

Using the toe of the shoe as a pointer, she took her bearing and found the next print and smiled. Either Eddie was crossing his feet when he walked, or he had his right shoe on his left foot. A distinct set of rabbit tracks paralleled the shoe prints then suddenly veered off to the right.

Amaya drew a deep breath. "I have his trail. I'll be back as soon as I can. Wait here."

She gradually increased her pace, keeping an eye on the uneven stride marked out in scuffled pine needles, dirt, and the occasional recently snapped twig.

In spite of her efforts to control her speed, her muscles ached and her breathing came heavily. Amaya stopped and sat, careful not to disturb the trail her quarry had left for her.

Without taking her backpack off, Amaya pulled a nutrition bar out of a small side pouch and peeled back the wrapper. While she ate and regained her wind, Amaya considered the path she was following.

The boy's stride was perhaps a foot at the most. Recalling other toddlers she'd seen, she knew approximately how fast Eddie could have traveled. With a departure time as early as sunset, he could have gotten quite a distance. Still, he was only a four-year-old. Even with his better human endurance, he would have likely tired at some point and stopped to rest.

Amaya finished her snack. Tucking the wrapper back into the side pouch of her pack, she resumed following the path the child had made.

She'd gone five minutes more when she had to slow down again. The ground became rockier, and trees became smaller. Brush grew more densely without the high canopy catching the majority of the light. The trail she'd followed no longer kept a predictable line but now wandered more as Eddie had to divert around obstacles. A large expanse of ruddy rock rose out of the dirt and formed a ridge on her right. There'd be no path to follow in that direction.

Amaya climbed to the highest point of the ridge. A dense line of jack pines arced around the rocky terrain to the northeast, east, and south. More of the ruddy rock spread out to the west and due north, and less than a mile in the distance, the top of the decaying wooden scaffold of the old iron mine rose above the trees. Until just a few years ago, if Eddie had wandered off that way, he would've found more of his own people, which might have been a blessing or a curse depending on who he stumbled upon.

Slipping her backpack off, Amaya pulled a pair of infrared glasses out of a side pocket and slipped them on.

Shades of color formed rainbows of heat and cold in all directions. The rocks around her appeared deep blue except where the morning sunlight had warmed them up to greens. Little red blobs in the turquoise tree branches had to be birds or squirrels. The images were much too small to be a child, and she couldn't fathom a four-year-old getting that far up a pine tree. No little footsteps or heat sources big enough to be a toddler were visible.

Amaya put the glasses away and returned to the last known place Eddie had been. She could start another circle search from this point, but she'd seen this reddish rock outcropping from the air. With very few breaks, the stony ground went for miles. She could still be circling when night fell.

Failing all else, she could have Talin meet her out here with an avicopter to continue the search from the air, but with Adri down and Essien and Kiva both exhausted after taking all the calls last night after Adri's injury, Hawk's Nest already ran a short staff today.

Amaya crouched to match her line of sight to a four-year-old human boy. There had to be a way to find him. She'd seen a toddler up close. Amaya simply had to put herself in that mindset, but she dreaded even trying.

With a heavy sigh, Amaya looked at the bracelet on her right wrist. Two years ago, she'd lost both her son and her husband to a sniper, and the pain hurt no less now. Nevertheless, she thanked God for the experience. With a little divine guidance, she might yet spare another mother the same pain that tore at her own heart.

A chill that had nothing to do with the air temperature unsteadied her hands as she thought about the family she used to have, but she shut all those emotions away. A lost and possibly injured child needed to be found. What kind of *kiand* would she be if she didn't do her duty with all her effort? She pushed the bracelet back under her sleeve and got back to the task at hand.

Eddie would have been here at night, so Amaya slid on her sunglasses and turned the small wheels on the temples to make the lenses as dark as she could. The rocky ridge to her right seemed as imposing as a wall, especially when she factored in a tiny human and loose-fitting shoes. Forward and to the left, the way looked more inviting.

Amaya began her search anew, walking in a forward-moving arc from the edge of the rock to the base of the ridge and back again until she found a partial shoe print in a patch of lichen. That gave her a general direction, and she continued searching forward. Several feet away, she found a few flattened, scraggly blades of grass sticking up through a crack in the rock. Connecting the two points, she had her vector again.

Less than fifty strides later, she came to an abrupt stop when the ground suddenly dropped away by most of a yard. The base of the miniature cliff marked the edge of the old iron mine. Miles of rusted tracks and wooden structures just beginning the long, slow process of decay filled a huge expanse. There had been a time when men had been as busy as ants around this area.

Almost a full stride straight below where she stood, Amaya found the blue overalls and red-striped shirt she'd been hunting for.

Eddie lay face down with one arm under him and the other out to the side. One knee was bent slightly, but the other was straight. From where she stood, he didn't appear to be hurt, but she doubted he'd chosen that spot for a nap. The nights still got frigid at this time of year.

Amaya jumped down into the loose dirt and gravel and sank to her ankles. She knelt beside the child and pressed her fingers against his wrist near the base of his thumb and found his pulse beating about seventy per minute. His skin seemed unnaturally cold, but that could have been the combination of her higher metabolism and the exercise she'd been getting on the way out here.

She took a thin, folded blanket from her backpack and draped it over him then fished out a transdermal viewer. The hand-length scanner had an emission port on one face and the viewing lens on the opposite. After tapping the on button, she set it aside to let it go through its start-up cycle. While that got ready, she took out a regenerative gel test kit.

If only this stuff had been around three years ago, then maybe—

Amaya bit her lip and cut the thought short. What good would such speculation do her? Those closest to her were gone, and she had no family nearby. Working with small children always brought her back to the loss of her own joy. Without another child of her own, she wondered if she ever would work past the grief, but every time she considered the prospect of remarriage, an equally strong grief for her lost husband shut out any possibility.

Amaya took a small paper packet from the regenerative test kit. The paper tore easily, and she used the sterile lancet within to prick the child's finger then drew the blood into a capillary tube containing the testing solution. Then she slid the tube under his shirt to keep it warm without overheating it with her higher body temperature.

The transdermal viewer chimed to indicate the end of the start-up cycle. Amaya held the cylinder up to her eye and adjusted the focal length with the wheel on the edge. She scanned along the boy's skeleton to find signs of damage, changing the depth of the viewer to get a peek at the farther side of his ribcage and skull and the arm under his body. The full-color, three-dimensional image showed nothing broken or misaligned, but he did have a knot on his head just inside the line of his bright red hair. She refocused the viewer on that part of his skull and found what could have been the thinnest of fractures.

Amaya put the viewer away and checked the capillary tube. No hint of the warning colors showed.

You're more fortunate than I in this regard, Eddie Osborn.

When she rolled him onto his back, she found the fist-sized rock that had given Eddie the egg-sized swelling. She dusted the dirt off his cheek and then gently opened each of his eyes one at a time and used a small flashlight to check the reaction of his pupils. One reacted at about half the speed of the other, the sign of a possible concussion.

Using a tube of regenerative salve and an applicator to avoid touching the gel herself, Amaya spread a generous layer of the medication on the bump on Eddie's head and watched the dense fluid absorb into his skin. She should see the beneficial effect soon. While she waited, she put the viewer and the test kit away then sat back to keep an eye on her young charge.

Eddie Osborn inhaled sharply. He clenched his eyes closed then opened them and blinked into the mid-morning light.

"You picked an interesting place for a nap, little one." Amaya smiled.

Eddie studied her with far more curiosity than fear. His broad, round face had the square jaw of his father and the blue, wide-set eyes and small ears of his mother. His red hair had been close-cut after the style of human men, and dozens of freckles dotted his nose and cheeks. Humans looked so strange compared to her own people. They were shorter and stouter, looking like an Eshuvani who had been vertically squashed and horizontally stretched.

"How do you feel?" Amaya asked.

"My head doh't huht no mo'." Eddie sat up.

"I'm glad." She smiled at the peculiar accent of toddlers. "Are you warm enough?"

"Uh-huh." His brow furrowed, and he darted to his feet, looking all around. "Mama? Daddy? Mama!"

Amaya rested a hand on his shoulder. "They aren't here, dear one. When they woke up, they didn't find you at the tent, and they thought you might be lost. They went to the Eshuvani police station for help because we know this area better. Your parents are waiting for us at the tent. They didn't want you to come back and find them gone."

"Yo' a poweesman?" he asked.

She smiled. "Something like that. My name is Amaya. I am a *kiand*, which means that I'm in charge of the Eshuvani police station called *Uloniya Varoosht Kiandarai* or 'Hawk's Nest.'"

"Wow." He stared at her for a few moments. "I didn't see a girl poweesman befo'."

"It's very common in the Eshuvani. What are you doing out here, little one?" She took in the expanse of the abandoned mine with the sweep of her hand.

"I wanted to pet da bunny. Bunnies are vewy sof', but he wan away an' I couldn't find him." He looked down at his shoes.

"I understand. Well, let's get your shoes on the proper feet, and then we'll get you back to your parents. They're very worried about you wandering off like that."

"'Kay."

He sat down in front of her and switched his shoes. Amaya tied them after the human fashion rather than the more typical knot her own people used. She shook the dust off the blanket and then folded it and put it in her backpack.

"Are you hungry, Eddie?" she asked.

"Uh-huh."

She took a nutrition bar out of her pack and unwrapped it for him. "Eat that while we walk."

Amaya slipped her backpack over one shoulder then picked him up and propped him on her other hip. Then she jumped up to the top of the ledge and landed easily.

Eddie looked at her, wide eyed. "Wow! You jump good!"

She chuckled. "I practice."

"Yo' even bettuh dan a bunny. Can we find a bunny to p'ay wif?" Eddie asked.

"We might find a bunny to look at, but wild bunnies don't like to play with us." Amaya adjusted his weight. "I think we scare them a little. I'll keep an eye out for tracks made by bunny feet, and maybe we'll see one."

"'Kay."

He stayed quiet while he ate the nutrition bar. Amaya kept her pace slower on the return trip. She'd weary too quickly with Eddie in her arms if she went any faster.

Eddie finished his snack. "How come yo' poweesman is named *kiand*?"

Amaya shrugged. "That's just what Eshuvani call their police captains. We have a different language than yours."

"But I know what yo' sayin' now," he said.

"I practiced for a very long time to learn your language."

"Do you have odder names for evwyting?"

"Yes, we do. Do you want to learn some of them?"

"Uh-huh!"

She set an unhurried pace and passed the time with the language lesson. Whenever she paused, he'd ask for another word. She'd forgotten just how curious little kids could be. Eddie bore little physical resemblance to her own child, but her heart desperately reached out to him.

Amaya walled off her most fervent wish. Too many other times, she'd tried to befriend a small child only to have the child or the child's parents reject her. She needed no more repeats of that pain, either. If God willed that she have an *urushalon*, Eddie would reach out to her.

After a long walk, they came close enough to the camp to see the back of the tent. Amaya looked off to the side of their path and saw a small rabbit reclining in a patch of sunlight that had worked its way through the canopy. She stopped and crouched.

Amaya pointed. "Look, Eddie. *Yharu.*"

He leaned over to follow the line of her long, thin finger. "Awu!"

The bunny looked straight at them and froze.

"Oh, you startled him," Amaya said.

"Eddie?" Mrs. Osborn called from the far side of the tent. "Eddie?"

"Mama!" Eddie yelled.

Amaya cringed and leaned away. Excitement she could understand, but a little less yelling in her ear would be nice.

"Eddie!"

Eddie pulled Amaya's chin, so she looked at him more directly. "How do you say, 'I wuv you, Mama?'"

"'I love you' is *Urusha-ve.* 'Mama' can't be used as a name."

"Uwusa-ve?"

"Yes. *Urusha-ve.*"

She set him down as Mrs. Osborn came around the tent, and Eddie ran to his mother. Amaya smiled in spite of the recollection of her own child charging at her when she walked in from a rescue or police call. She'd be with him and her husband again someday. For now, she would try to feel the vicarious joy of another mother's relief.

Eddie reached up for his mother. "Mama!"

Mrs. Osborn cried and laughed at the same time. She swept Eddie up in a tight hug and showered him with kisses.

"*Uwusa-ve*, Mama," Eddie said.

"What?" she asked.

"Dat's how Amaya says, 'I wuv you,'" Eddie said.

"I love you, too, Eddie," Mrs. Osborn said.

Mr. Osborn came up behind his wife and hugged them both.

"*Uwusa-ve*, Daddy," Eddie said.

"Huh?"

"'I love you' in Eshuvani," Mrs. Osborn whispered in her husband's ear.

"Uh-huh." He frowned and speared Amaya with a look. "I, um, I love you, too, Eddie."

Amaya came a little closer but stopped a few strides away out of respect. When she realized she was fiddling with her wedding bracelet again, she tucked it into her sleeve. Her hands quivered and felt cold, even to her. She thrust her hands into her pockets in what she knew was a useless effort to try to warm back up. She could sit in the middle of a fire and still not shake the brutal chill of grief.

Mr. Osborn interposed himself between her and his family.

Do you think I mean to harm them, foolish one?

"Where did you find him?" He propped his hands on his hips.

"At the edge of an abandoned mining site a couple miles north by northwest of here." Amaya pointed in the dead mine's direction. "He told me that he'd seen a rabbit outside your tent and went to go play with it. He came across the old mine and fell about three feet into some loose dirt and gravel. His head struck a rock, but he reacted well to the regenerative salve in my kit. The injury is healed, and he should have no lasting effects. I would advise that he rest for what remains of the day."

"An'-an' on da way back, an'-an' Amaya gived me some food, an' it taste wike apples, an' Amaya tol' me a bunch of names for t'ings, an' da bestest paht, we saw a weal bunny right there!" Eddie pointed to the patch of sunlight where the rabbit had been.

"Anna, let's strike camp. I want Eddie's pediatrician to have a look at him." Mr. Osborn leaned toward his wife and whispered, "In case she's done something else to him."

"I'm sure that's unnecessary." Mrs. Osborn rolled her eyes. "Amaya is a physician."

"A practitioner, not a physician, and my medical specialization is traumatic injuries, particularly in older children and adults. Infants and toddlers pose some unique challenges in both of our races." Amaya shifted the backpack on her shoulder. "A pediatrician might see something I wouldn't. The nutrition bar I gave him is fully compatible with human physiology, but if you would like one for your pediatrician to analyze, you may have it."

"No, my grandfather's friend gave me one once. It's very sweet, but harmless," Mrs. Osborn said.

"That's fine, but it's still a good idea that you take Eddie to his usual doctor. A second opinion about how your son fared in his adventure last night wouldn't hurt." Amaya reached out to pat Eddie's back but mutated the movement into a stretch of that arm.

"It doesn't bother you that I don't trust your medicine?" Mr. Osborn asked.

Amaya shook her head. "You are concerned for your son, which is reasonable and proper. By all means, take every precaution you feel necessary. My ego is not an issue here."

Mr. Osborn's brow furrowed and his head tilted as he regarded her. Some of the hardness in his gaze softened. Amaya followed them back around the tent, and Mrs. Osborn set Eddie on the picnic table.

"Thank you for finding Eddie and bringing him back safely." Mrs. Osborn glared at her husband while still talking to Amaya. "You did exactly what you said you'd do in less time than I would have dreamed possible."

Amaya nodded. "God provided all the guidance I needed."

Mr. Osborn sighed. "I apologize if I was abrupt. You aren't what I expected."

"All is forgiven. I understand too well the anxiety of losing a child." Amaya shivered.

Just a little longer, and then she could either go to her quarters and grieve openly for a while or bury herself in work and forget until the next time.

"We'll give you a ride back to your station," Mrs. Osborn said.

"I would appreciate that. I can get the rest of the information I need for my report on the way."

Eddie hopped down from the picnic table and ran over. She would have liked to pick him up, but his father might misunderstand. Instead, she went down to one knee to put them closer to the same height.

"Can I p'ay wif you some mo'?" Eddie asked.

If only ... "That will be up to your parents."

Mrs. Osborn beamed. "Certainly."

Mr. Osborn frowned. "We'll see."

"Honestly, Charles. You and your superstitions." She planted her hand on her hip and wagged her finger at her husband. "She rescued Eddie and brought him back to us safe and sound. What more do you want? Of course, you can see him again, Amaya. You'll be most welcome in our home."

Eddie cheered and collided with Amaya for a hug, and she had to adjust her balance by sliding her foot back. Was this happening? Was God blessing her at last?

"*Uwusa-ve*, Amaya."

"I love you, too, *Urushalon*," she said.

Warmth flooded through her and steadied her hands again. Maybe now, she'd be able to put an end to that particular pain. If she couldn't have her own family here, God was granting permission for her to borrow this one or at least Eddie.

Mr. Osborn turned the crank to start the car. "Let's go."

"You can see where your new friend works, Eddie" Mrs. Osborn said.

"'Kay!"

Amaya smiled and lifted Eddie into the back seat then climbed in after him.

About the Author

Originally from Michigan, Cindy Koepp combined a love of pedagogy and ecology into a 14-year career as an elementary science specialist. After teaching four-footers — that's height, not leg count, she pursued a Master's in Adult Learning with a specialization in Performance Improvement. Her published works include science fiction, fantasy, and GameLit novels, a passel of short stories, and educator resources. When she isn't reading or writing, Cindy is working as a tech writer, hat collector, quilter, and crafter.

Cindy can be found on the web at: ckoepp.com

Other books by Cindy:
Remnant in the Stars
Lines of Succession
The Loudest Actions
Mindstorm: Parley at Ologo
Condemned Courier
Like Herding the Wind: Urushalon Part I
Into the Open: Urushalon Part II
Animal Eye

Anthologies
Medieval Mars
Avatars of Web Surfer
Victorian Venus
Hero's Best Friend
A Chimerical World: Tales of the Seelie Court
Aquasynthesis Again
Friends Like These
Rise and Rescue, Vol. 1
Rise and Rescue, Vol. 2
Warrior's Tribute
Spurs and Six-Shooters
When Your Beauty Is the Beast
Nightmare Collective, Vol. 2
Moonlight and Claws
My Voice Has Power
Mythic Orbits, Vol. 2
Misfits and Unusual Heroes